Praise for *White Smoke*

"A suspenseful love story. . . ."
—*Morning Star Telegram* (Ft. Worth, TX)

"Greeley tells his story with charm and wit, and with more than a dollop of steamy sex. . . ." —*San Jose Mercury News*

"Once-you-begin-it-you-can't-put-it-down fascinating appeal that snatches your attention from the first sentence and doesn't release it for 384 pages. Some 2½ dozen of Greeley's publications are novels, of which there are more than 15 million copies in print. *White Smoke* may well be his best." —*Jackson Clarion-Ledger* (Jacksonville, FL)

"A ripping good read!" —*Milwaukee, WI Sentinel*

"Smoothly done, with delightful dialogue, wry observations by "Blackie" and an incisive style of writing that produces warm and engaging characters. . . . Superbly written. . . . Will captivate the reader."
—*Jacksonville Georgia Times-Union* (Jacksonville, FL)

"An excellent crime novel." —*Cincinnati Post*

"A thinking person's James Bond story. Along with plenty of action this book has plenty of substance. . . . Enormously rich in history, politics, international events, church history, scene description and in developing realistic characters. . . . Fast paced, enjoyable to read and thought provoking." —
Irish American News

"A lively story. . . . A real page-turner, exciting through to that last puff of smoke." —*Greenwich Time* (Greenwich, CT)

WHITE SMOKE

*A Novel about the Next
Papal Conclave*

ANDREW M. GREELEY

FORGE®

A TOM DOHERTY ASSOCIATES BOOK
NEW YORK

WHITE SMOKE: A NOVEL ABOUT THE NEXT
PAPAL CONCLAVE

Copyright © 1996 by Andrew M. Greeley Enterprises, Ltd.

"Because of the Stories," by Andrew M. Greeley, July 10, 1994.
Copyright © 1994 by The New York Times Company.
Reprinted by permission.

Cover photo by Telegraph Colour LIB/FPG International Corp.

A Forge Book
Published by Tom Doherty Associates, Inc.
175 Fifth Avenue
New York, NY 10010

Forge® is a registered trademark of Tom Doherty Associates, Inc.

ISBN 0-812-59055-4
Library of Congress Card Catalog Number: 96-1412

First Edition: June 1996
First mass market Edition: April 1997

Printed in the United States of America

0 9 8 7 6 5 4 3 2 1

None of the ecclesiastical characters in this story are drawn from life but they do represent the attitudes and feelings that exist in the inner circles of Catholic power. Thus the cardinals of Chicago—Sean Cronin in my world and Joseph Bernardin in God's world—are both admirable men but very different men. The former is not based on the latter. And vice versa. My story is not a roman à clef.

With the exception of Chicago, most of the cities to which I have assigned cardinals are not cardinalatial sees, so that no one can claim that my cardinals are drawn from life.

Recently, Pope John Paul II made some changes in the rules for a Papal election. The electors will continue to vote in the Sistine Chapel but will not live in the Sistine Palace but in "St. Martha's House," a new and motel-like residence with modern "conveniences" on the other side of St. Peter's near the Audience Hall. Moreover—catching up with Bishop Blackie—he imposed stern controls to frustrate electronic eavesdropping.

In memoriam
MARVIN ROSNER

A single star that broke heaven's darkling arch
A hint of dawn after a stormy night
A soft and warming wind in icy March
A smile which dissolved all unhappy blight
A shrug of shoulders and an easy grin
A lift of eyebrows and a roll of eyes
A conspiracy in which he dealt you in
And enough graceful charm to fill the skies

Spouse, father, presider at nativity
Advocate of our precious right to be free
And that parks and trees should remain the same
And Cubs, Bears, Bulls, and even Notre Dame
Democrat, sweet and gentle man of peace
Witness that life is too much to ever cease.

"THE CATHOLIC CHURCH HAS NOTHING TO FEAR FROM THE TRUTH."

—*Leo XIII*

"THE CATHOLIC CHURCH SHOULD BE MADE FROM WALLS OF GLASS."

—*Pope John Paul II*

Church at a Turning Point?
News Analysis

By Dennis Michael Mulloy

After a long, momentous, and controversial papal administration, the cardinals who will gather in Rome next week will find themselves at a turning point in the troubled and problematic history of the Catholic Church. Should they strive to recapture the enthusiasm for change which marked the years of the Second Vatican Council and the pontificate of Pope John XXIII? Or should they continue the attempts at stern and uncompromising legalism which have marked the last two papacies? Or should they try to compromise somehow between the two styles of governance?

Already a powerful, worldwide alliance of Catholic business leaders calling itself Save Our Church is gathering in Rome to use its wealth and power to influence the outcome of the election. Its organizer, American industrialist Timothy Ignatius ("Ty") Williams, was candid with *The New York Times* about its goals. "We don't intend to let liberal cardinals like Cronin turn the Church over to socialists, sodomites and secularists." The combination of Mr. Williams' organization and the right-wing Corpus Christi Institute will bring vast financial resources to bear on the outcome of the conclave.

Sean Cardinal Cronin of Chicago was unavailable for comment, but a close associate said, "As I remember his previous ventures into politics, Ty couldn't lead a pack of hungry vampires to a blood bank."

Cardinals tend to be conservative men, though occasionally the Vatican does make a mistake: No one claims papal infallibility applies to such appointments. The electors will be very nervous about any appearance of abrupt change in the Church. On the other hand, they cannot be unaware of the restlessness and dissatisfaction not only among the Catholic laity but among many if not most of the Catholic clergy. They may wonder if the attempts of the last couple of decades to restore unity to the Church have been counterproductive. The most perceptive of them know that many millions of Catholics feel alienated from the Church. The wise may feel that if there is not a drastic change, tens of millions more may be lost, if not to the Catholic heritage, then at least to the institutional Church.

A few of them may even know the wisdom expressed in Giuseppe Di Lampedusa's novel *The Leopard (Il Gattopardo)*, namely: We must change in order to remain the same.

The outcome of the age-old and dramatic ritual of the papal conclave, which will end with the traditional white smoke announcing a new pope, is likely to have a powerful impact on Catholicism for decades to come. For weal or woe.

Dinny

"Mulloy, you stupid son of a bitch," my editor had exploded in exasperation. "This is the story of the century! How often does the Catholic Church elect a new pope, a couple of times every hundred years?"

He had waved my analysis from the morning's paper at me.

"Eight or nine, anyway," I had said. "No big deal."

As I recalled the conversation yesterday in New York, the Alitalia jet was vectoring over Rome. I caught a brief glimpse of the sun-baked Tiber and the glittering dome of St. Peter's.

"There are a billion Catholics in the world. This may be the most important election in the history of the papacy. The future of the Catholic Church will depend on the outcome. For the next two weeks the eyes of the whole human race will be on Rome. Every important journalist in the world will be there. And you want to sit here in New York and feel sorry for yourself."

Low blow, that last line. Not like him or like the paper.

I had thought that CNN would probably send its ace Catholic anchorperson to Rome. All the more reason for not going.

"They claim that every time there's a conclave," I had responded. "Like I say, no big deal."

I knew I had lost the argument. The personal jab meant he was seriously impatient with me. I had better pack.

I admit that I felt a catch in my throat at the sight of St. Peter's. Actually, this *was* a very big deal. The oldest human institution in the world was about to roll the dice again on its future in an ancient and solemn ritual. Or, if one wishes, an archaic and stupid ritual (words I had cut from my brief and last-minute "analysis" piece because I knew they'd never get by the boss).

My editor was wrong about one thing, however. The Church of Rome, for all its enormous faults, had survived a couple of hundred appearances of white smoke. Its future was not in jeopardy.

Well, it had survived so far. Now, however, it was split wide open, with the late pope and the bishops seemingly on one side and most of the laypeople and the priests of the world on the other side.

Maybe this conclave was indeed a very big deal.

Despite myself and despite the damage that air travel does to my organism, my heart was beating faster. Maybe, like my editor had said, this would be the most exciting story I had ever covered.

"Even more than Rwanda?" I had demanded.

"Absolutely!"

"No way," I had replied as I listlessly rose from my chair. "Nothing more than the Democratic convention. Or maybe even the Republican convention."

"Dinny!" he had shouted at me. "Cut the bullshit! You're dying to go!"

"All right, I'll go home and pack."

The Alitalia pilot came on the plane's PA system.

"Because of the gathering for the papal election," he said solemnly, "security will be especially tight at the Leonardo da Vinci airport this morning. There may be some delays in clearing immigration and customs."

Why the special security?

Hell, they'd already tried to assassinate one pope. Why not a new one?

I glanced out the window. Not a speck of cloud in the sky. Yet there was a storm gathering. My heart began to pound, just like it always did when I'm getting involved in an important and dangerous story.

A very big deal, indeed, so much so that I felt stirrings of enthusiasm—until the plane taxied into the jetway and I had to shove myself into a standing position. Then the full weight of motion sickness, jet lag, and dehydration hit me.

All I wanted to do was find a bed somewhere and sleep for a couple of days. I wanted a drink too, but that was no longer a possibility in my life.

There were rumors that this time the white smoke might be a prelude to the announcement of the election of the first American pope. Our own paper had mentioned Chicago's Sean Cardinal Cronin as a possibility. Judging by his picture, he looked like a pope ought to look—a handsome, faintly dissipated, early Renaissance pope, with the political moves of the South Side Irish, like the various mayors Daley.

"Good morning, Mr. Mulloy." A pretty child, clipboard in her left hand, extended her right hand to me as I staggered into the international concourse. "Welcome to the Leonardo da Vinci airport at Fiumicino. Welcome also to Rome. Welcome finally to the pope's funeral mass tomorrow. I am from the Rome bureau and have been assigned to assist you in your coverage of the papal election. I am Paola Elizabetta Maria Angelica Katarina Brigitta Oriani. You may call me Paoli."

She pronounced the name as though it were Pa-OW-li. A cute kid, very cute, as a matter of fact. Even cuter because she was so solemn and serious. And maybe a little shy in the presence of the silver-haired Pulitzer prize winner. Only a few years older than my daughter.

I struggled to respond with my very best genial, shanty-Irish grin.

"Not 'Signorina'?" I said, shaking hands with her, my grip a lot firmer than my character.

She was wearing a businesslike blue suit, with white at the neck and the cuffs, a skirt just below mid-thigh, a gold cross at her neck, gold studs, but no other jewelry. There was but a slight hint of makeup on her lips and she wore sensible pumps. Her scent was discreet and expensive. Successful Roman businessperson with a face from Fra Angelico framed by a halo of tight black curls. She tilted her chin up and favored me with a slight hint of a smile.

"Only if you wish to be *very* formal."

"They told you at the bureau that I was a very formal person, didn't they?"

"They told me that you were very funny, do not engage in sexual harassment, do not drink anymore, are kind of cute in an elderly way, and write like an angel . . . now, if you follow me we will take you through customs."

An accurate-enough description of Dennis Michael Mulloy. Well, no, maybe a little too favorable.

She lifted my garment bag from the floor of the international concourse, where I had dropped it in bemused confusion. I wrestled it away from her.

"I'll take that. It has secret documents in it. Could launch a world war. You can carry my notebook-computer bag. If you lose it we will sacrifice you in the Tiber to ancient Etruscan deities."

"My family is Etruscan . . . this way please."

I followed her dutifully.

"This is really a huge, big deal, isn't it?" I said, changing the subject.

"The conclave? But naturally. Power is at stake, very large power, spiritual and temporal both. The careers of many people can be affected and the hopes of millions might be renewed or destroyed completely. Even someone like me who knows the Vatican all too well becomes excited."

How did she know the Vatican "all too well"?

"Power corrupts," I observed pontifically.

"And absolute power corrupts absolutely. Lord Acton was speaking of the papacy."

"Of course," I said, pretending that I had known that all along.

The concourse was teeming with people who looked like they might be conclave bound—TV crews carrying their minicams, reporters of every skin color under heaven (I can always spot a fellow reporter; the hang-dog, faintly paranoid expression is a dead giveaway, even among the women), clergy in assorted costumes, from the black suit and Roman collar to flowing Asian robes and towering hats. A couple of the Roman collar boys were wearing red socks or displayed red trim at the collar—cardinal electors, obviously.

With typical New York anticlericalism, I figured that the delegates to the Democratic convention on the whole would inspire more confidence.

I searched a crowd looking for possible assassins. I discovered only apparently rich Americans, come, possibly, to throw their weight and money into the conclave cauldron.

Everyone was deadly intense. A humongous, big deal. The tension isn't electric, I told myself, it's just your Brooklyn, Irish Catholic roots.

But the atmosphere was indeed tense. Rome and the Catholic Church, I would discover later, could do that to you.

My girl guide wove her way through the crowd like Barry Sanders ran through behemoth tacklers of the Giants. I struggled to keep up with her. Upon due consideration, Paola Elizabetta Maria Angelica Katarina Brigitta was more than just a cute child. She was a very lovely young woman, a diminutive china doll with deep brown eyes, a finely carved oval face, mobile lips kept in control as she bantered with me only by great restraint, a generous body, and, judging by my present view from behind, nice legs and a flawless rear end.

I had given up sex along with drink, so my libido didn't react during this evaluation. But if it had been operative it would have found her delectable, just as would the libidos of other dirty old men when they glanced at my daughter.

"Who's going to win the conclave?" I asked my pretty guardian angel.

"Naturally, Don Luis will win," she said with the serene confidence of the young.

"Menendez? He's the liberal Spaniard, isn't he?"

"He is a good man," she insisted firmly. "Many bad men will try to defeat him. Like those foolish Americans who could not find their way to a blood bank. But he will still win."

"I hear there's opposition building up to him. Does he have the votes?"

You live with a woman from Chicago for fifteen years, you learn to ask Chicago questions.

"Gesù and the Madonna will see that he wins."

That settles that.

"Can I interview him?"

"Until now he does not give interviews—even to *The New York Times*."

That's no way to win an election.

My angel and I, having successfully run for daylight, approached an immigration gate that was apparently closed.

"Your passport, please," she said.

"Uh, it's here someplace." I searched in my jacket pockets, my trouser pockets, the pocket on my garment bag, and then my jacket pocket again.

"Is this it?" Paoli had retrieved it from the pocket on the outside of my computer bag.

"Yeah . . . I guess I'm confused from the flight. Sorry."

I had learned always to apologize to women, even when I had done nothing wrong.

"No problem." My guide smiled benignly. "Naturally it is permitted that you be confused."

Her English was quite good. Syntax and vocabulary practically perfect and accent better than a lot you could hear in New York City from native-born Americans. However, her speech was formal and stiff, as though she wanted to be sure that she had chosen exactly the right word.

She gave my passport to a beaming young inspector who had materialized from nowhere. He stamped it with an elegant flourish and bowed to her and to me. The two of them exchanged what sounded like compliments in Italian.

The kid had clout.

"You have clout."

She dismissed it with a wave of her hand, which I would learn meant "It is nothing."

"You have more luggage?"

"Nope. Travel light. Presumably there are stores in Rome where I can buy clothes if I need them."

She considered my rumpled off-the-rack gray suit, and replied, "The most fashionable men's clothes in the world."

"Yes, ma'am."

I noticed a guy that I thought was a shade. He was lost in a long line. Maybe I could shake him completely.

But why were they tracking me, especially with a man who could be one of their best, a guy that looked like a successful commodities broker in the later middle years of life, if one who drank too much? Obviously I had a lot on them. My current investigation—into a network of small European banks and their link to them—might embarrass them considerably. And the boss had said that the Rome bureau had reported rumors in the city of a new financial scandal in the Vatican, one that would dwarf the Banco Ambrosiano scandal a few years back.

Just as obviously, they knew that if anything happened to me, the paper would instantly print all the stuff in my secret files. Were they afraid I might find out something more during the conclave?

Who are "they"?

The first thing you have to learn when you get on the international crime beat is that "they" are not a single group, nor even a loose alliance of a lot of groups—drug dealers, arms merchants, the Outfit, the Russian Outfit, crooked bankers, remnants of the CIA and the KGB and their agents, the diamond monopoly, and a dozen or so other international entrepreneurs of crime and corruption. The second thing you have to learn is that representatives of these various groups know one another and on occasion talk to one another when necessity demands—as when you want to kill a pope, like they tried to do back in the eighties. Any and all of these institutions might be interested in me, even if all of them were, I fervently hoped, afraid to kill me.

I was not supposed to spot the shade. But I usually picked them up at once. Comes of being the son of a cop.

What might I learn at a papal election that they most particularly did not want me to learn?

As I had said to the boss, "I'm on the international crime beat. Remember? What's that got to do with a papal election?"

"Give me a break, Dinny! You've heard about the Vatican Bank scandal, the Banco Ambrosiano, the Masonic Lodge they called P-2 which a lot of cardinals were supposed to belong to, Liceo Gelli and his bunch. Hell, you know enough history to realize that the Vatican has been corrupt since the Reformation."

"Before that."

"And there was that pope who died after only a month in office back in 1978. . . . What was his name?"

"John Paul?"

"No, that's the guy that just died."

"One and Two."

"Yeah. Anyway, there were a lot of stories that he was murdered."

"More likely died of medical neglect."

"Yeah, but is it possible to buy a papal election? Ty Williams seems to think so. He plans to buy it. That's a great story line!".

"Old stuff. It's been done a lot of times. Remember Rodrigo Borgia and his delightful kids—Lucrezia and Cesare by name?"

"That was a long time ago, Dinny. Could it still happen today? Besides, we want a Catholic to cover the conclave, even if it's an honest one."

"I'm not a Catholic anymore."

"The hell you're not. Once a Catholic, always a Catholic."

"I'm afraid you might be right."

My native guide continued her commentary.

"There is great excitement here at the airport. Rumors that a bomb will be planted in the Sistine Chapel and that there will be many assassinations. And even we cynical Romans know that the curtain is rising on a drama that is very old and yet somehow very new—just like the Church itself."

"Ah," I said.

The Roman sun in spring is so bright that for a moment you think you might be on another planet. No clouds. But still, I sensed instinctively that dark clouds were gathering. There were too many things going on for there not to be trouble. I felt the knot of fear and excitement that always assaulted my dubious stomach.

Paola Elizabetta etc. etc. inspected her clipboard.

"We can naturally hire a car here. In fact, however," she ran her pen down the board, "it would be quicker if we take the Alitalia train into the Termini station. Then it is but three stops on the Metro to Spagna. . . . Public transportation is often much faster in Rome these days."

She hesitated, not sure how I would take it and also not altogether sure that she liked me.

"Saving money on the elderly journalist, eh?"

"Forty-four years old is not *really* elderly, Mr. Mulloy. . . ."

"Dinny."

She giggled. "What a funny name!"

"They told you at the bureau that I was a funny man."

"Deeny?" she experimented with the funny word.

"Close enough."

"Moreover," she smiled brightly, having decided that she did like me, "you are to stay at the Hassler, which is not a hotel where money is saved."

The paper was taking care of its hero reporter, who maybe had not completely recovered from the bug he had picked up in Rwanda. Why not enjoy it?

"Yeah, but you expect me to climb the Scala di Spagna

all the way up to the Piazza Trinità dei Monti carrying this bag?''

See, kid, I know this city, too.

"I could carry it for you," she said uncertainly.

"And let me be ridiculed as an old man by those ruffians that hang around the Spanish Steps? No way!"

Actually, I am in pretty good condition for a man of my years. Getting back into shape was part of my therapy in giving up both Patty and drink and then again after the African bug left me.

She pulled a cellular phone out of her shoulder purse, which was almost bigger than she was, and spoke in rapid Italian. She closed the phone and shoved it back into the bag.

"It is necessary for you to walk at least an hour in direct noonday sun to recover from the circadiedic disrhythmia. For at least two days."

As she talked, she guided me across the glass-covered bridge to the terminal of the Alitalia train to Rome, made up of green and white cars like an old-fashioned ice cream truck.

"You mean the jet lag?"

"Naturally."

"Out in the noonday sun with the other mad dogs and Englishmen?"

She threw back her head and laughed, finally catching on to the Dinny Mulloy style of banter.

"Well, Deeny, you are not an Englishman."

"True enough."

"We could," she consulted her clipboard, "have you check in at the hotel, then we could walk down the steps and have lunch at Babington's English tearoom, where your poets, I mean their poets, used to eat, and then take the Metro to Ottaviano and walk over to San Pietro. That should give you at least an hour of the noonday sun. You could attend the pope's wake and obtain your press credentials.

The car would then take you back to the hotel, where you could file a story if you wish."

"Do you have an aunt who is a sister superior?"

"My great-aunt is a mother general," she said proudly. "She says I am more efficient than she is. . . .We get in here, Deeny."

Before I could comment on that, a young man, thin and with long hair, burning eyes, and a pale face, rushed by us on the bridge and collided with Paoli.

She screamed, spun around like she had been hit by a truck, dropped her clipboard, and crashed against the glass wall of the bridge.

I thought that she would shatter the wall and fall to the ground twenty feet below. But the wall held and she bounced back toward me

Then she tumbled forward toward the floor of the bridge. She'll cut her face and bang up her head, I told myself and reached out to catch her.

I grabbed her in midair and steadied her on her feet.

Instead of commending my quick reflexes, she launched a barrage of fierce Italian denunciations and at the same time gripped my arm firmly so I would not go after him.

Some of the other people on the bridge shouted imprecations after the fleeing youth, but no one seemed much interested in pursuing him.

"He tried to push you off the bridge!" I shouted.

"No fighting, Deeny," she ordered. "Not while I'm in charge of you!"

I picked up her clipboard.

"Are you all right, Paoli?"

"Naturally, I am fine. My suit and my nylons are undamaged. What else matters?"

She grinned weakly.

"Badly bruised?"

"Naturally not. I am fine. Come, we must not let that pig cause us to miss the train."

Had I imagined that the violence was deliberate? Was the romantic in me seeing a plot already?

Probably. Why would anyone want to dispose of a cute little journalist?

Still, I glanced around, searching for the shade. It could be the kind of trick his kind might play. Hurt her to warn me off. "They" had refined the art of pushing people off platforms to perfection. The CIA particularly liked it.

Warn me off of what?

"Yes, S'ter," I said, obeying her command.

She laughed again. Patty and I used to banter that way in our early years together. We both loved it. I'm not sure when it all turned sour. Sometime after Kevin, our second child, was born. Patty was determined that she could be both an anchorwoman and a mother of two toddlers at the same time and do it with a minimum of outside help—or help from me, as far as that goes. She was a good mother and a good journalist, but the strain of being both at her own high pressure was probably too much. She had lost her temper more often and her banter with me had turned nasty. I responded by going off to dangerous foreign places and drinking more when I was home. Before I realized what was happening, our marriage, previously extolled by our friends as a perfect match, had begun falling apart. Love had been replaced by constant strain. So to escape the strain I drank even more and had ended up by disgracing myself at Deirdre's graduation from grammar school.

The pastor, who was a fool, had preached at the graduation mass on abortion. I had just returned from Bosnia and had consumed too much Irish whiskey to steel myself against Patty's complaints and temper tantrums. Nonetheless, I should not have risen from the pew and denounced the pastor as a fool—at considerable length. Patty, not without just cause, had thrown me out of the house, took the kids back home to Chicago, and sued for divorce.

I had been relieved at the prospect of escaping from her and from my failure as both a father and a husband. There was no reason for our divorce to be acrimonious, except that Patty had been determined to make a big fight out of it. I had told my lawyer to give her whatever she had wanted. But that wasn't enough. She had wanted to denounce me in public and did so furiously.

I was glad to be rid of her, though I missed the kids, who seemed to like me at least a little—and were better able to deal with their mom's insults and rages than I was.

We had been so happy—and so convinced that we were deeply in love. I ran away from Patricia's energy and rage. But I knew, even then, that the failure was mine, not hers. That's why I avoided entanglements after the divorce. For all my charm and my wit, I just wasn't very good with women when the relationship became serious.

There was an Irish nurse in Rwanda, a lovely woman who'd been with me when we talked the Hutu militia out of killing a couple hundred Tutsi Catholics whom they had locked in a church (the Hutu were Catholics too). She was a very smart and a very brave woman. But once we got our flock across the border, I'd seen that the determined line of her lips and the defiant jut of her jaw were Patricia all over again.

Paoli ushered me through the door of the Good Humor train. I noted that my shade was just behind us.

"Tonight at nineteen-thirty, uh, seven-thirty," she continued, "the car will pick you up to take you to Ristorante Sabatini in Trastevere, on the Piazza Santa Maria in Trastevere. You will meet Bishop Ryan of Chicago. He will provide background information for you."

"Only a bishop?"

"He is on the staff of Cardinal Cronin."

"Ah."

"He speaks English, of course. Therefore it is not necessary that I accompany you."

"Your parents let you out after dark, Paoli?"

She laughed again. "My parents are very proud of me."

"Your young man wouldn't mind?"

She dismissed him with a wave of her hand. "He is a nice young man. Rather sweet at times. But he is harmless."

"Ah. What does he do?"

"He is a cop."

"You would like to meet this Bishop Ryan?"

The train started smoothly.

She shrugged. "It does not matter."

"Let me put it this way, Pretty Paoli. You're welcome to come along with me on this caper anytime you want."

She nodded, not committing herself to anything.

"What kind of cop?"

"Carabinieri. Intelligence."

"Kind of like our FBI?"

She nodded. "Nonetheless, he can be very sweet."

I decided that I would ask no more questions till she volunteered further information about this sometimes "very sweet" cop of hers.

"Have the cardinals decided yet when the conclave starts?" I asked, changing the subject.

"This is Sunday, naturally. The pope died three days ago. His funeral will be tomorrow, as you know. The rules say that the conclave itself must start no less than fifteen and no more than twenty days after a pope dies. The General Congregation—a daily meeting of all those cardinals who happen to be in Rome—decided that they would go into conclave a week from Tuesday night and begin voting on Wednesday."

"Bare minimum?"

"Naturally. Those who vote in the General Congregation for the first day or two are likely to be those resident in Rome. They want a quick election so that the outsiders cannot organize themselves."

"Dirty politics from day one."

"Naturally."

Well, it was the way politics often worked.

"*Conclavium* means 'lockup'," my guardian angel continued. "Today it is intended to keep the public outside. In its origins it was intended to keep the cardinals inside and uncomfortable until they elected a pope. When the citizens of Rome became irate at their failure to agree, they would cut the food supplies in half.''

"How many citizens of Rome were there in those days?''

"In the ninth century, perhaps five thousand. Goats grazing in the ruins of the Forum.''

In front of us a line of hills loomed up, probably dunes of the Mediterranean of earlier eons. A string of pine trees lined the ridge, a dark silhouette against the deep blue sky. I imagined Respighi's music in my head.

"I've been here a couple of times before, Paoli. Each time I arrive I'm excited. This is one of the great places in all the world. Then when it comes time to leave, I am happy to get out.''

She nodded solemnly.

"I know what you mean, Deeny. My family has lived here for ten centuries. They were the ones who locked up the cardinals and cut their food supply. I think we all feel about Rome just as you do.''

A thousand years in Rome? Very interesting. But I didn't want to touch that just yet. Instead I returned to the subject of Bishop Ryan.

"What is he like?''

She frowned. "They say he is an odd little man.''

"So?''

She glanced at her clipboard. "He is called "Blackie."''

"As in Boston Blackie?''

"I do not know. . . . He also is said to know more about politics than Mayor Daley.''

"Impossible,'' I snorted. "Absolutely impossible.''

Blackie

*K*laus," Milord Sean Cardinal Priest of the Holy Roman Church Cronin said, as he carefully sipped his post-prandial Benedictine, "this guy Menendez is the only one that can win for us. He's got to understand that it's either him or another decade and a half of the same thing."

Milord Cronin is a tall and handsome man whose ample blond hair is now mostly gray. He is one of the few cardinal princes who looks like a cardinal ought to look. You expect to see such a man in a picture by a Renaissance painter—a man with broad shoulders and a slender waist, haggard, perhaps, and reckless, but confident of his power and prestige. Perhaps he has a flagon of wine in his hand and a crooked grin on his face.

In fact, however, Sean Cardinal Cronin drinks very little and the crooked grin appears but rarely and then only when the hoods retract from his eyes and you see a manic gleam that would be more appropriate in an Irish gallowglass warrior. I understand most people moderately well. Though I am said to be his alter ego or his éminence grise, Sean Cronin I understand not at all.

"*Ja, ja,*" Herr Cardinal Klaus Maria Johann von Obermann, count bishop of Düsseldorf, agreed as he tossed off his second glass of schnapps. "To win we need two thirds plus one vote—seventy-four votes. Perhaps fifty cardinals already support him. Look at our lists—the Spanish and the Portuguese, of course; France, Germany, the British Isles, even some of the Italian residential bishops; the European Union supports him completely, with the exception of the Curial cardinals. Most of the Americans too, because finally they will vote the way you tell them to vote. Everyone knows him and likes him, even if they don't quite agree with him on everything. They all think we must have a regime that is somewhat different than the present one. Moreover, most of the Italians are so tainted by the scandals in the Christian Democratic Party that they wouldn't dare be candidates.''

We were finishing a very long lunch in a private dining room in a small restaurant in Borgo Pio, a narrow street just outside of Vatican City. The Borgo is in the shadow of the wall on the top of which the popes used to escape (in a carriage on a road built above the top of the wall) from the Vatican to the Castel Sant'Angelo (near Hadrian's tomb) when the city was being invaded by barbarians. An earlier version of the barbarians, that is.

The food was excellent, especially the pasta, of which I had three helpings. While the two cardinals consumed European liquors, I contented myself with a thoroughly American beverage, Bailey's Irish Cream.

Earlier in the conversation, I had wandered to the door of our private room and pushed it open. As I had expected, two young men—black suits, white shirts, black ties—had been lingering just outside the door. Doubtless, spies from the Corpus Christi Institute, trying to eavesdrop on our little conspiracy. Corpus, far to the right of the ultrareactionary Opus Dei, had replaced Opus during the last couple of years as the most influential force in the Vatican.

Surprised by my alarums and excursions, they staggered away from the door and almost into the lap of Timothy Ignatius Williams. That worthy, a caricature of the successful Irish Catholic entrepreneur (fat, silver-haired, ugly), had been acutely embarrassed. He had responded as was his wont—stupidly.

"You should watch where you're going, Ryan," he had yelled at me, his face turning purple.

"No blood bank in there, Sir Timothy," I had said

mildly. "And no sodomites either. Not on our side of the door, anyway."

His title is from some ancient and irrelevant papal knighthood, irrelevant even when it wasn't ancient.

I bowed politely and returned to our table. Neither Milord Cronin nor his ally had noticed my absence.

The count bishop of Düsseldorf was even taller than Chicago's delegate to the conclave and notably heavier without being exactly fat. He wore his thick blond hair long and attacked the food with almost as much gusto as I did, but more noise. He looked like a red-faced Viking prince turned hippie in an ample purple sport shirt—in great contrast to Milord Cronin's off-white knit shirt. Despite these rather heavily Teutonic characteristics and his title—Graf Von Obermann—the German cardinal was as authentic a democrat as one could find in the Sacred College; he had often gone head-to-head with the Vatican on reception of the Eucharist by divorced and remarried Catholics. Such behavior was unusual for the Germans because they are paid by the government, not by contributions from the people (cardinals receive the salary of a field marshal, which is nice work if you can get it), and generally see no reason to engage in confrontational behavior with the Vatican. However, they were apparently fed up with the constant interference of the Roman Curia in their daily work, an anger shared by most other Catholic bishops, even the most conservative.

"Fifty," Sean Cronin shoved away the papers on which he had been counting votes, "but we will need at least sixty, better, sixty-five on the first vote, or many of these fools will run."

"Ja, ja," von Obermann agreed with a yawn. "We will get more. The Africans depend on us for their money. We will persuade them to vote our way."

"You can hold them after the first ballot?"

"Everyone knows how everyone else has voted as soon as the count is over. They are not supposed to know." He chuckled. "But they know. We will tell the Africans that and they will vote our way until the bitter end.''

"I wish I were as confident about my American colleagues,'' Sean Cronin said bitterly. "With the exception of Mick Kennedy, you put them all together and you hardly have a single human brain. They'll vote for the winner once it's clear that he's the winner. I have to remind them every day that Don Luis is the winner. But he has to start acting like a winner.''

"Don Luis'' was Luis Emilio Cardinal Menendez y Garcia, bishop of Valencia.

"Everyone thinks he will win,'' our Teutonic knight agreed. "But then, they say that he who goes into the conclave as pope comes out a cardinal.''

"Like Pacelli and Montini,'' I added. Both men, who later became Pius XII and Paul VI, had been favorites before the conclaves that had elected them.

The count cardinal (or was it cardinal count?) looked up in surprise, noticing my presence perhaps for the first time. I am the most insignificant and inconspicuous of people. People hardly notice that I'm there. I am the little man who isn't there again today. It is a most useful trait. Von Obermann absorbed my comment thoughtfully.

"Ja, ja,'' he roared. "That is very good. Very good. You should say it often. They were what your cardinal calls the winter-book favorites and yet they won.''

I was not at all sure that the good German knew what a winter-book favorite was or had ever heard of the Kentucky Derby.

"They wanted to be pope, despite their pious disclaimers. They were willing to campaign, discreetly, of course. But they spoke out and hinted broadly what the Church would be like if they won. Don Luis won't do that. It took him a day to realize that he had to release the exact quotes of his statement on abortion before the Corpus goons destroyed him completely on that issue.''

Cardinal Cronin is South Side Chicago Irish, which is to say that he loves the political game. He saw himself, not unrealistically, as playing Tim Degnan to Cardinal Menendez's Rich Daley. Unlike most of his colleagues in the Sacred College, he understood clearly that the Holy Spirit does not whisper names in their ears but rather works through the ordinary political process of an election. Hence he was a passionate counter of votes, an enjoyable activity if you are of his ethnic background, but one that is hard on the blood pressure.

His sister-in-law, Senator Nora Cronin Hurley, had cornered me that morning at the North American College after breakfast with the cardinal and before she returned to the Flora Hotel.

"I'm worried about him, Blackie. Very worried."

Naturally. That is one of the things women are for: to worry about men.

"Ah?"

Senator Nora, a handsome white-haired woman in her early sixties, was beyond doubt the love of the cardinal's life. No one doubted that the love was platonic and had been so since her remarriage to a genial and ingenious sports broadcaster after the death of the cardinal's brother, Senator Paul Cronin, a quarter century ago. As to the years before that, the nature of their relationship was none of anyone's business, especially not the business of his harmless and inoffensive auxiliary bishop, John Blackwood Ryan.

Nora was in Rome because the Senate, alas dominated by those who are to politics what the New York Knicks are to basketball, was in spring recess. Ed Hurley, her husband, would come to Rome after the end of the NCAA tournament.

"He does not take care of himself, Blackie. You know that. His blood pressure isn't very good. He works too hard. He doesn't sleep well at night. It's an impossible job."

"Indeed."

I have learned through the passage of years that some women can be irresistible at any age in life. Nora certainly was one of them.

"Promise me that you will take care of him."

I reflected that Sean Cronin had displayed marvelous taste in women, a charge he had often leveled against me, without the slightest justification.

"I'll do my best," I had said, hedging my promise.

"I know you will." She had brushed her lips against my cheek, an undeniably pleasant experience.

Yeah, I'll do my best to tame the whirlwind.

"The Corpus people are out whispering against him," Sean Cronin continued. "They say he is soft on abortion and a bad administrator."

"They lie." Von Obermann pounded the table.

"So what else is new. . . . But they're running things now and have created the illusion that they will continue to run things. They have aced Don Luis out of preaching at the week of funeral masses. If he wants to describe his platform, he's going to have to find another occasion to do so."

The Corpus Christi Institute, a rich, secretive, and reactionary organization of priests and laypeople that had built up enormous power for itself during the papacy which had just ended—and enormous resentment among residential bishops, who distrusted its independence and often suspected it of being a Catholic version of the Moonies. Not without reason. During the reign of the late pope, Corpus had infiltrated key offices in the Curia. The pope's physician, his press spokesman, and many of his financial advisers were members of Corpus.

The main reason why Cardinal Menendez y Garcia might not be elected was that he would be an ideal pope. A gifted historian and dean at Salamanca, his appointment as archbishop of Valencia had been a surprise. He had, however, made the transition from scholar to pastor with remarkable ease and was worshiped for his piety, his clarity, his intelligence, and his dedication by everyone in his diocese—rich and poor, right and left, young and old. He had lectured and given retreats all around the world and had discreetly preached the values of pluralism in the Church as opposed to the centralization of the present (now past) regime. "Pluralism" was the buzzword around which the conclave would be fought. Everyone wanted it, but everyone defined it differently.

For Don Luis, as for Sean Cronin, it meant that local bishops governed together with the pope and were, by divine institution, responsible for their own dioceses. They were not lower-level bureaucratic functionaries to be harassed every day by the Roman Curia—often on the basis of complaints by Corpus and similar ultrareactionary groups that they were shocking the laity. As the cardinal had put it with notable lack of delicacy, "their goddamn spies are everywhere."

Even outside our dining room here in the Borgo.

"They call me about a homily a young priest preached last Sunday," Sean Cronin launched his usual litany of complaint, "a comment in class by one of the seminary professors, a remark made at a high school sex course, an unnecessary hysterectomy at a Catholic hospital, an alleged feminist liturgy in a local convent, a penance service at Christmas, a parish where they wash the hands instead of the feet on Holy Thursday. I have to investigate each complaint and then report back that nothing erroneous or imprudent happened. Hell, I'm a cardinal and a successor to the Apostles. I know Chicago better than all of them put together. Yet they think their spies know it better than I do. I finally told them that if they came to me with one more frivolous complaint I'd quit and let them send to Chicago that dumb punk from Alton who is telling everyone he is my designated successor. I also told them that the laity are rarely scandalized except by the authoritarianism of the Vatican and the Curia."

Klaus Maria was impressed. "And they said?"

"They backed off. Afraid of me, I guess."

"Ja, ja. That is good. Keep them that way. We have even more trouble with them. Rome is closer to Germany than to the United States."

"Distance does not matter, Klaus. We live in the worst of all possible worlds—an authoritarian Renaissance papacy with all the tools of modern communication. I dread the day they go on E-mail. Don Luis has to speak up. Now, before it is too late."

The downside of statements by Cardinal Menendez was that he might specify too clearly what he thought decentralization and pluralism would mean for the Church. If the Curia was conceived of as working for the bishops instead of vice versa, no major decision would ordinarily be made without intense consultation with residential bishops. Thus unilateral decisions like the late pope's letter on the ordination of women would be rare—if they happened at all. It would be a very different Church, one in which the local bishop would represent his priests and people to the universal Church, just the opposite of his present role. Cronin and von Obermann would not mind that kind of democratization at all. Many of the Sacred College would be profoundly uneasy with such a change, including most of the American cardinals, who didn't understand yet that a little bit authoritarian was like a little bit pregnant.

"Ja," von Obermann agreed, "but he does not want to campaign. He will be pope if asked by the Sacred College, but he will not seek it."

"He has to let people know where he stands." Cardinal Cronin pounded the table. "He has to respond to the Corpus people. You're his closest friend among the cardinals. You've got to tell him he must at least reply."

"Ja, I'll try, but I don't know...."

"Perhaps," I said with my characteristic diffidence when in the presence of cardinal princes, "he could be persuaded to make presentations on the condition of the Church at the North American College and the Germano-Hungarian College. Academics, especially when they have turned to administration, cannot resist the temptation to get back into the classroom...."

Again von Obermann seemed surprised by the voice of someone who wasn't really there.

"Ja, ja. That is good, very good. Ja, ja. We do it, Sean. *Nein?*"

"Ja, Klaus, we do it."

"We make some discreet arrangements to have the media there," I murmured, "perhaps *The New York Times* and CNN. . . ."

"Blackwood here has clout with the media. He's having supper tonight with the reporter that the *Times* has sent to do the color on the conclave. CNN has pulled their Chicago anchor and sent her here. With those two in our camp we can dominate the world media. I presume you can do the same with the EU media."

"Ja. No problem . . . that is very, very good, Bishop Blackwood."

"Call me Blackie."

The cardinal and I rode back to the North American College on the Janiculum Hill, overlooking the Vatican, in a taxi. We would not join the occasional mad dog and English person under the noonday sun. Neither would we use one of the limousines the college had reserved for one of its distinguished guests. The cardinal did not approve of the rector of the college. Not at all, *not at all*. Sean Cronin, Irish politician that he was, did not trust men whose disloyalty was patent.

"Ja, we have our ways with the African cardinals," I commented with the accent of the Gestapo agent in the old war films.

"You are an incorrigible shanty-Irish bigot, Blackwood." He laughed. "I just wish that Klaus was not so easygoing."

"One of the unindicted co-conspirators should keep his blood pressure under control."

He laughed again. "You've been talking to Nora . . . ? Let me see that list of cardinals again. We have to win the first morning to keep all our uncertain voters in line. Sixty-five votes on the first ballot of the first scrutiny. Then seventy-five or more on the second. It's white smoke then, or it will be a very long conclave.''

I kept to myself the thought that it would be acceptable for the white smoke to soar the first afternoon, instead of the first morning.

As the counting of votes continued, I reviewed in my head what I knew about this Dennis Michael Mulloy person with whom I was to have supper. Typical Irish Catholic journalist—magical with words, a fall-down drunk, divorced, fallen away from the Church. On the other hand he was said to have been on the wagon for three years and not to have remarried. His brief piece in the paper yesterday showed that he was not unacquainted with the dynamics of contemporary Catholicism. It was reasonable to assume that he felt lonely, guilty, and sorry for himself. Thus the male of the Irish species.

Interestingly, his former wife was the Celtic Diana whom CNN had sent to Rome, not entirely, I presume, because I had suggested her. Oddly enough this combination was not the result of plotting on my part.

She had not remarried either. Doubtless she felt lonely, guilty, and sorry for herself. Thus the female of the Irish species.

I had to resist the clerical impulse, ancient even at the time of the Bard's Friar Laurence, to reconcile apparently star-crossed lovers.

Unless, of course, they patently wanted to be reconciled.

Dinny

My first brutal shock of the day came at the top of the Spanish Steps. I had climbed all 137 of them, without a whimper of complaint about my age and infirmities and the heat of the noonday sun. I was acutely conscious that my sister superior was deliberately walking slowly so as not to embarrass me by bounding ahead of me. I resolutely refused to permit the smallest gasp that would hint I was out of breath.

I might, of course, die before I made the top.

I gasped loudly at the top, however, as we turned into the small Piazza Trinità dei Monti. In solemn high procession— two cars and a truck—the Cable News Network pulled up to the hotel next to the Hassler. Out of the lead car, an enormous Lancia, appeared my ex-wife in full sail.

Queen Boudicca, a.k.a. Patricia Anne Marie Elizabeth, my wife. My ex-wife, that is.

I was in trouble.

Along with her entourage, she swept into the hotel with characteristic heedless, exuberant, five-foot-ten-and-a-quarter, red-haired grace—Queen Maeve the Passionate charging into battle and doubtless fuming at any delay to her headlong charge through life. Well, she wasn't fuming at me, for which I thank God. Should there be a God. My wife, my ex-wife, that is, was a congenitally impatient, combative, angry woman whose attack on life was never once marred by self-examination, regret, or apology. Enormously attractive on the TV screen—long red hair, flashing green eyes, flawless cream complexion—witty, brilliant, and untiring, Patricia McLaughlin (pronounced, in case you were wondering, as though it were spelled "McLofflin") lived as though she were one of the half-mad goddess queens of Ireland—Sionna, Bionna, Erihu, one of that crowd of berserking hellions.

Maybe she was. But, thank God again, she was no longer my goddess queen. If I got too close to her or let her get too close to me, my three successful years as a recovering drunk would be wiped out in a day.

"CNN," Paoli observed.

"Right."

"The Hotel de la Ville is very nice," she said. "But not as nice as the Hassler."

"Naturally."

"Perhaps you will wish to spend fifteen minutes orienting yourself; then we have lunch."

"That much time!"

Not a word from her about Queen Maeve. Had she not noticed her or did she already know about her?

Paoli checked me in and sent me to my room. My hands were trembling in the elevator.

The Hassler-Villa Medici was clean, elegant, and luxurious, if somewhat faded. The employees oozed discretion like a street gang would ooze menace. In my room I pulled open the curtains and looked down the Spanish Steps and over the city of Rome.

The steps are one of the most striking vistas in the world, dense with polychrome spring flowers, the kind of Roman scene Disney would design if someone had not beat him to it. Several of the male loiterers had made what sounded like lewd comments to Paoli as we climbed the steps. Before I could even think of taking a poke at them, she had shouted them down with a stream of vitriolic Italian. They instantly backed off. One did not trifle with practically perfect Paoli.

Where, I asked myself ironically, had I met a woman like that before?

I had little time to do more than look at the inviting king-size bed and drop my computer and my garment bag. I desperately wanted to throw myself on the bed and recover from the shock that my ex-wife would be next door to me all through the conclave.

Mother General was waiting.

I would have bet much of my month's salary that she would glance at her watch as I emerged from the elevator. I would have lost. She was not quite as bad as Peppermint Patty.

Rome is a crumbling, old museum filled with crazy people on motor scooters (*motorini*) without helmets and tourists who want to see "everything" and couldn't possibly go home without a picture of themselves in front of the Trevi Fountain. The city is saved by flowers, a litany of joy on every balcony, roof, and stairway in Rome, blossoms that somehow make the city seem young again—if you can momentarily drown out the noise of the motorini, ignore the stained and dirty walls, and avoid the glazed eyes of the tourists.

An odd thing had happened on our way down the steps, which are steep and narrow, not exactly designed for an American with size-twelve shoes. I had to be careful not to stumble on them and make a fool out of myself—old man who can't walk down 137 steps without falling.

I'd heard someone running behind us. I'd turned around and seen a thin, handsome young man with blazing eyes rushing down the steps, a young man who had looked like the one who had bumped into Paoli at the airport. He was wearing a black suit and a white shirt. In the blink of an eye during which I had observed him, I figured he was a very young priest.

Then he had collided with me and shoved me forward. I lost my balance and teetered on the edge of the step. Sixty more steps down. For an instant I had hung suspended in space, like someone about to leap off a high dive with second thoughts at the last moment.

I'd make an awful mess at the bottom of the Spanish Steps, I'd mused.

CLUMSY PRIZE WINNER BREAKS NECK IN ROME
MULLOY FALLS DOWN HISTORIC STEPS
Condition Called Critical

That's how the paper would have announced my accident to the world.

However, my life, such as it was, did not pass before my eyes. Instead I had lunged in the opposite direction, grabbed for Paoli, missed her, then fell toward the low wall, and finally collapsed against two women who were selling beads as they crouched on a tattered, old blanket.

If I hadn't hit them, I would have surely tumbled down the remaining sixty or so steps.

"Are you all right, Deeny?" my guardian angel had asked anxiously as she helped me up, placated the women with several ten-thousand-lire notes, and dusted me off.

"You should have let me hit him at Fiumicino."

Out of the corner of my eye I'd seen the shade slipping up the steps, easily, smoothly, rapidly. Not exactly Sean Connery, but perhaps a kind of James Bond at that.

"It was not the same boy," she had said. "I am sure of it."

Like Patty, she was a woman occasionally in error and never in doubt. Maybe she was right. Still, two accidents of the same sort within two hours were too much of a coincidence, especially since "they" specialized in such accidents. Someone didn't like us very much. For Paoli they had intended no more than a warning. For me they had sent a message that they really didn't care much about how badly they hurt me.

Well, I'd played with their kind before and I was still alive. I'd wait them out and see what they were up to. If I had not been jet lagged, I would not have been so reckless.

"Are you all right?" Paoli had demanded again. "You look confused."

"I look that way most of the time."

"Are you sure?"

"Let's eat," I'd said, cutting her off. "I'm starved."

Mark

As he walked down the back street in Trastevere toward the *pensione* where he would meet his second contact, Mark still felt guilty about the young woman he had knocked over at the airport.

He should have stopped and apologized to her. His mother would have been very disappointed in him. Always apologize when you bump into someone, she had told him. Especially a woman.

His mother had raised him to be polite and courteous at all times, not that courtesy had done him much good either in the seminary or in the marines. Still, she was right. One should always try to be civilized, even when one was on a mission of critical importance.

Yet the girl had been rude to him. Women that said things like that to men should be taken out and shot. She was probably a feminist as well as a whore. She should be taught manners with a horsewhip, before she was shot.

That did not, however, excuse his lack of courtesy. No matter what they do, his mother had insisted, you must always be civil.

The girl probably had had at least one abortion already. A murdering whore. They all should be taken out and shot.

How many of the cardinals were no better than she was? They condemned abortion, all right, but they didn't support the pro-life movement like they should. Why didn't they say that killing abortionists was like killing a guard in Hitler's concentration camps, legitimate defense of innocent victims?

They were cowards, no different from the abortionists and the bitches who helped kill their own babies.

And this man who everyone said would be the next pope. He was soft on abortion, too. What would happen to the Church if a baby-killer was elected pope?

Mark had wanted to be a priest. They had asked him to leave the seminary because of his concern about abortion. Baby-killers everywhere. But he would be known as a martyr eventually and even perhaps be a canonized saint. That would show them all.

He looked up at the number of the house on his right. A dump, but it was fine for a future saint. His friend would be inside waiting for him. The friend, known to other friends in America, would give him what he needed and then leave.

Mark already felt the smooth bore of the rifle beneath his tender fingers.

Dinny

*Y*ou have walked," Pretty Paoli consulted her watch, "precisely twenty-eight minutes in the noonday sun. You must do at least thirty-two more minutes."

We were eating lunch, pasta for both of us, in Babington's tearoom, which did indeed look very English, though most of its clients looked and spoke middle-western American. She had declined wine with her pasta. I had insisted that she not worry about me. My problems had nothing to do with what other people were drinking.

The man I thought was shadowing me had come in a few minutes after us and was sitting at the far side of the tearoom. He was a shade, all right, no doubt about that.

"Arf," I growled, doing my best to sound like a mad dog.

She giggled. She was giggling a lot. My rusty shanty-Irish charm was working.

"After we have finished our lunch," she picked up her clipboard, "we will walk down the steps to the Metro and ride to Ottaviano. It is a ten-minute walk to the Vatican. We will pick up your credentials at the Vatican press office and then visit the late pope in San Pietro. Then we will walk down the Via della Conciliazione and have our tea in front of the Hotel Columbus. We were thinking of putting you there because it is so close to San Pietro. But the Hassler is much nicer and, as you will see, the Metro brings it very close to the Vatican."

She took a deep breath and continued, "The car will take you back to the hotel. When you have to file a story you can fax it from the hotel. You do have a portable printer, do you not?"

"Of course. Doesn't everyone?"

She frowned. No wit was permitted when she was going through the agenda.

"Then you will have time to rest, although I do not recommend a nap. We will pick you up, as I have said, at nineteen-thirty for your dinner with Bishop Ryan. Do you have any questions?"

She looked up, pen poised in her hand.

"Only one. Will Mario join us for dinner?"

"Mario?"

"Your young man."

"Naturally not." She did her best to try to sound like she was offended by my interest in the young man. "Additionally, he is called Niko."

"Do I get to meet him?"

"Only if you are very good."

"Lot of people flocking into the city for the funeral and the conclave, Paoli?"

"Crazy people!" she exploded. "As if we don't have enough already. The pope is not buried yet and already there are demonstration lines around the piazza: priests who want to marry, priests who don't want to marry, married priests who want to be priests again, nuns who want to be priests, nuns who don't want to be priests, pro-abortion, anti-abortion, Buddhists who are still angry at the poor pope, Muslims who are angry at Israel, Jews who are angry at Pius XII—everyone is here, Catholic radicals, Catholic reactionaries, Catholics who are gay or lesbian, Catholics who are not gay or lesbian, and everyone with angry signs in bad Italian. Bah!"

"Plus the usual collection of sightseers, hangers-on, international thieves, and corrupt bankers. And, naturally, journalists hungry for blood."

"And already they try to influence the conclave; Corpus people are swarming everywhere, trying to persuade everyone that Cardinal Menendez is a bad man. At the sala stampa—the press room—you will see that Maître de Tassigny will bow all over you once he learns that you are *The New York Times.*"

"Who's he?" I sipped my apricot tea.

"The pope's spokesman. Head of the sala stampa. Corpus, of course. Bah! He is, how do you say idiomatically, ah, I know . . . he is a creep. I cannot stand him."

Mother General was not a woman of weak opinions. I knew others like her.

"You do not approve of Corpus?"

"Pigs! They believe women are inferior."

"While you and I know that they are superior, do we not?"

"Naturally!"

This time she didn't giggle.

"Does this Don Luis agree that women are superior?"

"Naturally. He seems to like women."

"Good for him. But he is not Italian?"

"Neither are the cardinals who are Italian. Italian men like women."

I guess I knew what she meant. Sort of.

"Your family see things the same way?"

"Naturally. My father will open his best sparkling wine if Menendez is elected. They were friends long ago. My father is interested in history."

"And Niko?"

"Of course!" She grinned. "Naturally."

Lucky Niko, I thought. As long as, unlike certain men I knew, he could cope with a strong woman.

It was time to change the subject, especially since I was now convinced that she was the source of the rumors the Rome bureau had picked up about another scandal in Vatican finances.

"Can you tell me a little bit more about the rumors of financial scandal that seem to be floating around?"

She became very serious, almost intense.

"There are always such rumors," she said softly. "One learns to discount them. But there are so many more this time. Mama and Papa usually laugh about them. These rumors they will not discuss."

"You think they know something?"

"I'm not sure. Perhaps they have suspicions. They do not want to share them with their journalist daughter, who they have always said has very large ears."

She lifted her shoulders in resignation.

"Not," she added, "that I blame them."

"Any content to the rumors?"

"The Vatican had a small positive balance at the end of last year. For the first time in many years. One hears it said that there had to be some trickery."

"What kind of trickery?"

"If they reported a small profit, there must have been a larger one . . . I know that sounds absurd. It is the way people think around here, however."

"I'll try to track it down after the funeral. Are there names or places?"

"A bank in the Netherlands may be involved."

I'd check it out with our stringer there. In recent years, The Hague had become a center for dubious dealings.

We left Babington's—after she had paid the bill in the name of the Rome bureau—and descended to the Metro again. Three stops, no more than five minutes later, we came to the end of the line—Via Ottaviano. The Metro wasn't really a Metro. It ended in the middle of town. The street was a crowded shopping thoroughfare, filled with bustling people, even though as best as I could calculate, it was siesta time.

"Do you take a siesta, Paoli?"

"Naturally not. It is a waste of time. If I had a lover it would be different, perhaps. But I do not have a lover."

"I understand. . . . You sound like an American when you talk of wasting time."

"I take that as a compliment."

We crossed the Piazza del Risorgimento, where every tram and bus in Rome seemed to be moving dangerously in one direction or the other. Paoli took my hand to guide me across the piazza, lest I take a wrong step into an oncoming tram.

"You must be very careful here unless you have been a Roman all your life."

"I believe you."

On our right the walls of Vatican City loomed. Real walls, designed to keep out invaders from long ago.

We passed through the rim of the Bernini columns and turned left into the Via della Conciliazione.

"This was once an old Roman neighborhood to which people were loyal. That pig Mussolini tore it down so there would be a view from the Tiber to San Pietro. Now everyone says that the Basilica was much more striking when you came upon it suddenly. The pope didn't stop him, either."

"What pope was that?"

"Pius XI, also a pig."

"Are there any popes who were not pigs?"

"Pope John. Papa Luciani, John Paul I, too. The man whose body we will see soon, he was only a stubborn *straniero*, a foreigner."

"Won't Menendez be a straniero too?"

"His mother was Roman, *romana a Roma* like I am. Irrelevant it is that her father was an ambassador here. She was still born in Rome. He speaks Italian like a Roman. The Tuscan tongue in the Roman mouth."

I guess if your family has lived in Rome for more than a thousand years, you are entitled to strong opinions.

The sala stampa is in a building at the very top of the Conciliazione, on the left as you come down from San Pietro. On the ground floor, we encountered a small auditorium in which a number of journalists, most of them looking seedy and impoverished, were curled up sleeping. They weren't any more seedy looking than I was. And I wished I was curled up somewhere sleeping.

On the large-screen television at the front of the auditorium one saw the Piazza San Pietro, complete with a long line moving in the portals and another line moving out. The lines seemed to be moving pretty rapidly. Sure enough, just as Paoli had said, there were groups of picketers walking around the circle created by the Bernini columns. A man and a woman were standing on either side of the obelisk in the center of the piazza haranguing small crowds of followers while teenage boys sat on all the other vacant spaces on the obelisk, the San Pietro version of the drugstore corner of the American past. Gaggles of nuns in garb from the traditional to the modern flight-attendant variety floated briskly across the piazza, some of them apparently reciting the rosary. The Roman city police and the carabinieri were watching indifferently, apparently not wanting to make any unnecessary trouble for themselves.

"Niko out there?" I asked my guide.

"Naturally not." She dismissed the possibility as absurd.

"I've noticed that there are now women cops in those two-person patrols they have around here."

"In the *polizia* and the *municipale*."

"Not in Niko's outfit?"

"They are pigs, but not Niko. He wants women in his unit."

"What do you think about that?"

"Naturally I approve. They are less likely to take chances They don't want to be heroes like the men."

My guardian angel must be very confident of herself—with reason, I supposed.

The next room was the press room—long tables with typewriters, faxes, and phone lines. A few journalists, mostly Italian, were eating their lunches. A couple of others were napping, including one American press association correspondent that I knew slightly but didn't want to know any better.

"Over here is where we get your credentials." Paoli nudged me toward what looked like a theater box office. Three men and a woman waited patiently in line ahead of us. A large, flabby-looking man in a dirty suit was shaking his head negatively at a black man who had trouble with Italian.

"They were very busy this morning with all the reporters flying in for the funeral tomorrow. They will be even busier tomorrow. As you will observe, they take their time."

We waited a half-hour before the functionary got to us. He turned his back on us and began to write something on a sheet of lined paper. Paoli became irate with the delay and shouted at him in angry and rapid Italian. He ignored her. She reached in the window, grabbed him, turned him around, and waved her press card at him. He smelled of strong garlic and other aromas I did not want to name. I gathered she was telling him that he dared not treat *The New York Times* so contemptuously. He glanced at her card and then decided he had better deal with us.

He looked at my application, my ID, my passport, and

the two passport photos I had been told to bring. He looked at them again. Then again.

"Impossible," he murmured and shoved everything back at me.

Paoli exploded. I noted with interest that unlike most women's voices, which become shrill when screaming, Paoli's voice sunk into a lower register and sounded menacing. I guess that's what half a hundred generations in Rome will do for you.

A short, sleek man in a Giorgio Armani blue suit, impeccably groomed down to his manicure and neatly trimmed mustache, appeared behind the functionary.

"Surely, Carlo, we must make special arrangements for *The New York Times*. I will see that the matter arranges itself."

He turned to me and extended his hand.

"Welcome to Rome, Mr. Mulloy. I am Alphonse de Tassigny. I am afraid I am responsible for this place. When I heard *carissima* Paola's voice, I realized that the *Times* was here. We know your work, of course, Mr. Mulloy, and admire it very much. Here, Carlo, I will stamp these documents for Mr. Mulloy."

He stamped the papers, fixed my picture to the press card, glanced at the photo, and passed the card to me.

"You are more handsome in reality than in the photo, Mr. Mulloy."

"Most people say just the opposite, Maître," I replied. "Thank you for the assistance."

"You should have someone else here, Alphonse," Carissima Paoli, still simmering, insisted. "Carlo is a pig."

"I will consider your suggestion, carissima," he said, patting her head with a patronizing gesture, an action that I thought put his life in danger. However, Pretty Paoli simmered down. After all, the *NYT* played it cool, didn't it?

"Thank you for your help, Maître," I said evenly. "I am happy to be duly accredited for this historic event."

Paoli made a face at me behind his back.

"Incidentally, Mr. Mulloy, your former wife was with us not a quarter hour ago. Patricia McLaughlin will represent CNN here. She is duly accredited also."

It was a kind of warning: *We at Corpus know everything.*

"I was aware that she was in Rome, Maître," I said blandly. "Actually, she is still my wife."

"Ah? I had heard you were divorced. . . ."

"Civilly," I said.

Neither Mad Maeve nor I had sought an ecclesiastical annulment.

"So? She is a very beautiful woman." He smiled complacently. "And very, ah, determined."

"Tell me about it."

"So," Paoli said as we left the sala stampa and turned toward the piazza, "you put him down nicely. He pretends to know everything about everyone."

"Does he know about Niko?"

"Everyone knows about Niko." She smiled contentedly. "But you and Signora McLaughlin are, ah, hedging your bets?"

"Nice try, Paoli, but no way. We are both thoroughly sick of one another. I guess we just don't believe in annulments."

"How long have you been divorced?"

"Four years."

"And neither of you have remarried?"

"No."

She sniffed skeptically.

I did not respond to the sniff.

Outside the sala stampa young men and women were passing out handbills with crude cartoons. One of them depicted the late pope throwing gays and lesbians into gas ovens. Another portrayed a crowd of bishops sexually assaulting women. Yet another showed dead embryos scattered in an alley.

Nothing about the death penalty, however.

"Pigs," Paoli whispered to me.

"Kind of pathetic, though. Poor kids."

There were nuns everywhere—almost as many of them as there were pigeons—for the most part ignoring the protesters, as did the solemn priests who strode around importantly, as though the very future of the Church depended on them.

I must confess that nuns produce a visceral revulsion in my stomach. They never liked me when I was in grammar school. I knew too much and caught them too often in mistakes. One of them dubbed me "the walking encyclopedia" and the label stuck until I got to Manhattan College. I hated her and all of them. If I hadn't been such an idiot, I would have known that you don't catch teachers in mistakes, nuns or not.

"You always were a smartass," my ex-wife would tell me when I complained about nuns.

"Didn't they give you a hard time about your good looks?" I would reply.

"Only a few of them. I had the sense not to judge the others by them. The sisters do ninety percent of the good work in the Church."

Down in flames again.

We slowly walked across the piazza as I tried to absorb the atmosphere. More protesters; kids running around as kids always do; speakers shouting their rage against the Church; cops watching more closely than I had thought when I watched the screen in the sala stampa; tourists waiting to see the pope's body, a bonus for their trip; and above it all the looming, outsize masterpiece of the world's largest church.

Beautiful place. It cost us—if I was still part of Catholicism—Germany because Martin Luther, not unreasonably, objected to the sale of indulgences to pay for it. Beautiful and just a little sinister. On the facade the Borghese pope who had built it received more prominent notice than did Saints Peter and Paul.

"What do you think of it, Deeny?"

"Beautiful. And just a little sinister."

"Yes," she said simply. "Just so."

We ignored the line and walked up to the portal on the far right, where two handsome Swiss Guards stood at rigid attention, pikes very firmly in hand.

"You may not enter here," one of them said, in excellent English.

Paoli handed them her card. Both men snapped to attention and presented arms with their pikes. You've never been saluted properly until you've been saluted by a Swiss Guard.

"You may enter here," the guard said, gesturing toward the door behind him, "and approach the bier from the right aisle. Our colleagues in front will direct you."

He smiled approvingly at my guide.

Was that *Times* clout or did Paola Elizabetta Maria Angelica Katarina Brigitta have her own special clout? She sure knew her way around.

We strode by the *Pietà* and down the long side aisle of the immense church. A plainclothes cop, papal gendarme, I assumed, stopped us halfway up. Paoli displayed her card and he too saluted—after glaring his disapproval of her miniskirt.

San Pietro is overwhelming, possibly excessive, to use one of my kids' favorite words. Too big, too much beauty, too much history, too much great art. It was a long way from Galilee. Downhill.

The event wasn't like a wake ought to be. That is, it wasn't like an Irish Catholic wake in America. There was no one with whom to shake hands and tell that you were sorry for their trouble, no murmur of friends and relatives in the background, no politicians working the room, no one kneeling in prayer. Moreover, the crowd pouring through the basilica chattered noisily. No respect, I thought, neither for the church nor the dead. Since it was obvious that we were not to be permitted to stop at the bier for a prayer, I began my Our Fathers and Hail Marys and Eternal Rests on the way up.

Addressing my prayers "to whom it may concern."

Or to "occupant." Possibly "Occupant."

At the front of the aisle, a Swiss Guard inspected Paoli's ID again and led us to the line passing the bier. He deftly eased us in. I glanced at the dead pope, who looked very old and very tired, and mentally grieved for all of us who are born to die. Then we were walking down the side aisle on our way out. Maybe we had a second and a half at the bier.

"You prayed for him?" Paoli asked as we emerged from San Pietro and shielded our eyes against the sunlight.

"I figured it wouldn't hurt. You?"

"Naturally. . . . Do you believe prayers are heard?"

"Some people's."

I wanted a gelato in the worst way. But I was afraid to break away from Mother Superior and I did not want to tell her that whenever I thought about Peppermint Patty for more than a few minutes I developed a fierce hunger for ice cream. Instead I suggested we have a cup of tea.

"And ice cream!" she said with the enthusiasm of my younger daughter.

"Why not!"

A few minutes later we were sitting at the outdoor café in front of the Hotel Columbus halfway down the Conciliazione, sipping tea and eating chocolate ice cream, which Paoli had brought from inside.

"We have a room reserved for you inside, if you want to stay here during the conclave itself," she informed me. "It's a lovely old palazzo, owned by the Knights of Malta, but I'm afraid the rooms are not too comfortable."

"I continue to be astonished at the red carpet treatment."

She shrugged her pretty shoulders. "The *Times* values you very much, Deeny. You must know that."

My shadow was sitting three tables away. Persistent fellow. I needed a picture of him.

"I keep wondering how long it will last."

"Your wife is truly beautiful?"

"Knockout. Wait till you see her on CNN. Whenever she's on, their ratings go up. Bright as they come and persistent."

"You loved her very much?"

"Once."

"And she you?"

"Once."

"I ask too many questions?"

"Ask as many as you want, but don't expect that I can explain what went wrong. It just did, that's all. Mostly my fault."

"Children?"

"Three teenagers. Two girls and a boy. One of the girls goes to college next year."

"They blame you?"

"I hope they don't blame either of us. They seem to like me, though God knows why."

"You will see her here in Rome, naturally."

"Not if I can avoid it."

"But would it not be the time and the place to reconcile?"

None of her goddamn business. Which she probably knew. But women invest a lot in the durability of marriage, any marriage, all marriages.

"No," I said firmly. "It would not."

An elegant black Lancia pulled up next to us. It had some kind of crest on it, probably from the limo company.

"That is your car, Deeny," Paola informed me. Now remember . . ."

"I go back to the hotel, unpack, maybe take a shower, file a dispatch, rest but do not nap, and be at the door at seven-thirty. To meet Bishop Blackie, an absurd name if I ever heard one. Right?"

"You might also find time to watch your wife on CNN."

"I might," I said as I climbed into the car and the chauffeur closed the door. And then again, I might not.

Was I more afraid of encountering Peppermint Patty or of not encountering her?

Damn the little brat. Why didn't she mind her own business? What did she know about marriage anyway?

Blackie

Sean Cronin bounded into my room, eyes glowing in triumph.

"We did it, Blackwood. You were right as always. Don Luis couldn't resist the offer to speak to the students. Idiot face doesn't like it, but how can he say no, especially since Louie might be the next pope?"

"Indeed."

I was trying to link my notebook computer with AOL's European network so as to establish quick links with both my staff at the cathedral and my family on the South Side of Chicago.

"You'll let the media know?"

"Every journalist in Rome will be there, of that you may be sure," I replied. "When?"

"I figure not the day after tomorrow. Too close to the funeral. Nor the day after that. Let the other side get its people out. Then we turn Louie loose. Right?"

"A not unreasonable strategy. . . . Are you sure your man will say the right things? He always has before, yet he is an unusual man."

"You seem to have distributed copies of his quote on abortion to the right people."

"Indeed?" I plugged in a phone line to the modem of my notebook.

"I hear that the redheaded woman from CNN raised

bloody hell over at the sala stampa this afternoon.''

I smiled complacently. ''I don't doubt it for a moment. It was useful to suggest to CNN that they send her here.''

''I hope they don't have anyone like you on their side.''

''Most unlikely.''

I activated AOL. Sure enough, it seemed to work. Remarkable.

''And you see the guy from the *Times* tonight?''

''In Trastevere.'' I addressed a message to Mkate@LCMH.com, Mary Kathleen, my sister the psychiatrist, at Little Company of Mary Hospital.

''He's likely to be on our side?''

''I gather from the literature that reporters always take sides at conclaves. He certainly won't be on the other side.''

''Great!''

''Now is perhaps the time for your siesta?''

''Funny.'' He grinned. ''I just talked to Nora on the phone and she said the same thing.''

He dashed out of the room, not to a siesta, of that I was sure.

I composed my message to my sister the psychiatrist:

You may tell the mayor of Chicago that his presence is not required here. Sean Cronin is in charge. Arguably we will win this one. It will not be worth any damage to his health, however. After a few days in Rome I wonder whether the system will ever change. The Church is still being run by men who would not pass an MMPI test.

In any case, please dispatch specialist on cardiology and circulatory problems to Rome as soon as possible. I will make reservations for her/him at the Park Hotel.

Blackie@aol.com

N Y T

Vatican Prepares for Papal Funeral
Protesters Swarm at St. Peter's
Spanish Cardinal Denounced

By Dennis Michael Mulloy
Vatican City.

Not since Geoffrey Chaucer made his pilgrimage to Canterbury has the Roman Catholic Church attracted such a colorful and disparate collection of people to one place. As workmen prepare the altar and the grandstands for the funeral of the late pope tomorrow, protesters from every cause under heaven have appeared here in Vatican City. Armed with angry orators and colorful posters whose messages are often written in bad Italian, they swarm in the centuries-old Piazza San Pietro, in the shadow of the world's largest church, a church that, as someone remarked today, cost Catholicism Germany.

Nuns in old-fashioned religious habits, priests in cassocks, bishops tinged in purple and an occasional cardinal tinged in crimson stride through the piazza, oblivious to the protesters, who have no votes in the upcoming conclave and, like the rest of the 900 million Catholics around the world, really don't matter.

Crowds of mourners file past the catafalque inside St. Peter's, many of them tourists, for whom a papal wake will be one more thing to talk about when they return home. There are few signs of grief in the rapidly moving line, supervised sternly by Swiss Guards and papal gendarmes. The latter have responsibility for the miniskirt patrol, which obliges them to turn away women who display too much thigh. What is "too much" is a secret that may be known only by the Deity.

Journalists from all over the world, many of them innocent of any knowledge of Catholicism or conclave, corner the occasional passing cleric, desperately seeking a story that might be called "exclusive." Operatives of the supersecret Catholic "secular institute" Corpus Christi buttonhole journalists and ecclesiastics with whispered stories that attack the character of Luis Emilio Menendez, the winter-book favorite for the next pope, who is still accused of being "soft" on abortion though documents released today by the Spanish College indicate that the accusations are false.

Behind closed doors the cardinal electors are presumably "consulting" with one another, though one experienced Roman observer says they are more likely taking long siestas today. Worn from jetlag, one finds oneself speculating about beautiful women manipulating the strings of power in old but elegant palazzos. But this is not a Fellini film, and that kind of manipulation, regrettably, perhaps, ended several centuries ago.

The ambiance here the day before the burial of a dead pope and a week before the election of a new pope reminds one of nothing else in the world save the quadrennial conventions of the Democratic Party in the United States. However, the Democratic National Committee does not lock itself up in an old building and signal the nomination of a candidate by sending white smoke out of what seems to be an unstable chimney. Maybe it should.

The pageant goes on against the backdrop of the world's largest open-air museum, an intensely lived-in city whose women are supposed to be the most beautiful in Italy and whose men are surely the most surly. Romans, who have long memories, have yet to forgive the papacy for destroying their republic more than a century ago. Not so long ago they would cheer for the pope in the Piazza San Pietro and then vote Communist in Rome's municipal elections. Even today they sneer at clergy on the streets.

None of this has much to do with religion, to say nothing of grief for the death of a fellow human being. But it has a lot to do with politics, old and new. On the other hand, if Jesus wanted his church to be free of politics, he should have turned it over to angels.

Mark

Though his heart was pounding rapidly, Mark tried to seem casual as he climbed the stairs of the office building. No one was in the offices because it was siesta time. How stupid to waste the afternoon sleeping when God's work had to be done. Mark paused at the top of the stairs, winded from the long climb. The man who had met him in the pensione had assured him that the door to the roof would be open. It had been open for years, he had insisted.

That morning he had awakened happily from a dream in which his parents were still alive and his brother and sister were still with the family. For a moment he had felt free of obligations. He did not have to kill anyone.

Then he had realized that the dream was foolish. His father had died in a rundown hotel room of a liver infection caused by chronic alcoholism years after he had left the family. His brother and sister could not stand his mother's piety and had left the family.

Until she died, Mark had been Mom's only remaining joy. She had been so proud of him in his seminarian's black suit and then in his marine uniform, a uniform just like the one his father wore before he turned to drink.

On her deathbed she had made Mark promise that he would always fight against abortion. Mom hated abortion.

Still thinking of his childhood happiness, Mark turned the handle of the door to the roof and pushed. The door did not budge. Furiously he pushed harder. It still did not open. This was not fair. He had come to Rome to do God's work and now God was not helping him. He threw the full weight of his body against the door. It sprung open and Mark hurtled out onto the sloping tile roof toward the end. He fell on his face at the very edge. He lay on the roof, panting and frightened as he watched the people and the cars four stories down. No one seemed to have heard him. Gasping for breath, he tried to concentrate his energies, focus his attention.

I wish I did not have to do this, he thought to himself. *But I promised Mom. I must do it for her.*

He crept to the side of the roof away from the street, where no one could see him. Then, when he had calmed down and regained his breath, he crawled around the corner and peered toward St. Peter's. The line of sight was perfect. He had several yards of unobstructed view.

He removed from his jacket pocket the small but powerful telescope that had the same magnification as the scope on the rifle. At first all he could see was a blur of the great church. Then he focused it carefully. The balcony of St. Peter's came into view, seemingly only a few feet away.

Perfect. He couldn't possibly miss.

As he walked down the stairs to street level, a man stared at him curiously and said something in Italian. Mark brushed the dust from the roof off his trousers and ignored the man.

Fuck them all.

Dinny

I did as I was told. I unpacked, took a shower, read the Italian papers (which I could understand, more or less, because of my high school Latin), wrote a story, watched as the hall porter faxed it to New York, and returned to my room to "rest."

Before my rest, however, I put a call in to a certain number in Dublin, a phone in a certain office of the Financial Services Center on the Ana Liffey River.

"Mulloy here."

" 'Tis yourself?"

" 'Tis."

"And you'd want to know about?"

"The Agriculture Bank of Den Haag."

"Ah, 'tis that you want to know, is it?"

If you wanted to talk to the Irish, you had to talk that way.

I sighed loudly.

" 'Tis."

"Well, I'll tell you one thing: You have no business messing around with them gobshites, and yourself with three fatherless children back home."

She never missed that jab.

"Why not?"

"Aren't they thugs now? And killers? And stupid too?"

"Good, pious Catholics, I'm told."

"Haven't they been good, pious Catholic crooks and killers for the last four generations? Doesn't the Divil take care of his own?"

"Up to anything bad recently?"

"Sure, aren't they always up to something bad?"

"Derivatives?"

"Isn't that what they're all doing?"

"Will they get away with it this time?"

"There's them that says they won't."

"Vatican involved?"

"There's them that wouldn't be surprised at all. Aren't your men all papal knights?"

"OK. Thanks for the information. I'll see you sometime."

"Dennis," she abandoned the west of Ireland nonsense and spoke bluntly, like a good Irish mother does on occasion, "stay the fuck away from those fuckers."

"I'll try."

Then I began my "rest."

I did not turn on CNN, however. Not at first. Cute little witch was not going to tell me what to do.

I picked up one of the Italian papers and a dictionary. Was time I worked on my vocabulary.

My head began to nod. I had been strictly forbidden to take a nap. Perhaps I should turn on the TV to keep myself awake. Why not CNN?

I dozed off anyway and indulged myself in erotic dreams, the woman in the dreams being a blend of Paola Elizabetta Maria Angelica Katarina Brigitta and Mad Maeve, my wife. No, my ex-wife. Not in God's view, however.

Then I heard that woman's name and stirred into consciousness. Where in the world was I? Oh, yes, in the Eternal City, where I was doomed to be eternally sleepy.

C N N

ANCHOR: For all the details of the politics of electing a pope, we take you to Patricia McLaughlin in Vatican City. Are Church politics like all other politics, Patty?

(PM is standing in front of the sala stampa, radiant in a white, short-sleeved dress with gold buttons down the front.)

PM: They're worse, Tessa. They make the Chicago politics of a couple of decades ago look honest and straightforward by comparison. Just a few moments ago, Alphonse de Tassigny, the head of the Vatican press office, admitted in an exclusive interview with CNN that he is a member of the radically conservative Catholic organization that is slandering Luis Cardinal Menendez, the front-runner for next week's conclave. (Cut to tape. PM holding mike for AT)

PM: Don't you think it is inappropriate for conclave campaigning to take place before the funeral Liturgy for the pope tomorrow, M. de Tassigny?

AT: (smoothly) I quite agree, Patricia. There should be respect for the dead. Moreover, there are really not campaigns before the conclave. The electors in the Sacred College must clear their minds to be open to the inspiration of the Holy Spirit.

PM: Yet isn't it true that members of Corpus Christi Institute have been circulating distortions of Cardinal Menendez's position on abortion all day?

AT: (somewhat nervously) I'm sure they are not the ones.

PM: Everyone else in Rome thinks so. Isn't it strange that the Vatican press office does not have copies available of the actual text of the cardinal's remarks, which was distributed by the Spanish College today?

AT: (now wishing to escape) We direct anyone who asks for a copy to the Spanish College.

PM: Isn't it true that all the cardinal said was that the Catholic tradition does not tell us when the human person appears?

AT: Ah, I believe so.

PM: So there is no question about his orthodoxy?

AT: Certainly not.

PM: Isn't it true, M. de Tassigny, that you are a member of the Corpus Christi Institute?

AT: (angry) That is a personal question!

PM: Don't you think it is unfair that the Vatican press office be controlled by an organization that is trying to destroy Cardinal Menendez's reputation and prevent him from being pope?

AT: I am terminating this interview. (walks off camera) (Cut to PM live on the Conciliazione, St. Peter's in the background.)

PM: So, you see, Tessa, the cards seemed to be stacked against Cardinal Menendez. Catholics believe that the Holy Spirit influences the outcome of conclaves. Just now it would seem She has Her work cut out for Her if She is to overcome Vatican corruption.

This is Patricia Anne McLaughlin, CNN, Vatican City.

Blackie

"Wow," said Mick Kennedy, cardinal archbishop of Albany. "Did she stick it to him! Good for her!"

Mick had played basketball for Manhattan College in his youth and now, though utterly bald, radiated vigorous good health from every inch of his six foot five inch frame.

"Pretty effective, if you ask me," Sean Cronin said with a beatific smile. "And she cleared Louie of that crazy business about being soft on abortion."

"Arguably," I murmured.

"I agree that she was effective," observed Cardinal John Lawrence Meegan of Miami Beach. "But the woman is a shameless hussy."

John Lawrence is a small, bookish-looking man, with

thick glasses and a repertory of fluttery, nervous actions. He alone wore a crimson watered-silk sash and zucchetto and a cassock with crimson buttons. "He sleeps in his robes," Sean Cronin had insisted, "so that no one can take them away while he's in bed."

We were sitting in the faculty common room, reserved for cardinals and their aides during the pre-conclave period, everyone sipping scotch except Milord Cronin, who indulges every day in one tumbler of Jameson's (special reserve) straight up. I was uncharacteristically drinking iced tea because I was eating supper with *The New York Times* and did not want to commit the blasphemy of falling asleep in such august company.

"She surely does generate sexual appeal." Milord Cronin sighed, appreciatively, I thought. "Wholesome eroticism, however. Irish Catholic eroticism."

All the more seductive, I thought, because it was wholesome. Well, almost wholesome.

"I hear she left her husband and has a lesbian lover living with herself and her children."

"I can guarantee you that is not true," Sean Cronin said crisply. "Is it, Blackwood?"

"No lover of either gender." I sighed. "She is the most virtuous of matrons."

"I'm glad to hear that," Meegan said in the tone of voice of someone who didn't believe it at all. "But she does terrible harm to the faithful by broadcasts like that. The simple laity all over America will be shocked by her insinuations."

"We all know she's telling the truth," Mick Kennedy observed. "If people are shocked by the truth, it's our fault for tolerating what goes on here."

"The laity," my cardinal said, "are beyond shock. They just assume that this place is corrupt. The Banco Ambrosiano mess did that for us."

"As well," I murmured again, "as the reading of fifteen minutes of Catholic ecclesiastical history."

Dinny

Peppermint Patty, I thought, as I stirred out of my chair and turned off the TV, still had a great instinct for the jugular.

And she radiated a lot more sex appeal than the "Peanuts" character.

The problem between us had nothing to do with professional envy. We admired and respected each other as journalists and rejoiced in each other's triumphs. Moreover, we both felt free to be critical, as mature professional colleagues should feel. I had learned a lot from her and said so. She never admitted to learning anything from me, but was always tolerant of my suggestions.

No, that was not the problem at all.

"Admit it!" my shrink had shouted at me. "Nothing in your life prepared you for intimacy with such a woman!"

"That's true," I had conceded.

"Face it, Mulloy, you may be a hero who has saved hundreds of lives, you may be good at martial arts, but when it comes to women, you are a wimp."

She had been absolutely right.

"That's not completely true," I had said.

"You can't even cope with me when I shout at you."

"That's not true!" I had shouted back. "But I can't deny what you just said. In our house, when I was growing up, no one ever shouted because it upset Mom."

"That's better . . . you understand that your mother ruled by using a passive-aggressive strategy. You learned how to charm women, but not how to fight with them when fighting was necessary to sustain an intimacy. Wimps lose strong wives.''

For sure.

I started going to this shrink after I had stopped drinking. She was much better than the feminist counselor that Mad Maeve had chosen for us. Most of the ''counseling'' had been a joint attack on me for my failures of manhood. Finally I had walked out on it all and Patty had walked out on the marriage.

''I didn't think I was supposed to fight with a woman I loved.''

''Now you understand that love implies conflict and reconciliation?''

''In theory. I don't know that I can do it in practice. I don't think it would have done any good with Patricia.''

''What would have happened if you had said to her, for example, 'Goddamn it, Patty, will you shut up and listen to me for a minute or two?' ''

My stomach had clutched at the very thought.

''Frankly, I don't know.''

''Yes, you do.''

''Do I?''

''Certainly.''

''Well, you think that she would have shut up and listened and I suppose you ought to know because you've treated people like her.''

''I can guarantee you that she would have done just that.''

''Maybe.''

''You understand that, given the noise and contention in which she was raised, your wife tests reality by charging into it. When it charges back, she is delighted because she understands where she is.''

''It doesn't seem fair.''

''I didn't say it was fair. I make no case for her behavior at all. But your response of running away was not fair either. Lovers must draw lines for one another.''

I had not drawn many lines for Pugnacious Patty during

our marriage. Yet I remembered a few times when I had tried it. As the shrink had predicted, she'd backed off, wept a little, and then embraced me and told me how much she loved me.

I suppose that was a kind of an apology, but she never once said she was sorry.

"Lovers should always be ready to apologize," my shrink had insisted. "But you never demanded an expression of regret, did you?"

"No," I had admitted.

In my room at the Hassler, my stomach clutched again at the very thought of confronting Queen Boudicca with such a demand.

I had learned at least one thing from my shrink: I had failed as a husband. Maybe Queen Boudicca had failed as a wife too. But that wasn't the point. I hadn't been the kind of husband she needed. She needed someone who hadn't spent much of his life in conspiracy with the rest of the family to tiptoe around our mother, lest the whole structure of our family life come tumbling down at her first tear.

Queen Boudicca had been stunning as well as brilliant in her dismantling of Maître de Tassigny. Despite her height Patricia was not what could be called Junoesque. Rather, she was slender and willowy with glorious breasts that caused a man to gasp even when they were fully covered. Her intelligent, mobile face was neither beautiful nor even pretty, but it was striking. When you saw her face on the screen, you had to stop channel surfing. Her alabaster complexion, varying from becoming rose to appealing scarlet when she blushed (which was often), was indestructible. The combination of her long, burnished red hair, neatly fitting white dress, and big golden buttons during her destruction of the papal spokesman, had set my fingers twitching as she had destroyed him—despite the fact that I had unbuttoned her clothes hundreds of times in the course of our ill-starred intimacy.

"But never that dress and those buttons," my surly libido muttered.

I could be celibate with relative ease unless Patty happened to be around.

I took another shower and dressed for dinner with this Bishop Ryan from Cardinal Cronin's staff. I had never heard of him, but I had to assume that, despite his odd name, if he had been vetted and approved by Paola Elizabetta Maria Angelica Katarina Brigitta, he must be worth an interview.

Just to show Mother Superior that I was a good boy, I presented myself at the entrance to the Hassler at seven-twenty-five.

Promptly at seven-thirty, the Lancia pulled up and Paoli hopped out.

"Ah," she said, glancing at her watch, "you are punctual."

"I'd be afraid not to be."

She giggled and dismissed me with a wave of her hand. No clipboard tonight.

Tonight I was favored by a much more glamorous Paoli—sleeveless gray shift with a skirt, if anything, shorter than the one she had worn at the airport, more-elaborate makeup, and sparkling jewelry, real diamonds, unless I had lost the ability to tell the fake from the real.

"You look lovely tonight, Paoli," I said.

She blushed and replied, "Thank you, Deeny. That suit is much better than the one you wore today."

"It's my other suit."

"We must have our tailor come to you in the hotel." She guided me into the car and closed the door.

I was given no opportunity to reply or to protest that I should be holding the door open for her.

"So," she began as our driver cautiously eased his way into Roman traffic, "you watched your wife on CNN?"

"Yep."

"She was excellent, no?"

"A little above average for Patricia Anne."

"She is extremely attractive, no?"

"Dazzling."

"You still love her?"

I should have told the nosy little snoop that it was none of her business. Truth to tell, I liked talking about Patty.

"I'm a human male, Paoli. So I still desire her. But I am terrified of her."

"You will see her in Rome?"

"I fervently hope not."

Paoli sniffed derisively. She then turned to the subject of the Church of Santa Maria in Trastevere. It was probably the first Christian church built in Rome: founded by Calixtus I in the third century, remodeled and rebuilt in the thirteenth century. The mosaic of Mary nursing the baby Jesus dated from that time, yet was so bright that it seemed made only yesterday. Trastevere itself was very old. Some of the people there were certainly descendants of those who had first settled the district in pre-Christian times. They spoke their own peculiar dialect and kept their own peculiar superstitions, probably dating back to Etruscan times. They had great fear of blindness from the evil eye, which was frequent among those born at the turn of the century because of trichinosis caused by the polluted waters of the Tiber River.

"Were the people here a long time before your family?"

"Oh, yes. I'm afraid my ancestors had to fight them often."

We wound through the darkening streets of Rome, down alleys and through silent piazzas, crossed the Tiber somewhere, and then crawled along even narrower streets.

Finally we turned a corner into a square, on the other side of which loomed a very old church whose dazzling mosaics on the facade were illumined by a floodlight.

"As beautiful as you said it was, Paoli."

"Very beautiful. In those days they were not ashamed to admit that the Madonna had breasts."

"Useful for feeding children," I said, feeling ashamed of my lust for my former wife.

"And for ornaments to attract men," she added.

"Really?"

She giggled.

This time the driver was permitted to open the door of the Lancia for me and I was permitted to help Paoli out of the car. Lucky Niko, I thought, as the movement of climbing out of the car briefly displayed fresh young breasts and even more thigh.

For someone who had given up sex, I was in a thoroughly tumescent state. All Patty's fault.

"You wish to sit outside?" She gestured at the array of tables in front of the restaurant that encroached on the piazza.

"Great idea. Do you know what this Bishop Ryan looks like?"

"Naturally not. But you have been described to him."

"What the fuck are you doing here?"

Oh, oh. It was the aforementioned Maeve the Mad. My stomach turned over several times.

"Patricia," I began hesitantly.

"What are you up to? Did you steal my source?"

"Uh, no, I don't think so."

"I've been waiting an hour for my source and I'm leaving."

I have often wished that when Queen Boudicca was in full sail she would turn ugly and shrewish. Alas, she looks even more beautiful. She was wearing a black wraparound dress whose neckline plunged in the general direction of her navel.

"This is . . ."

"I know: your most recent bimbo. You're robbing cradles now, aren't you, Dinny?"

I experienced the sensation that Mount Vesuvius was about to erupt beside me.

"Would you just shut up!" I yelled at her. "Shut your big shanty-Irish mouth for a moment and listen to me."

An experiment.

Score one for my shrink. Peppermint Patty recoiled, her aquamarine eyes widened, and she shut up.

Before I could figure out what to say next, an odd little man, wearing black slacks and a Chicago Bulls windbreaker, drifted among us. His eyes, behind thick glasses, blinked rapidly as though he were lost.

"Bishop Ryan!" Queen Maeve said sweetly. "I didn't know you were in Rome!"

"Arguably I am. I am to sup with *The New York Times*, which I believe has sent a delegate to the conclave. But he seems to be lost."

"Not at all, Bishop." Always a priest fan, she continued to be sweet. "May I present my ex-husband, Dennis Michael Mulloy, prize-winning correspondent for *The New York Times*. Dinny, this is Bishop John Blackwood Ryan of Chicago, Cardinal Cronin's auxiliary bishop."

"How romantic!" The bishop extended his hand to me. Then he added, "Call me Blackie."

I couldn't quite believe he had said "how romantic." This guy was weird, all right, but arguably (to use his word) very bright and very dangerous. He saw too much.

"And this is my colleague from our Rome bureau, Bishop: Paola Elizabetta Maria Angelica Katarina Brigitta Oriani."

With astonishing grace, he kissed Paoli's fingers.

"*Principessa.*"

"*Monsignore.*" Paoli beamed. Then she added, "Are you *really* a bishop?"

"I'm afraid so. I fear I have forgotten my ring." He searched in his pockets. "Perhaps I can find another badge of office."

He reached into the jacket of his windbreaker and, with some difficulty, produced a large and very unusual pectoral cross.

"*Ah, La Croce di Santa Brigitta, mia patrona carissima. Bellissima!*"

"What's this princess business?" I demanded.

"The Principessa Paola Elizabetta Maria Angelica Katarina Brigitta," he replied, "is a daughter of one of the great families of the black nobility, which patently does not mean in this context African-American, but papal, in contrast to the white nobility, which were those noble families that opted for Vittorio Emanuele when the Piedmont monarchy came to Rome. The black nobility have been distinguished for their loyalty to the Holy Father and for the beauty of their daughters, who until recently tended to marry elderly bankers."

Paoli was beaming happily. She had decided that, weird or not, she liked this little bishop. It was in fact hard not to like him.

"But now fall in love with young cops," I added.

"Net improvement," he said.

Paoli giggled happily. "Cops whose fathers own a computer company as well as vineyards . . . now shall we stop talking about my disgraceful ancestors and find our table?"

She moved into the restaurant.

"I'm not part of the group, Bishop," Queen Maeve said with considerable charm and a fetching blush. "I've been stood up by a source who found someone more important. I hope I can see you later."

She smelled delicious. Soap, water, and spring air.

"Why don't you join us, Patricia?"

The words tumbled out of my mouth. I didn't mean to say them. Honest, I didn't.

"You really wouldn't mind?"

"Certainly not. CNN will owe the *Times* one."

"I . . . uh . . . I'd like that very much."

In the slight confusion of going into the restaurant behind Paoli, who did not seem happy at all about Patty's presence, my former wife managed to take Mother Superior aside. I watched as Paoli listened to her, stony-faced and imperious.

Surely Mad Maeve is not apologizing.

But apparently she was. Paoli's face melted. She smiled and touched Patricia's arm in a gesture of forgiveness.

Well, I'll be damned.

We arranged ourselves around the table, Paoli asked permission to order for us, I turned over my wineglasses (a gesture that my ex-wife did not miss), Mother Superior ordered our food and drink as though she owned Rome, and Bishop Blackie waited patiently for the interview to begin.

Out of the corner of my eye I saw the shade arrive, a little breathless and a little late. I had to find out more about this guy.

"What is an auxiliary bishop?" I asked Bishop Ryan.

He looked around the table, his pale blue eyes, shrewd but kind, taking in everything.

"It is safe to assume that you all have seen the motion picture *Pulp Fiction*?"

We all nodded.

"You will remember the role Harvey Keitel played in the last segment?"

"Sure," I spoke for all of us.

"The Sweeper?" Patricia Anne added.

"I play the same role for Milord Cronin."

We all laughed, though I wasn't altogether sure that he was merely joking.

"May I take notes?" Patricia looked at me. "I'll check with you if I am going to use anything."

"Bishop?"

"If you find anything worth recording."

My ex-wife pulled out glasses that she hadn't used to need, drew a notebook from her purse, and opened it on the table next to her wineglass. She began to scribble on the notebook.

"Is Cardinal Cronin going to be the first American pope?" I continued with the obvious next question.

"In the same sense that General William Tecumseh Sherman was elected president of the United States."

"The guy who said, 'I will not run if nominated, I will not serve if elected'?"

"Indeed."

"But then," my former wife took over the interview, "who will be elected?"

She clutched her pen more anxiously and scrawled more furiously than she had in yesteryear. The strain of being at the top and of fearing a fall from the top was catching up to her

"I advance the hypothesis that it might not make any difference."

Dead silence around the table.

"Pardon?" Patricia filled the silence.

As she leaned forward I spotted a bit of black lace in the cleavage of her dress. Suddenly I imagined myself ripping off that lace and caressing again those glorious pale breasts—with her hands pressing against mine as if to forbid me ever to stop.

Dangerous fantasies.

"Does it matter who is the monarch of the United Kingdom?"

"Not really."

"Why not?"

"Because the queen or the king is a symbolic leader with no real power. But doesn't the pope have awesome power?"

Four large plates of antipasto arrived.

"Does he? Consider by way of example my own family. Three sisters and a brother. A psychiatrist, a judge, a writer, and a lawyer. Numerous nieces and nephews and now grandnieces and grandnephews whose number I cannot keep up with. All of them Catholic to their fingertips. Unthinkable that they could not be. Deeply involved in the work and activities of the Church. They will cheer enthusiastically for the pope when he comes to our city, but, instead of being present in Grant Park for his Eucharist, more likely than not they will watch him on television unless there is a Bears' game or a Bulls' game. They admired the last poor man's piety and stage presence. They were mildly happy when *Time* chose him as Man of the Year. But they had nothing to learn from him. They had long ago made up their minds on birth control and other matters such as artificial insemination and in vitro fertilization. They think it odd that a man who knows nothing about marriage and, in fact, little about married people would pontificate about marital intimacy or the context of marriage. They are embarrassed by his seemingly reactionary attitude towards women, but it does not trouble their allegiance to Catholicism. They bought his book when it came out and did not find it utterly unintelligible. Neither did it respond to any of their spiritual needs nor address what they think is the great weakness in the Catholic Church.''

"Which is?" Patricia asked, scooping up a forkload of pasta.

Her dress had a long slit in the side, which exposed an appealing area of nylon-covered thigh—a muscular but enchanting thigh, as I remembered it.

"The disgraceful quality of Sunday homilies."

"So you conclude . . . Sorry, Dinny," she said, touching my hand and sending an electric shock through my body, "this is not my interview."

"Go right ahead," I said. "The *Times* does not mind our exploiting your talents as an interviewer. Do we, Principessa?"

I had forgotten the silky softness of Patty's fingers. She had changed to clear nail polish.

The black noble smiled benignly, displaying a perfect row of shining white teeth. "Not at all. We may even pay for your dinner."

General laughter.

Why do women bond together so quickly against the rest of us?

"As to what I conclude," Bishop Blackie frowned at his plate, as if he suspected someone had stolen some pasta from it, "it seems to me patent that for them and for millions of Catholics in the United States, there is nothing more that we—popes, bishops, priests—can do to drive them out of the Church. We have done our best in the last three decades and they won't go. Defection rates have not changed for a half-century. They would like to have a pope that inspires them as did Pope John during the early nineteen sixties. They would be content with a pope who does not embarrass them. But in their ordinary daily lives, the pope is not relevant to their Catholicism. I do not argue that this is the way matters ought to be, but only the blind in this city really believe that it is not the way they are.''

''But,'' Patty protested, ''the pope is the Vicar of Christ!''

If we were still married I would take her home to my suite at the Hassler, gently and slowly remove her clothes, play with her for a long time, and then engage in sweet and tender love with her.

Shut up, I told my libido. I'm not married to her anymore.

''The poor man whose body lies over in St. Peter's admitted that the title was not altogether appropriate, though tolerable. For the first thousand years the pope was called the Vicar of Peter, a much more modest and more accurate title.''

''So where are we?''

''For all practical purposes, as far as the laity and even the parish clergy are concerned, we are back in the ninth century, when this young person's,'' he gestured toward Paoli, ''rural ancestors descended on Rome and attempted to restore order.''

''Eight popes died in eight months, most of them poisoned,'' Paoli said. ''One of them dug up his predecessor from the grave, convicted him at a trial, and executed him. Some of my female ancestors were papal mistresses, others brokered papal elections.''

''And in such matters generally made intelligent decisions,'' the bishop sighed loudly. ''It was not the worst way of doing things.''

''You wouldn't do that today, would you, dear?'' Patricia turned to my principessa.

''Naturally I would,'' that worthy replied calmly. ''I

wouldn't be anyone's mistress because that is an oppressive and degrading role. But I'd love to broker a papal election."

I tried to focus on Paoli instead of my luscious ex-wife. Mother Superior's slender neck, I noted, was like an ivory pillar, smooth, flawless, utterly unblemished by age.

"Consider what I mean," the bishop continued. "In that era, the pope was very lucky to have influence in Rome. Beyond Rome the peasant people and the peasant clergy, to say nothing of the various warlords who dominated Europe and fought off the barbarians with differing degrees of success, knew there was a pope somewhere, but he was, for reasons of transportation and communication, utterly irrelevant to their lives. So it is today, despite faxes and E-mail and supersonic jets. The outcome of the conclave will be important to the electors, to bishops around the world, to theologians, and to some, but not all that many, parish clergy, and to journalists like yourselves. The combination of instant communication and Renaissance absolutism which has marked the papacy during this century matters very little to most Catholics."

"Is all of this off the record, Bishop?" I interjected.

"I can't imagine saying anything important enough to keep off the record. All the comments I have made so far are patent to anyone who knows any Catholic history and the recent studies of Catholicism around the world. Only the pope and the Curia and some bishops have been able to keep their heads in the sand."

I had yielded the floor to Peppermint Patty because I didn't trust my power of speech. It was a glorious spring night in Trastevere. A full moon had risen over Santa Maria; the smell of flowers and blossoming trees permeated the air; street noises and bits of conversations suggested that we were indeed in a neighborhood not unlike the one I grew up in; I was sitting between two glittering women, with both of whom I wanted to engage in prolonged sexual play.

Fat chance.

I was enough of a trained journalist to absorb everything

the funny little bishop was saying. But my mind, despite the stern warnings I tried to impose on it, was preoccupied with my former wife. It was not just lust, I told myself. I felt residual affection for her. I was indeed besotted by her cleavage. I did indeed want to strip away her dress and the black lace beneath it. But hurt her even a little bit?

Good God, no! I wanted, rather, to ease the pain that occasionally flashed at the back of her green eyes.

Well, then stop objectifying her! She's not a sex object, is she?

Well, sort of.

Women usually know when a man is doing something like that. I presumed that in some corner of her mind Patricia did perceive what was happening. But she was too busy with her interview to pay much attention or care.

Or, heaven knows, perhaps she even enjoyed it.

I avoided Mother Superior's eye. I wanted to see neither her approval or disapproval. Nor did I want to permit fantasies about her breasts.

"How did this happen, Bishop Blackie?" Patty said as she gulped from her wineglass.

Could she be nervous too? I had no monopoly on fantasies, did I?

"Two things happened, Patricia. First of all, the Second Vatican Council, and secondly, the birth control encyclical in 1968. The council was an attempt, under Pope John's benign guidance, to reform the administration of the Church. It was shaped by the great European theological minds that emerged from the cataclysm of the Second World War. It stirred great hope and enthusiasm around the Catholic world. Then the bishops and the theologians went home and the Roman Curia did what any bureaucracy does: It set about undoing the changes which were a threat to its monopoly on power. Many of the council reforms have survived, the Mass in English, for example. But reform of the institutional structure never occurred. The proposed decentralization of power frightened Pope Paul VI, who was elected after Pope John died. The man whom we bury tomorrow arguably centralized power more than ever before."

"Did you ever meet him, Paoli?" I asked the principessa.

"Naturally. He is, uh, was a nice man. He liked women, which is more than you can say for some of the others. But I don't think he ever knew any women, not well. He gave us a lecture once about purity. Some of us will be pure and some of us will not, but the Church will have nothing to do with either decision."

"It was sex that undid it all." The bishop sighed, an Irish sigh just like my mother's, though apparently meaning something very different. "The council wanted to discuss birth control and probably would have voted overwhelmingly for change. It was a critical turning point. Dr. Rock's pill—the first widely used oral contraceptive—required some kind of reevaluation. Pope John set up a commission of advisers and postponed conciliar discussion. When he died, Pope Paul, a nervous and timid man, I'm afraid, withdrew the issue from the council and expanded the commission. He was not sure what he wanted. On the one hand he wanted a good reason for a change in the traditional teaching. On the other he was afraid that change would shake the people's faith in the authority of the papacy. So he stacked the commission with bishops and experts who could be expected to vote against change. However, the married laypeople on the commission persuaded the other members of what every married person in the world and most parish priests know."

"And that is?" I asked uneasily.

"In effect, that human sexuality is distinct from the sex of other primates in that it is for bonding as well as for procreation. The bond between husband and wife stretches like a rubber band." He moved his hands apart. "Then, when it is at the breaking point, the force of passionate love draws them together again." He brought his hands together.

I was afraid to look at Patty. I'm sure she was afraid to look at me. Was he saying that for our benefit?

The waiter brought our veal piccata. I waited uneasily for him to slip away. I was not particularly eager to hear the bishop say anything more about sex. I stole a peek at Patty. Her eyes were glued on the veal.

I remembered our wedding night. She had been frightened, but game. Desperately eager to please me. Which she surely did.

"Sex in humankind," the bishop went on, "heals the hurts and the frictions of the common life. At the end of the final meeting of the commission, in 1966, the fifteen bishops voted with only three dissenting that birth control was not intrinsically evil. The laity, consulted on the subject of their marriage relationship for the first time in history, thought they had won. But the Curial cardinals went to work on the pope's conscience after the commission had gone home. They persuaded him that he would be violating the teachings of Jesus if he approved of change. Two years later he issued the famous birth encyclical in which he listed the reasons his own commission had advocated as grounds for change. He did not reply to them but simply dismissed them. The issue wasn't sex, it was papal power. The reaction from the world's hierarchies was underwhelming. The pope wept in sorrow for himself and announced that in twenty years he would be hailed as a prophet. He staked his papacy on that decision. So did the man who died a few days ago. But the laity and clergy of the world rejected the decision. The hopes at the end of the council turned sour and bitter. The wisdom of the Catholic heritage on human sexuality was taken out of the equation as our species argued over sex. In a crowning irony, a decision made to protect papal authority in fact diminished papal authority. The pope for most Catholics became a figurehead."

"How sad," Patricia Anne said sadly.

I glanced at her. She really was feeling pain. Not like her to worry about something in the past.

"The veal piccata is excellent," I said, hoping to change the subject.

"Neither of them knew any women well enough," Principessa Paola observed, "to ask them what sex was for. Or what it meant to a woman."

"Or any married men either," Bishop Blackie added.

"So the conclave will be about sex?" Patty renewed the interview.

I imagined my ex-wife striding through the four fields of Ireland with flaming red hair and a huge battle sword, Ycats's Kathleen ni Houlihan. Most men would follow her even when it was raining, which was usually the case in that soggy land.

"Not at all. It will be about power. The late pope, raised as he was in a time of crisis in his native country, believed in the discipline of the garrison—strong centralization, authoritarian power, absolute obedience. He was indeed the most gifted pope of the century, perhaps the most gifted ever to sit on the throne of the Fisherman. Yet it does not follow that he was a democrat.

"Still, it must be remembered that as a young bishop he exercised considerable influence on the side of the progressives. He read with fascination the works of Küng and Congar and Rahner and Schillebeeckx, the decisive intellects of the council. Yet as pope he persecuted Küng and Schillebeeckx. In Krakow he ran a flexible archdiocese. It was the liberals who voted for him in the second conclave of 1978. And they were led by Franz König of Vienna, who had proposed him before the first conclave of that year of the three popes. König apparently made a speech from the floor in his favor. But when König retired, the pope appointed successors without consulting with him, men who opposed everything that König stood for. A few years ago, König, in his nineties, went into open opposition on birth control. The pope spoke constantly in favor of human rights, but he did not see that these rights should also be recognized in the Church."

"What happened to him?"

"There are many theories, most of them pointing at the

Polish Church's long battle against foreign governments. They say he saw no other way to govern the Church. You have to be authoritarian and rigid when you perceive that the Church is under attack . . . an odd position for the man who helped to compose the joyous and optimistic document *Gaudium et Spes*, which celebrated the promise and possibilities of the modern world.''

"It is all very sad,'' Kathleen ni Houlihan said. "Tragic.''

"Given enough time,'' I observed, "most things go badly.''

"Oh, yes. The bishops of the world, even the conservative men that he had appointed, found that instead of the freedom to govern their own dioceses as successors to the apostles, indeed in union with the pope, but mostly without his interference, they had become low-level civil servants under the constant supervision of the Roman Curia and their spies. The reform of the Vatican Council, which implied more day-to-day power for the residential bishops, had not only been aborted. It had been reversed. The bishops have been subject to constant harassment. The pope and the Curia, it seemed, trusted their own appointees less than they trusted the writers of crank letters or spies from Corpus or the Opus Dei or other such groups. The word 'pluralism,' which you will hear often during the next week, is the buzzword of bishops who would like to be left alone to run their own ship without constant interference from Rome.''

"So they're voting for more freedom for themselves but no more freedom for us?''

"And, good Patricia, more freedom from your friends in Corpus, whom you so nicely skewered this afternoon.''

She flushed attractively, a usual Maeve-the-Mad reaction to a compliment. Especially when someone praised her when she was stark naked.

"Thank you, Bishop. But we still don't count any more than those people on the birth control commission did thirty years ago.''

The waiter came with zuppa inglese. Paoli dispensed us

from any dieting obligations on the grounds that this was the best zuppa inglese in all of Rome.

"I'll run two extra miles tomorrow," Patty promised, then asked, "What did he think of Americans?"

"Not much, I'm afraid. At least one European intellectual who was invited to his annual seminars declined after the first couple of times because he could not tolerate the pope's dislike for a country that he, the visiting intellectual, admired so greatly. We were sex-mad materialists almost as bad as the Soviet Communists. He felt that the whole of Western culture was doomed and that the faith would vanish in the West. That's why he appointed so many bishops, particularly in Europe, who were unsympathetic to their priests and people. He wanted bishops who shared his contempt for the West."

We were silent for a moment at that revelation.

"Is the Catholic Church corrupt, Bishop?" I asked bluntly while I slopped up the dessert.

"It's your beat, Dinny." His shrewd blue eyes blinked rapidly behind his Coke-bottle glasses. "You know about the scandals of the last two papacies, you've written about the Banco Ambrosiano scandal. No one knows what happened to all that money or what, if anything, the Church got out of it."

"It is my impression," I said cautiously, "that it didn't get anything, but was taken for a ride by some of the more shady elements in Italian international finance."

"Yet it was said that the money went to Poland to support Solidarity."

"I could never find any proof of that."

"But no proof that it didn't happen either." The bishop extended his hands in a gesture of helplessness. "The Vatican is an old and secret bureaucracy which doesn't have much money and needs a lot of it just to pay its bills. To whom does it report? God? She is silent on such matters. No one is in control. No one watches the books, much less watches those who are supposed to watch the books. Who can say what happens?"

He shrugged his shoulders.

"It is only because of the media and a somewhat more diligent Italian government that the Banco Ambrosiano scandal became public knowledge," I observed.

"Money," he sighed, "corrupts. In many Catholic countries, including this one, a priest is assumed to have responsibility for all the members of his family because, poor as he might be, he is less poor than they are. Tips and gifts are commonplace when one wants small favors from the Curia or even dispensations, which theoretically should be free. Small problem, I suppose. It would be much better if we paid our staff a decent salary."

"Grubbing for money all the time," Patricia said. "How awful!"

"It was happening even before my family came," Principessa Paoli agreed. "We have paid much money in bribes through the centuries."

"I know of an American bishop," Blackie continued, "now lamentably no longer among us, who used to give high Curial officials a thousand-dollar bill and ask them to say a Mass for his mother. A Mass stipend or a bribe?"

"Were there payoffs for him?"

"Oh, yes, most certainly. The papal nunciature in America is a lucrative post. The nuncio receives a large stipend from every bishop at whose ordination and installation he presides. One of the men who held the post twenty years ago boasted he returned home a millionaire. In those days a million dollars was a lot of money. Is that corrupt? Who is to say?"

"How much did you have to pay, Bishop?" Patty asked.

His round, bland face crinkled in a leprechaunish gleam.

"The nuncio informed me that he could come for my ordination, rather unusual in the case of a lowly ecclesiastical Harvey Keitel, but he had heard that my family was not without resources. The stipend would be twenty thousand dollars.''

"And you said?''

"I invited him with all due respect to go jump in the Potomac River.''

"In those very words?''

"Oh, yes.''

"Naturally,'' my princess-guide said, beaming her approval.

"You will never make archbishop!''

"I trust I can count on that.''

"Will a new pope be able to clean up the mess?''

"Perhaps. But pluralism comes first. Cardinal Menendez is patently the candidate of the pluralist party. Many of those who will vote for him, most, perhaps, want only to be left alone by the Curia and the papacy. Some of them, however, including Menendez himself and Milord Cronin and Klaus Graf Von Obermann, realize that pluralism means they will be consulted often about decisions here. Hence there will be no more unilateral statements about such matters as women's ordination. In their turn they will consult routinely with their clergy and laity. The Holy Spirit, who speaks through the laity to the hierarchy as well as vice versa, will be freed finally to say all the things She wants the ordinary people of God to say in Her name. It will take a little time, such cardinals will tell you quietly, but it will happen. Alas, if most of the supporters of Menendez were imaginative enough to foresee such an effect as an inevitable result of their own freedom, they might well have second thoughts.''

"It would be a very different kind of Church, wouldn't it?''

"Somewhat different, Patricia. One must realize that in the course of history papal authority has taken many different forms. It has not always existed in the present centralized and authoritarian style and it need not always exist in such form. For the first thousand years a papal decree was considered to be valid only when it was accepted by the whole

Christian people. The kind of Church which Cardinal Menendez and his inner circle of supporters want would obviously be much more acceptable to our separated brothers and sisters.''

"I've heard bishops say that the Church is not a democracy," Patty said.

"They don't know what they're talking about. As a statement of fact their assertion is undoubtedly true. As a statement of historical description it is patently false. Thus when this young person's ancestors were trying to restore order to Rome, on the frequent occasions when the cardinals—the parish priests of Rome—were called to St. John Lateran to select a new pope, they would choose one of their number and bring him forth to the balcony. If the waiting crowds cheered, he was crowned. If they booed, the cardinals went in and tried again. Perhaps it is a form of election which left something to be desired, but I'm not sure that it was any worse than the present procedure.''

"Photographs?"

A shapely young woman with rather too much makeup and a large Polaroid camera who had been wandering through the restaurant taking snapshots of the customers paused at our table.

"Bring them home as a remembrance of a supper in Rome?"

Paoli looked at me uncertainly. Probably she identified with this young woman of her generation trying to make a few extra ten thousand lire by working at night.

Why the hell not?

"Sure," I said, giving her a hundred-thousand-lire note.

"Four pictures?" The child seemed surprised.

"Grand.''

Patricia looked uncomfortable. I noted that she leaned toward the bishop instead of toward me. The photographer snapped four shots, waited for them to develop, peeled off the cover sheets, and presented them to me.

"*Molte grazie, signorina,*" I said, giving her an extra twenty thousand lire.

Both she and Paoli smiled their approval.

"Since I paid, I'll divide them up." I chose one for myself, slipped it into my jacket pocket, and distributed the others. The women expressed considerable pleasure with their pictures.

"I don't look half bad," Patty admitted.

"You could never look bad," Paoli announced as though she were speaking with full papal authority.

"You're sweet, young woman." My sometime-wife flushed modestly. "I'm glad you like me."

Unindicted co-conspirators.

"Fascinating," Bishop Blackie said, looking at me instead of the picture.

Had he spotted the shade too?

The picture I had chosen offered the best shot of the shade's face. He was an arrogant son of a bitch. He hadn't even bothered to get out of the line of sight of the camera. He must have really thought he was good.

Maybe he figured that they'd get me on the way back to the hotel. Then the pictures wouldn't make any difference.

"Will he win, Bishop?" I asked. "Cardinal Menendez, I mean."

"Arguably. However, both Corpus and the Curia will do all in their power to stop him. While some elements of the Curia lose no love for Corpus, they see in Menendez a resurgence of the Second Vatican Council and their final defeat. Pope John XXIII has been marginalized and trivialized during this recent pontificate—a foolish old man who almost ruined the Church. The Curia thinks it smells John XXIV."

Patty's eyes flickered at me and then turned away.

I could probably seduce this woman if I wanted to. Not tonight. Well, maybe tonight and presumably with my girl-guide's approbation. But, if not tonight, surely before the new pope was elected. She was as lonely and as hungry for physical love as I was. I had seduced her often enough before. That was marital love, an ongoing cycle of successful seductions, wasn't it? The most recent one was not necessarily any less glorious than the first one. What harm would there be in it?

Why not one more time?

There were a thousand reasons why not one more time.

Only, at the moment I couldn't remember any of them.

"It should be an exciting week, shouldn't it?" Patty asked.

"Perhaps." Bishop Blackie sighed.

"Why all the secrecy, Bishop? And the white smoke?"

"The Church is more often good theater these days than good religion. The secrecy originated in this century. Before the collapse of the papal states, the cardinals used to vote in St. John Lateran and live in the Lateran Palace. Each day they would walk down the street to the basilica of St. John Lateran for their day's work and chat with the populace. After the Piedmontese arrived . . ."

"Pigs," Paoli snorted. "They were without dignity or style."

"Arguably. Even when the conclave was moved up to the Sistine Chapel, there was little attempt to keep the events secret. Everyone knew at the end of the day what the count was and who had voted for whom. The secrecy was imposed to protect the cardinals from the Roman emperor, that is to say, the Austrian emperor, whose ambassador had vetoed an election in 1903."

"There isn't an Austrian emperor anymore," I said.

"You've noticed?"

"Are you cold, Dinny?" My wife, ex-wife, future concubine, whatever, asked.

"Someone walked over my grave," I replied.

"Don't say that!" Paoli pounded the table.

I had shivered because my desire for Patty had been transmuted into something even more dangerous—respect, admiration, affection. I was perilously close to the most insidious emotion of all.

Whatever else I did, I must not fall in love with her. Not again. Not now. Not ever.

"So this is pretty much like any other election?" Patty flipped a page in her notebook.

"In the sense that humans are voting, it is. However, this is a special class of electors. Many of them think their task is so important and they are so special that the Holy Spirit will whisper in their ear how to vote and they don't need to go through the useful processes of the political enterprise. Of lesser men it would be said that this is the sin of tempting God, of expecting Her to do our work for us."

"But are not some of them out there campaigning?"

"Some. The Curia play their usual game of dropping hints to favored journalists, whispering in the ears of other cardinals, spreading rumors of the outcome as though they already knew it, and manipulating the process—like the choice of speakers for the funeral masses for the late pope. Corpus is out there maligning Cardinal Menendez to anyone who will listen. The others? A few like Milord Cronin are campaigning like members of the Cook County Regular Democratic Organization. The others are sitting around waiting for the Holy Spirit to murmur in their ear. Some of the Americans are more interested in the NBA playoffs and the baseball season."

"You make the cardinals sound like they're not very bright men," I commented.

"It was never written in the law of the Church that you had to be intelligent to be named a cardinal prince of the Holy Roman Church. On the whole, however, our process is better than that of the Mormons."

A waiter brought a dessert wine. The little bishop, who had sipped only one glass of Frascati throughout the meal, shook his head. Virtuously, I did the same.

"I'm not driving," Patty said, lifting the bottle. "Neither are you, Paola."

"No, Patty," my traitorous guide agreed, tilting her nose in my direction. "You may call me Paoli. Everyone does."

My sometime-wife filled both their glasses.

"To John XXIV." Patricia raised her glass.

"John XXIV," Paoli echoed.

I joined in by raising my glass of sparkling Pelegrino.

"Indeed," Bishop Blackie agreed softly as he finished off the remnants of his Frascati. "Poor dear man."

Dinny

I really appreciate this, Dinny," Perilous Patty said as she shook hands with me in the piazza. "The dinner and the interview."

Her expressive green eyes wavered, not willing to look directly into mine. Vulnerable gratitude was not her shtick. Yet it notably increased her erotic appeal. I had never thought that I had to take care of Patty, to protect her from pain. Fragility turned out to be an aphrodisiac.

"Nice to have you with us," I said blandly. "How are the kids?"

"They're all fine. Doing very well . . ."

"Give them my love when you talk to them."

I said it to cut her off before she started talking about the kids in detail. It would break my heart to hear about them.

She had been dangerously close to kissing me and would have done so if I had not stepped back. A kiss, however harmless, would have sent me into an ultimate tailspin. And Patricia's kisses were never harmless.

"I'll call you before I use any of this." She held up her notebook.

"If you want to, but it won't really be necessary. We work in different worlds."

She nodded and climbed into the waiting CNN car, a Fiat, not a Lancia.

The bishop insisted on finding a taxi. So Paoli and I rode back to the Piazza Trinità dei Monti by ourselves. I sunk into the seat in complete exhaustion. Had I been in Rome less than twenty-four hours?

"You will sleep well tonight, Deeny."

"An instruction, Principessa, which I will be happy to obey."

"You love to play with names."

"I'm Irish."

"What did you think of the little bishop?"

She crossed her legs next to me. The silky sound of legs brushing one against another took my breath away.

"Amazing man. I don't think he'll ever be an archbishop and I'm sure he couldn't care less."

"He was telling us exactly what he wanted to tell us and, naturally, what his cardinal wanted us to hear."

"Patently," I said, using one of his words.

I hadn't thought of that possibility at all.

"I do not mean that it is not all true."

"I'd sooner have him on my side than the whole Corpus crowd put together."

"I, too."

We had managed to find the Tiber, a great, languorous silver snake.

"Tomorrow we will pick you up at ten-thirty to take you to the funeral Liturgy. You will have plenty of time to sleep."

She looked up at me with a smile of admiration and mute appeal for my approval. Why did two gorgeous women feel the need to be vulnerable in my presence?

Maybe I should go to a monastery.

"Me need sleep?"

"We can get you a seat in the press gallery."

I thought about it.

"Better that I hang around with the crowd. Maybe walk

into the sala stampa and watch some of it on TV, do a mood piece, then wander around Rome."

"I will bring a portable phone so you can stay in touch, if you wish."

"I might get lost."

We crossed the Tiber in silence.

"Your wife is very beautiful."

"I warned you that she would be."

Now it comes.

"She loves you very much."

"She tell you that?"

"Not exactly, but I can tell."

"Can you, now?"

"She loves you even more than you love her, if that be possible. She would have been very happy to sleep with you tonight."

Women, like I say, have serious investments in spousal reconciliation.

"It wouldn't work, Paoli. It didn't work the first time. Too many things have happened."

"Perhaps."

A long and thoughtful silence followed as the car wended its way down dark streets. There were, however, lots of people in the streets. The siesta, I presumed, would enable you to stay up half the night. But I didn't have a siesta. Apparently they were forbidden on this assignment unless one had a lover.

"Yet you would not be able to escape if she tried to recapture you while you're in Rome."

I gulped. She was probably right. But that wasn't the scenario. I was the one who had the option of seducing Peppermint Patty, not vice versa.

I laughed uneasily. "I don't think that's going to happen, Principessa. If it does I'll let you know."

"Oh, I'll know," she said confidently. "I'll know."

I suppose she would.

"Well, don't hold your breath."

"We will see."

The argument ended because our Lancia had somehow found its way to the door of the Hassler.

"Thank you for all the help, Principessa Paola Elizabetta Maria Angelica Katarina Brigitta Oriani," I said, touching her hand. "You are the greatest junior journalist in the whole world."

"You exaggerate," she said primly. "But I am pleased by your approval."

The Lancia turned across the Piazza Trinità dei Monti and down the Via Gregoriana into the night. I strolled a few yards along the Via Sistina and leaned against the wall of the hotel next door—The Hotel de la Ville—too tired to go right to bed and bemused by the sense of pleasant lassitude that the Roman spring evening had created, a feeling of sleepy well-being that one might have after pleasant sex while expecting even more pleasant sex in a quarter of an hour or so.

I should have gone up to bed immediately.

"What are you doing here, you fucking son of a bitch?"

Patricia had emerged from a car that had come up the one-way Via Sistina, her mood totally transformed. Her jaw was tight, her voice raw, her eyes dark and hard. Still beautiful, of course, and still sexually appealing.

"I beg your pardon?"

"Why the hell are you hanging around here?"

"Because that's my hotel," I replied, waving vaguely at the Hassler.

"How dare you stay next to my hotel? I've got enough problems as it is without you lolling around with your hang-dog expression, expecting me to sympathize with you!"

"Ah?"

I thought I sounded a little bit like Bishop Blackie.

"Besides, you stole my source. I know him from Chicago. What right did you have to interview him first?"

The Patricia McLaughlin galleon was in full sail, all guns blazing. Such quick changes of moods went with the territory. One minute she was ready to kiss you. The next moment she was ranting at you. I should have just turned my back on her and walked into the hotel. I didn't need a fight at this hour of the night.

I did, however, wonder if her rages were nothing more than a cover-up for the vulnerability she had cautiously displayed earlier in the evening. Then I remembered what my shrink had said about my inability to fight with a woman. Hell, this could be good practice.

"Would you shut the fuck up!" I shouted at her.

My words had come out very nicely. I could learn to enjoy this.

"What?!"

"I said would you shut your loud shanty-Irish mouth and act like a reasonable adult human being instead of a spoiled prepubescent brat."

One advantage of being a prize-winning journalist is that you've learned to use a lot of words. "Spoiled prepubescent brat" was rather good, if I did say so myself.

"What do you mean?" She simmered down just as my shrink had said she would.

"I mean you've gone a long way in your career on your reputation of being a ranting red-haired Medusa, but if you're not careful your loudmouth paranoia will get you in real trouble. People are getting tired of it."

"Oh." Her eyes were wide, doubtless in surprise.

"I don't want to run into you during the conclave any more than you want to run into me. But it's going to happen. And when it does I expect you to act like a responsible journalistic colleague instead of a screaming shrew. Bishop Ryan set up the interview with me, probably because he wanted to appear in a quality medium. Our Rome bureau didn't try to find out where you were staying and put me next door because they wanted to hassle you. If you don't like it you can move out of the Hotel de la Ville and go somewhere else. And in the future I would appreciate it if you didn't insult my colleagues."

She stood absolutely still, her eyes wide, lovely lips wide open. I could almost feel sorry for her. But I didn't. Well, not much.

I turned to walk away. "Ranting red-haired Medusa" was pretty good too. Then I thought of something else.

"And would you stop this nonsense about my cheating on you? I was never unfaithful to you and never have been, though God knows why. I'm the fallen-away Catholic and you're the good Catholic, or so you'd tell me. Have you ever heard of the virtue of charity?"

I thought she might have swayed a little, but I didn't wait to make sure. Sir Francis Drake sailed into the lobby of the Hassler and up to his suite with a victory pennant flying from his topmast.

Scratch one galleon.

Only when I had collapsed into bed did I wonder if I had indulged in overkill just for the pure fun of it. And to get even.

Well, if I had it was only part of evening the score. She'd leave me alone from now on.

My shrink had been absolutely right.

At the end of my tirade her eyes were clouded with self-doubt and hurt. Poor woman.

I could not permit myself to feel sorry for her. When one mixed tenderness with lust, one was edging close to the most dangerous of all human emotions.

I slept as though I had been drugged. Perhaps I dreamed about her, but the next morning I had no recollection of any dreams. In fact, I wasn't sure where I was.

Blackie

The great dome of St. Peter's glowed in the moonlight—the dome of the Pantheon on top of the basilica of Maxentius and Constantine. A heroic idea. The Church leaders of that time were men with huge faults. Better, doubtless, than the petty faults of our contemporary leaders.

I disliked the whole place intensely. The Catholic heritage and the Catholic institution would not change if the whole creepy Vatican establishment, including the obscene obelisks, the sputtering fountains, the tired, old palace, the tiresome museum, the gross, costly church, and all the cynical, unsmiling bureaucrats were abandoned. We did not need them and they were an obstacle both to the sophisticated, who saw through them, and the unsophisticated, who worshiped them.

I would spare the Swiss Guard, the frescoes, and young princesses like Paola Elizabetta.

The conversion of the bishop of Rome into a sacred person isolated from the rest of humankind was evil. If we didn't have a pope we would have had to invent one. But he didn't have to exercise his office as though he had a direct pipeline to God—which he didn't. Vicar of Christ, indeed!

The man whose body lay under the *baldacchino* inside had doubtless been the most gifted pope of the century, maybe the most gifted ever. Philosopher, actor, poet, musician. Leave out Milord Cronin, and the IQ scores of all the American cardinals put together would not add up to his score. His tragic flaw was that he really did not trust the Holy Spirit to guide his brother bishops or the Catholic laypeople. But the Polish hierarchy and clergy were authoritarian by necessity. Or they thought it was necessary. Medieval princes. Consultation was not a word in their vocabulary.

No one ever really told him that authoritarianism does not work in most of the modern world. It is not enough to teach, you must also persuade. He could never understand the need for persuasion. And so his pontificate was a tragic failure, despite his immense talents. He set out to bring unity to the Church by issuing a steady stream of orders. He divided the Church more than it had been when he began. The Curial cardinals were celebrating the marvelous unity and stability he had imposed on Catholicism. But they could be sincere in their celebration only if they were blind to the actual condition of the Church.

Poor dear man, as my female siblings would say.

I walked slowly toward the stands that they had erected for the funeral Liturgy. He would not yet be in his tomb, and plans for the dismantling of his creation would be underway. So soon does the world dispose of our most treasured efforts.

If Milord Cronin and his allies were successful and Cardinal Menendez became John XXIV, the demolition of the previous papacy would be complete, though gradual. Even if the other side won, the authoritarianism would become more humane and more languid. All but a handful of cardinals—and the ever-present Corpus—realized that it was time for a change. The late pope's style would be repudiated by the very men he had appointed to the Sacred College.

Our lives are so very short. Most of us try to do our best. Yet we are limited by our backgrounds and our lack of knowledge and by our physical weaknesses. With best possible intentions we make a mess of things.

It is Your fault, I mused, for not handing Your Church over to angels or some other superior creatures.

Maybe they'd foul up, too.

We didn't need the big basilica. We didn't need the worn,

old palazzos. We didn't need that big museum. We didn't need the elaborate ceremonies, the superb choir, the faded glory of the past. We didn't need the bizarre method of electing a successor Peter—who was no prize a lot of the time. We didn't need superannuated and inept leaders. We would probably be better off without them.

Did I sound like Martin Luther?

Anyway, no one planned to tear that gross building down.

All right, all things human fail. But the failures are different. And our present failure was pretty bad. I'd spoken the truth when I'd told those young people that the man whose body lay inside had become a figurehead. We could use someone who was more than a figurehead, I believed, but it would be a long time before anyone put the troubles of the last thirty years behind us, before healing eased the blighted hopes and the soured dreams.

Sean Cronin and Klaus Maria von Obermann would go home happy in their victory. Luis Emilio Menendez would have to stay and try to put Humpty-Dumpty back together again. Poor man.

I didn't like any of it. On the other hand, however much we fail, I believe, we must do our part.

Those two reporters tonight, I thought, were obviously still in the grip of a great love that had become twisted. It was not yet dead and perhaps would be renewed. If it was not, I feared that their lives would be ruined.

Why do You let that happen to good people? I asked. You may argue that you have sent them a guardian angel in the principessa. I admit that it is an ingenious idea: Etruscan black nobility saves love between shanty-Irish Catholic-Americans. Even the good Dinny would like that line.

Indeed, at the end of that troubled and troubling day I ventured the thought that in her generosity and her concern, in her stern principles and her incorrigible romanticism, that young woman represented the Church at its best far better than do all the cardinal princes.

E - M A I L

From MKATE@LCMH.COM

To BLACKIE@AOL.COM

Drs. Ron and Janet Stewart arrive Fiumicino day after tomorrow. Will stay at Excelsior. Since all cardinals probably need psychiatric attention, my Jungian husband and I will accompany them. Please provide transportation from Fiumicino. Omit bands.

Love,

Mary Kathleen Ryan Murphy, M.D.

:-)))

Dinny

I ate my breakfast in my room, discombobulated, befuddled, and disoriented. Besides confused.

I managed to persuade myself that everything that I thought had happened yesterday was a dream. There was no papal princess running my life. I had not met a bishop in a Chicago Bulls jacket. I had not lusted for my wife during most of dinner. Ex-wife. I had not excoriated said ex-wife at midnight at the top of the Spanish Steps. All of these images were too implausible to be taken seriously as anything but bad dreams.

I showered, put on my "other suit," and rode down the elevator. It would not do to keep the principessa waiting.

An American couple was already on the elevator. Early sixties, flushed faces, silver hair, expensive clothes, a little overweight. Wealthy, spoiled, pampered Irish.

Ty Williams and his consort.

"Did you see this?" The man jabbed a copy of the *Herald-Tribune* at me.

I looked at the front page:

VATICAN PREPARES FOR PAPAL FUNERAL
PROTESTERS SWARM AT ST. PETER'S
Spanish Cardinal Denounced

The crowd in New York had wasted no time in getting my piece into print. It read pretty well, considering how confused I had been.

"Shameful," I agreed, returning the paper to him.

"Who the hell is this fellow Chaucer?"

"I don't know."

"This guy, what's his name . . ."

"Dennis Mulloy."

"Yeah. He's probably a pinko and a homo too."

"Arguably."

"*The New York Times* is a pinko, homo paper. If you really want to get at the truth, you gotta read *The Wall Street Journal*. They tell it like it is."

"I think there's some pinkos working for their news staff."

"Yeah, probably."

"And that woman on CNN yesterday," his wife joined in the conversation, "wasn't she a disgrace!"

"The one with the red hair?"

"Looked like a hooker for sure. Probably a lesbian."

"You'd think that if a man is the Holy Father's press spokesman, he'd be entitled to a little respect."

"You certainly would."

We stepped out of the elevator.

"Well, let me tell you something," her husband poked my chest, "we're not going to let the homos and pinkos take over the Catholic Church. We're both dead set against abortion, and I don't care how much money it costs, we're not going to let an abortionist be elected pope!"

"Or a man who supports the death penalty!" I said naively. "Wasn't the late Holy Father against both?"

"Two different issues," the man grumbled. "Completely different."

"He didn't seem to think so."

I eased away from them. Lord deliver me, should there be a Lord, if they ever found out that I was Dennis Michael Mulloy, one-time white basketball star from Manhattan College.

Outside the Hassler, Rome's fickle spring weather had changed. The sky was gray, the temperature had dropped, there was a hint of rain in the air.

I glanced at my watch. Five minutes before the arrival of la bella principessa. Should I go back to get an umbrella?

Certainly not. She would bring one for me.

Naturally.

"Dinny . . ."

A familiar voice.

"Patricia . . ."

She was wearing a black dress, hem substantially below the knees, and a black scarf that could double as a veil. What your proper Catholic matron wears to a papal funeral. Just tight enough so there will be no doubt about the size and elegance of your breasts. Which Peppermint Patty would it be today? My stomach clutched again.

"Fine article this morning."

"Thank you."

"They let you get away with a lot . . . no, what I meant to say is that they really value what you do."

"I liked the way you skewered Maître de Tassigny yesterday. You did a great job. I hope you get a shot at some cardinals before this is over.''

"Thank you . . . uh, the kids all send their love back.''

"Great.''

My ex-wife was uncharacteristically hesitant. What was going on? She was breathing rapidly and thus tormenting me with the movement of her breasts.

Irish male fixation.

"I apologized to your colleague last night.''

"I noticed.''

"And to you for taking over the interview.''

"I called the Villa Borghese. They said the other leopards were not changing their spots.''

"Good line.'' She laughed nervously.

"I write.''

"Now I want to apologize to you for my behavior here last night. Maybe I had too much to drink—''

"I doubt it.''

"Anyway, you were absolutely right. I've already had a lot of trouble because of my temper and my mouth. I'm sorry.''

I touched her face with my fingers and grinned, my absolutely best Irish-charmer grin. "Apologies accepted, Patty.''

Her cheek was as smooth as fine Irish linen. I moved my fingers ever so slightly in a hint of a caress.

"I'll try,'' she gulped, "to be a responsible professional colleague through the rest of the conclave.''

"Me too.''

I removed my fingers, reluctantly, from her cheek. Instantly I regretted the lost opportunity.

"You had some great lines—'ranting red-haired Medusa.' ''

"And how about 'spoiled prepubescent brat'?''

We both laughed. Two professional companions sharing a joke.

"I laughed at them when I finally pulled myself together.

Then I realized that they were very accurate.''

"Overkill."

"I won't keep you, Dinny. There's your sweet and gorgeous little princess with her car. The two falcons on the crest are the family seal."

"See you."

"One more thing, Dinny?"

I turned toward her.

"Yes?"

"I believe you about . . . about the other matter. I guess I always have."

"Thank you, Patty."

I turned back toward the car.

"*Ciao,* Dinny."

I turned again. Her face was radiant with her most blinding smile. But now it was a vulnerable smile, a plea that I take care of her pain and never hurt her again.

What do I do with a radiant and vulnerable Peppermint Patty?

I do what comes naturally. I grin my most charming shanty-Irish grin and say, "*Ciao,* Peppermint Patty."

And then get the hell out of there before we're both in serious trouble. Before I fall in love with her again.

I was sure that said gorgeous little princess had seen me lollygagging with my former wife. However, she said nothing about it when I got into the car—into the backseat with her parents. She was sitting in the front with a teenage punk.

"Mama, Papa, this is my colleague, Mr. Dennis Michael Mulloy of *The New York Times.* You may call him Deeny."

The poor kid said "colleague" with great pride.

"Deeny, these are my parents, Antonia and Ricardo. This is my brother, Tonio."

I had expected that her parents would be elderly, white-haired people. But they were about my age. The mother looked like Sophia Loren on a smaller scale and the father like Marcello Mastroianni thirty years ago.

Both women were encased in black, long skirts, long

sleeves, copious black mantillas and thick veils, none of which left any doubt about the subtle appeal of their graceful bodies. The father and son were wearing white tie and tails, sashes across their chests, and large silver medallions featuring two falcons over a river backed up by mountains.

I high-fived the grinning punk, who responded with a low-five. Then I said respectfully, "Principessa, Principe."

They both laughed. "Please, Deeny," her mother said, "we are Ricki and Tonia."

"And we are delighted to hear that you find our daughter's assistance helpful."

"Best darn guardian angel west of the Pecos River, sir!"

"We are, of course, very proud of her," his wife added. "But we are not without our prejudices."

"Only two flaws, ma'am. She's not very efficient and is a little too calm for my taste."

Everyone roared.

"Yes, that's what we think too," Tonia said. "We have always felt that if only she were more efficient she would make a fine journalist."

My blushing guardian angel tilted her defiant little chin high in the air. But she was eminently pleased with herself.

"I feel kind of sorry for poor Niko. It must be hard to cope with such a disorganized young woman."

Again there was much laughter and rolling of eyes and a disdainful snort from herself.

"Naturally you will meet Niko this morning."

Which of us, I wondered, would be showed off to the other?

"He is a very nice young man," Tonia observed. "I tell Paola Elizabetta that she should treat him with more respect."

Another loud snort from the front seat. Paoli turned her back on the lot of us.

"I suspect he knows how fortunate a young man he is," I said, pulling out all the plugs of traditional Irish blarney. Her parents smiled happily.

''I think he does,'' Ricki agreed.

''Naturally,'' his daughter chimed in.

Her parents were both *avvocati*—lawyers—because, as Ricki said, there was not much money to be made in the black nobility business. They were delighted that their child had chosen journalism. To be a reporter for *The New York Times* was much more important than to be a mere lawyer.

They seemed to mean it.

They grieved at the death of the pope. He was a good man who meant well, but he did not understand about married people or young people. And especially about women.

Being a papal noble apparently did not prevent you from having your own opinions. But I suppose it wouldn't, not if you've been around for ten centuries.

I wondered if they still hunted with falcons. Most unlikely.

''This is the portable phone you will use,'' my efficient guardian angel informed me. ''You press this button and you may call or receive. You press zero-one and 'Send' and naturally you find me. You press zero-two and you will find the bureau. You press zero-three and you will find Niko.''

''Niko?''

''If you need help from the carabinieri.''

Actually, Pretty Princess, I just might need such help.

We arrived at Vatican City and were waved through barriers and gates, directed down narrow streets, and saluted by Swiss Guards at every turn.

Everyone around Vatican City, I began to suspect, knew Paola Elizabetta Maria Angelica Katarina Brigitta Oriani. It would be hard not to. No wonder she had so much clout.

Above us the rain clouds were lower and were scudding across the sky, which seemed only a few feet above the Vatican Palace.

We ended up in a courtyard that looked very much like pictures I had seen of the Cortile del Belvedere. All kinds of people, mostly men, dressed up in funny clothes were waiting for the funeral to begin, including over in one corner some Knights of Malta in flowing white robes. No cardinals, however.

"I hope your gallery has a roof," I said to the Orianis.

"But it leaks!" Tonia laughed.

A young man in a black suit approached our Lancia as it stopped, saluted, and smiled. I had figured that Niko wouldn't be in uniform. Too important a cop to have to wear a uniform.

He was slim and of medium height with curly black hair and twinkling blue eyes. His face looked like that of a Giotto angel. Paoli and her young man were throwbacks to medieval paintings.

He held the door open for us, helped us out, and brushed my princess's lips with a kiss. She did not pretend that she did not like it. Poor Niko was trapped.

"Deeny," she said, now using the informality of the young, "this is Niko. Niko, this is Deeny."

He saluted again and grinned. "I hope my Paoli is treating you well, Deeny."

"Best darn guardian angel west of the Pecos."

She snorted and gave me a very official-looking document. "This pass will permit you to leave here without getting arrested. Naturally it will also permit you to return here and sit in the car if you wish to avoid the rain. If any gendarme tries to make trouble for you, tell him my name."

"With that name," Niko rolled his eyes, "you could probably get as far as the papal apartments."

She ignored him. "Here also is a plastic rain sleeker—is that the right word?—it will keep you dry for a time. I will phone you at the Hassler after the Liturgy is over. Are there any problems?"

"None at all."

I shook hands with her parents and then with her. They walked toward the other side of the *cortile,* where a group of similarly clad men and women waited for them. Niko followed her with admiring eyes.

"Can I have a word with you, Niko?"

His eyes changed quickly from dreamy to intelligent. Smart kid to have achieved rank so young in life.

"But of course."

I removed the Polaroid shot I had put in my jacket pocket the night before.

"Ah, what a nice picture," he said approvingly. "I believe I know that young woman. And the other *bellissima* is from CNN. And the funny little man in the jacket?"

"A bishop . . . but I'm interested in this man at the table against the fence."

"Ah," Niko said, peering closely at the picture. "An American."

"Former CIA, I think. Perhaps rogue CIA. He has followed me ever since I left New York. He assumes that I am too much a dumb journalist to spot him. He's good but not that good."

Niko nodded solemnly. "Any reason he should be following you?"

"My beat is international crime. But I can't imagine why any of his potential clients would worry about my covering a conclave. Unless there are money problems around here."

"Do you know any of the recent history of the Vatican, Deeny?"

"Yeah."

"So that answers your question. There is not enough control yet to prevent such scandals. Too many dubious and incompetent men."

"But I thought the Vatican does not have much money."

"Compared to, let us say, Baring's Bank in London or the Dawai bank in Tokyo, it does not. Yet it fascinates many criminals. I will find out who this man is and if possible why he is following you. I urge you to be careful. If he follows you, we will follow him. As I said before, this could be serious."

"There have been one or two accidents which might not have been accidents."

"Then it might be very serious. You would not mind if

we, ah, kept you under surveillance? If we think it necessary for your protection.''

"Not in the least.''

"You can count on us, Deeny.''

"Thank you, Niko.''

"You will take good care of my Paoli for me?''

"You bet.''

I had a smart cop on my side. Good.

I shivered, and not because of the cold wind or gently falling raindrops.

Blackie

I vested for Mass somewhere in the bowels of the Vatican with many other purple-robed people. None of them seemed very friendly and I was in no mood to try to strike up a conversation.

It is my firm conviction that any liturgical ceremony that lasts more than an hour does violence to the Roman liturgy. I try, almost always successfully, to avoid such acts of violence. I could pray just as effectively to a God who is everywhere in front of a TV screen as in a rain-drenched piazza. However, I continued to be uneasy about Milord Cronin. He insisted that at his last medical checkup his heart and blood pressure were in excellent condition and that he felt fine.

"Blood pressure is in the normal range with the medicine I take,'' he informed me curtly. "Let Nora worry about me, Blackwood.''

"In my Harvey Keitel role I must worry about you.''

He always found that line funny.

I was more worried about exhaustion. He drove himself

ruthlessly, as though he were a man in his middle twenties with unlimited energy. He almost commuted between Chicago and Washington and Chicago and Rome. He attended every major church dedication and anniversary in the archdiocese and accepted virtually every lecture invitation from a secular entity.

In Rome he was alleged to have engaged in several shouting matches with the pope, which must have been some of the great scenes of the twentieth century. How did he get away with it?

"The big Pole likes me. Hell, I like him. So we shout at each other and then shake hands and smile. He says to me, Cronin, you are a very difficult man. And I say it takes one to know one and we both laugh. He knows he'll never hear bullshit from me."

"That is patent."

He had not been sleeping well since we'd come to Rome and was restless and irritable, especially with the ineffable John Lawrence Meegan and Archbishop Schreiber, the rector of the North American College, whom he despised. I feared that he was at the breaking point and that he would drive himself beyond that in his efforts for victory in the conclave.

So I would endure the long ceremony and the potential for being drenched in the rain so that I could keep an eye on him.

Though what I could do if he should keel over in the cardinals' gallery, I did not know.

I adjusted the Brigid Cross—La Croce di Santa Brigitta, as the principessa had called it. It was sufficiently large and sufficiently different to attract attention. My cousin Catherine Curran, who had made it for me, designed it with just such a purpose in mind.

"People don't notice you, Blackie. But they'll notice this cross."

"Doubtless," I had agreed.

A couple of Italian bishops, having seen the cross, were

whispering among themselves. Pagan curses and incantations, no doubt. So I took advantage of the situation.

"*La Croce di Santa Brigitta, la Patrona Irlandese. Il sole è Cristo,*" I made the motion of the sun moving across the sky, "*la Luce del Mondo.*"

They smiled and murmured their approval.

"*Santa Brigitta, sì, sì!*"

"*Bellissima.*"

"*Grazie.*"

I lacked sufficient Italian to explain to them that Santa Brigitta had been converted from a pagan goddess responsible for poetry and spring and new life to a Christian saint with roughly similar responsibilities.

"Bishop Ryan?" A young priest was at my side.

"Sì, I mean, yes?"

"Will you come with me for a moment?"

In the corridor outside I encountered in full watered-silk choir robes the cardinal archbishop of Valencia, Luis Emilio Menendez.

"Blackie." He shook hands vigorously. "It is good to see you again."

Naturally he remembered me. Tons of cardinals, as my nieces and nephews would have said, came through Holy Name Cathedral. None of them noticed me, because by grace and nature and intent I evaded notice. But not Don Luis Menendez.

He was perhaps five feet ten inches tall—tall for a pope—with wavy brown hair flecked with gray. His skin was dark, as were his brown eyes. He was trim, agile, and possessed a wonderful smile that revealed perfect snow-white teeth. He was drop-dead, movie-star good-looking. Zorro, maybe. Or the Cisco kid. A distinguished historian, a highly successful pastor with a balanced and cautious mind and a gift for words in a half-dozen languages. As pope he would win over the world with his charm, his wit, and his smile.

All of which, naturally, were good reasons for not electing him.

"You are of course responsible for this invitation to speak at Collegio Nordamericano. It is the sort of thing you would think up."

He knew me only too well.

"Who, me?"

He laughed. "I would say 'who, I' and be wrong. Sean and Klaus must think me a complete innocent not to know what they're doing."

"Arguably."

"Here is the text. Will you read it?"

"Of course."

"Now."

I went quickly through his text. It was, as I would have expected, perfect. A campaign platform that would delight Sean Cronin. And the world media.

"Perfect," I said, slipping the pages into my pocket.

"You're sure?"

"Absolutely."

He didn't object to my keeping the pages, so he didn't mind what he knew I might do with them.

"You understand why I hesitate?" He smiled, a little sadly, I thought.

"Sure. You're not crazy, so you'd rather not be pope. But you don't want the Church to fall into the hands of the Corpus crowd."

He nodded. "Exactly. I am told that they have three attacks on me. The first one was the abortion issue. That collapsed yesterday, especially because of that beautiful woman on CNN. You know her?"

"She is from Chicago."

"Magnificent. De Tassigny will never recover. Now they are talking about financial scandal in Valencia."

"Ah?"

He shrugged expressively. "It is nothing. Two months after I arrived, I realized that one of my predecessor's staff had been stealing from us. I dismissed him and invited the state prosecutors to investigate. We will respond effectively to this charge too. But . . .''

''If they throw enough mud, some of it might stick.''

He shrugged again. ''If it does it will be God's will but, as much as I dislike it, I will respond.''

''And be all the more eager to fight them?''

He grinned. ''Cronin always says you know too much.''

''Arguably.''

''The media will be at the Collegio Nordamericano when I talk?''

''Every TV camera in Rome.''

He winced. ''So be it. There will be questions?''

''Not if you don't wish it.''

''If I do this, Blackie, I will not hide.''

''Sound policy.''

''There will be the usual questions, I suppose. Abortion, ordination of women, birth control, celibacy?''

''You can count on them.''

''I have answered them before.''

He shook hands briskly. ''Thank you very much. Doubtless I will see you at the Collegio Nordamericano.''

''Arguably.''

Small wonder, I thought as we walked out into the rain, the Sistine choir, and the lightning and thunder, that Milord Cronin wants him to be pope.

I had forgotten to ask him one important question: What might the third charge against him be?

CNN

ANCHOR: Was the funeral for the pope rained out, Patty?

PM: (in black dress, rain slicker, and holding an umbrella against a dark sky) Yes, it was, Tessa. And they don't give rain tickets for a replay.

The Catholic Church today buried the late pope in a rainstorm which sounded like a Wagnerian opera. The rain held off until after the homily, delivered by Wojdmeres Cardinal Madaj of Gdansk. Some of the seventy-three-year-old cardinal's words, however, were drowned out by thunder.

(Cut to cardinal preaching in weak voice against a dangerous sky streaked with lightning.)

The cardinal, however, made his point despite the noise: The late pope had restored discipline and order to the Church and protected it from the dangers of Communism and capitalist consumerism. He alone was responsible for the collapse of Communism. The cardinals owed it to his memory to select a successor just like him to continue his work.

(Cut to procession at beginning of Mass. Sistine choir voiceover.)

Cardinal Madaj's homily was a direct attack on the candidacy of Cardinal Luis Menendez of Valencia, who stands for a very different approach to Catholicism than the late pope's.

(Cut to clip of Cardinal Menendez listening to the homily and showing no emotion.)

As if to emphasize the implacable opposition of some cardinals to the archbishop of Valencia, another attack on him appeared in *Il Foro*, the same right-wing Italian paper which only the day before yesterday distorted his position on abortion. This time *Il Foro* accused Cardinal Menendez of financial incompetence in his administration of Valencia. *Il Foro* has close ties to the Corpus Christi Institute, which has enormous power in the Vatican and which is bitterly opposed to the cardinal.

(Cut to clip of people rushing from the piazza as rain pours down.)

Even as the rain drove the mourners to temporary shelter, CNN learned that the scandal is well known in

Spain and that it occurred before Cardinal Menendez became archbishop. He uncovered it during his first months in office and took immediate steps to correct it. Apparently his enemies do not hesitate to lie about him even as the pope's funeral is being observed.

(Cut to piazza under blue sky and sun. Mass drawing to a close.)

The sun reappeared before the end of the Liturgy, perhaps a symbol of new light for the Catholic Church. Now, however, as people leave, more rain is closing in. Tessa?

ANCHOR: It sounds like a lot of dirty politics, Patty.

PM: Very dirty politics, Tessa. I'm a practicing Catholic and I feel humiliated to have to report this story.

ANCHOR: Will there be more of the same?

PM: I wouldn't bet against it. . . . Now the heavy rain is sweeping towards us again. This is Patricia Anne McLaughlin, CNN, at the papal funeral Liturgy, Vatican City.

Dinny

I was stopped by every papal gendarme, Swiss Guard, and cop between the Cortile del Belvedere and the piazza. Each one inspected my pass and saluted.

I went into the sala stampa and read the morning papers, which were filled with the allegations of financial mismanagement against Cardinal Menendez. I didn't believe a word of the stories, but the mud was flying thick and fast. If they could throw enough of it, they could do him in by the sheer weight of it.

The auditorium was crowded with reporters who thought it was a much better idea to watch the ceremony from the comfort of the sala stampa than in the rainstorm that was closing in on Rome. I should have brought my notebook computer.

I read the text of Cardinal Madaj's homily: Out of gratitude to the late pope, the Church ought to elect someone just like him. Had he not freed the world from Communism?

Logic and historical fact were invisible in the homily. Gorbachev deserved the credit. But for those from Eastern Europe, it surely had a powerful emotional appeal.

The TV showed the procession emerging from San Pietro as the Sistine choir started up the music of mourning, which also had a strain of triumph in it. As Catholic mourning should, I guess.

I put on my rain "sleeker," as herself had called it, and ventured outside.

I was reminded of Bishop Blackie's remark about great theater. The rites at the far end of the piazza were dramatic and powerful. But where I was, at the fringes of the crowd, they seemed to have little effect. The crowd was watching a spectacle, not participating in a worship service. Moreover, even though it was a funeral Mass—or whatever they call them these days—I saw no signs of grief, except from a few nuns and in the Polish section up near the front of the crowd.

I grabbed a taxi and went back to the Hassler. I arrived just in time to hear the end of Cardinal Madaj's homily and the tumultuous applause from the Poles. The worst of the rain came right after that. Lightning danced across the sky. Thunder drowned out the Sistine choir. Under a phalanx of umbrellas, Mass went on.

I turned on my computer and wondered for a moment what I'd do if my wife, my ex-wife, seriously attempted a reconciliation.

It would be a terrible mistake for both of us. But how long could I resist her?

N Y T

Papal Funeral Rained On but Not Out
Cardinal Calls for Pope Like Predecessor
Little Grief Seen at Service

By Dennis Michael Mulloy
Rome.

Rain spoiled the pope's funeral today. Since the Catholic Church does not give rain checks, the Mass continued despite the rain.

Nor did the rain prevent the celebrant of the Mass, Wojdmeres Cardinal Madaj, from calling for the election of a new pope in the image and likeness of the old one. While thunder drowned out many of Cardinal Madaj's words, there was no doubt that they were part of a concerted program on the part of the Vatican power structure to preserve the status quo. Charges of financial incompetence were leveled this morning against Luis Emilio Cardinal Menendez, archbishop of Valencia, in a paper closely associated with the Corpus Christi Institute. The movement, compared by some Catholic observers to the Unification Church of Rev. Sun Myung Moon, is seen as bitterly opposed to Cardinal Menendez.

The charges were easily refuted in a statement issued at the Spanish College just before the funeral Mass began. However, some churchmen think that the repeated accusations against the archbishop may damage his cause irrevocably even if they are without substance.

Until it rained on the papal funeral, the ceremony was elaborate, solemn, and stately. The procession of cardinals, bishops, priests, and papal nobility—whose women are alleged to be the most beautiful in Italy—was both colorful and somber in its blend of red and black. The vestments of those actually celebrating the Mass were white, symbolizing the Church's belief in the eventual resurrection of the late pope and of all humankind. The soaring music of the Sistine choir hinted at the possibility that life might conquer death after all.

However, one did not have to be very far from the service to realize that the crowd was largely passive and—at the very fringes— irreverent, as little boys chased one another, and tourists shopped for souvenirs. Some nuns dabbed at their eyes with tissue, and in the section reserved for the late pope's Polish countrymen and -women genuine mourning was evident. But until the rain spoiled the splendor of the rite, the rest of the congregation, if it can be called that, displayed few signs of grief.

C H I C A G O   S T A R

New Candidates Emerge in Rome

Rome.

As the late pope's body was being laid to rest today, sources close to the Vatican said that with the fading of the candidacy of Luis Cardinal Menendez of Valencia in Spain because of repeated charges against him, three front-runners have emerged for the conclave next week to choose a new pope.

The favorite, with strong support in the Roman Curia, is Vincente Cardinal Monastero, 72, president of the Congregation for the Making of Saints. An accomplished and affable diplomat, Cardinal Monastero is seen as likely to continue the late pope's policies but with greater tact and charm. It is expected that he will also get the votes of the cardinal electors who think it is time to return at least temporarily to the tradition of Italian popes.

Also receiving prominent mention is Astride Cardinal Valerian, a native of Kenya who works in the Curial office responsible for supervising the behavior of priests. If Cardinal Valerian is elected he will be the first Black African to serve as pope, the head of the world's 900 million Roman Catholics. It is said that many of the third world cardinals believe that it is time that one of their men becomes pope. Cardinal Valerian is known as a stern disciplinarian.

Sources also say that Wojdmeres Cardinal Madaj, 79, of Gdansk has moved into contention today after his stirring funeral oration at the papal funeral Mass was greeted with a thunderous ovation. Cardinal Madaj called for a continuation of the policies of the late pope, which, he said, had brought down the Communist dictatorships in Eastern Europe.

Timothy Williams, leader of the influential Catholic lay organization Save Our Church, was among those who applauded Cardinal Madaj's homily. ''That's what we need in the Church,'' he said, ''more discipline and order.''

Mark

M ark walked casually down the stairs from his chosen fire point. The crowds were pouring down the street from the funeral mass. Poor pope. After all the work he had done to protect life, it was a shame that he died knowing that his successor might undo all he had accomplished.

Mark did not always agree with the pope. He was certainly wrong when he linked abortion with the death penalty.

Criminals deserved to die for their crimes. There should be more executions rather than less.

That's what Mom had always said.

For a moment he wished he could go home and forget his obligation to Mom. She had never said he should kill anyone, had she?

Couldn't he go home and start life all over again—maybe find his sister and brother and their families and reconcile with them? They had never disliked him. Then he saw a young woman with long black hair and he forgot about abandoning his sacred mission.

"*Buon giorno*," he said.

She nodded in return.

He must appear on the stairs every day, so that by the time it was necessary to do his work, the people in the building would take his presence for granted.

The woman was a cunt. He could see sin in her eyes, in the way she considered him and then dismissed him. It might be interesting if she got in his way on the big day. Then he would have a good reason for ridding the world of one more whore.

Dinny

"Father Ryan speaking."

"Dinny."

"Ah."

"You said I could call."

"Of course."

"You get wet?"

"As the pretty princess would say, naturally. But now I will have an excuse to avoid wearing my medieval robes."

"You see these stories in the Italian papers about the three candidates?"

"Indeed."

"What should I think of them?"

"They were written by journalists who are in the pay of the Curia or of Corpus. Madaj is senile, Valerian was driven out of Africa by his own priests because he is a sociopath. Monastero is their real stalking horse. They argue that his policies will be like the late pope's, only nicer. Authoritarianism with an Italian face."

"How long can Menendez survive these attacks?"

"Arguably, longer than they think. Perhaps they are dirty fighters but not clever ones. If they were really clever, they'd send Ty Williams home."

"Is Menendez ever going to speak out?"

"Certainly. I have it on very good authority that he is going to deliver a lecture to the students at the North American College the day after tomorrow at ten-thirty and subsequently to the students at the German College."

I wrote it down on the notepad next to my telephone. "Worldwide media coverage?"

"One might expect that."

"He will say important things?"

"Arguably."

"You can get me the text beforehand?"

"Perhaps."

"If I honor an embargo till he begins speaking?"

"Arguably."

"Who should I interview over there? Whom, that is?"

"Doubtless, the eminent prince of Miami Beach."

"He's a clown, isn't he?"

"Some believe so."

"But good copy?"

"Oh, yes."

For some reason the bishop's master plan called for a clown tomorrow and Cardinal Menendez the next day. Made sense.

"Will he give us an interview?"

"Oh, yes. He believes that he is good with the media and that he has an obligation to reassure American Catholics that nothing is going to change in their Church."

"I'll get the principessa to set it up for us."

"Naturally."

"I suppose you've told CNN about Cardinal Menendez's talk?"

"You're accusing me of double-placing?"

"You know the words . . . ! We are not really competitors, you know."

"Not in the media world, at any rate."

I paused. Damn priest knew too much.

"We very much enjoyed the dinner with you last night."

"Ah?"

"My wife and I are, uh, estranged, as you probably gathered."

"Patently."

"I assume your rubber band metaphor was aimed partly at us."

"Totally."

"Marriage is not an easy thing, Bishop."

"So I am told."

"We tried it once and it didn't work."

"Should you try it again, you should not begin with the attitude that you are trying to see if it might work a second time. Rather, you should begin with the assumption that this time there is no question of it not working."

I paused to consider that hard wisdom.

"Yeah, I guess so. Maybe the two of us will sit down and have a talk with you sometime."

"Priests have a vested interest in reconciliation because that is the paradigm of humankind's relationship with the Deity."

"He has a reputation for being tough in such circumstances."

"Wrong God. Like all mothers, ours is a pushover."

"I'll see you around."

"Doubtless."

After I had hung up I noticed that my palms were sweaty and my heart was beating rapidly. I was terrified at the possibility of falling in love with Maeve the Passionate. Yet if she wanted me back, she could probably entice me into it.

If she were going to do it, she should do it soon, before I lost my mind from hunger for her.

I pushed Paoli's number on the cellular phone. It rang a long time.

"Oriani," she answered, breathless.

"Took you long enough. What's happened to my practically perfect principessa?"

"I do not take the phone into the shower with me."

"Got soaked, huh?"

"My hair is ruined for the rest of my life."

"I hear from a certain mutual friend that I ought to do an interview tomorrow with the cardinal archbishop of Miami Beach, a certain John Lawrence Meegan."

"Very well. In the morning."

"As early as possible so I can make the deadline."

"Very well. Nothing, perhaps, need be done tonight."

"There's not much taste in that crowd, but at least they'll give the pope one night in the grave before they begin lying."

"Perhaps."

"Have a good time tonight."

Would she wonder how I knew she had a date? Probably not. She'd know I was guessing.

"Thank you, Deeny. You liked my Niko?"

"Good kid."

"Naturally."

I did not permit myself any fantasies about the principessa climbing out of her shower, drops of sudsy water glistening on her pert young breasts. Well, only enough to realize that I had truly become a dirty old man.

Or maybe only a man who should have a wife.

Actually, as the bishop would have said, I had a wife.

That was the whole problem.

I turned on the TV.

The hotel phone rang.

"Mulloy."

"You're the only guy in this whole damn paper who could get away with that line about the women in the papal nobility!"

"It was a Catholic ceremony, so naturally there were sexual hints lying around."

"You've seen Patty yet?"

"How can one not see her?"

He wanted a reconciliation as did all my colleagues, who thought we were perfectly matched.

"How about a sidebar on the papal nobility?"

"How about a background piece written by one of them?"

"That sounds good. Do you know one that can write?"

"We got one working for us in the Rome bureau."

"No shit!"

"Yeah, and before your dirty mind starts working she's a kid, my daughter's age."

"I can't guarantee we'll use it."

"You'll want to."

"OK. Tell her to file it tomorrow."

"Right."

"Keep your stuff coming."

"Have I ever not kept it coming?"

The phone rang again. I picked it up and it still kept ringing.

It was Paoli's phone.

"Dennis Michael Patrick Mulloy."

"Niko."

"Oh, I thought it was a young woman with six names."
He chuckled and then got right down to business.

"I'm calling about the man who is trailing you. His
name is Peter Rush. He was a CIA station chief in South
America. Also a professional killer. Went rogue, as you
Americans so colorfully put it. Also became a little
sloppy, as you yourself noticed. We have put some of our
best men on him."

"Why is he following me?"

"Do you know anything about a bank called the International Agricultural Bank of Holland in Den Haag?"

I rustled around in the files in the back room of my brain.

"Family bank. Small-time involvement in the scene.
Mildly crooked. Not very bright."

"Anything more?"

"No. He's working for them?"

"It would appear so. Three of their executives have
rented a small villa up in the Alban Hills. Some Dutch hard
guys with them. Very interested, it would seem, in the conclave."

"Why?"

"We don't know. We found out about them only when
we began tracking Peter Rush. We are in touch with the
police in Den Haag."

"Quick work. And good work."

"Thank you, Deeny." There was a smile of pleasure in
his voice.

"Tell you what. Is there any way you can infiltrate an
agent or two into their operation?"

"Servants at the house, perhaps?"

"Yeah. A house in the hills sounds like a kidnap try."

"We will do it. Naturally. But why?"

"If I had to guess, Niko, I'd say that they're afraid someone with my background might stumble into something this
week that they don't want anyone to stumble into before the
conclave."

He was silent for a moment.

"That is certainly possible."

"Keep me posted."

"Naturally."

I was sure that he would take care of me and my guardian angel. Nonetheless I was worried. There were heavies out there who were up to no good. Also, presumably there was one hell of a story.

I pushed the principessa's button.

"Oriani."

"Mulloy. I got an assignment for you from New York. A thousand-word background piece on the papal nobility. Can do?"

"Naturally."

"I hope it won't interfere with your date."

"I will do it before Niko comes. Thank you very much, Deeny. You are a good man."

"Maybe."

Peppermint Patty appeared on the screen. I turned up the volume. She was on one of her rolls, precision and carefully controlled rage.

The woman was really good at what she did, better than I was at what I did. She had to have split-second reflexes and the ability to talk in sentences when hell was breaking loose all around her.

Even if I didn't love her anymore, there was nothing wrong with me admiring her, was there?

What target would Bishop Blackie set up for her tomorrow?

Blackie

That woman," John Lawrence Meegan's hands fluttered like prairie grass in the wind, "is positively *evil*. I will write to my friend Mr. Turner and suggest he dismiss her."

"I'll bet he doesn't," Mick Kennedy said with contempt in his voice. "She's too good at what she does. Why blame her for the dirty politics that's going on around here? Blame the people that are linking this junk to *Il Foro* and the Italian papers."

We were in the faculty lounge at the North American College, theoretically reserved for the cardinals and their close advisers. However, Archbishop Eugene Schreiber, the fat, bald, oleaginous rector of the North American College, took it upon himself to preside over the gatherings as though he were the chairman of the board as well as the host. I did not like him much. Sean Cronin detested him.

"What do you think, Cardinal Cronin?" He nodded at Sean as if he were the moderator of *Meet the Press*. "Will these assaults on Cardinal Menendez weaken his chances?"

"More likely strengthen them," Milord Cronin said with a grunt, indicating that he didn't like being quizzed by the rector. "None of our voters are impressed by this kind of stuff. They know how the Curia and Corpus and their paid journalistic hacks operate. Each time they try another one of their sneaky tricks, our people grow more angry."

To some extent Cardinal Cronin was whistling in the dark as he crept by a graveyard. There were some indications in the calls from our precinct captains—Klaus, Tim Whelan from Castlebar, Jaime Sanchez from Davao, Dick Llewelyn from Cardiff, and Ives Michner from Saskatoon—that fury at the Curia was increasing as was contempt for Corpus. But they had also reported that some of their "delegations" were uneasy.

Klaus said all the Africans were rock solid against Valerian, whom they despised.

But the situation was very fluid. No one could be sure what would happen in the week ahead as the Roman establishment strove to keep its control of the papacy.

"I don't trust the bastards, not for one moment," Cardinal Cronin had muttered to me before supper.

"Our bastards or theirs?"

"All of them."

Well, he might be dubious. The American cardinals were no worse than any of the others. Yet only a few of them had any grasp of what was happening. As they had done most of their lives in the Church, they would do what they were told. Presently, all of them were prepared with varying degrees of enthusiasm to go along with Sean Cronin because he seemed to know what he was talking about, even the fluttery John Lawrence Meegan, when push came to shove. Only Mick Kennedy from Albany had similar deep convictions on the matter. The others wanted to be able to say when they went home that they had backed the winner from the beginning.

As in the Chicago political dictum, "Don't make no waves, don't back no losers!"

Indeed, all of them wanted to be free of harassment from Rome and from the Corpus spies. But they didn't want to get caught voting against the Curia if the Curia seemed likely to win.

So at the supper table we talked about the White Sox and the Yankees and Michael Jordan, not about the issues and the candidates.

"She's from Chicago, isn't she, Sean?" Egbert Winter of Omaha asked.

If Meegan was the most fluttery of the cardinals, Egbert was the slowest. He was so slow, in fact, that even the other cardinals realized it and tried to update him by using simple, declarative sentences when at all possible.

"Who's from Chicago?"

"The dame on TV."

"Patty McLaughlin? Yeah, she's from Chicago."

"City itself, Blackwood, not the suburbs?"

I nodded on the premise that whenever you could, it was better to nod than to say anything.

"Goes to church?"

I nodded again.

"Every Sunday," the cardinal responded. "So what?"

"Couldn't you make her tone it down?"

"Easier to stop a prairie fire," Milord Cronin replied forcefully. "Only make her worse. Or better, depending on her perspective."

"Well," said the rector, "she certainly doesn't seem to care about the good of the Church."

"Maybe," Mick Kennedy interjected, "she defines it differently than we do."

"Well, I think I can clarify things a good deal tomorrow." Cardinal Meegan squirmed in his oversize chair as would a woodpecker preening itself. "I have an interview with *The Times*."

"*Miami Beach Times*?" the rector asked, revealing just what a fool he was.

"Certainly not! *The New York Times*!"

Sean Cronin glanced at me, his lips betraying ever so slightly the hint of a grin.

"Congratulations, Your Eminence," he said to John Lawrence, his irony hidden from all but me. "You are the first one of us to be approached by them."

"I will definitely clarify matters," Cardinal Meegan said complacently.

Our conversation turned to the baseball season again.

Cardinal Cronin rose to leave the room. "There's one more thing. Sorry I didn't mention it to you before, Archbishop Schreiber, but these have been very busy days. Cardinal Menendez has agreed to present a lecture here to the students day after tomorrow at ten-thirty. Klaus von Obermann invited him to speak at the Germano-Hungarian College in the afternoon and asked me if we wanted him in the morning. Obviously I couldn't say no. I doubt that we can keep the media away. So we'd better do everything we can to be nice to him. Good night, everyone.''

There was a murmur of approval from the cardinals. Americans that they were, they believed in fairness to everyone.

I noted as I gently closed the door that there was a look of pure hatred on Gene Schreiber's fat, flabby face.

"Get that man out of the room," I said to the cardinal, once we were outside. "He is a spy, certainly for the Curia and probably for Corpus too."

"I'll tell him bluntly that we wish to be alone so that we can talk privately. It will infuriate him again, which I will enjoy. Incidentally, whom are you turning *la bella* Patricia loose on tomorrow?"

"I thought we might try your man from Castlebar."

"Tim Whelan?" The crooked grin appeared on his face. "Wow! That's good talent if there ever was any! The folks at Turner Broadcasting will love it."

"As, hopefully, will the people of the world."

"It's getting to be more and more a media war, isn't it, Blackwood?"

"It would appear so."

"I'm not sure that's a good thing."

We had climbed a stairway and were walking toward his suite, the one reserved for the senior American cardinal.

"Ours at least tell the truth."

"There's that."

"Most of the other cardinals are like our own. They watch television—BBC, RAI, Skytel—and read the Italian papers and the *Herald-Tribune* and *Time* and *Newsweek*. Those are the voices they think belong to the Holy Spirit. CNN is naturally their favorite."

"Because of Patty?"

"Doubtless."

"It was smart of us to persuade them to pull her out of Chicago, wasn't it?"

"Arguably."

"And the guy from the *Times* is her ex-husband."

"That may be an open question, but humans, as you well know, are all too skillful at resisting grace. . . . I have, incidentally, been informed by reliable sources that my sister Mary Kathleen Ryan Murphy and her husband are arriving from Chicago tomorrow. I will meet them at the airport."

"Psychiatrists? I thought you would get a cardiac specialist for me. By the way, before supper my blood pressure was one-thirty-five over eighty."

"That, however, was before you had to listen to your colleagues and our good host, Mean Gene Schreiber."

"There's that."

Patricia Anne

You got me into this mess and it's Your job to get me out of it!

Don't You ever answer anyone, not even here in the church of Trinità dei Monti?

I've fallen for him the second time around as badly as I did the first time. I'm a horny old cow. Whenever I'm with him, my body betrays me. When he touched my face this morning I almost fell into his arms.

He looks great, he's obviously on the wagon and likely to stay on, he's his old, genial, charming self, the man I fell in love with.

I've read that women's desires become stronger as they

grow older. That's another one of Your dirty tricks on us!

He wants me. When men undress me in their imaginations, I'm usually offended. When he does it, I turn hot and wet all over.

I want him. It's been so long since I've enjoyed physical love. You don't want me to be a celibate for the rest of my life, do You? I'd make a lousy nun with my temper and my mouth.

So, if we're not careful, we'll fall into bed with each other and all the old problems will come back. This time around they could destroy both of us. We were badly matched and we're still badly matched, whatever our lusts are.

I'll be honest, especially since You know anyway. I want to feel his hands all over me, demanding, caressing, invading, reassuring. I want his tongue and fingers exploring all my secrets. I want him inside me, filling me up, thrusting and pushing and driving me out of my mind with pleasure. I want to feel the glowing heat intensify within me. I want to feel his power within me. I want to twist and squirm and yell and then burst with pleasure and joy. I want to be rent open, cleaved, joined, not only to him but to everything in the universe. I want to belong to him totally. I want to lose myself totally in him. All day. Every day. For the rest of my life.

I'd never do that, of course. I could never give up control completely.

Remember how shy and modest I was as a kid? I've come a long way, haven't I? And that's Your fault too.

Bishop Blackie's rubber band snapping us back together again. Only, the rubber band doesn't know that we shouldn't be back together again.

You know that. So why did You bring us both to the same story and put us in adjoining hotels? If I don't stay away from him, You know what will happen and it will all be Your fault.

I'm so lonely. When I'm working it's all right. I don't notice the loneliness. At night it's terrible. Maybe I should have an affair. You know I'm not the affair type. I shouldn't have let the divorce happen. If he had stood up to me, there wouldn't have been a divorce. He joined AA without my insisting. That should have been enough. He's not an ordinary drunk. I drove him to it. When he got away from me, he stopped drinking. It's my fault I lost him.

Look, I know that I'm more to blame for what happened between us than he is, poor lout that he is. I worked it all out with my shrink. I was a bitch. I *am* a bitch. I will always be a bitch. I can't help it. I can apologize now, which is something of an improvement. But I'll do the same thing all over again, the next minute, the next hour, the next day, no matter how hard I try.

OK. He is to blame too. But he's not a bitch, he's only a wimp, and then only with noisy women like me.

If I ever try to apologize to him for everything, I'll die. I'll simply die. And he'll own me. As much as I want him, yes, all right, as much as I love him, I don't want to be owned by him or anyone else. No way.

Well, You can own me. But only You.

But You still have no right to put me in this awful mess.

Well, all right, yes, You do.

What do You want me to do? They say human love is like Your love. Do you want me the way I want him?

But I couldn't ruin Your life like I ruined his.

I don't want to do it again. No way.

Still no answer, damn You.

Sorry, I didn't mean that.

Anyway, I have a pretty good idea what You want.

Well, I'm not going to do it.

So I'll light my votive candle and go home.

I'm stopping here at the door of the church, looking out on the Piazza di Spagna. I have one more request.

Please take good care of him. Don't let anything bad happen to him. I love him very much.

Please.

REUTERS

Conclave Favorite Advocates Changes in Church

The Roman Catholic cardinal who is rapidly emerging as the moderate favorite in the upcoming conclave today called for change in the Church. "We must change to remain the same, but we must appear to be the same in order to change," said Vincente Monastero, cardinal president of the Congregation for the Making of Saints at today's Mass for the late pope.

Cardinal Monastero, who has had wide experience in papal diplomacy and administration, appears to be positioning himself at some distance from Cardinal Wojdmeres Madaj of Poland, who yesterday called for a continuation in both substance and style of the last papacy, according to Vatican observers. He is presenting himself as a middle-of-the-road pope between men like Madaj and Cardinal Luis Emilio Menendez, who stands for a return to the openness and pluralism of the Second Vatican Council.

Significantly, Cardinal Menendez has been excluded from those who will preach at the funeral masses this week. Thus he has not been given an opportunity to develop his view of what paths the Church should take in the years to come.

While not the first choice of the powerful Corpus Christi Institute, who would prefer hard-line African Cardinal Astride Valerian, it is thought that Cardinal Monastero would be acceptable to them because he would not interfere with their influence in the Church.

Monastero, according to a prominent English ecclesiastic, would be the late pope with an Italian face. Nonetheless, many in Rome think that is what the Roman Catholic Church needs today.

TIME

Luis Loses It

As the first day of the conclave approaches, the odds against Luis Cardinal Menendez becoming the next pope have increased dramatically. "Luis has lost it," a veteran American member of the papal government observed. "If you were picking a pope on the basis of popularity or good looks, he'd be a sure winner. But the pope must be a man of proven administrative ability and stern doctrinal orthodoxy. Luis is the candidate of the media, but no one else supports him anymore. This is not the nineteen sixties."

Few astute Roman observers would disagree. The Vatican Council was a long time ago. The late pope has reshaped the Church. Conservatives are far more important than they were back in 1965. The cardinals have to take into account such powerful institutions as the Corpus Christi Institute and the Opus Dei. The liberal era ended in the Catholic Church long before it ended in American government.

Such once-controversial issues as birth control, priestly celibacy, and the ordination of women were definitively decided by the late pope. Further discussion on them is possible. The tightening up of central control has reassured Catholics who had begun to wonder whether their faith meant anything at all.

Cardinal Menendez's life has been that of an intellectual. His experience as dean of a college at Salamanca did not prepare him to administer his small Spanish diocese. In his first year there he encountered serious financial problems that many Spanish churchmen thought were too much for him. He could hardly be expected to assume the much more complex role of governing almost a billion Catholics. While there are no serious questions about his personal orthodoxy, informed Roman sources report that the Congregation for the Defense of the Faith once did a preliminary investigation of some of his public remarks.

"The Church does not need a John XXIV," an Italian journalist close to the Vatican remarked. "One Pope John a century is enough and more than enough. This is a time for consolidation, not for more reform."

It would appear that Cardinal Menendez is one more proof that the man who comes to a conclave "papabile," leaves it still a cardinal.

His decline is likely to benefit two elderly Italian cardinals who in substance are like the late pope but in style are more in the tradition of Italian popes, Vincente Cardinal Monastero of the Congregation for the Making of Saints and Gregorio Cardinal Alabastro, president of the Rota, the Church's supreme court. Both would be elected as transitional popes who would serve for several years and bring the Sacred College more in line with the present realities of the Church.

"There is need for some change," a European cardinal told *Time*. "But not too much change. The Catholic people need a long period of stability to recover from the mistakes of the nineteen sixties."

C N N

ANCHOR: Our correspondent at the Vatican, Patty McLaughlin, more than met her match today when she interviewed an Irish cardinal.

(Cut to Rome. PM standing near Bernini columns in bright sunlight. Next to her, in cardinal red, is Timothy Joseph Cardinal Whelan, archbishop of Castlebar.)

PM: We're talking with Timothy Cardinal Whelan, archbishop of Castlebar and Primate of All Ireland[1] . . . do I have the title right, Your Eminence?

TJW: (a tall, lean, craggy man who seems to carry a perpetual scowl) Well, you might want to add that I'm the successor of Saint Patrick.

PM: Sorry, Cardinal. It would never do to forget Saint Patrick.

TJW: And yourself bearing his name.

PM: Cardinal, do you think the Church is ready for an Irish or an Irish-American cardinal?

TJW: I'm the only Irish cardinal and God knows the Church isn't ready for a crazy old man like me. As for your Americans, well, your man isn't the worst of them at all, at all. And that's a compliment where I come from.

PM: You mean Cardinal Cronin?

TJW: Haven't I said so? But America is too rich for the pope to be from there.

PM: Can I ask who you will vote for, Cardinal?

TJW: You can ask, young woman, and I'll answer you. There's only one of us who's fit to be the next pope and that's your man from Spain. I'm sick of all these vile attacks on him from your Curialists. He's a great man and he'll be a great pope, despite your lying blackguards at *Time* magazine.

PM: You believe there is need for drastic change in the Church?

TJW: I believe that the next pope should turn the Church upside down and shake it hard so that all the riffraff and liars and crooks and schemers and petty thieves would fall out. 'Tis springtime for the Church, young woman. We need fresh air and the scent of flow-

---

[1]The Primate of All Ireland and the successor of Saint Patrick is in fact the archbishop of Armagh. For the purposes of this book, however, the see is moved so that no comparison will be made with actual cardinals.

ers and the sound of children's voices and the laughter of young men and women and the song of blackbirds in the trees instead of all them caterwauling and wailing and warning and complaining ecclesiastical zombies.

(As he talks, the cardinal's eyes soften and a beatific smile transforms his face.)

PM: You make me proud to be Irish, Cardinal.

TJW: Sure, young woman, cheap poetry from an old priest is not much to be proud of. But I'll tell you one thing: As long as the Irish race produces beautiful and brave and smart young women like you, won't there be plenty to be proud of!

PM: (embarrassed) Thank you! I've never been complimented by a cardinal before!

TJW: 'Tis high time, then, sure you're not the worst of them at all, at all.

PM: (turning to camera) This is a furiously blushing Patty McLaughlin, not the worst of them, CNN Rome.

ANCHOR: (laughing) It would be fun to watch those two all day long.

Blackie

*E*minenza!'' Cardinal Monastero embraced Milord Cronin with considerable enthusiasm. "I am so glad we have encountered each other here."

Sean Cronin does not take to being embraced by men, especially when they have garlic on their breath as a chronic condition.

"Cardinal," he said mildly.

"You of course know Cardinal Alabastro?"

"Certainly."

The proceedings paused to give Milord Cronin an opportunity to congratulate Cardinal Monastero on his sermon at the Mass for the late pope that morning (which I had fortunately missed because of the obligation to meet my sibling at Fiumicino). No congratulations was forthcoming.

"Let us take a little *passeggiata* here."

"Sure."

Milord Cronin could be courteous to people he despised— when it suited his purposes.

Our "encounter" took place in one of the marble corridors of the Vatican Palace, a place as warm and comforting as a mausoleum. I had come to join Sean Cronin after he had left a meeting of the committee of cardinals responsible for inspecting the rooms where the conclave would occur.

"Setup" would have been a better name for the meeting.

"Bishop Ryan, it is so nice to see you again. You know Cardinal Alabastro, do you not?"

Never met the man in my life. But I was spared the necessity of responding when the cardinal grabbed my hand and pumped it up and down enthusiastically.

As I have remarked before, people do not notice me. When they do notice me, I smell of something stronger than garlic.

The two cardinals were both short men, shorter than me, that is, which is under five foot seven and three quarters— if I stretch. Monastero's head was covered with bushy, untidy, white hair. Alabastro was egg bald. Both affected expressions of deep and gentle piety, which, for all I knew, were accurate reflections of the state of their souls.

Though I wouldn't have bet on that.

Monastero asked about Senator Cronin and said that he had heard she was here in Rome at the present time. Milord grunted. Alabastro asked about young people in Chicago. Cronin replied that they still seemed to be around, though they had the interesting habit of receiving the Eucharist while living in sin. The two Curialists mouthed expressions of dismay.

"So," Monastero said as we reached the end of the corridor and turned to continue our walk in the opposite direction, "I believe that we are in basic agreement about the qualities of the next pope?"

"Arguably," said Cardinal Cronin, inexcusably stealing my line.

"Surely we need a change. God sent us the poor pope just when we needed a strong man to bring order and stability back to the Church. But now we need, how shall I say it, a different style. More open. More sensitive. More willing to consult with others, is that not true?"

"I agree that we need a different style."

"Of course, of course. As our friend from Valencia keeps telling us, there are many different ways the Petrine Office can be exercised. We should not cling to one style. Do you not agree?"

Sean Cronin grunted, a Chicago political response that can mean everything and nothing. In this case it meant very little.

"Yet these transitions are very delicate. We must change to remain the same, but we must appear to be the same in order to change."

Bullshit.

"Doubtless."

Another one of my lines.

"All of this should go very smoothly, should it not? Without the appearance of strife or conflict as our brothers in the Lord listen to the voice of the Holy Spirit."

"Sometimes conflict is necessary."

"Surely, Eminenza, surely, but it must also be very delicate conflict. Very delicate. Don't you agree?"

"Uhm."

"After the conclave there will be some necessary changes here in Rome. New officials in the Curia. I have heard many say, Eminenza, that you would make an excellent secretary of state, perhaps with enhanced powers to reorganize the rest of the papal administration."

Cardinal Alabastro nodded vigorously.

Ah, at least we had come to the point.

"I'm afraid I don't have sufficient delicacy for the job."

They both laughed nervously.

"Come now, Eminenza, we all know your diplomatic skills. There is no more discreet administrator in the Church."

Sean Cronin said absolutely nothing, the most favored of all Chicago political responses.

"And, Bishop Ryan, with your background and experience, you could guarantee continuity in Chicago."

There were many things I could have said; the most pleasing to me would have been to suggest sexual intercourse for the cardinal and for the horse he rode in on. However, I continued to be the soul of discretion.

"Arguably."

"This has been a very interesting conversation," Sean Cronin said as we reached the stairway that would bring us down to the Belvedere. "I'll keep it in mind."

"*Benissimo*, Eminenza." Cardinal Monastero's hand clutched Sean Cronin's arm, reminding me of the hand at the end of the film *Carrie*. "We will have a serene conclave."

Out in the clear air and the sunshine of the cortile the cardinal turned to me.

"Was I mistaken, Blackwood, or were you offered my job?"

"It would seem so."

"Were we being bribed?"

"It would seem so."

"Do they think we might be interested?"

"Doubtless."

He paused to consider.

"What infuriates me is that they are so damned dumb."

"You noticed that too?"

"Am I right in thinking they will float that as rumor before the day is over?"

"Oh, yes."

"So, we issue a denial?"

"Before the rumor starts."

We then turned to the matter of lunch with the excellent Dr. Murphy and her entourage.

"And the cardiac specialist Mary Kate has brought along."

"But, Eminenza, it will all be very delicate."

C N N

ANCHOR: An Irish cardinal called today for a transformation in the Catholic Church. Patricia McLaughlin in Rome has the story.

PM: (in front of the Sistine Chapel wearing an empire-waist spring dress in a floral print) In very poetic language, Cardinal Timothy Whelan called today for a dramatic change in the Catholic Church.

(Cut to original interview, which CNN has been playing all day.)

TJW: I believe that the next pope should turn the Church upside down and shake it hard so that all the riffraff and liars and crooks and schemers and petty thieves would fall out. 'Tis springtime for the Church, young woman. We need fresh air and the scent of flowers and the sound of children's voices and the laughter of young men and women and the song of blackbirds in the trees instead of all them caterwauling and wailing and warning and complaining ecclesiastical zombies.

PM: Cardinal Whelan indirectly endorsed the candidacy of Cardinal Menendez of Spain.

TJW: There's only one of us who's fit to be the next pope and that's your man from Spain. I'm sick of all these vile attacks on him from your Curialists. He's a great man and he'll be a great pope, despite your lying blackguards at *Time* magazine.

PM: There have been other developments. Antonio Cardinal DeJulio, a Dominican and archbishop of Verona, also came close to endorsing Cardinal Menendez in an interview with CNN.

(Cut to DeJulio interview, also in front of Bernini columns.)

PM: Cardinal, do you think it will be a short or a long conclave?

AD: (tall, genial man with square and honest face) Very short, Patricia. The obvious man will be elected the first day.

PM: And that is . . .

AD: (quick smile) You know who that is, Patricia. You Americans will not be unhappy!

PM: But there is so much talk about stability in the Church. It is said that the era of reform is over—

AD: (frowning as he interrupts) What the Church needs today is a return to the spirit of the Second Vatican Council, a spirit whose fruition has been delayed but cannot be destroyed.

(Cut back to Patricia in floral dress.)

PM: In a related development CNN has learned that some Italian newspapers will report tomorrow morning that Sean Cardinal Cronin of Chicago has agreed to a compromise in which he will withdraw his support for Cardinal Menendez in return for a promised position as papal secretary of state in a "moderate" papacy. Cardinal Cronin's office issued a denial even before the rumor was published.

(Reads from paper.) "Cardinal Cronin has no intention of leaving Chicago under any circumstances for any other place, unless it be heaven. Or, in lieu of heaven, purgatory."

That seems pretty definite. Patricia Anne McLaughlin, CNN Rome.

Mark

Mark watched the cardinals coming out of their meeting. It was not difficult to pick out his target—dark skin, handsome, gleaming teeth. A spick. Some even said he was a Jew. Mom had said you should never trust Jews. Yet in the marines, a Jewish boy had been nice to him.

Perhaps this Jewish cardinal ought to be executed as a murderer even before the conclave began. Would that be right? Why wait till a killer became pope to blow away his pretty face?

But maybe he shouldn't kill anyone. He was having dreams at night now in which Mom kept repeating one of her favorite phrases, "What will people say!"

Why couldn't she make up her mind?

Mark walked back to Trastevere in deep thought.

N Y T

American Excludes Spaniard as Pope
Cardinal Meegan Fears Shock to Laity;
Other Americans Disagree

By Dennis Michael Mulloy
Rome.

A prominent American cardinal today excluded the possibility that Luis Emilio Cardinal Menendez y Garcia, archbishop of Valencia, would be elected the next pope of the Roman Catholic Church. "He is too much of a change from the previous pope," said John Lawrence Cardinal Meegan of Miami Beach. "He is a fine man and I personally would have no problem voting for him, but I fear our good, simple laypeople would be shocked by such a different pope."

The cardinal gave a long and candid exclusive interview to *The New York Times* in his suite at the North American College on the Janiculum Hill overlooking Vatican City.

Cardinal Meegan, a diminutive, slender man with thick glasses and quick hand gestures, pointed out that the Archbishop of Valencia was an intellectual and had taught at a university, that his father had served as an ambassador to Italy of the Communist-dominated Spanish Republic in the 1930s, and that his public stances, while certainly orthodox in themselves, were often couched in terms which troubled "the good, solid laypeople."

When it was argued that the late pope had also been a university professor, that Cardinal Menendez's parents had been shot by anarchists in the late 1930s, that Cardinal Menendez is reputed to be enormously popular with the people of Valencia, and that his administration has been marked by a strong religious revival in that city, Cardinal Meegan did not modify his position.

"I don't doubt any of those things, but it is the appearance of great change which I fear will have a profound negative affect on Catholic laypeople all over the world. At this troubled time in Catholic history, we cannot afford to confuse people even more than they are already confused."

It was pointed out to the cardinal that a new *New York Times*/NBC poll of American Catholics showed that they support, in overwhelming numbers, both the general principles of moral pluralism and decentralization in the Church and the specific qualities of Cardinal Menendez. He dismissed the findings with the observation that he had never been interviewed in a survey and doubted that this one reflected the feelings of "our good, devout Catholic laity. People like my good friend Ty Williams, a successful Catholic businessman."

In fact, the demands for change in the style of papal administration are especially likely to be endorsed by those who go to Mass regularly, according to the survey.

Cardinal Meegan, who wore his full cardinalatial robes, including skull cap and cummerbund during the interview, expressed his vigorous disapproval of Cardinal Menendez's custom of wearing shirt and tie instead of clerical collar. "Our people expect a priest to look like a priest. I insist on it in my diocese. My people would be shocked by a pope in lay garb."

However, the *New York Times*/NBC poll showed that 75 percent of American Catholics agreed with the statement "I wouldn't mind a pope who dressed in a shirt and tie sometimes."

Cardinal Meegan spoke warmly of Vincente Cardinal Monastero, who preached at the Mass for the late pope this morning. Without committing himself to voting for the president of the Congregation for the Making of Saints, Cardinal Meegan noted approvingly the cardinal's call this morning for cautious change: "We must change to remain the same, but we must appear to be the same in order to change."

Asked to interpret the meaning of that enigmatic phrase, Cardinal Meegan, hands waving, said that it represented "*soavità*," which he interpreted as "smoothness," the ability to deal with the fears of the Catholic laity in such a way as not to upset them.

Cardinal Meegan also declined to say whether other American cardinals agreed with his analysis of the upcoming conclave and in particular his fears about Cardinal Menendez.

"All I will say is that I think many of them are leaning in my direction."

He denied vigorously that the Monastero "boom" was a product of certain Italian media which are closely allied with members of the Roman Curia. Did it really have any substance? he was asked.

"It must have substance or he would not have been chosen to say the Mass today."

Not everyone at the North American College agreed with Cardinal Meegan. Another ecclesiastic, encountered in the corridors of the school, commented, "Like his good friend Ty Williams, John Lawrence could not lead a band of starving vampires to a blood bank."

What about the good, simple laypeople? this churchman was asked.

"Most of them exist," he replied, "only in John Lawrence's head."

Dinny

After I had faxed my piece off to New York, I turned on CNN to see what herself was up to today. For Patty-watchers it was a banner day. CNN played her interludes with Cardinals Whelan and DeJulio over and over on its *Headline News*. As well it might, Peppermint Patty's red hair blended nicely with the cardinalatial crimson, and her mix of respect and audacity was perfect.

When she was "in the zone" she was tremendous, and she was getting better with the years.

The cellular phone rang.

"Vincente Monastero."

Silence for a moment, then laughter. Male laughter.

"Niko here."

"*Sì*? Whatta you want?" I did my best to mimic the cardinal.

"We found out more about the Agricultural Bank of Holland."

"Ah."

"It is in deep trouble with derivative purchases. Not as bad trouble as Baring's Bank in London was when their man ran up a billion-dollar debt, but serious enough trouble for a bank its size. You have not heard about it?"

"Nope, but I don't hear about everything. What kind of derivatives?"

"Swaps, put and takes, straddles."

"Dummies."

"We will continue to watch them. Naturally. We also have two of our people in their house now. But we cannot understand why your presence in Rome for the conclave has caused them unease."

"Any known links with Vatican officials?"

"None that we know of. As you can imagine we must be very cautious in exploring that possibility. But we will do it nonetheless."

"Keep in touch, Niko."

"Naturally I will do that."

Odd stuff. A Dutch bank, of all things. Odd, and somehow sinister.

I returned to the TV screen. Peppermint Patty should be an anchor on network news. But, despite her smashing good looks and her intelligence, she didn't quite fit into anyone's affirmative action quota. So she stayed with CNN at a much lower salary. While she was ambitious enough, these distinctions in prestige and remuneration bothered her not at all.

When she decided to dump me and Washington and take her kids, *our* kids, I suppose, away from me and Washington, her agent applied for a job on all the Chicago channels.

The best he could get for her was a job as beat reporter. Again she didn't quite fit in anyone's quota. So she settled for CNN's one-person Midwest bureau in Chicago. Eventually they decided to create an anchor role for her in Chicago, not that they cared all that much about the Windy City, but they did care about having her on prime-time news every night. Now every news director in America was fuming that she had stolen all the conclave action away from his station.

With some help, I was willing to wager, from the ineffable Blackie Ryan.

"She really didn't want the divorce, did she?" My shrink had railed at me. "If you had refused, she would have backed off, wouldn't she?"

"I didn't think of it that way then."

"And now?"

"I was so damned tired of it all, I just wanted out."

"You joined AA, you stopped drinking, you went into counseling with her, you were ready to leave Washington. . . ."

"And they destroyed me in that counseling."

"Yet you didn't resume drinking."

"No."

"Do you think you're an addictive personality?"

"Probably not."

"So are you a true alcoholic?"

"I have to live like I am."

"Fine. You should. I suggest, however, that you drank at first to escape her tirades and then let her end the marriage, so there was no need to drink anymore."

"That may be true," I had conceded reluctantly.

"In the end, however, despite your pose of being the guy who was tossed out of the house, you were the instigator of the divorce."

"She sued."

"I know that. And you manipulated the relationship so it

looked like she ended the marriage despite your honest efforts to save it.''

I'd had to think about that before answering.

"Maybe."

"Not maybe."

"I didn't think of it that way then, but I guess you're right."

"So rather than stand up to her, you cut and ran and made her look bad."

"That's pretty harsh."

"But it's true."

"I guess so."

"And now you have lost her and you miss her terribly."

To my surprise, I had buried my face in my hands and wept. "If we tried again, I'd start drinking again."

"If you were unwilling to change your responses to her mercurial temperament, you surely would."

Why was I playing that scene over again?

"She needed your help," the shrink had ended that session. "Instead you became a drunk and ran away."

Well, so what?

No, I had been driven away.

Was there any difference?

The phone rang. I reached for the cellular phone and then realized it was the hotel phone.

"Dinny?"

Familiar voice.

"Julia Roberts, is it?"

"Crazy as ever."

"More so, maybe. By the way, you were great today. Marvelous. The boys in the Curia won't be pleased with you."

"I'm sure Blackie set me up with those two. Weren't they sweet?"

"Bewitched is the word I'd use."

Pause.

"You interviewed Cardinal Meegan today?"

"Yeah. I don't know why Blackie set that one up. The man's a real asshole."

"Maybe so bad that the other cardinals will realize it."

"Could be."

"Isn't it astonishing how they could create that boom for Monastero out of nothing?"

"Smoke and mirrors."

Pause again. Was she going to propose an assignation? God help me, but I'd come. I would have any time in the last couple of years.

"I'm going to do an analysis and commentary tomorrow on smoke and mirrors in Vatican politics."

"Neat idea."

She hesitated.

"And I wonder if I could see your piece tonight so I could quote it tomorrow. I won't use anything from it till I see the *Herald-Tribune* tomorrow morning. I promise."

"Why not? A lot more people will hear it on CNN than will ever read it."

"Could you put it in my box at the hotel sometime today? It's 144."

"I'll be going out about seven. That all right?"

"Perfect. Thanks awfully, Dinny."

"My pleasure to help."

I was ready to hang up.

"The kids send their love."

"Great."

"They really do love you, Dinny."

"I'm glad they do."

Another pause.

"You'll be at the North American for Cardinal Menendez's talk tomorrow?"

"Wouldn't miss it."

"See you there."

After a friendly conversation, I could hardly say, "Not if I see you first."

So now I knew her room number.

Well, so what?

Blackie

$\mathcal{H}$ow many cups of coffee is that today?'' My sister, the virtuous Mary Kathleen Ryan Murphy, M.D., demanded.

''Only five.'' Cardinal Cronin permitted himself a lie, which perhaps was not sinful because he did not expect to be believed.

We were eating dinner—the Stewarts, the Murphys, Milord Cronin, and I—in the restaurant of the Grand Hotel, across from the Stazione Termini. The food and wine were of the highest quality and the view of the hotel's lobby, a half floor below us, was excellent.

I was thus able to see the admirable Patricia Anne McLaughlin, gorgeously arrayed in blue, come in the lobby and up to the other end of the restaurant with an English writer of many romantic conquests about whom many things were said, of which *cad* was the least serious. I reflected to myself that Dinny Mulloy was a fool.

''Punk?'' The good doctor turned to me.

''Ten would not be an excessive number.''

''More like twenty. Minimum.''

''Maybe,'' the cardinal, an old pro at charming women, said with his most genial smile.

Knowing my sister, he should have known better.

''Ron and Janet might be impressed with this blood pressure record.'' She pushed the paper that the cardinal had given the two cardiologists across the table at him with a dismissive gesture. ''It doesn't impress me at all. You look like hell, Sean. You're not sleeping, you're nervous, irritable, and worn out. I don't care what your last EEG or EKG said, you're a prime candidate for collapse of one sort or another. What's your heart rate?"

Oblivious to the fact that he was a cardinal and she an attractive woman in the middle years of life, she reached across the table and grabbed his wrist. The Stewarts looked shocked. Joe Murphy, her long-suffering Bostonian husband, winked at me.

"A hundred and two. A caffeine high. You're living on a caffeine high, Sean Cardinal Cronin, by the grace of God and favor of the apostolic see, whatever the hell you are."

"This is a critical time, Mary Kate," he argued. "We're electing a pope."

"OK, so you get into the conclave and you freak out on a caffeine binge, then who the hell is going to be this Spaniard's campaign manager . . . ? No, *cameriere*, Eminenza has had his last coffee for the night."

"That won't happen, will it Janet? Ron?"

Ron Stewart glanced at his wife. She looked at him. She was the one to respond.

"I never argue with Mary Kate's diagnoses of my patients. She's always right."

"Just like her brother," I murmured.

"All right," Mary Kate continued. "That's settled. Five cups a day. Absolute maximum. None after supper. Take one of these in the morning and the evening. Walk at least an hour. Outside. In the sunlight. I know you well enough to know you won't do these things, but don't blame me if you flake out in the Sistine Chapel."

"Prozac?" the cardinal asked hopefully.

"No, I don't want you dumbing out in there either. Then the Punk will have to wire the whole thing, not, God knows, that he's incapable of that."

"Punk" is an affectionate nickname that my siblings and their children use. As in "Uncle Punk, that's a totally cool nickname."

"I should take one of these green things now?"

"*No!* Before you go to bed."

"They don't interact with alcohol," Joe Murphy said mildly.

"Right. You can drink as much as you want. *Cameriere*, Eminenza will have a B and B. Large. Monsignore will have a Bailey's Irish Cream. Also large."

While there was a touch of crimson at Sean Cronin's Roman collar—not that it earned him any respect from my admirable sibling—I wore no such mark of office. Indeed, it was only after a desperate, last-minute search that I had found a Roman collar. The waiter seemed surprised at the title.

"On ice, *signora*?"

"They're Americans, aren't they?"

General laughter.

In defense of my sibling, I must note that she suited her style to her patient. While hardly a passive personality, she was far less directive with her husband and children. When she tried to order them around, they simply laughed at her. Then, O saving grace, she would laugh at herself. However, in a phone call before dinner I had admitted to her that it was not just Nora Cronin who was worried about the cardinal.

"Mkate@LCMH," I said, "the man's a wreck. He is, to use one of your currently favorite terms, overinvested in this conclave affair."

"It is kind of important, isn't it, Punk?"

"Moderately important, but not worth his life. Still, he'll be better if he's cool. Today in my presence he said to *The New York Times* that one of his colleagues could not lead a pack of starving vampires to a blood bank."

She laughed. "Can he?"

"Oh, no. But it was not a *politique* remark on the record. Fortunately, I persuaded the gentleman from the *Times* not to attribute the quote. Thus people will think I was the one who said it—after all, he did steal it from me—and no harm will be done."

"He probably heard it from you anyway."

"That is irrelevant."

"Does the outcome of the conclave hinge on him?"

"Our coalition is soft, especially in the absence of a strong stand by our candidate. If Sean is out of it, we could be losers."

"That's candid enough."

So Mary Kate had played her assigned role perfectly. The best that could be expected was that Milord Cronin would cut down somewhat on the coffee and maybe get some exercise each day—maybe walk down from the Janiculum to the Vatican. He had promised Senator Cronin before she returned to Washington that after the conclave he would take a week off at Amalfi.

"What's going to happen, Cardinal?" Joe Murphy asked, deciding that Mary Kate's shock therapy had been as successful as it was likely to be. "Are we going to win?"

The cardinal threw up his hands in desperation. "We're in trouble. The Curia is playing its usual game of acting like everything is settled. The Corpus Institute people have a new calumny against Louie every day. Their media hounds are phonying up stories that are pure fiction. They have produced this 'stability' issue out of thin air, as if the Church is not in deep crisis and more of the same won't make it worse. All our guys want to vote for the winner, and some of them are beginning to think that Louie isn't a winner. He'd better be good tomorrow."

I noted that the Englishman had paid the bill and stalked out of the Grand Hotel. Alone. Doubtless the pious Patty had long experience brushing off boors.

"Punk?" Mkate@LCMH glanced at me. "What do you think?"

"With a few breaks, which I believe we can generate, the grace of God, and the good health of Milord Cronin, we will win."

"That is a clear enough prediction," Ron Stewart agreed. "I hope you're right."

"You guys certainly have CNN and the *Times* on your

side," Joe Murphy said. "That gorgeous woman is devastating."

"She's more than a pretty face, if you ask me," his wife added. "And a great body, too. Isn't she, Punk? She seems to have a first-class mind."

My sibling has never felt the need to withhold an opinion until she is asked.

"Oh, yes . . . there are some indications that she will do a commentary tomorrow on smoke-and-mirrors politics as it is practiced in the Vatican. I think it will not displease our side."

"First I've heard of it," the cardinal complained.

"I didn't want it to be on your conscience."

I observed the pure Patricia leaving the hotel, head and shoulders bowed. She too must have a breaking point. I would leave it to heaven to make judgments about Dinny Mulloy.

When we left the Grand Hotel, the cardinal and I did not return immediately to the Janiculum. Rather we asked our driver to take us to the Germano-Hungarian College over near Santa Maria Maggiore. Klaus Maria Johann had summoned a meeting of our precinct captains at eleven-thirty.

Most of them were already there when we arrived.

I noted that Francis Ulululu, from the island of Yap, had joined us. The youngest of the cardinals, a tall Polynesian who looked like he might be a recently retired linebacker for the hated Niners, Ulululu was not highly regarded. The late pope, it was said, had named him to the Sacred College over the objections of his advisers because he wanted to show that the Church's concern extended even to the smallest of countries.

In fact, he had been only a second-string linebacker at Ohio State University.

"Hi, Blackie." He encompassed my hand in his massive paw. "Good to see you. This stuff is a crock of shit, isn't it?"

"Inarguably."

So he remembered me and my name. Might be dangerous after all.

We were gathered around an oak table, which may have been the largest in the world, in the "study" of the count cardinal—a room that would have fit nicely in an elaborate, baroque castle of a robber baron on a mountain overlooking the Rhine. To enhance the mood, the lighting suggested that we were in a cave hewn out of the mountains below the castle. Elves perhaps lurked behind the closed doors. Or Siegfried and that crowd of howlers.

I only mix historical eras when the mix fits the reality.

Klaus was still wearing the purple shirt—or maybe he had a closet filled with them—and was ensconced on a throne at the head of the table.

I looked around. We hadn't lost anyone: Tim Whelan from Castlebar, Jaime Sanchez from Davao, Dick Llewelyn from Cardiff, and Ives Michner from Saskatoon. And we had picked up Tony DeJulio, OP of Verona, Armande Henri LeClerque from Bordeaux, and Ulululu. The best and the brightest, to remember an unfortunate phrase.

None of us were dressed like Wagnerian characters, however. Rather, we were attired in every kind of clerical garb from von Obermann's purple shirt and black trousers to DeJulio's black cassock. The only sign of crimson in the room was the edging around the gap in Sean Cronin's Roman collar. Astride Valerian, who had been reported likely to denounce the propensity of priests not to dress "like priests" at the funeral Mass, would not be pleased.

I was the only one in the room who was not a cardinal, but that was all right because no one noticed me anyway.

"Ja, ja," Klaus began, "We are here because we are worried about this issue of stability and shocking the people that the Curia and Corpus have created. It has influenced many cardinals, including some of our own. They still favor our friend Don Luis but they are now not so sure."

"It is a red herring!" Sean Cronin exploded. "Order has not been restored in the Church, only the semblance of order at the very top. The Church is not united. There is more division than ever. The clergy are restless, the people are dissatisfied, there are sex scandals in every country, the pope has become a figurehead as far as the priests and the people are concerned—not only on sex but on everything else—and these damn fools are trying to tell us we have a stable and orderly church! Hell, if we had some barbarian invaders we'd be back in the ninth century. This is order? This is stability? This is unity? That asshole from Miami Beach told the *Times* yesterday that Menendez would frighten the good laity because he wears a tie! Meegan is the one that scares them!"

He was working on his first cup of coffee since dinner. I would endeavor to spill it the next time he pounded on the table. The line about the ninth century was, needless to say, mine.

"They claim that they have another charge against Don Luis, this time sex!" DeJulio added, his saturnine features drawn up in a fierce frown. "Can you imagine anything more absurd!"

"Focking bastards!" Whelan pounded the table even more fiercely than Milord Cronin had.

LeClerque, a round little man with dark skin and brooding black eyes, clutched the table with both his hands and glared at all of us. "Rezak of the Holy Office has prepared a document to be issued the day we go into conclave. He warns that most of what the late pope did was infallible because everything was accepted by the bishops of the world. Anyone who suggests changes is guilty of heresy!"

"So if we vote for Don Luis," a grim-faced Llewelyn said through tight lips, "we are all heretics. Perhaps then our vote is invalid."

"Corpus might argue that!"

Milord Cronin pounded the table again. I tipped the coffee cup with hardly any effort. He did not even notice that I was clearing away the mess.

These cardinals were by no means radicals. Many of them

had been appointed by the late pope. But they were fed up.

"Ja, ja." Our host tried to calm us down. "First of all, we must hope that Don Luis makes a good presentation tomorrow."

"He will," I said softly.

"You have seen it, Bishop, ah, Bishop . . . ?"

"Oh, yes."

"I know!" Sean Cronin said with a shrug that implied despair when it came to dealing with his Sweeper. "I didn't ask."

"Ja, Bishop, that is very good. We will assume that he will say the right things. . . ."

"In the paper. Who knows what will happen in the question period. Might I suggest that as many cardinals as possible show up for the talk at one or the other of its venues to indicate their support? It would be a shame, of course, to miss Cardinal Valerian's remarks tomorrow morning."

General laughter.

"Ja, but that is very good, Bishop, very good. I myself will come to the talk at the Nordamericano and stay for lunch."

"Bishop Ryan," the cardinal put my name out on the record, "will be happy to see that there is an adequate supply of schnapps."

"Though you might want to sample Bailey's," I said softly, very softly.

"Then," Michner continued, "we must talk constantly about the need to revive the spirit of the Second Vatican Council."

"We will strongly imply that the troubles in implementing its reforms," DeJulio added, "were caused by Curial rigidity, by the very stability which they praise. The Conciliar Reform has—"

"Not been tried and found wanting, but found hard and not tried," the linebacker from Yap concluded with a bright smile that was as big as he was.

"Ja, that is very good, Franz! Very good."

"We should be careful," Jaime Sanchez of Davao spoke for the first time, "of seeming to repudiate the late pope."

Sanchez was a precise little man with an unreadable face, a canon lawyer with a lawyer's concern for small print.

"We should not offend the pious unnecessarily," DeJulio agreed.

"One might say," Llewelyn, the Lion of Cardiff, suggested, "that we want to continue the work of building Church unity begun by the late pope, by continuing the implementation of the Vatican Council. No one would quarrel with that."

"Not properly interpreted, of course," my cardinal added. "Still, I am worried about this baloney that the good and pious laypeople are shocked by change and would be scandalized by decentralization of authority and respect for pluralism. Bishop Ryan, could you speak to that?"

Another setup.

"I am reliably informed that both *The New York Times* and CNN are going to report tomorrow, well, it's today now, on polls taken of American Catholics. I am afraid that His Eminence of Miami Beach will be profoundly shocked to find that the laypeople to whom he talks are not typical."

"Ja, ja, that is good, Bishop Reen, very good."

"Call me Blackie. . . . If I might suggest that in many of your countries it should be possible to do phone surveys during the day and report them in various media outlets tomorrow . . ."

"Grand idea! Super!" exclaimed his lordship of Castlebar. "Haven't they been using this 'simple laity' line with us long enough? Let's knock it down once and for all."

The precinct captains left with their enthusiasm enhanced. My own cardinal, not to put too fine an edge on the matter, looked like hell.

"I'll sleep well tonight, Blackwood," he informed me in the car as we returned to the Nordamericano. "It's been a long day."

"Arguably."

"You did tip over my coffee cup. I saw you."

"Every cardinal in the room would deny it."

"Mary Kate is tougher on me than Nora."

"Such is the nature of the women of the ethnic group involved."

"Nora and I were lovers once, you know."

"No, I do not know."

"Sure you do. No point in trying to hide anything from you, Blackwood. I want someone else besides the two of us to know it."

"Indeed?"

"Positano. We would never dare be there at the same time again."

"Prudent."

"I don't regret it for a moment."

"Ah."

"I mean I regret the violated vows, though I'm not sure that my late brother was capable of any kind of a promise, much less a marriage promise. I don't regret the love or the passion, but of course I am sorry for the sin involved."

"Indeed."

I wondered in my own head whether there was enough freedom to make serious sin possible. Fortunately only Herself needs to judge these matters and She has made it clear that She is indulgent to Her children.

"Only once and we'd never do it again. When he killed himself I wanted to leave the priesthood and marry her. She would not hear of it. She's kept me in the priesthood. Kept me alive. Kept me human. I kind of want to make this conclave a present to her."

We Irish, I thought, are not only romantics. We are crazy romantics.

"So I'll stay alive, don't worry about that."

"My charge is merely to supervise your coffee consumption."

Why tell me about this youthful romance?

Perhaps because at this decisive time in his life, he had to have a confidant. Besides, as he said, I knew already.

We were silent for some time. As the car pulled up the Janiculum, I asked him, "How many of those men would you classify as radicals?"

"Good question. Not many. Little Armande LeClerque must have anarchist bomb throwers in his background somewhere. He is the most angry of all, so angry he can hardly talk. But he is nothing more than an honest man who has been driven to the edge by what's been going on the last fifteen years. Besides me the only real radicals are Llewelyn and Tim Whelan, all three of us Paul VI men."

"All three Celts."

"I hadn't thought of it that way. The real bomb throwers."

"Pikes, more likely."

We got out of our car. The rector would have one of his assistant spies watching for our return. He would try to pry out of the driver where we were and who else's cars were there. Fine, let them know.

In truth, they were terrified of us. The Curialists, anyway. The Corpus Institute people were probably more confident. They figured they were more clever than we were.

"A peaceful people till they are pushed too hard—farmers, cattle raisers, horse trainers, poets."

"Yeah. Tomorrow will be an interesting day. Our turn."

"Arguably."

"Don't worry. I won't drink any coffee before I go to bed."

"I am edified. Nor, I presume, will you forget your green pill."

Indeed, it would be an interesting day.

Yet I wondered what the opposition thought they had on Don Luis, as I had discovered he must be called.

Was there a Nora Cronin lurking somewhere in his past? If so, all bets were off.

Mark

Mark had dressed in black trousers and a white shirt so that he would look like a seminarian. He had been a seminarian not so long ago, but was forced out of the seminary because the rector thought he was obsessed with abortion.

How could you be obsessed with mass murder? The rector was as guilty as the abortionists. He had told him so.

He could not use his rifle in this crowd. So he had crammed a .25-caliber pistol in his pocket. It was a very efficient weapon so long as you were close enough. He would have to get very near his target, pull the weapon out of his pocket, and put its mouth right between the eyes of the baby murderer. It would not be easy, but Mark believed that he was resourceful enough to do it. He would not escape, but that did not matter. He would have made his statement.

Because he knew how to play the seminarian game, it was easy to slip into the auditorium. At least a dozen TV cameras. He would bear witness and perhaps become a martyr before the eyes of the whole world.

Dinny

Actually I didn't go out the previous night. I had told my ex-wife that to maintain my image as someone who was coping just fine with divorce. I wasn't coping just fine at all. I didn't sleep much either, too many thoughts and guilt feelings about the kids.

Good kids. I had reason to be proud of them. No I didn't. I was not part of their lives.

"You are quiet this morning, Deeny."

We were driving from the hotel to the Janiculum because it had been decreed that it was too hot to walk from the Ottaviano station up to the top of the hill.

I thank heaven, such as it may be, for that.

My guardian angel was watching me closely. As a concession to the heat, she had forsaken her suits and was now wearing a neatly tailored beige skirt and matching blouse. Still strictly professional, but now hot-weather professional.

"Heat is getting to me."

"Yes, it is unseasonable. More like August weather."

I should ask her something. What the hell was it? I was as thoughtless with her as I was with my own kids. Charming at first and then ignore them.

Oh yeah, her piece on the black nobility.

"You file your piece?"

"Naturally."

"Are they using it?"

"Naturally!" She smiled happily.

"Hey! Congratulations!"

I thought about hugging her and decided that a handshake would be better.

"The editor said," she poked her nose very high in the air, "that he might just call you back and let me cover the rest of the conclave."

"Great idea!"

"Naturally, he was only joking."

"Do I get to see it?"

Solemnly she handed me two pages of computer output. The headline was perfect for the new and more playful *Times,* though the old one would have winced at the thought of using it:

FOR PAPAL NOBILITY CONCLAVES ARE OLD STORY
THEY LOCKED UP POPES TO FORCE ELECTION

By P. E. Oriani

Rome.

In the Colonna palace in the heart of Rome, the chair that should be at the head of the table in the ornate dining room stands instead at the wall—awaiting the election of the next Colonna pope. It does not matter that no Colonna has emerged the winner from a conclave in the last three hundred years. For a family that claims to be descendants of Mark Anthony, three hundred years is only yesterday. The chair will remain empty after this conclave too because there are no Colonna cardinals. The Colonnas nonetheless are confident that history is on their side.

The papal nobility, called the "black" nobility in distinction to the "white" nobility, which aligned itself with the House of Savoy after 1870, has witnessed scores of conclaves. It has on many occasions cut off the food supply of the electors to force them to choose a new bishop for Rome. Popes come and go but the princely families go on.

Among the famous families who spurned the House of Savoy (and laugh now at those who supported it) are the Orsini, Ruspoli, Sacchetti, Lancellotti, Massimo, Aldobrandini, and Giustiniani-Bandini.

They were all at the funeral mass the other day, men in white tie and sashes and medallions, women in long black dresses and black veils. They look and often act like characters in a Fellini film. The men tend to be short and some of them grow stout with the years. The women, whatever their age, are always radiantly lovely. In the past, women from the papal nobility have been mistresses to popes and have sired popes. Whether they are born into the noble family or marry into it, they all share a strong determination to make their opinions heard and prevail.

Many of the families were once fabulously wealthy. In the palace of the Doria Pamphili family, there is a bust of one of the princes made by Bernini and a painting by Velàzquez. Some of them retain their wealth, though not because there is any money to be made anymore by being a papal noble. Either they have made shrewd investments in land (often vineyards) or they have married into wealthy families. Others are successful professional men and women, not rich, but hardly poor. Still others live on handouts from the more affluent families. The members of the black nobility are not always fond of one another, but they share a common history they do not want to lose.

Do they become excited over the prospect of another conclave? "Of course we do," a princess said to a *New York Times* reporter, "but we are discreet about it. We learned long ago to be discreet about everything and remain close to the pope but not too close."

Despite all the splendor of their history and their pride of family, the black nobility have little influence on the papacy. It is not clear that most of them would wish to.

"We are indeed anachronisms," Prince Ricardo Benedetto Antonio Oriani, a successful attorney, said recently. "But perhaps at certain times anachronisms can become relevant."

When asked what he meant, the prince shrugged indifferently. "I don't know," he said, "but that seems to be what a character in a Fellini film might have said."

He paused thoughtfully.

"Early Fellini, of course."

(Ms. Oriani, of the *Times* bureau in Rome, is herself a papal princess, the first one to ever work for the paper.)

"Great work," I said enthusiastically. "No wonder they liked it. I won't say, Pretty Principessa, that you'll be a fine journalist someday. You're a fine one now. They shouldn't make you play nursemaid to an aging journalistic bum."

"Guardian angel. I asked for the task."

"Why?"

"I wanted to see how a truly great journalist worked, what made him, how do you say it, tick."

"And?"

She shrugged her very pretty shoulders.

"I don't know yet. But thank you for your kind words about my sidebar. I have at least learned that great reporters can be decent human beings."

She turned and considered me very carefully.

"Perhaps I will never understand you."

I felt my face go warm.

"There may be no one there, but if you do figure me out, let me know."

She changed the subject.

"What Don Luis says this morning is very important, is it not?"

"It's make or break for him."

"Which will it be?"

"What do you think?"

I gave her the copy of the text that Bishop Blackie had somehow purloined for me. She read it carefully.

"It is perfect. . . . My parents are friends of his, you know. I have met him. He might be one of the best popes since my ancestors came here."

"With their swords and their falcons and their beautiful women."

"The most beautiful in Europe, according to *The New York Times*, so it must be true."

"All the news that's fit to print."

"Did he give it also to her?"

"To Peppermint Patty? No, I did. She needed it for a commentary she's doing today."

"That was very generous." She smiled her approval.

"I don't hate her, Paoli. I'm kind of proud of her, to tell the truth. I just don't want to live with her."

"My parents wish to have a little party for you tomorrow night because you have been so kind to me. Will you come?"

"Naturally."

"It is entirely up to you: Shall we invite her?"

"Who . . . Oops, *whom*?"

"Your wife?"

"Ex-wife."

"Well?"

"Look, practically perfect princess, I'm not going to be put in a position of saying whether Patty should be invited to a party. If you want to ask her, ask her. I won't stamp out of your apartment. I won't even make nasty faces at her."

The parking lot at the Nordamericano was jammed with cars and vans with television equipment. Sweating seminarians and Roman cops were trying ineffectually to control the mess. Already set up, CNN camerapersons were shooting it all.

Despite the press of vehicles and people, our Lancia

coasted right up to the entrance. Paoli's clout seemed irresistible.

We arrived at the same time as another Lancia, out of which stepped Luis Emilio Cardinal Menendez y Garcia. An enormous cheer swept the throng. He and the young priest with him were unable to move, until a phalanx of cops surrounded him and moved them slowly toward the entrance of the college. He was wearing a black suit and a white shirt with a dark blue tie, a slim, handsome, almost fragile man with dark skin, an intelligent face, and a wondrous smile. He waved in our direction. Paoli waved back.

She could get me an interview with him. I wouldn't need Bishop Blackie. Not that it mattered.

Anyway, I didn't want to interview him just yet. Timing wasn't right.

The American cardinals were waiting for him, all but Sean Cronin in their robes. My friend from Miami Beach looked most unhappy.

"You have written your story?" Paoli asked me.

"About this? Yeah, but subject to revision."

A new lead was banging around in my head: "Perhaps the outcome of the conclave was decided today."

We eased our way from the car and promptly encountered herself. She was wearing a light green, double-breasted, one should excuse the expression, summer suit with a white scarf at the neck and looked radiant. And cool. She was also on an excitement high.

"Great footage, Dinny. There's at least twenty-five cardinals here, in addition to the Americans. This could be the turning point!"

"The high tide, King Alfred cried, the high tide and the turn!"

"Tennyson?"

"Chesterton."

"We're carrying it all live on both CNN and *Headline News*! They'll replay it all day long in the States if it's any good."

"A guy could use a lead suggesting that the outcome of the conclave was decided today."

"A guy could." She grinned. "Don't worry, I won't steal it."

"You're doing your commentary afterwards?"

"I'm doing it here. I'm not sure when. Depends on when Atlanta wants it."

Then, mike in hand, she dashed away from us, and headed right for John Lawrence Cardinal Meegan. Poor man.

Sean Cronin looked terrible, I thought. The strain and the conflict of the campaign must be getting to him. Glancing back once, I saw the shade. Still tracking me despite the crowd.

Paoli's pass and her determination got us into the college and then to the auditorium. I noticed a young man who was near the Spanish cardinal get pushed out of the way by a burly cop. From the expression on his face, I thought he would kill the cop.

Talk about cult of personality.

"Mr. Mulloy? Signorina Oriani? Bishop Ryan has a seat for you up front.

"Naturally," I said before herself could say it.

Mark

Mark was less than a foot away from the baby-killer cardinal. His hand tightened on his weapon. Only a few more seconds . . .

Then a pig of a cop shoved him out of the way and the cardinal passed by him. Mark shoved back at the cop. If he could not kill the cardinal, he would at least kill the cop.

The man turned on him angrily and pushed him hard.

Mark reeled back and fell against a seminarian, who also shoved him aside. He pulled the weapon partway out of his pocket.

Then he shoved it back in. It would be foolish to sacrifice himself. He would wait for another day.

He turned away from the crowd and fought his way out of the college. He wished he had enough weapons and ammunition to kill them all.

Blackie

We had not counted on Archbishop Gene Schreiber. As rector of the Nordamericano, he assumed the right to introduce the guest speaker and moved to the podium before Milord Cronin could get there.

"Your eminences, your excellencies, reverend fathers, ladies and gentlemen of the media, I bid you welcome. We are not used to such interest in our academic lectures."

Pause for laughter. None came.

The next ten minutes were unbearably painful for everyone. Fortunately, as Schreiber rambled on, the TV folks turned off their lights. He spoke of the difficulties of growing up Catholic in his hometown, where most people were, as he put it, "non-Catholic," and of the great love we all should have for the Church. He warned the seminarians not to be swept along by "novelties," which threatened the Church we loved so much, and even warned the cardinals, "whom we are honored to have among us," of their solemn obligation to protect the Church "from those who would harm her."

"Institution worship," Milord Cronin whispered in my ear.

"Idolatry," I replied.

Doubtless the archbishop hoped that it would be reported to the Curia and Corpus that he was blunting Menendez and that it would be so counted to his credit.

It was inconceivable to him that the forces that had run the Church for so many years could possibly lose.

Finally he shut up. His introduction of Don Luis was brief and perfunctory.

Don Luis

CLIPS EXCERPTED FROM THE TV FEED.

I have been asked to speak about the future of the Church. That may seem an odd subject for a historian, whose specialty is the past and not the future. And indeed it may be an inappropriate subject for me to discuss. Nonetheless, the historian has a perspective from his knowledge of the past which enables him to evaluate the present in which we live, necessarily, if I may say so . . .

(Laughter.)

. . . and in which we must work at the construction of the future.

On the basis of my knowledge of the past history of the Church, I am compelled to say that the present is one of the most exciting and challenging times we have seen in the last nineteen hundred years. It is, to use the Greek word, a *kairos*, an appropriate time, a pregnant time, a time of great grace and promise which we must not ignore.

Only now do we begin to realize what a critical turning point in our history was the Second Vatican Council. Only now do we begin to understand where the spirit of that council may lead us if we have the courage and the faith and the confidence to follow that spirit which is also the Holy Spirit. Like the council we must be open and sensitive to the "signs of the times," we must understand that each bishop in his own diocese should speak for the whole Church to his own people and for his people to the whole Church. Like the Council we should realize that a large number of our laypeople are well-educated, intelligent, and dedicated and eager to help us. Like the Council we must listen to the Spirit wherever the voice of the Spirit is to be heard. The pope must listen to his brother bishops, the bishops must listen to their brother priests, and the priests must listen to their people. Only when we are ready to admit the possibility that the Spirit speaks wherever She wishes to speak, and that therefore we must listen always and everywhere, will we be able to discern the work of the Spirit in the world.

Today, because of the marvelous resources of instant communication, there is hardly a place in the world in which the Spirit cannot speak to all of us.

Above all we must not be afraid. We must not be afraid of our well-educated laity; we must not be afraid of the artists, scholars, and thinkers whose background is Catholic and from whom we can learn so much, even if just now they are angry at us; we must not be afraid of the new cultures from all over the world that we are only now beginning to appreciate; we must not be afraid that the Lord will not continue to protect us; we must especially not be afraid of the demands of women, who have always given so much to the Church and now, as fully equal human beings, can give us so much more; we must not be afraid of the new insights into the nature of human nature that science has made available to us. We must not be afraid to make ourselves the patrons of social justice all over the world. We must not be afraid to change, as Cardinal Monastero said so well the other day: We must change in order to remain the same. We must not confuse what is essential in the Church with that which is mutable, no matter how ancient it may be. The Church has presented itself to the world in many different forms since it left Jerusalem. No custom and no tradition which is not of the essence of our message, no matter how old, should escape reexamination. And no custom and no tradition, no matter how new, should be abandoned until we carefully consider the costs of doing so. We must be willing to experiment, to modify, to refine before we change.

We must be open, sensitive, and above all hopeful. We must be ready to dialogue with everyone. We must question no one's good faith. We should not fear that we will be contaminated and corrupted by those who disagree with us. While we must certainly recognize the presence of evil in the world and the threats to human dignity and freedom that evil poses, we must also recognize the goodness and goodwill in the world and become partisans of goodness and goodwill.

It must be admitted honestly that many of our people have a negative impression of our institution, as of course do many who know us only from outside the Church. They view us as harsh and unbending, as narrow and uninformed, as arrogant and unsympathetic. Are we prepared to say that there are no reasons to justify that view of us? Are we prepared to say that there is nothing in our manner, our style, our institutional organization, our narrowness of vision which has given them that impression?

I for one am not ready to say those things. I candidly believe that we are our own worst enemies because we have often seemed to worship not the Father in heaven but our own institutional being. We should not, my fellow Catholics, worship the Church, we should not make the Church an end in itself. The Church clearly is only a means. When the means gets in the way of the end it has become the object of idolatry. When we seem to want to impose that idolatry on others, we appear to many to be religious imperialists. Are we so sure that we never act like idolaters and religious imperialists?

I am not.

We must listen to our critics, to those who hate us, to those who will not listen to us, because God's spirit might well be telling us through them something we desperately need to hear. Can we not say even to them, Come reason with us? Come, let us know each other better and let us part, if not in agreement, at least in mutual respect?

We must learn that it is not enough merely to preach the truth. In the world in which we live today, we must also seek to persuade. If we are content with laying down our rules and regulations, our laws and our doctrines, then we may be preaching to empty halls. I do not say that we should stop preaching what we believe. I merely say that we must preach in a way that women and men of good faith and goodwill will be able to see that there is a point to be made for what we say and that we are not merely arrogant and doctrinaire. I am not suggesting that we compromise any of those things we believe in, but only that we change our way of talking to those who do not believe the same things, especially when for one reason or another they are of the household of the faith. It may be that, if we do that, we will find less disagreement than we would have thought. And more insight.

It will be very difficult to change a style of communicating with others that was appropriate for another era but which is utterly destructive of our message today.

I believe that we have no choice but to go in the directions of which I have spoken, better sooner than later, but surely later—with many wasted opportunities—if not sooner.

Will there be chaos if we attempt to follow this new way of being Catholic, a way which I believe is as old as Saint Mark's Gospel?

My friends, I have studied the history of the Catholic Church for thirty-five years. I cannot find a time when there has not been chaos. Chaos is part of the human condition. The divine guidance in which we believe guarantees only that we will not, as you say in English, self-destruct. A church which is human will always be in chaos. When it does not seem so, the reason is that the dangers and the possibilities which come with chaos have been so effectively repressed that they are not visible. They are still there, however, and may at any time explode.

The present crisis in the Church, I believe, is the result of the fact that after the Second Vatican Council many of us who are leaders lost our nerve. We tried to repress rather than to understand the energies, some of them admittedly terrifying, which the Council unleashed. But we could not repress them and thus we lost our ability to focus and direct the changes. We stopped being leaders because we no longer had the courage to listen carefully to our followers. The worst failure of a leader, any leader, is the failure of nerve.

That, I submit, must change. We must not isolate ourselves from our people any longer.

So many of our laypeople believe that ours is a church of rules, that being Catholic consists of keeping rules. They do not find an institution which is like that very appealing. Nor should they.

In fact, we are a Church of love. Our message from the Lord Himself even today is the message that God is love and that we are those who are trying, however badly, to reflect that love in the world. I find that in my own city that notion astonishes many people. How we came to misrepresent that which we should be preaching above all else is perhaps the subject for many doctoral dissertations.

More important for us today, however, is the reaffirmation that we exist to preach a God of love, we try to be people of love, and we want our Church to be, insofar as we poor humans can make it, a Church of radiant love.

Does such a Church have a future?

How could it not?

(Thunderous applause.)

Blackie

*W*ithout a single note!'' Milord Cronin murmured to me.

"Photographic memory, among other things. As my siblings' children would say, 'Like, totally awesome!' "

"I hope he doesn't blow the questions."

"He'll say what he thinks."

"Not a good political strategy."

"Sometimes the best strategy."

I noted that three Corpus people had made it to the microphones.

C N N

PM: We are carrying live from the North American College in Rome a talk by Luis Emilio Cardinal Menendez y Garcia, archbishop of Valencia. The archbishop is now about to answer questions.

Q: Is it true that you are a Jew?

A: Are we not all Jewish? Is not our religion a product of the religious culture of Second Temple? Is it not proper to say that we are a Jewish religion, a sister or a first cousin, if you wish, of rabbinical Judaism? As for my own ancestry, there are those that say that all Spanish names which end in "ez" are Sephardic names. That is not certain and there is no memory in my family of such origins. But if it were true that I am part Jewish I would be very proud of that because it would mean that I would be, in a very remote fashion, a relative of Our Lord and Blessed Mother and Saint Peter, who is honored in the massive church just below us.

While I'm on the subject of Judaism, I deplore all forms of anti-Semitism. I believe that for more than a millennium and a half the Church has been guilty of it and has helped to create an environment in which the Holocaust became possible. We will have apologized enough at the end of the next millennium and a half!

(Applause from seminarians.)

Q: Do you favor a change in the Catholic teaching on abortion?

A: No. But I am not prepared to say that all those who are not Catholic on the other side of the argument are devoid of good faith and goodwill.

Q: Why are you not properly dressed?

A: (looks at his clothes in surprise) I think I am properly dressed. This is an academic meeting and I am dressed as an academic. If it were a liturgical ceremony, I would dress for the Liturgy.

Q: But Cardinal Valerian said this morning that all priests should be sternly obligated to wear appropriate garb at all times.

A: I think what I'm wearing is appropriate. If the cardinal means clerical garb, then I am afraid that he and I disagree, though not on a matter of grave import. Saint Peter did not wear a Roman collar when he preached in this city. Nor did Saint Paul appear in cardinal red. I know enough of the history of the papacy to know that such customs have often changed. What we wear as priests is not nearly so important as the kind of priests we are . . . perhaps I should have worn a crimson tie!

(Laughter.)

Q: Do you favor the ordination of women?

A: I don't favor any abrupt change in any Church custom, as I said in my remarks. The issue is a historical one: Have women ever presided over the Eucharist in the history of the Church? As a historian I find the evidence now tilting in the direction that they have done so, particularly in the very early days.

Q: Do you think the practice of birth control is a serious sin?

A: In this matter I agree completely with the late pope that the laypeople, in virtue of the charisma of the sacrament of matrimony, have a unique and indispensable contribution to make to the Church's understanding of human sexuality. Certainly it is evident now that human sexuality is different from that of all other higher primates, precisely because it is designed to bind men and women together, as it were, to drive them towards reconciliation in their often turbulent and painful relationships. When we listen to the experience of the laity, as the late pope insisted we should, then I think that many of our problems in this most important part of life will diminish. Moreover, if we look at the history of the development of many of our teachings on sexuality we will see that they were designed to protect women from exploitation. For many men the so-called sexual revolution has merely meant greater opportunity for exploiting women. We should denounce such exploitation masquerading as liberation.

Q: Do you favor married priests?

A: How can I not favor them when many of our fellow Catholic priests in the Byzantine tradition are married? Do I think that experiments should be made in the Latin Rite, with married priests? I surely do, especially in those countries where needs are great. As a historian I know that even in the Latin Rite, for a thousand years and more there were in fact many married priests.

Q: Do you expect to be elected pope?

A: (laughs; audience joins in laughter) I don't know! I would hope I will not be and I am honest when I say that. Yet, having urged everyone to follow the grace of the Spirit this morning, I cannot say that I would resist the Spirit if that becomes an obligation for me.

Q: Are you not advocating an abandonment of everything the late pope did?

A: No. I don't believe I am. I am saying that rather we should continue what he began, perhaps with some changes in style and structure but no changes in basic conviction. . . . Now I see that Bishop Blackie Ryan is becoming nervous, which means I had better stop talking. I have been promised a real American lunch—hamburgers and french fries—and I better eat it before it gets cold.

   (Tumultuous standing ovation.)

PM: Cardinal Luis Emilio Menendez y Garcia has just finished a lecture and question period here at the North American College in Rome. The reaction of the audience suggests that the cardinal has many friends here at the Nordamericano. I am told that all the questions after the talk were asked by members of the Corpus Christi Institute and were designed to embarrass the cardinal. He did not seem very embarrassed.

   We are trying to get to the cardinal . . . Don Luis . . . Don Luis . . .

A: Yes?

Q: Do you have anything to say to the Catholic people of the United States?

A: I studied in America for a year, at the University of Michigan. I wish to greet all my friends in America and all Americans, whatever their religion. You have a wonderful country, better than perhaps you realize. And to my friends in Ann Arbor I wish to say, 'Go Blue!' "

   (The cardinal is eased away from the camera.)

PM: (dazzled) Thank you very much, Don Luis. Notre Dame fans, eat your hearts out! This is Patricia Anne McLaughlin, CNN, at the Collegio Nordamericano, Rome.

Mark

Goddamn bastard!'' Mark seethed. He didn't condemn abortion, not once. *He has to die! And he's going to die! On the day he is elected.* That would show the world that you can't diddle with the teachings of God about the sacredness of human life.

Blackie

Don Luis was sipping the best port we could find. Well, *I* could find in a hurried visit to Rome's better purveyors, a list given to me by the good principessa.

Sean Cronin was nursing his favorite B & B. I was, in the name of virtue, limiting myself to iced tea.

"They will never give up," Don Luis said with a sigh, not unlike my patented West of Ireland version. "They are absolutely convinced of their own righteousness. Like the Communists, they believe that any action taken in the name of their cause is moral. They will be a thorn in the side of the next pope."

We were in the parlor of Cardinal Cronin's suite waiting for the elongated Mercedes (I knew it had to be that) from the Germano-Hungarian College, which was to take Cardinal Menendez to that Rhenish bastion.

"He will have to get rid of them all, will he not?"

Don Luis nodded sadly.

"First of all, he will have to find out who and where they are. Then he will have to replace them slowly, one by one. The pope would not want to risk looking like he was engaged in a pogrom."

"Or the Saint Bartholomew's Day massacre, for example."

"In effect, he will have to take the papacy back so that it is his and not theirs. The pope should warn their leader that they are on very thin ice. It will not be easy."

I offered him another small sip of port.

"No, no, Blackie." He grinned up at me. "I cannot afford to fall asleep in an afternoon lecture, though I don't believe they take siestas over there. Did you buy this port yesterday or this morning?"

If he were indeed elected, Corpus and the Curia would have a very perceptive foe.

"Yesterday. Milord Cronin runs a tight ship."

They both laughed at that.

"Do you have any idea what their third shoe is?" my cardinal asked.

"Third shoe . . . oh, as in waiting for the other shoe to drop. No, none whatever. I suppose it will be something false again."

"We will have to be ready to respond promptly," Sean Cronin said, again looking tired and haggard.

"I will be ready to do so."

A bell rang. I picked up the phone.

"Father Ryan."

"Blackie," my gifted curate, Jaimie Keenan, said, "the Krauts are here. You were right, a 600 stretch."

"Ja, ja."

Don Luis put aside his port and rose from his chair.

"They are not," I said, "thousand-pound gorillas."

"What do you mean by that?" Don Luis seemed puzzled by my perfectly obvious comment.

"Like all true believers they have one major flaw: They

are not very bright. Sending their guys in to harass you this morning was monumentally stupid. It gave you a chance to cut them down with the whole world watching. They will overreach."

He sighed again.

"I hope you are right."

So, as a matter of fact, did I.

REUTERS

African Cardinal Calls for Stricter Discipline

Rome.

An African cardinal who is among the leading contenders in the papal election called today for a return to strict discipline in the Catholic Church. Cardinal Astride Valerian, president of the Congregation for the Clergy, said that a smaller Church would be a better Church. "The Church should be a saving remnant of those who believe firmly in everything that the Holy Father teaches. The others should, as the Gospel says, be cast into the fire and burned." He added that "It is impossible to be a pilgrim people if the pilgrimage is slowed down by those who will not follow the commands of the leader of the pilgrimage."

In a related development, Father Leonard F. X. Richardson, English-language spokesman for the Vatican press office, criticized Cardinal Luis Menendez for giving talks at the North American College and the German College on the same day as Cardinal Valerian's homily at the Mass in St. Peter's. "One would have hoped that His Eminence would have had more respect for his brother in Christ."

Copies of Cardinal Menendez's talk in several languages vanished from the Vatican press room almost as soon as they were placed there.

NYT

Menendez Describes His Platform
Wins Ovations at Two Colleges
Supports Second Vatican Council

By Dennis Michael Mulloy
Rome.

If the upcoming conclave had been held today in the auditoriums of either the North American College or the Germano-Hungarian College, white smoke would be pouring from either or both buildings. Luis Emilio Cardinal Menendez y Garcia presented a "platform" for his possible papacy and won ovations and demonstrations which would remind one of American political conventions in the old days when the outcome was in doubt.

Cardinal Menendez called for a rejuvenation of the Spirit of the Second Vatican Council but insisted that such a development must build on what the late pope had accomplished. He presented an emotional picture of a Church which existed to preach love.

"We exist to preach a God of love," he said, "we try to be people of love, and we want our Church to be, insofar as we poor humans can make it, a Church of radiant love."

The two venues were chosen for his "platform" speech by Cardinals Von Obermann of Düsseldorf and Cronin of Chicago because the Roman Curia, which is reported to be bitterly opposed to the Spanish cardinal, had refused him an opportunity to preach at one of the masses this week.

In both colleges the seminarians were especially enthusiastic and cheered wildly as the cardinal fended off hostile questions supplied by members of the Corpus Christi Institute. However, many bishops and virtually all of the thirty cardinals who were present at the talks also applauded vigorously.

Cardinal Menendez indicated he could not accept a change in the Church's teachings on abortion but said he would not condemn as lacking in good faith and goodwill those who disagree. He favored experimentation with married clergy in countries where the need for more priests is great and pointed out that Byzantine Catholics already have a married clergy. Speaking as a historian, he said that he was inclined to believe that historical evidence indicates that women did preside over the Mass in the Church's early history. He indicated on the subject of birth control and other sexual matters that he felt the Church should listen to the experiences of married laypeople, and quoted the late pope as saying the same thing.

"It was a standard, moderate liberal speech," another cardinal remarked afterward, "but it was couched in language which would offend no one except those who wanted to be offended. He combined sincere piety and intelligence with rich historical knowledge which is appropriate because he is a historian."

Cardinal Menendez is a polished and appealing speaker in both English and German and had special messages for friends in Germany and the United States—including those at the University of Michigan, where he studied for a year.

It now appears that if the cardinals reject a man who seems to have such an appealing papal image, they will do so in the face of the enormous pro-Menendez sentiment that television rebroadcasts of his presentations are likely to generate all over the world.

CNN

ANCHOR: Our Patty McLaughlin had a chance today to observe firsthand the way dirty politics works at the Vatican.

PM: (in front of San Pietro) That's right, Tessa. It's terribly hot here in Rome. They say it is like August heat. Everyone is edgy, especially at the *sala stampa,* the Vatican press office. Maître Alphonse de Tassigny has turned over daily briefings and supervision of the press room to Father Leonard F.X. Richardson, an American priest, like de Tassigny a member of the Corpus Christi Institute. Father Richardson treats journalists with ill-concealed contempt and does his best to completely ignore female journalists.

Today we experienced a kind of mystery in the sala stampa. Twice, copies in five languages of Cardinal Menendez's lecture at the North American College have been delivered to the press room. Within a very few moments these copies were snatched up and destroyed. No one seemed to know who was engaging in this physical censorship of a speech by a cardinal. So CNN attempted to track down the villain.

. (Cut to clip.)

In this picture you see Father James Keenan, a member of Cardinal Cronin's staff, arranging the documents, a different color for each language, on the table. Note that the man in the left-hand side of the picture ducks out of the room. That is Father Richardson. Father Keenan leaves. A few moments later Father Richardson appears carrying a wastebasket.

(Richardson is a young priest, quite bald. He wears a cassock and a sash and a very high Roman collar. As the camera watches, he sweeps all of Cardinal Menendez's texts into the wastebasket. CNN tries to interview him.)

PM: Father Richardson, I am Patricia McLaughlin of CNN. Could you tell me why you are destroying the texts of Cardinal Menendez's lecture this morning?

(Light on video camera goes on.)

LR: (startled) They are unauthorized. No unauthorized papers may be left on this table.

PM: I've never heard of that rule. Look at the table: It's littered with many different piles of paper. Why is this set of texts removed almost instantly?

LR: I don't have to explain what I do to you!

PM: The people of the world who will see this tape may wonder why you are trying to suppress news of Cardinal Menendez's remarks. That's what you're doing, aren't you?

LR: (furious) You have tricked me! I forbid this!

PM: Is the Corpus Christi Institute so determined to defeat the cardinal that it will destroy his texts? Are you going to burn them, Father, like books were burned by the Inquisition?

LR: Get out of my way, you filthy bitch!

(Pushes PM. She staggers back and falls against the wall. He pushes the camera away, it spins and captures a shot of the ceiling of the sala stampa.)

PM: (back in front of the camera) This is what freedom of expression means in Vatican City. Patricia McLaughlin, CNN, Rome.

ANCHOR: Did that priest really hit you, Patty?

PM: I guess he did, Tessa. I'm still in shock.

ANCHOR: You didn't hit him back.

PM: I'm a Catholic, Tessa. I'd never hit a priest. I never expected to be hit by one either.

ANCHOR: Then they threw you out of the Vatican press office?

PM: Vatican security people confiscated our camera and removed the tape. Father Richardson tore the tape apart as we watched. Then banned us forever and threw us out. ˙

ANCHOR: You had already changed the tapes, however?

PM: And put it in my purse. Within an hour Cardinal Cronin of Chicago protested to Cardinal Jacques Moreau, the camerlingo—the acting pope—and our camera was returned to us with apologies. Cardinal Moreau is reputed to be close to the Corpus Christi Institute. We can go back in tomorrow morning if we don't bring our camera.

ANCHOR: You'll bring the camera, however?

PM: You bet your life, Tessa. ˙

Blackie

*T*oday settles it," Egbert Winter sighed expansively, like a man letting out his belt after a large dinner, "that man is going to be the next pope. I've made up my mind. I'm voting for him."

Cardinal Winter made up his mind slowly, but once made up, it was made up.

We were in the faculty lounge of the North American, sipping our after-dinner drinks and watching television. The dinner table conversation for once had actually been about the conclave. Rather, it had been about the astonishing impact of Don Luis on the audience at his lectures earlier in the day—and through TV—on the whole world.

CNN, without my having to suggest it, had done on-the-street interviews in America. They couldn't find anyone who was not an enthusiastic Menendez supporter.

"I must confess," John Lawrence Meegan confessed,

"that most of my doubts have been removed. He is a memorable man. He would make a fine pope."

Milord Cronin was silent, pensive. Doubtless worried about the third shoe that Corpus might drop.

"Hell," Mick Kennedy said, "if we go home after they've elected someone else, we'll be lynched."

Nat Ferraro of San Diego shook his head dolefully. "My diocese is half Hispanic. Can you imagine what they will do to me!"

Then CNN turned to the current chapter of the ongoing miniseries of the Corpus Christi Institute vs. Peppermint Patty (as her husband—in the eyes of God—called her). Milord Cronin and I were prepared for this because the aforementioned modern version of Grace O'Malley had stormed up to the Janiculum—trailing fire like a comet—immediately after the contretemps at the sala stampa.

"My God!" murmured Mick Kennedy. "We're in deep shit now!"

"Oh, yes," I observed, more complacently, I confess, than I should have.

"He hit a woman on national TV," Egbert Winter moaned. "How could he be so dumb!"

"Well, yes," John Lawrence Meegan admitted. "But they did trap him, didn't they?"

"They trapped him, John Lawrence," Sean Cronin thundered, "stealing my papers!"

"Of course, of course," the archbishop of Miami Beach said, as always, frightened of Sean Cronin's anger. "He should not have done that."

"Damn right!" The cardinal poured himself another cup of post-prandial coffee. In public I would not try to dissuade him and would only attempt to spill the cup when I could do so unobtrusively.

"So you stormed up to see the camerlingo immediately?" Mick Kennedy asked.

"Got him out of his siesta. That little Corpus jerk who is his secretary wouldn't wake him until I threatened to do so myself. I demanded the video camera and wouldn't leave till I got it. He was all apologies. No ban on CNN. Only, don't bring the camera tomorrow. I said I couldn't guarantee that. He said that the young man was imprudent but that he was trapped. So I yelled that he was trapped stealing copies of a talk given by a cardinal and brought over by one of my staff. You know Moreau, sweet old man. He dithered and he apologized and wrung his hands and said he would write to the woman. He told me that he was going to vote for Don Luis and I think he means it . . . heaven knows how many times he'll change what passes for his mind.''

"This Richardson kid is an American himself," Mick Kennedy said, pounding his knee. "How can he hit a female journalist on camera and call her a bitch? And Patty, of all people!''

"He figured he was going to be able to confiscate the tape," I said. "Moreover, Corpus is on the record as believing in the inferiority of women.''

It was a long speech for me in that milieu. I was angry because the punk had pushed around one of our own. I was also delighted that he had been caught pilfering Don Luis's talk. It could not have been done more splendidly if I had orchestrated it myself.

"She's one of mine," Sean Cronin continued, echoing my thoughts. "Those dirty bastards pushed around a woman from my archdiocese. I demanded that he be replaced. Moreau said he agreed, but he won't act on it because Corpus won't let him. I'm going to write a formal letter of apology to CNN and to her.''

That was a new idea and an excellent one; again someone had a devious idea before I had. *Blackwood, you're slipping.*

"I'll sign it with you if you don't mind." Mick jumped out of his chair. "Damn them all! I don't know whether to be angry because they're so boorish or because they're so stupid . . . the rest of you will sign?''

They all agreed, John Lawrence less promptly.

"Good." Sean Cronin smiled. "I'll go write it and we

can get it off to her tonight. Where's she staying, Black-wood?''

"According to usually well informed sources, she's stay-ing at the Hotel de la Ville up by the Piazza di Spagna.''

"Let's get it done.'' He rose and strode out of the room, his color and vitality restored by the smoke of another battle. I noted with satisfaction that he had barely sipped the cup of coffee.

"Stop gloating, Blackwood,'' he commanded me. "We haven't won yet.''

"Indeed not . . . I wonder, will they decamp?''

"Who? Corpus and the others like them?''

"Will they do what Archbishop LeFevbre's crowd did and walk out? It is said that the founder of Opus Dei thought of joining the Orthodox after the Vatican Council. Corpus is newer but there are hints every once in a while that they are the authentic interpreters of the faith.''

"I never thought of that.'' Sean Cronin stopped in his tracks; weariness and strain returned to his haggard face.

"They might start hinting about that if things begin to look bad for them.''

"Blackmail with a threat of schism?''

"Also give the new pope, should he not be theirs, some-thing to worry about. They will not go silently into that good night.''

"Will their people go with them?''

"Some might. Many of their rich allies, however, will hesitate to do so. They will not be missed, but it is the threat of their departure that worries me rather than the fact.''

"What's the French saying, 'He who eats the pope dies of the pope'?''

"Precisely.''

"Anyway, right now, we need a letter of apology. See to it, Blackwood.''

"Naturally.''

Dinny

We have to stop meeting like this," I said to Peppermint Patty as we collided at the top of the Spanish Steps.

She frowned at me, a frown which I knew all too well. It meant that fury was waiting in the wings.

"I didn't think that was a very bright idea."

"Which not very bright idea?"

"Inviting me to dinner at Paoli's house. Didn't I tell you I didn't want to see you?"

"I seem to remember that."

"I don't want to sit all night at a party while you ogle me."

"I'll try not to, but it will be hard."

"How dare you cook this up!"

"Look, stupid, I didn't cook anything up. I'll admit that our mutual friend asked if I minded if she invited you and I said I wasn't making decisions about her family's social life. It didn't make any difference to me either way. Did she say it was my idea?"

"No . . ."

"Why don't you call your therapist and tell her that you're falling into another spell of paranoia?"

That was dirty pool. I shouldn't have said it.

"It's not a date, understand?" she said cautiously.

"You're projecting, Patty. Who said date? We can go and return in separate taxis."

"That would be silly, Dinny. Besides, the little schemer said she'd have the car pick us both up. . . . I'm sorry."

"I'm sorry about the paranoia line. That was dirty pool."

"I'm afraid it was true."

"You know what?"

"No, what?"

"I called the Borghese today and they said sure enough, a lot of leopards were changing their spots."

"They say which gender?"

We laughed together.

"Nice job at the sala stampa this afternoon. You really did that asshole in."

"It's almost too easy, especially when you're a bitch on wheels."

"Only sometimes."

"It shook me, Dinny. I never expected physical abuse by a priest. This place is rotten to the core. It makes me want to vomit."

"So the Church is human, all too human. You learned that from the nuns in grammar school, didn't you?"

"And you're the fallen-away Catholic!"

"Once a Catholic . . . but there's another side to it too, Patricia Anne Marie Elizabeth. Don Luis, for example. That's the Church at its best and that is damn good."

"Or Bishop Blackie . . . and his damn rubber band."

She didn't look at me when she said that. I think she didn't. I don't know for sure because I didn't look at her. Well, not at her eyes. I couldn't help notice the sharp movement of her breasts as she caught her breath. Anyway, I changed the subject.

"What happened to your commentary?"

"They postponed it till tomorrow. Too much Patty Anne Marie Elizabeth for one day. I'm a little nervous about it."

"No one to fight with?"

"No, just me and the camera. This is the biggest story I'll ever have in my life and my commentary might be the biggest part of it. I don't want to blow it."

"I'd bet that you won't."

"Thanks."

"You really were great today."

"I feel bad about it. We set that guy up, poor man."

"He set himself up."

"Would you have hit him back?"

"Man hits my ex-wife, I hit him back. That's the way we do it west of the Pecos."

"No, you wouldn't, Dinny. You're just like me. You'd never hit a priest."

"I guess not."

We parted at the door of the Hotel de la Ville (having walked past the Hassler), if not friends, at least colleagues again.

Poor woman, I thought. She's going through hell. It's mostly my fault.

I was falling in love again. That wouldn't help either of us. The only way to stop it was to get out of Rome.

In my suite I discovered that someone had made a mistake and delivered the wrong laundry and dry cleaning to my room.

I investigated more closely—two suits, one blue and the other brown slacks with a beige sport coat, a half-dozen ties, six dress shirts, four knit sport shirts, a dozen underpants and pairs of socks. All of them were of excellent design. The fellow who was missing his laundry must be worried about it.

Two pairs of brightly polished shoes, one black, one brown.

Then I looked more closely. The lot of them were not laundry. They were all brand new!

"What the hell!" I exclaimed.

I tried on the sport coat. It fit perfectly.

I sat on the edge of the bed. There was no point in trying on anything else. It would all fit perfectly.

But how would the little imp have known my sizes?

Obviously she had help. Moreover, help that would not only remember my sizes, but my sizes eight or ten years ago when I was in the same shape I was now.

There was a conspiracy going on and there was nothing I could do about it.

So I gave up and laughed.

REUTERS

American Cardinals Apologize to Reporter, CNN

Rome.

Acting as a body, all the American cardinals in Rome for the papal election apologized last night to reporter Patricia Anne McLaughlin and to the Cable News Network for an incident at the Vatican press office yesterday. A deputy director of the office, Rev. Leonard F. X. Richardson, physically pushed McLaughlin when she, her producer, and her cameraman recorded him removing from the press room copies of a lecture given by Luis Cardinal Menendez earlier yesterday at the North American College. Subsequently, Vatican security guards confiscated the CNN camera and ejected the CNN team from the sala stampa, the press office. Father Richardson destroyed what he thought was the tape depicting his assault on McLaughlin.

"As men who are in part responsible for governing the Church during this interregnum," the cardinals wrote, "we wish to express our deep regrets to you and to the Cable News Network for the unconscionable behavior of a staff member of the sala stampa. A physical assault on a woman is always repugnant. When it is committed by a priest on Church property it verges on sacrilege. We are embarrassed, humiliated, and ashamed by what happened."

The apology letter was given to Ms. McLaughlin last evening by Cardinals Sean Cronin, Egbert Winter, and Michael Kennedy.

Cardinal Cronin is believed to have recovered the confiscated video camera yesterday afternoon. A spokesman for CNN in Rome said that their team would return to the sala stampa this morning with the camera.

There was no word as to whether disciplinary action will be taken against Father Richardson.

CHICAGO STAR

Catholics Face Possible Schism

Rome.

When the cardinals go into conclave next week, they will face for the first time since the Reformation, the possibility of schism in the Roman Catholic Church. Veteran Americans in the Vatican and observers from other countries warned of this possibility today as a head-on collision between the supporters of left-leaning Luis Cardinal Menendez and more moderate cardinals loomed.

"They don't understand what they are doing," said one experienced American observer. "Electing a pope is a very delicate matter. If you choose someone that is too liberal, many of those who are committed to traditional Catholic doctrines and practices will begin to wonder if there is still room for them in the Church."

Another Vatican expert did not rule out the possibility that if Menendez is elected, some of the more conservative cardinals will go elsewhere, elect a pope of their own, and assert that the Sacred College and the pope and the majority of the cardinals elected are in heresy and schism from the Catholic tradition. "It will be the first time since the fourteenth century," he said, "that Catholics will be forced to choose between two men, both claiming to be successors of Saint Peter and the legitimate head of the Catholic Church."

The likelihood of a bitter conflict in the conclave increased yesterday when Cardinal Menendez delivered radical lectures at both the North American and the Germano-Hungarian Colleges, so radical that the Vatican press office refused to distribute them.

Cardinal Menendez, according to some theologians here, did not go over the edge into heresy. But he came close to it on several occasions in that he did not adequately explain and defend traditional Catholic doctrine. "Don Luis is a clever and good historian," an Italian theologian commented, "but he would be a disaster as a pope and might well drive many loyal and dedicated Catholics into schism. If Menendez is elected it will be like having Bill Clinton for pope."

A P

Cardinal Discounts Schism Talk

Rome.

A powerful Italian cardinal today dismissed as absurd, published stories that the Catholic Church might face schism if Luis Cardinal Menendez y Garcia is elected pope.

"It's just the far right wing of the Italian press engaging in their usual fiction," said Antonio Cardinal DeJulio, archbishop of Verona. "I don't know of a single cardinal who would even dream of leaving the Church, much less trying to elect an anti-pope. Even those who are not inclined to vote for Cardinal Menendez do not dispute either his orthodoxy or his respect for Catholic tradition. As a historian he knows the tradition better than most of us and hence understands how it has grown and developed and changed. That may frighten people who think that tradition is the way things were done in 1955, but they are simply wrong in that regard."

Asked to distinguish between the late pope and Cardinal Menendez, Cardinal DeJulio said that there was little to differentiate them in terms of their basic beliefs. "Don Luis is a moderate, very moderate. There are many cardinals who are more radical than he is. His style, if he were elected, would be different than that of the last pope's because he is much more hopeful about human nature and the modern world and is more ready to share power with his brother bishops. Neither of those issues have anything to do with Catholic orthodoxy. There is room for both orientations in the Church."

Cardinal DeJulio also praised the talks that Cardinal Menendez gave yesterday at the North American College and the Germano-Hungarian College. "I was at both of them," he said, "and I cheered as enthusiastically as anyone did. Far from shocking the Catholic people, the surveys which have been done around the world show that almost all Catholics would be delighted to have someone like him as pope."

Blackie

Milord Cronin tossed aside the morning papers in disgust. "More bullshit, Blackwood."

We were seated in his study just after breakfast. He was drinking his fifth cup of coffee.

"Pure, unadulterated cow plop," he continued. "Now they are about to threaten us with schism, just like you suggested they would last night. Want to bet there will be an 'accidental' meeting after the General Congregation this morning with anguished appeals to prevent a return to the Great Western Schism?''

The General Congregation, a daily meeting of the cardinals which served as a kind of governing body during the interregnum, took place in the Hall of the Synod above the massive and ugly "modern" audience hall, which Pope Paul VI had caused to be erected on the opposite side of the piazza from the Vatican Palace.

"Doubtless. One might note that such an unfortunate event is not likely to occur because there is no French monarchy to sustain a schismatic Church at Avignon or anywhere else."

"Thank God!" He rose from his chair and buttoned the crimson buttons. "There's nothing they won't do, is there? The world media are replaying the pictures of that asshole zapping Patty Anne and these morons fill the pages of the Italian papers with talk about an anti-pope! We look worse every day."

"You propose to denounce the affair at the sala stampa today?"

"Sure. We could even vote to fire that asshole, but it won't do any good. The Curia does whatever it wants no matter what we say."

"I thought the cardinal prince of Verona did an excellent job responding to these rumors of impending schism."

"Without our suggesting it to him."

"Precisely."

"He was right about a couple of things. First of all, Don Luis is not as radical as the three Celts we have discussed, nor even as radical as Mick Kennedy, another Celt, incidentally. Secondly, in his psychology he is as different from the late pope as day is from night."

"The battle is not over psychology," I said. "It is about power. Always has been. Often, however, differences in psychology, when reinforced by power concerns, translate into differences in substance."

"Yeah, well, that's what they want to make it. Anyway, you want to come over with me? See the fun at the General Congregation, visit the conclave area with me, watch for the next plea to compromise?"

"Why not?"

The General Congregation was not without its interests. Sean Cronin ranted about the disgrace of a priest physically attacking a female reporter. No one in the hall attempted to disagree, though a few argued that the CNN behavior was "provocative."

Milord Cronin, growing grayer by the day, acted out again his tantrum that it was more provocative for a low-level functionary to "expropriate" texts that he himself had caused to be translated and duplicated.

No one tried to respond to that.

Poor old Cardinal Moreau dithered and fretted about "this appalling affair."

Finally our friend from Cardiff, Cardinal Llewelyn, took him off the hook with the suggestion that Cardinal Cronin convey to the parties involved the "sense of this meeting," that we had made our thoughts one with those already exposed by the American cardinals.

Since most of those present were not altogether sure what the "sense of this meeting" meant, there were no objections and Cardinal Moreau instructed Milord Cronin to convey the message.

"Crafty old Welshman pulled a fast one," he murmured in my ear.

"Indeed, yes. We can assume that this resolution will not be reported in the briefing at the sala stampa. However, we can also assume that the media will be waiting for us when we come out of this atrocious building. We can tell them what occurred and then they can go over to the sala stampa and raise Cain with them."

"There's that," he agreed.

I was encouraged indeed by the General Congregation's willingness to admit that something inappropriate had happened. But even more by the fact that, studying the faces of those assembled, I saw the beginnings of a grim determination that nothing like that would happen again.

CNN

(As Sean Cronin emerges from General Congregation, he is mobbed by the media, who fling questions at him. An inoffensive little cleric in a black suit stands in the background, almost invisible even to the eye of the video cameras.)

SC: Just a minute, gentlepersons, I have a statement to read. If you'd just back up a minute so I can get it out of my pocket. Well, I put it in one of these pockets. . . .

(A master at stage presence, the cardinal removes the paper, unfolds it, looks at it, blinks, and then turns it upside down.)

He reads:

There was considerable discussion at the General Congregation about the despicable incident yesterday at the sala stampa. There was strong agreement with the position taken last night by the North American cardinals. No one rose to defend what was done. Finally Cardinal Llewelyn of Cardiff suggested that I convey to the aggrieved parties the sense of the meeting, and I quote, ''that we make our thoughts one with those already exposed by the American cardinals.'' There being no objection, Cardinal Moreau directed me to convey this expression of regret to those involved. I do so now orally and will do so in writing before the day is over.

(The cardinal is bombarded by questions as to whether this is a public apology and whether Father Richardson will be sacked.)

I don't think at this moment and in this context I should say any more than I have. Now if you'll excuse us, Bishop Ryan and I must go into the conclave area and see what our quarters will be like.

Dinny

I showed up to witness the scene at the end of the General Congregation. It was still unbearably hot. My guardian angel was in tow. Or rather I was in her tow. She was wearing a very thin summer sundress with a matching jacket. I joined in the spirit of things by wearing my new brown slacks and a matching knit sport shirt. Right out of a Fellini movie.

Well, not quite.

"Ah, you look very nice this morning, Deeny," my self-anointed guardian angel informed me. "Your new clothes fit perfectly."

"Who is paying for them?"

"We will see how much expenses you run up while you're here. Actually you are rather low-priced as visiting reporters go, since you don't drink."

"Hmm . . ."

"You might at least say that we had good taste."

"You and the other one have good taste."

"And?"

There was no choice.

"And thank you for pushing me in the direction of chic. I'll never quite make it, but it's a nice try. *Mille grazie.*"

"*Prego,*" she said, all too content with herself.

We drifted into the crowd waiting for Sean Cronin.

"What are you doing here?" Queen Maeve the Mad demanded.

"Covering the international scandal of a brutal attack on an American woman journalist."

"It wasn't really brutal."

"Yes, it was."

"I don't want you to think that I need you to defend me."

"God forbid."

The red-haired Irish queen was clad in a pink summer suit that doubtless had stopped traffic on the Conciliazione. Naturally enough she displayed no hint of being even slightly warm. She smelled of cool, brisk spring. New scent.

"No violence, do you understand?" She glowered at me. "I can take care of myself."

"No one of us can take care of ourselves," the principessa said with a pious smile. "Not even guardian angels."

She broke the ice, which is what guardian angels are supposed to do. Patty Anne relaxed and laughed with us.

"OK, I appreciate your show of support. And I like your new clothes."

"Mille grazie. Isn't it amazing how Paoli knew all the right sizes?"

"Amazing."

"There is a small problem with our dinner tonight," the guardian angel said, changing the subject. "It is naturally very awkward. My father encountered Don Luis yesterday and invited him to join us for dinner tonight. My mother and I were quite displeased. If you object, we will call Don Luis and make other arrangements."

"You will tell the next pope that he can't come to dinner because we were invited first?"

"You, Deeny, are a colleague. You, Patty, are in a certain sense a colleague. That makes you more important to my family and I than a mere *papabile*. We have had many of those in our palazzo in twelve hundred years."

I think the little imp was putting us on. But, if so, she did it with a perfectly straight face.

"I guess I can put up with him if I have to. What about you, Patricia?"

Maeve the Passionate looked at me like I was about to lose my mind, caught my wink, and said, "I don't have any objections, Paoli."

"Good. The cardinal said he was very eager to meet the two of you because he admires your work. He did not impose any limitations on the conversation, but naturally I think it would be proper if my father might assure him that everything said is not only off the record but also off background."

"Can we permit ourselves to admire him a little?"

"Naturally that is permitted."

Then Patty giggled and so did my principessa and thus spoiled the formality of the conversation.

I had forgotten how much Patty's giggle transformed the atmosphere of the most serious conversation into comedy. Indeed, I had forgotten how much a comic she was. Even in bed. Especially in bed.

I had forgotten a lot.

"Congratulations on that splendid piece in the *Times*, Paoli," my ex said. "It was wonderfully well-written and droll enough so that the intelligent reader would realize it was very funny."

Just then Cardinal Cronin appeared with his éminence grise lurking in the background, the latter blinking into the bright sun and looking more like a hobbit than ever. The cardinal read his statement.

"How about that!" my ex-wife exclaimed. "We won!"

Without saying a word, the three of us turned toward the sala stampa. Perhaps we could raise a little hell. Patricia's producer (known only as Dee Dee) and her cameraman (Billy Joe) trailed behind us.

"How were they when they came over last night?"

"Very sweet, though Cardinal Cronin did all the talking. I was in the shower when the concierge rang my room. I probably didn't look too presentable."

"Probably not."

I grinned. She blushed.

"I thought Cardinal Cronin does not look well," Paoli said.

"He's working too hard, poor dear man."

The sala stampa scene was disappointing. Maître de Tassigny presided and quoted verbatim Cardinal Llewelyn and Cardinal Moreau without comment.

So there was nothing to fight about. Someone asked him about the incident and he said that the action of the General Congregation spoke for itself.

"Come on, Principessa, we have work to do. See you tonight, Peppermint Patty."

My ex-wife nodded, not, apparently, too happy about a date with a cardinal, especially since she would be stuck with me.

"I will admit it," Paoli said as she raised an imperious finger for our card. "Your wife is somewhat, ah, mercurial. . . . Is that the right word?"

"She's under a lot of strain, Principessa. It is hard to be a mother to three teenagers from four thousand miles away."

"Tell me about your children, Deeny."

"They're good kids, poised, mature, articulate."

"That's not what I mean, and you know it."

"Yeah. . . . Well, Deirdre looks like her mother, red hair and all, though not as tall. High school senior. Great basketball player. Witty. Class president. Hunting for a college. More mature than either of us. Kevin is a sophomore at the same school, St. Ignatius. Bright, top student. Looks a little like me. Too deep to figure out. Brigie is just turning thirteen. Sweet, sensitive little kid. Pretty as a picture. Prays a lot."

"It is a difficult time in life for all of them."

I often thought the same thing. It made me feel guilty.

"I know."

"That is true," my girl guide said, "especially when the children do not really have a father."

When women gang up on you, you just can't win.

Blackie

Blackwood, this joint makes our seminary look like a Four Seasons Hotel. At least we had johns that worked in each room and comfortable beds."

The room the cardinal and I were examining was small and uncomfortable, a twin bed with an iron frame, a hard wooden chair. A small wardrobe in which a cardinal's robes would barely fit. A table with a water pitcher on it, four sheets of paper, a pencil that had not been sharpened recently, a pad of Kleenex, and a red-shaded lamp from which only a dim light shone.

Even Trappist monks did not live so austerely.

He measured with his eye the length of the bed in which he would sleep. It was obviously too short for his long frame.

"Fit for neither man nor beast. Feel that mattress, it's nothing more than a cotton pad."

I felt it gingerly.

"No wonder they want to get it done in a hurry. You wouldn't like to stay in this place too long if you were a sick or feeble old man. This is just an office they have converted. If you're lucky you get a big room with marble walls and frescoes. But the same furniture. You could bang around a lot at night in one of those places."

"The local populace wanted results. They still do. So does the world."

"That may be why the Big Guy didn't modify the rules so we could use that new hotel on the other side of St. Peter's—a hundred thirty rooms with all the amenities—including air-conditioning. You could have a much more thoughtful conclave there. But then, maybe you don't want the cardinals to think too much."

"Arguably."

"We may have created a Frankenstein's monster, Blackwood. Ever think of that? If our guy loses, God forbid, the world is really going to be very angry at the Catholic Church."

"If our guy loses, the world would have reason to be angry."

The cardinal sat at the edge of the bed, looking wearier than ever. "God, it's a long way from Galilee, as you are fond of saying. There's gotta be better ways."

"And worse ways. As I have remarked, the Mormons simply give it to the oldest of the surviving apostles."

"Paul VI, before he lost his nerve, wanted to have all the presidents of the bishops' conferences from around the world made temporary cardinals so they could vote. Needless to say, the Curia shot that down, too."

"What are we doing to Don Luis?"

"Nothing that he does not know better himself than we do. Yet he is willing to do it."

"There's that . . . you know we are supposed to sweep this place for bugs before the cardinals and their valets come in."

"The bugs will come with them."

He sighed. "I guess so."

"It is said that at the election of John XXIII Cardinal Spellman signaled the CIA Resident over at the American embassy the results as soon as they were announced in the Sistine Chapel. Doubtless, the technology has improved in forty years."

"Sounds like something he'd do."

"And Pius XII brought in his housekeeper, Madre Pasquelina, as his valet. Moreover, they all knew about it and still elected him. I guess that's why Paul VI banned all *conclavisti*."

"I suppose every rule has been broken many times. . . .

What exactly are we doing here, Blackwood?

"You and me?"

"Yeah."

"We are engaged in the ancient and honorable art of politics, second only to poetry in Plato's view of things. We are attempting to elect a pope who will not stand in the way of either the Holy Spirit or Jesus' message of love."

"Seems a long way from that." He gestured around the room. "Why do people stay in?"

"Because they like being Catholic. Nothing which will happen here in the next few days will drive them out of the Church. We have done our best for thirty years and they will not go."

"You always say that. What do they like so much?"

"Christmas and Easter, May crowning, processions, first communions, angels and saints, Mary the Mother of Jesus, the appeal of the local parish, all the sacraments and rituals, the whole panoply of Catholic imagery and story, which for all our weaknesses and corruption, we clergy have never been quite able to destroy."

"Yeah, you're right. I guess. But this nonsense is a long way from any of those things."

"One does what one can in the context in which one finds oneself."

He pondered that for a moment.

"One can enjoy the game too much."

"Politics? Oh, yes. Especially if one is Irish."

He thought about it all for a moment and then, a man of action more often than a man of reflection, he heaved himself off the bed.

"Let's go check the doors."

They all seemed reasonably secure. However, there were probably dozens of sophisticated listening devices located in buildings all around the Sistine Chapel that could pick up every word which was said. Nothing is secret anymore, which, as far as the Church is concerned, may not be a bad thing.

We ended up in the Sistine Chapel, overwhelmed by the restored Michelangelo frescos.

"If anything can make the guys think about what this is supposed to mean," Milord Cronin said in an awed whisper, "it's this stuff."

"After the first night in those beds and the first couple of meals of what I am told is rotten food, they'll hardly notice."

"Well, we get them out for lunch."

"I will be satisfied with getting them out without a second night in here."

"Maybe. Oh, by the way, Blackwood, you'll be in here with us."

"Indeed?"

"Your job will be to make sure that all the doors are sealed and that there are no bugs. Like you always say, no one will notice you. Don't worry, I got it through the General Congregation yesterday. No one objected, but only because they don't know who you *really* are."

"Indeed."

I did not pretend to be surprised. I did, however, pretend that I was not delighted.

"Why?"

"So someone will spill my coffee."

"If I may make a suggestion?"

"When have you not?"

"We should instruct our guards to make sure that no portable radios are brought in. Perhaps you would wish to announce it at the General Congregation."

"Hey, if I want to find out what the Chicago Bulls—" the cardinal began.

"One can depend on it: The Corpus people will have the place bugged. They will endeavor to learn the votes as soon as you and your colleagues do, perhaps sooner. Should we be held over to the afternoon for want of a vote or two, they will begin to broadcast news that support for Don Luis is slipping when in fact it is not. If cardinals inside should hear . . .''

"Gotcha! No portable anything."

"I doubt that the Corpus group would be concerned about an oath of secrecy, because as we know they believe whatever contributes to the success of their work is defined as virtuous."

I thought as we walked out of the conclave chambers that he walked unsteadily. I hoped it was nothing more than a semipermanent caffeine high.

Our carefully planned "accidental" meeting occurred in the middle of the piazza, more public than the last one. This time the cardinals were what one might loosely call "Hispanic" (if one struggles to say that Portugal is at least part of the Iberian Peninsula)—Suarez of Tampico in Mexico and Schlossmann of Brazil, the latter the head of the Congregation for the Appointment of Bishops, an exile from his native country because he was too conservative for the still liberal Brazilian hierarchy.

They were a cut above the last two, Suarez a dark, tough-looking Indian who, if there were ammunition belts crossed over his chest, might have been mistaken for Pancho Villa, and Schlossmann, blond and blue-eyed, as were so many of the Brazilian bishops with German names.

"We have been waiting for you, Eminence," Suarez said candidly. He was the kind of man who could only be candid, even if he were on a conspiratorial mission in which candor might be a liability.

"I hope we haven't kept you waiting." Sean Cronin's smile was easy and relaxed. Momentarily, at any rate, his vigor was restored by the thrill of the game.

"We worry about the conclave," Schlossmann added. "We wish to discuss a compromise."

"Discuss it, then."

We had not counted either one of them in our camp. Schlossmann, despite his intelligence and ability, we had put in the Curial camp, though not as an ally of the Corpus

Christi Institute. Suarez was a "probable" on our side on the second ballot.

"We take the possibility of schism seriously," Suarez began, "if Don Luis is elected. I myself will vote for him, of course, but we fear that should he be elected, many will leave the Church."

Who had put them up to this? I wondered. Probably some nervous Curial Italians.

"How many? How many Mexicans, Cardinal Suarez? How many Brazilians, Cardinal Schlossmann?"

They looked at each other. They were prepared for Cardinal Cronin to be difficult. He was always difficult. No *bella figura* here.

"Not very many ordinary people, Eminence," Schlossmann said, trying to sound soothing. "But some important segments of the Church that we do not want to lose unnecessarily."

"Corpus."

"Among others."

"So you're prepared to give a veto right to an institute, rich but small in comparison with the whole Church, indeed, a right to veto beforehand a choice of the Sacred College. Sounds to me like the Austrian ambassador all over again."

That was an apt comparison. I had not thought of it myself. When the light of battle gleams in his eyes Sean Cronin is often absolutely brilliant. It is hardly necessary to say that the two cardinals were taken aback.

"What we wish to propose," the Mexican said, moving his big peasant hands back and forth, "is a compromise which will not please them any more than Don Luis, but which would keep them in the Church."

"So?"

"We could promise that Cardinal DeJulio would be elected by acclamation on the first ballot, if Don Luis should withdraw in his favor."

"Ah!"

"If anything he is perhaps a little to the left of Don Luis.

Yet he would be acceptable to all because he is Italian and because he uses more traditional language and because he is not so clearly in opposition to the Corpus Institute. It would be a happy compromise for everyone. Truly, Don Luis means what he says when he says he does not want to be pope."

"It would save the Church much trouble," the Brazilian concluded.

"But Cardinal DeJulio insists that he will not be pope."

"He insisted that the Church was not yet ready for a Dominican pope and that the corruption in Italian public life also meant that the Church really was not ready for another Italian pope."

"We believe," Suarez said carefully, "that he would change his mind if he saw how his election would soothe the transition back to the era of the Second Vatican Council."

"Perhaps."

"And if you made the argument to him."

"I understand."

"Will you present the argument to him?"

"Be your messenger?"

"If you wish to put it that way." Cardinal Schlossmann frowned.

"Are you sure that the election will be by acclamation? Can you promise it?"

They both nodded solemnly.

"Well, then," Cardinal Cronin concluded briskly, "I will deliver the message. Objectively. I will tell Cardinal DeJulio to be in touch with you, Cardinal Suarez, if he agrees. I presume he will discuss it with Don Luis before he makes any decision."

They nodded. We exchanged polite good-byes and Sean Cronin and I began our hike back to the Janiculum.

"Opinion, Blackwood?"

"They may think they can deliver the votes. They may even have promises. I'm not so sure that we can trust the other side to honor such promises if they once cause chaos in our midst."

"And?"

"I think both the Curia and Corpus were astonished at how much resentment they had built up through the long years of the last administration. They really didn't take Don Luis seriously as a candidate. Suddenly they are confronted with a large block of men whom they once thought docile or harmless who are prepared to vote resoundingly for change. Their attacks have not been successful. They see defeat looming. They are trying to salvage something. They use these two as go-betweens because they are more admirable than most of their kind. Suarez, at any rate, seems honestly worried by the possibility of schism."

"Hmm."

"We will, of course, pass the offer on to your friend Tonio, with the warning that, while our messengers are probably sincere, at least Suarez is, there is no telling what others might try to do when our camp is thrown into confusion."

"That is a reasonable strategy. I will phone him and propose supper in one of those little trattorias over near the Piazza Pilotta he loves so much. It will be interesting to see how he responds."

By which he meant that it would be interesting to see how the balance between ambition and honor worked itself out in Antonio DeJulio's soul.

He strode rapidly up the Janiculum, like a man transformed. As I have often said, about Sean Cronin I understand nothing at all.

Upon our return I dutifully phoned my sibling.

"He is consuming your green pills."

"How do you know?"

"I take the liberty of counting them whenever I'm in his room. He is walking back and forth from here to the Vatican every day, which will suffice, I believe, for exercise. He seems to climb the hill on our return with no greater difficulty than I experience.''

"That doesn't prove anything."

"And I am able to spill an occasional cup of his coffee.''

"You *spill* it?"

"Discreetly, of course."

"But he hasn't cut down?"

"Not as far as I can observe."

She sighed. "Well, we'll have to wait till he collapses and then intervene. If he is fortunate it will only be from exhaustion, overwork, and a sustained caffeine binge.''

I did not find that reassuring. In Sean Cronin's absence anything could happen inside the conclave.

CNN

ANCHOR: For a commentary on the momentous events in the Vatican this last week, we call in CNN's special conclave correspondent, Patricia Anne McLaughlin.

(PM in the Vatican gardens, wearing pink suit, appearing more thoughtful than confrontational. She is reading from a TelePrompTer.)

PM: Tessa, the late Tip O'Neill, longtime speaker of the House of Representatives, once said that much of politics is smoke and mirrors. By which he meant fantasies and deceptions. He also added that smoke and mirrors were finally not enough.

We are seeing Speaker O'Neill's dictum confirmed here this week. The right-wing elements in the Roman Curia and their allies were not ready for this conclave. They have dominated the institutional Catholic Church for so many years that they could not imagine that the time would come when they might not be able to do so any longer. They underestimated the resentment of bishops around the world against the Curia's constant meddling in the affairs of the local Church. Suddenly they have found themselves facing a formidable candidate in Luis Emilio Cardinal Menendez y Garcia. They also discovered that a large coalition of cardinals supports his candidacy, perhaps close to the required two thirds plus one.

Since not even in a conclave can you defeat someone with no one, these churchmen have spent much of the last week trying to destroy Cardinal Menendez with personal attacks that have proved to be unfounded and with rumors that support for him is falling. They have expressed worries that many pious Catholics would be shocked by his election. This morning they reported that some conservative Catholics might go into schism—break with the Church—if Cardinal Menendez is elected. Each day they propose a new "favorite" for the conclave, regardless of the fact that some of them are mentally or physically sick or tainted with corruption or extremely unpopular with their own people and their fellow cardinals.

These rumors and innuendoes—smoke and mirrors— are generally launched in Italian newspapers that are closely allied with the extreme right in the Church and in Italian politics and are fed to reporters from around the world by compliant Italian journalists who are often in the pay of the Catholic conservatives.

Moreover, they assiduously pretend that Cardinal Menendez does not exist by excluding him from the role of celebrant in the Masses that are being said this week and by confiscating texts of his lectures given at two seminaries in Rome. They spread rumors of a third and devastating charge that they will launch against Cardinal Menendez in another day or two.

CNN has investigated all this smoke and mirrors propaganda and finds it without substance. Cardinal Menendez is not a radical but a charismatic and intelligent moderate. Surveys taken around the world show that by huge majorities, Catholics want a pope like him—the first time, by the way, since the tenth century that the laity have had a chance to express their opinions. Right-wing groups like the Corpus Christi Institute will hardly go into schism, because they will lose many of their rich supporters if they do.

Yet all of their smoke and mirrors might still work. Cardinals tend to do what they're told. The conservatives here act like they're still in charge and through their smoke and mirrors are telling the cardinals how to vote. If they throw enough mud at Cardinal Menéndez, some of it could stick to him. Cautious men that they are, many cardinals in the secrecy of the conclave might lose their nerve.

However, there is another factor that they must consider—world opinion among Catholics who watch the latest smoke and mirrors every night and who express their opinions in the instant surveys that are now technologically possible for the first time in the history of conclaves.

The Church has not returned to the situation of a thousand years ago. In those days, if the Romans gathered together in the piazza booed a man who had been elected, the cardinals went in and tried again. Nonetheless, many of the cardinals today, and all the smarter ones, know that the world is watching them very closely.

As a Catholic who believes that church leaders are human just like everyone else, I still must say that my experience of the present regime here leads me to believe that it is insensitive, dishonest, and often corrupt. Whether they are smart enough to win one more time with only smoke and mirrors remains to be seen.

Patricia Anne McLaughlin, CNN, in the Vatican gardens.

Mark

Mark focused his tiny telescope on the CNN van in the piazza. The cunt wasn't there now. But she'd be there when the new pope came out on the balcony. If the man they elected wasn't the baby killer, then he'd shoot her. She was certainly pro-choice despite her claim to be a Catholic and therefore she deserved to die too. He'd send a message to the world one way or another. If the murderer was the new pope, he still might be able to shift his rifle in the direction of CNN and kill her too. Two mass murderers for the price of one. The world would never forget him. Neither would all the cunts who wanted to kill their own babies. They could never be certain that the next moment an angel of death might not blow their stupid brains out.

Mark grinned to himself. He could hardly wait for the conclave to begin.

He put the small scope into his pocket and wandered down the stairs of the building smiling at everyone and exchanging greetings with them. Most of them already took him for granted. Except the young woman with long black hair who always regarded him suspiciously.

Third bullet for her.

NYT

(Editorial)

The American cardinals in Rome to elect a new head of the Roman Catholic Church showed commendable wisdom and courage yesterday when they forced the entire College of Cardinals to apologize to Patricia McLaughlin and the Cable News Network for the assault on her by a priest staff member of the Vatican press office.

Those who are not Catholics may well be mystified by the secrecy and the conspiracies that are apparently part of the process of electing a pope. One only hopes that the cardinals in Rome realize how unattractive the process looks from a distance. Perhaps they will learn that the ancient Catholic tradition seems narrow and rigid and even corrupt during the preparations for this conclave. There must be a better way for choosing the religious leader of 900 million human beings.

Dinny

Would you run through it again for me, Paoli? What are the various Vatican financial agencies?"

"I don't blame you for being confused, Deeny. My papa says that they are supposed to confuse."

We were in the Rome bureau, in Paoli's tiny but convent-neat office. Naturally the paper has air-conditioned offices, but since it was not May 15 yet, the air-conditioning system had not been turned on.

So Paoli had removed the jacket from her sundress and increased the temperature in the office several degrees. No question of making a pass at my adoring young colleague—not that it would have done much good anyway. But she did have lovely ivory shoulders.

"Air-conditioning," Paoli had explained, "does not start in Italy till May fifteen. As a matter of definition it is not required till then."

"Ah."

"Just as swimming in the sea doesn't start till May fifteen, no matter how warm the water is. Even now you could swim easily in the sea, say down at Nettuno, which is only an hour's train ride from here. But no one does, except American tourists, who do not know that it is not yet swimming season. Which shows how stupid American tourists are. Italians may take sun on the beach, but they know the rules and won't go into the water."

"Real rules?"

"Naturally not. And don't try to open the window because it has never been opened and it would just bring in more heat."

"I see. Does the air-conditioning work in your palazzo?"

"Naturally we do not live in a palazzo. The palazzo Oriani is now a museum. We live in an apartment in Parioli, just off the Piazza Ungaria. Not as ornate as the palazzo, but much more comfortable. And naturally the air-conditioning works, though tonight it may be cool enough so that we can eat with the windows open and perhaps—"

"Have a drink on the balcony? Make sure you have a large supply of Pellegrino."

"Naturally."

"Why does the air-conditioning work in your apartment and nowhere else? Why don't the Italian rules apply to you?"

"Because we are Etruscans."

"I see."

There were times when it was difficult to tell whether Paola etc. etc. was joking about her family history and when she was dead serious. Most likely her father had insisted on getting the system working for his dinner and had maybe bribed someone to do it.

"You should bring your wife down to Nettuno for a day. It would be relaxing."

"Nice try, Paola Elizabetta Maria Angelica Katarina Brigitta. But no thanks."

"She suffers much stress. You do not help."

"I suffer much stress, too. And she does not help."

"But you are not afraid of her. And she is afraid of you."

"Of *me*? That's absurd, Paoli."

"But then why does she recoil every time you reprimand her?"

"Recoil?"

"She becomes, how do you say it, ah, 'hyper'; then you tell her to stop and she recoils."

So it was working as my shrink had predicted it would.

"Oh, that. It's just that's she's surprised. I didn't use to do that."

"Never?"

"Never."

She pondered that information silently.

"No wonder your marriage broke up."

"Tell me about it."

Then I had asked her again for a description of the finances of the Vatican.

"The first thing you must understand is that the Vatican has very little money. When the Piedmontese pigs came down here they confiscated all the Church lands. Since then the balance sheets have always been tight. They had to borrow money to bury Benedict XV in 1922 and again for the burial of John Paul I. In 1929, when Mussolini and Pius XI—both pigs—signed the Lateran Treaty, Italy paid the Vatican eighty million dollars in compensation for all the papal lands they had confiscated. This a pittance, yet the Church has been living on it ever since. Its investors have just managed to keep pace with your Dow Jones for the last three quarters of a century—and that was in part due to illegal speculation in precious metals after the Second World War. The worth of the endowment,'' she glanced at her notes, ''is about that of your Harvard University. It earns perhaps two hundred million dollars a year, which is barely enough to pay the expenses. That is the Vatican's main source of income.''

''What about all the golden chalices and the art treasures in the Vatican museum?''

''You sound just like an American tourist—and a Protestant one at that. Who is going to buy the frescoes in the Sistine Chapel or the marble in San Pietro? The Mormons or the Southern Baptists? Is there a market for secondhand basilicas or secondhand papal chapels? As for all the treasures in Vatican City, your American Department of Health and Human Services spends more in one day than the combined worth of all the Vatican art. Bah, Deeny, they are poor over there.''

''And corrupt?''

''Everything in this country is corrupt.''

''What are the agencies over there?''

''First, the famous Vatican bank, the IOR or Institute of Religious Works. The *O* stands for 'opera' which means 'works' in Latin.''

''I studied Latin in high school.''

''Naturally. No one knows exactly how much money it has in its deposits. Probably less than most people think. It is a bank for religious orders around the world, founded during the Second World War to ease problems of currency exchange. Vatican City employees, we papal nobility, and certain other important Romans are able to use it. Like all banks it invests money. No one knows how much or with whom. As you recall at the time of the Banco Ambrosiano scandal, it was revealed that the IOR had written letters of comfort for the Banco Ambrosiano to support the loans it was seeking for some very mysterious Caribbean banking ventures. The money disappeared. The IOR was not held liable since a letter of comfort is not the same as a loan guarantee. The best that can be said is that the IOR was involved with some very questionable people. But then, it's hard not to be in Italy.''

''Does your family use the IOR?''

''Absolutely not!'' She sounded offended by the very idea. ''Papa says that just because we are an old and decadent family, it does not mean that we're fools!''

''They handle the endowment?''

''No, they do not. You must understand that IOR is thought to be 'outside' the Vatican. Inside there is the PEA, the Prefecture for Economic Affairs, which is supposed to coordinate all Vatican financial matters. It has almost no power. Your American cardinal John Fletcher is the prefect of it. You may remember that he left his archdiocese after driving it to the edge of bankruptcy. He is perhaps the only one over there who would talk to you, but don't expect to learn much from him, because he doesn't know much.''

''That's the oversight agency?''

''Oversight? Oh, I see what you mean. Yes, that is the agency that supervises all the other financial matters in the Vatican. All it really does is issue reports every year, which are probably honest, as far as they go.''

''So no one is in charge?''

''No one is really in charge of anything in the Curia. Pope John called an ecumenical council to get around it. Pope Paul used Cardinal Benelli as a deputy pope to get around it. The late pope had his own little Polish government-in-exile up in his offices to get around it. It is a Hydra-headed monster.''

''I like Hydra-head.''

She smiled complacently. ''I read the paper every day.''

The bureau chief stuck his head in the office. ''Turn on CNN; they're going to rebroadcast your Patty's commentary. It was damn good. Hey, nice shirt, Dinny. Someone with taste must be buying your clothes again.''

We turned it on and watched Patty. Damn! She *was* good.

''She should do that all the time. A think piece four or five times a week. It would be a hell of a lot easier than doing anchor work out of Chicago four or five hours a day and running around the Midwest to cover big stories.''

"You will tell her this?''

"I have no right to tell her.''

My principessa's pretty shoulders tightened into knots of anger.

"If you don't tell her, I will tell her what you said.''

"I'm outnumbered. Hey, Paoli, I was going to tell her anyhow.''

"Deeny, you are *impossible*.''

"All men are. . . . But now let's get back to Vatican finances.''

"Very well.'' She rearranged her notes. "There are a number of agencies which handle money in the Vatican. The Congregation for the Evangelization of Peoples and the Congregation for the Fabric of Saint Peter's both have their own budgets. The first provides money for the missions from collections taken up all over the world. It does not have much money. The second tries to keep San Pietro in repair with income from votive lights and other contributions in the basilica. It barely makes ends meet. Is there corruption in either or both offices? Perhaps. But, given that this is Italy, nothing to pay much attention to.''

"So who does invest the funds?''

"That brings us to the heart of Vatican finances, the Administration of the Patrimony of the Apostolic See. It has two sections. The first they call 'ordinary.' It pays the bills. The second is 'extraordinary.' That is where the investments are made. No one in either department will talk to you or any other reporter. Perhaps especially not to you because they remember your articles on the Banco Ambrosiano affair.''

"Who is critical in making the investment decisions?''

"Always a layman that a pope or a cardinal thinks is a financial genius, though that brilliance escapes other people—Bernardino Nogara, who speculated in illegal currency transactions after the war; Michele Sindona, who lost a hundred million dollars, between five and ten percent of the endowment in the 'Immobilare' scandal; and now this pig called Arturo Buonfortuno, who was once a clerk in a bank in Milano and has reportedly made tens of millions of dollars for the patrimony. No one knows for certain.''

''Let me guess: He is a member of the Corpus Christi Institute.''

''Naturally.''

''And he doesn't give interviews.''

''Naturally not.''

I thought about it. Might this Arturo Buonfortuno have ties with the International Agricultural Bank of Holland in The Hague? If he was actually bringing in large amounts of money, might he be playing in the derivatives market, investing in all kinds of complicated and convoluted swaps and straddles?

The derivative game was only for the big guys, and some of the big guys, like Proctor & Gamble and Baring's Bank and the Daiwa Bank of Tokyo, weren't big enough.

A bank clerk who was the favorite, possibly a relative of some Vatican official, messing in derivatives? Bad business.

I had not told Paoli about my conversations with Niko. Presumably he had not told her either. Should I now suggest to Niko that he might check up on this Signor Buonfortuno?

I thought about that. If the endowment was really worth about a billion and a half dollars, it was hardly small potatoes, though a B-2 cost more. If anyone should find out before the conclave that someone had lost a lot of money playing in the derivatives game, the next pope would have to clean the operation up once and for all. If he were an ''outsider'' pope, he might be especially dangerous. That would not please powerful people, nor the Corpus Institute, nor the International Agricultural Bank.

No smoking gun but it all seemed plausible, especially given the past performance of Vatican portfolio directors.

If it got around that Niko and his guys were looking at something like that, he might be called off. Not good. Better to wait till I had enough material to write a story.

A lot of trouble for a lot of people would flow from that decision, but I still think it was the right one.

"Deeny? Are you all right?"

"Sorry, Principessa, I was thinking."

"You looked very serious."

"I don't think very much, that's why it looks kind of different. Could you call Cardinal Fletcher at the," I glanced down at her notes, "PEA and tell him who you are and that Dennis Michael Mulloy of *The New York Times* newspaper would like to have a couple of words with him?"

For the moment I thought it would not be a good idea to be seen around the Vatican financial offices. I'd play it as a matter of passing interest.

While the practically perfect principessa was making the call, I glanced out the window. Yep, the shadow was still out there, apparently reading the day's issue of the *Herald-Tribune*. Down the street from him were two thoroughly disreputable-looking young toughs, loitering on the street corner. Niko's crowd.

If they disappeared, I'd start to worry.

All the time I thought I was the one who might be in danger. Bad mistake.

My girl guide introduced herself as Principessa Paola Oriani and, as best as I could translate her rapid Italian, she asserted that she was making a call from *The New York Times* Rome bureau. A call on behalf of the *Times*'s investigative reporter was, in her description, at least as important as a call from the pope. Or, at this time between popes, a call from the camerlingo. Or maybe from Sean Cronin.

She smiled and handed me the phone.

"Hi, Dennis, good to hear from you."

From this voice I would never buy a used car.

"Good afternoon, Your Eminence. I don't want to bother you with a long interview because I know you're busy with your job as well as preparing for the conclave."

When I put on that mask I wouldn't buy a used car from me.

"We sure are busy, Dennis. I have to make my report on

the Church's finances to the General Congregation tomorrow. But I have time for a few questions."

I pictured him glancing at his watch—the busy, efficient CEO of a major American corporation.

"I want to do a little sidebar on that very subject, nothing major."

"We issue reports every year."

"I have the last four or five here," I said

As we talked I had lined them up and noticed something.

"Then you are aware that we are not fabulously wealthy, as some would like to believe?"

"Basically you have the endowment from the Lateran Treaty and change."

"You got it."

"But I see that the income from the endowment has gone up sharply in the last two or three years."

"Yes," he said complacently. "Good thing, too. A wage increase for our workers was long overdue."

"Might I ask why the increase in income, particularly in years where the world markets were generally quite flat?"

My girl guide smiled and nodded her head in approval. *Good for you, Deeny.*

"Very wise and very sound investment policies. We're quite proud of that."

"Signor Buonfortuno?"

Great name for a gambler.

"Well, there's a board which must approve his decisions, but we feel that we have good reason to be content with his work."

"I should think so. . . . Any chance of my talking with him?"

"I'm afraid not, Dennis. That's against our policy at the present time. Perhaps in a few years we can change that. But the Vatican is not a public organization, as you know."

"With a billion members, it's hardly private. Didn't the late pope say it ought to be a glass house?"

My guardian angel rolled her eyes.

"I take your point." His voice was beginning to show some exasperation. "However, I can assure you that we don't invest in cigarette companies or companies that make birth control pills or abortifacients. Nor have we begun yet to reinvest in South Africa. When we get out of the problems we currently have, we'll probably be happy to list all our investments, item by item."

"Uh-huh. I note that income from Peter's Pence was only sixteen million dollars last year."

"That was up from the year before."

"I see that. But if there are a billion Catholics in the world, why is the annual contribution to the support of the pope so small?"

"Many people ask that. The simple answer is that most Catholics in the world are poor. Peter's Pence comes chiefly from the English-speaking countries and Germany. The Germans take it out of the church-tax money the government gives them."

"I'm told that the collection is less than half of what it was twenty-five years ago—without taking inflation into account."

"That's true," he said hesitantly.

"What explains that?"

"I'm afraid our people in the English-speaking countries are not as generous as they used to be, Dennis. Too much consumerism. Too much materialism. Particularly in the United States. The Church is very hard-pressed there, too. We're closing parishes and schools because we simply don't have the money to keep them open."

"So I understand."

But what a self-serving argument: Blame the laity because the clergy never do anything wrong.

"Could part of the reason also be objection to the late pope's policies?"

"The pope, Lord have mercy on him, was very popular

in America, Dennis. Wasn't his book on the best-seller list?''

''Indeed it was. . . . Well, thank you very much, Cardinal. I won't take any more of your time.''

I hung up, thought for a minute, and then snapped at Paoli, ''Get Blackie for me.''

She blinked at my brisk style.

''I don't have a trench coat with me, so I have to sound tough.''

''We will see about that the next time we shop for you.''

''Belts are back in fashion.''

''Naturally.''

''Father Ryan speaking.''

''Dinny Mulloy here, Bishop.''

''Ah?''

''Sources tell me that Cardinal Fletcher will report on Vatican finances at the General Congregation tomorrow.''

''How would he know anything about them?''

''Fair question. I note that there is a sharp increase in income from the, uh, patrimony in the last couple of years.''

''Indeed?''

''And during several of these years the world markets were flat.''

''That is my understanding also.''

''Your boss may want to ask whether the Church has been trading in risky derivatives—swaps, put and takes, straddles, that sort of thing. There is nothing illegal about them, but as the world knows by now, they are very risky.''

''We hear of these things even in Chicago.''

''I've heard of the Chicago Board of Trade, Bishop . . . and the Merc. It might just be possible that foolish risks have been taken and that substantial sums of money may have been lost. Some people might not want a pope who would take too close a look at such matters.''

''Arguably.''

''Your boss might demand a list of the Vatican invest-ments. He might demand that Signor Buonfortuno, the man who makes the investing decisions, present himself before the General Congregation.''

"He will not get either.''

"I don't suppose he will, but it should raise many questions on which his colleagues will want to ponder when they go into conclave.''

"You have other information, I take it?''

"Nothing I can talk about yet.''

"I see. . . . I presume that this Signor Buonfortuno is a member of the Corpus Christi Institute.''

"Oh, yes.''

"My phrase, Dinny. We'll do what we can. Presumably I would not be out of line to suggest this as the kind of question that someone might want to ask at the sala stampa tomorrow after the General Congregation.''

"It would make a good CNN story. By the way, I assume you saw her commentary this morning.''

"She is very good at that kind of thing. She should do it all the time. Presumably after this unfortunate affair is over she will be a very hot property, I believe the term is, and can make reasonable demands on her employer.''

"I'm glad you said those things, Bishop. I can cite you as in agreement with me when I make the same case to her.''

As I hung up, Paoli smiled triumphantly. However, she did not ask about my suspicions on Vatican finances.

"Do we have a bureau in the Netherlands?''

"A stringer in Amsterdam.''

"Get him for me . . . please.''

"Her.''

It took the princess some time and many impatient frowns before she was able to hunt down Harriet Van der Stappen in Amsterdam.

"Good afternoon Ms. Van der Stappen, this is Dinny Mulloy at the Rome bureau.''

"The whole world knows who and where you are, Mr. Mulloy.''

"Thanks," I said with my most self-deprecating, charming shanty-Irish chuckle.

"I wonder if you could do us a favor. We're interested in the investments the Vatican is making. In particular we are concerned about whether Signor Arturo Buonfortuno, their investment officer, might be playing in the derivatives market through the International Agricultural Bank of Holland at Den Haag."

"*Very* interesting. They are a well-known Catholic bank, closely held by members of a family who, it is said, are affiliated with one of those extremely conservative Catholic groups."

"Corpus Christi Institute?"

"I believe so."

"Is the bank in trouble?"

"It appears to be. There are many articles in the papers about it. Our police are investigating."

"I don't want you to alert them by doing any direct interviews. But if there are papers on the public record—"

"I understand. The law here, unlike that in Switzerland, requires relatively full disclosures. Let me see what we can find."

"You can reach me here in the Rome bureau or at the Hassler Hotel. I'm working with a woman named Paoli Oriani. If you can't find me, you might talk to her."

"I now understand why the paper wants to put you in places like the Hassler, Deeny."

"No story so far."

"But what a story it could be."

"Yes . . . and possibly a very dangerous story."

I didn't know the half of it.

Patricia Anne

I had stopped crying before I got back to my hotel. I don't cry much. In our family you shouted and argued and fought, but you didn't dare weep because that was thought to be unfair tactics. Looking back on it, crying as a form of intimidation is nothing more than a woman's response to the louder voice of the macho male. Knowing that, however, does not make it much easier to cry.

If I had ever wept on poor Dinny, he would have absolutely collapsed.

But these people had made me sob.

I had stopped in at Trinità dei Monti on my way back from San Pietro to say my daily prayers. Dee Dee is so used to it that she stops the car without my asking. I was utterly exhausted from the heat, the strain, the excitement of my commentary, which I made them do five times before I was sure I had it right. I was worried about the kids—though they had sounded fine on the phone, but then they always sound fine on the phone.

I was also trying, with no success whatever, to shake my schoolgirl crush on my ex-husband. I did not want to accompany him to dinner at the Orianis. No way. Not even if the next pope would be there. Even if it were not exactly a date, the tension between us would build up and then explode, one way or another. That wouldn't be fair, not to him and not to me.

I had all these things on my mind when I left the church, after lighting my daily votive candle. I had paid little attention to the American couple standing in the back of the church as I left, except to notice that they looked like they were Irish and they were dressed in very expensive clothes.

I had walked out in the glare of the sun, blinked at the obscene obelisk, and suddenly they were all over me.

"You have no right to pray in a Catholic church," the woman had snarled.

"You disgrace the church by your presence," the man, pompous and very red in the face, had shouted. "Do you realize all the harm you've done this week?"

"Do you have any children?" the woman had continued the attack.

I had been so surprised that I had answered her question. "Three teenagers."

"They must be ashamed of you every time they see you on television. You're absolutely shameless."

"Why don't you go back to them where you belong instead of earning all that money by attacking the Church?"

"I'm only reporting the truth."

"The Church doesn't need truth. It needs faith and obedience."

"And respect."

"Surely if a man works in the Holy Father's press office he deserves to be treated with respect."

"The Holy Father is dead."

I felt I had been backed into a corner, unable to reply effectively to these two virulent haters.

"And aren't you happy about that! It gives you one more chance to attack him and the Church to millions of people."

"How many abortions have you had?"

"None," I had said, turning and running down the stairs to escape from them.

I had sobbed most of the way back to the hotel.

If you're in my business you are going to meet people who love you and people who hate you. It goes with the territory. But this was different. Or maybe I was in a different mood.

What, I wondered as I took my shower, if they're right? Are we exploiting the Church with our reporting? Someone had quoted a pope, I think it was Pope Leo XIII, who said the Church had nothing to fear from the truth. We were reporting the truth. The Church was wonderful copy. Maybe it had always been wonderful copy. But these days it was wonderful copy because there were so many terrible things going on. The story had to be told, didn't it? That was the only way there would ever be change, wasn't it?

Some good and pious Catholics, who had been educated to believe that the Church was perfect, would be shocked. Most would not, according to our surveys. Quite the contrary, they were on our side. But maybe 10 percent were furious. Ten percent of American Catholics is, what? Six million people. Would they all hate me the way these two did?

Well, they didn't have to watch CNN, did they?

Was I building my career by attacking the Church?

It might look like that to some people.

I knew the answers and I knew they were right: Our job is to get the story and tell it as accurately and as precisely as we can—in clips that vary from thirty to ninety seconds. Good came from telling the truth. Bad from covering it up.

That is true, isn't it?

After my shower, I sat at the small vanity table and began to brush my hair. And thought about poor Dinny some more.

He used to love to brush my hair. I can't imagine most men even thinking about it. Yet often he would take the brush away from me and very gently and very lovingly run it through my carrot top. I would lean back against him and melt with pleasure.

Hair brushing as foreplay, I would say with a laugh. But that's what it was anyway. So sweet, so gentle, so kind. And I had driven him off. Maybe I wasn't completely aware of what I was doing, but, like my shrink said, I pushed him and pushed him and pushed him, poor dear man, until he finally could take it no more and left.

I removed my wedding ring from the secret jewel box in my vanity case. I carried it with me to use as protection if some jerk got a little too friendly. I should wear it tonight, should I not, especially since we would eat dinner with the next pope? I slipped it on my finger. It still fit. Why wouldn't it still fit? What would Dinny think? He'd proba bly not even notice, the jerk!

I took it off but left it on the vanity, in case I changed my mind.

Why had I ever accepted this invitation? It was a setup. The little imp means well, I thought, but she doesn't understand. Or maybe she does. Only too well.

I've taken enough chances in my life. I don't need to take this chance.

But I was locked into it. I had no choice. Besides, the man was pretty likely to be the next pope. How could I pass up an opportunity to meet him? Maybe after the election he'd give us an exclusive interview. . . .

So I finished dressing, wrapped my scarf around my neck—for purposes of modesty, not, heaven knows, warmth, and headed out the door. Then I remembered that I had left the wedding ring unprotected on the vanity. I went back to my room, picked it up, opened the secret box, and then, in a mood of absolute recklessness, put it back on my finger.

To hell with it.

Dinny

Peppermint Patty, you look delicious."

"Stop gawking," she said sullenly.

My ex-wife really did look delicious. She had piled her flaming hair on the top of her head, which added a couple more inches to her height—no shrinking violet, our Peppermint Patty—and transformed herself from being merely regal to being "totally" (as the kids would have said) imperial. She was wearing a long slip dress—high front, almost nonexistent back, long slit at the thigh—with a floral print that would have caused the Via Veneto to settle into a daylong traffic jam. She had looped around her neck, for purely symbolic purposes, I assumed, a scarf made of the same light and filmy material.

"No one will notice me when I walk in with you on my arm."

"I won't be on your arm."

Another fight. I'd done pretty well so far, but how long could a guy keep this up? Why not just forget about my shrink's words?

"Suit yourself."

"I don't want to do this."

All right, once more into the breach for England, Harry, and St. George.

"I don't give a damn, Patty, whether you do it or not. Make up your mind and stop acting like a nervous child."

"That little troublemaker set it up."

"Come on, everyone that knows us has tried to set up things like this. Why should she be any different?"

"You connived with her."

"And you're a member of the Corpus Christi Institute."

"I am *not*!"

Patty was a wreck. Should I keep on playing tough with such a troubled woman?

"Well, I'll have the next pope to myself."

"I don't give a damn."

"Good. Then go back to your room and sulk. In fact, in your mood you'd ruin the evening for the rest of us."

"I'm going to do just that."

She turned on her heel and started to walk back into the lobby of the Hotel de la Ville.

Just then the Oriani Lancia appeared. The driver hopped out and opened the door.

"Patricia Anne?"

She turned back, a tornado brewing on her face.

"Yes!"

"Get in!" I gestured brusquely at the open door.

She hesitated, torn between demons I could not imagine. I noticed my shade getting into a taxi behind us down the street. He would have a lot to think about before the night was over.

"I said get in."

She laughed happily and tumbled into the car, like a teenage hoyden.

"Thank you, Dinny." She touched my hand as the car eased away from the curb. "You are actually getting quite good at coping with my moods."

I took her hand in mine. "It would have been a shame for you to miss it, especially since you look so beautiful."

"Thank you."

I thought she might try to free her hand from mine. Instead she held it tightly.

I was making too much progress now. We were not, after all, teenagers on our first date.

Were we?

"You are very good on that commentary. Bishop Blackie

and I both think you should concentrate on doing that kind of thing.''

She sighed. ''I'd really love that. But they'd never let me do that.''

''As the good bishop observed, you'll be a hot property before this thing here is over. You can name your own terms.''

''Do you really think so?''

''Yes.''

She pondered that. ''It would make life a lot easier.''

''And a lot more satisfying. It would say that there is a woman on CNN whose commentary opinions are worth listening to.''

She nodded.

''That would be wonderful. Did you think I sounded too harsh, too, uh, masculine?''

''Not at all. You are not a yapper, Pretty Patty. The Religious of the Sacred Heart taught you grace and good manners. And besides, you're too beautiful ever to appear masculine, especially when you're vulnerable, as you are most of the time these days.''

She sniffed. A choked-off sob?

I thought about stroking that wonderful bare back and decided that I'd better not. But I didn't let go of her hand.

Then she told me how my two friends from the elevator in the Hassler had beat up on her.

''I know they're wrong, Dinny, but I guess they just got me at the wrong time.''

''They came here to buy the papacy with their money. Not the first time, as our mutual friend Paola Elizabetta Maria Angelica Katarina Brigitta would doubtless tell us. But you know what, Patty Anne, I don't think they have enough money to do it this time around.''

''I hope not.''

Blackie

My kind of Chicago Irish politician believes that you wait till dessert before you turn to business. But Sean Cronin is cut from a different kind of cloth. We had hardly seated ourselves in the Ristorante Arbruzzi, just around the corner from the Piazza Pilotta in the Piazza Santi Apostoli, and begun to sip our wine, when he jumped into the matter at hand.

"We have a message from the other side for you, Tonio."

DeJulio leaned against the brown-slatted wooden wall.

"Really?" He turned up his aristocratic Roman nose in dismay, as if he hated to see a perfectly good dinner ruined by the mention of them.

"Delivered through Schlossmann and Suarez."

"There are worse."

"They say that if you run as a compromise candidate who will prevent schism, they'll guarantee victory on the first ballot."

He put down his glass of the Frascati of the house, a plain water tumbler.

"Do they speak with authority?"

"They claim to. They're both honest men, Suarez especially. I wouldn't trust those who sent them."

We were all wearing sport shirts, Milord Cronin and I in black trousers, the cardinal archbishop of Verona in light gray.

"They must see in me two character defects of which I am unaware."

"Oh?"

"They must think that I would be easier on them and on Corpus than Don Luis would be."

"More likely they feel that since you're Italian you'll more easily be corrupted," Cardinal Cronin said bluntly.

He smiled, a tight, thin little smile. "Some of us remain honest, especially those of us who know what they are."

"And the other character defect, Tonio?"

"They must think I would betray a good friend because of ambition."

"It is more than likely," I put in my small comment, "that they think anyone would do that."

"You must bring them a reply?" He picked up his wine tumbler.

"They'll probably hang around me after the General Congregation tomorrow morning."

"Very well, tell them I said no—which is, of course, what you've known I would say."

I wasn't so sure we were that sure.

"Just plain no?"

"Yes, say that DeJulio says no. Let them figure out what that means."

"Fuck you and the horses you rode in on?"

Tonio relaxed and laughed. "You Anglo-Saxons have such colorful insults."

"Celts, actually," I observed in the name of accuracy and precision.

"Of course. We Italians from the north are also of Celtic origin, but a long time ago."

"It never goes away," I noted.

"Do you know anything about this fellow Buonfortuno who does the Vatican investments?"

"My banker friends in Milano say he is a fool. Why should he be different from any of the others?"

"Corpus?"

"Certainly."

"Who isn't?" I muttered.

"I am reliably informed," Milord Cronin continued,

"that he may be trading in derivatives. Hence the increase in income on the patrimony over the last several years, during some of which the markets were flat. Either he is a brilliant trader or he has been very lucky in that dangerous gambling den."

Cardinal DeJulio shook his head sadly.

"Don Luis will begin here just as in Valencia, with a big financial crisis."

"It could be that the reason some people do not want him to win is that he would uncover a potential financial mess because, based on the Valencia experience, he would be looking for that possibility."

"Fletcher will make his report tomorrow. He is not very intelligent."

"Tell me about it," Sean Cronin said, his English enhanced by the indirect influence of adolescents (through me).

"We should ask perhaps about the investments the patrimony is making and demand to see the list," DeJulio said thoughtfully. "And also demand to hear from Signor Buonfortuno. Neither of our demands will be met, but we will raise the possibility that something inappropriate and perhaps criminal is occurring. Everyone knows Buonfortuno is Corpus."

"I'll warn Don Luis to stay out of it. He probably would anyway."

"They will say that all investments are approved by a board of cardinals."

"Then we'll say that board does not represent the General Congregation and we have the right to know," Sean Cronin said, his hooded eyelids opening wide and revealing the bright light of battle. "So we'll set up our own board."

"Poor old Moreau will dither and vacillate and nothing will come of it . . . except to raise the possibility of yet another Vatican financial scandal if the same people are left in charge."

"The media will be alerted," I said softly. "Cardinal

Cronin will have his usual press conference in front of the audience hall before the one at the sala stampa."

Cardinal DeJulio, still not sure who I was, glanced at me. "You think of everything, don't you?"

"That's what auxiliary bishops are for."

Milord Cronin consumed only two cups of coffee at the meal and those only because my most diligent efforts to spill them were unsuccessful.

"He will be Don Luis's secretary of state [kind of the pope's prime minister], I take it," I said in care, going back to the Nordamericano.

"No doubt about it."

Back in my room I pondered the many events of the day. I then dialed a certain Chicago phone number.

"Reilly Gallery, Annie Reilly speaking."

"It is as I would have expected."

"Blackie! Where are you?"

"Rome, I believe."

"You sound like you're over at the cathedral. . . . You and the cardinal are really raising a lot of hell over there."

"Only the cardinal. I need some advice on matters related to police work."

Annie's husband was a relative of mine named Mike Casey, sometime acting superintendent of the Chicago police department and an expert on criminology. In our family he is known as Mike the Cop, as though there were another Mike Casey who was not a cop. But he is the only Mike Casey in the family.

Since he has married Annie, his childhood sweetheart of yesteryear, Mike has taken up painting, an art form at which he is reputed to be very good.

"Hi, Blackie, what do you need?"

"One, no, two, of those gizmos that intercept all attempts of probe into a room with distant electronic ears."

"How big a room?"

"Oh, about the size of the Sistine Chapel."

"Gotcha. No problem. Could I ask why?"

"For reasons that are not altogether clear to me, Milord Cronin has arranged it so that I am in charge of secrecy and security at this conclave. I don't believe all that much in the secrecy, but I am resolved that if our guys are bound by it, so will the other side be."

"Right. I'll send them over FedEx this afternoon."

"I am also led to believe that there are very new advanced 'sweeping' devices which enable one to detect bugs and that these are so simple that even a neophyte security expert like myself can work one."

"Sure. I'll send two of those also, in case one doesn't work. . . . Doesn't the Vatican have its own sweepers?"

"Oh, yes, but I'm not sure I would trust them. I will follow them through before each scrutiny, as it is called, to make sure that they are adequate to their responsibilities."

"What's a scrutiny?"

"An interlude of ballot casting, one in the morning, one late in the afternoon. Two ballots at each scrutiny."

"And you figure there will be bugs? Who will bring them in? The cardinals?"

"Arguably. Or cooks or doctors or even security personnel."

"Is everyone crooked over there?"

"Not quite all of them, but enough so you learn not to trust anyone."

"You guys got the votes?"

"It is good to hear a sensible Chicago political question. It appears that we do, but following the rules of the game, as we learned it at our mothers' knees, we always run scared as if we may not."

"There's a lot of support over here for your friend."

"That does not surprise. But, alas, there's only one Chicagoan voting in this conclave."

"I didn't think he looked all that good on television."

"He is exhausted and he drinks too much coffee, but my good sister, whom you may remember, is here with a team.

We are trying to deprive him of the coffee.''

"Bring home a winner, Blackie.''

"We don't back no losers, Mike. That's also something we learned from our mothers.''

Dinny

How did you ever become a cardinal?'' I asked Don Luis.

He smiled, his characteristic charming, diffident smile.

"The issue is how I became archbishop of Valencia. I think they made a mistake!''

We all laughed softly. It was that kind of evening, gentle conversation, soft laughter, much said by indirection and implication, an evening of relaxed charm.

My ex-wife, who I finally noticed was wearing her wedding ring, was remarkably quiet. She listened, she smiled, she radiated beauty; when she occasionally said something, she glanced at me for approval. Her creamy shoulders glowed invitingly in the candlelight.

Perhaps it will take another thousand years before we American shanty-Irish can feel at home in such a refined atmosphere.

On the other hand, I told myself, when the Oriani clan were goat farmers living in smelly huts out in the Campagna, we were the light of Europe. That fact didn't reassure me. That was then and this is now.

Paoli and her family lived in a spacious and elegant apartment on the fashionable Viale dei Parioli, the kind of apartment building into whose driveway you had to be buzzed by an unseen guard—just off the Piazza Ungaria, north of the Villa Borghese, the big park in the center of Rome. In the fading light, as we pulled up to their apartment complex,

I noted many well-dressed, well-maintained matrons strolling the streets, some with their dogs, some with men, some by themselves. Their clothes were suited to keeping them cool in this hot weather and the men who saw them warm. If it were true that Roman women were the most beautiful in Europe, the sample had probably been drawn from neighborhoods like this one.

"Stop staring at the women," Patty Anne, still holding my hand, had adjured me.

"It's either them or you."

She'd merely laughed.

I'd noted that the top of their building was not decorated with the usual array of obstacles to invasion by saucer-born aliens; only one discreet antenna probed the sky. The owners had actually been able to cooperate one with another, an unusual phenomenon in Rome.

When we had left the car, I recaptured the hand of the woman with the wedding ring. "You've always been a beautiful woman, Patty Anne. Yet I've never seen you more lovely than you are tonight."

Dumb thing to say.

She had kissed me lightly.

"You're so sweet, Dinny, that you break my heart."

Odd response.

Great kiss, however.

The apartment was quietly luxurious, modern paintings on the wall, thick carpets, pastel drapes, plush furniture— the whole a mix of old and new that disregarded consistency of style in favor of quiet charm.

Cardinal Menendez was already in the apartment when we arrived, my sometime-wife on my arm, despite her earlier protestations that she would not be. Perhaps the cardinal had come earlier for a more personal conversation with his old friends. He wore a somewhat rumpled dark blue suit, which probably cost half of what mine had, and a crimson tie, "To please Cardinal Valerian," he had said with a laugh.

Naturally he had kissed Patty's hand. Naturally she had blushed. Naturally my girl guide had beamed. It was a different world, one in which Patty, because of her striking beauty, fit much better than I did. At about five ten, the cardinal was shorter than Patricia in her stocking feet. But, wearing heels and displaying the pile of dazzling red on the top of her head, she towered over him.

"I believe, madam," Don Luis had said with a bow, "we have met before, but only very briefly."

Up close, this slender man with the flecks of gray in his black hair seemed surprisingly frail, almost as though a strong draft would blow him over.

"Go, Blue!" Patricia had replied.

"And you, Mr. Mulloy, have done a fine job in assisting this young woman," he had gestured at my girl guide, "in covering the interregnum for the *Times*."

"I just do what I'm told," I had said. "We Irish men learn that very early in life."

"It is a pleasure to work with such a distinguished and prize-winning journalist," Paoli had said, doubtless for the record. She and her mother, who did indeed look like Sophia Loren, though on a smaller scale, were wearing off-the-shoulder spring dresses, with symbolic scarves like Patty's. I would not be intoxicated by the "creature" as the evening wore on, but I was already halfway drunk on womanly beauty.

Paoli had rolled her eyes and made an *O* of her mouth when she saw Patricia Anne Marie Elizabeth. Then, behind my ex-wife's back, she had raised an eyebrow in what was probably a challenge. She had spotted the wedding ring long before I had.

We had stood on the balcony for our drinks. The apartment, behind the home of the American ambassador, I was told, overlooked a large green patio, five floors down, outlined with thick trees and filled with masses of flowers whose perfumes filled the air and added to the allure of the three women. Only an occasional and very distant sound of the *motorini* spoiled the allusion that we were pleasantly cut off from the turbulent and troubled urban world.

My Perrier was brought to me with solemn devotion by my guardian angel.

"Niko would love you in that dress," I had said.

"Naturally," she had said, turning up her nose, "he loves me no matter what I wear. Or don't wear."

That had settled that.

Our conversation on the balcony had been aimless and relaxed—Roman weather, the temperature of the water of the Mediterranean, the terrible corruption in Italian politics, basketball, kids (Tonia and Patty agreed that they were much better than their parents at the same age).

Only at the supper table, sparkling crystal, gleaming white plates, candles in holders that might have been half a millennium old, did we turn to the subject on everyone's mind and I asked the blunt question about how Don Luis had acquired the crimson.

"I was dean at Salamanca, a much easier job than it is in American universities, Dinny, and expected I would remain in that position until I retired. Corpus is very powerful there and it had fought my election as dean with all the power it had. To my surprise they lost. They do tend to overreach, you know. Then my home diocese fell vacant. A terna was submitted to Rome. My name was not on it, which did not surprise me. But there was no Corpus candidate either. The pope waited a year, and then to my astonishment the nuncio called me to tell me that the Holy Father himself had just decided that I was to be the next archbishop and that as a matter of holy obedience I must accept. I was so surprised that I never thought of trying to refuse. Corpus was furious; my fellow priests were quite pleased that one of their own would be the new archbishop."

He shrugged. "I wake up some mornings and still don't quite believe it."

"The old man rarely turned down Corpus, did he?"

"More often than most people think, especially after he

had made a few very bad mistakes because of them in Holland and Switzerland. When there was bitter resentment in a diocese, he tended to look for a compromise candidate. I gather that I was the compromise.''

''He must not have known much about you.'' Patty said cautiously.

''On the contrary,'' the cardinal lifted his wineglass, ''he knew too much about me, though perhaps he would have thought later that it was too much of the wrong things. You see, he had read my dissertation.''

''He made you a bishop because of your dissertation!''

''Tell him the story, Don Luis,'' Tonia insisted.

''I wrote my dissertation,'' he smiled happily as academics always do when they get a chance to talk about their own work, ''about the Khazars, a Turkic people who lived north of the Black Sea and presided over a large and powerful empire of their own in the second half of the first millennium of the common era. They were like many others of the powerful kingdoms that flourished in that era on the fringes of what was left of Rome. The only thing unusual about them is that they were Jewish.''

''Really!''

''We know very little about them, as we know very little about Europe during the so-called Dark Ages. They converted to Judaism in a sense not unlike the Germanic tribes converted to Christianity. Judaism was much more a missionary religion then than it is now. Some scholars argue that a quarter of the Roman empire, or at least the urban parts of it, were Jewish or Jewish proselytes at the time of Jesus. That seems too much, but they were certainly ten percent of the empire. We know nothing, except legends, about the story of the conversion, only that suddenly there was this large and powerful tribe of Jews on the fringes of the empire.''

''Not ethnic Jews?''

''What's an ethnic Jew, Dinny? The Hebrews were, after all, a collection of disparate desert tribes that became a people at Sinai. Judaism becomes an ethnic group only because of a religion. If you wish to say that the Khazars were not Palestinian Jews, you would probably be right. But then, who and where were the Palestinian Jews? My presumably Sephardic ancestors? Perhaps, but who can say?"

"So the pope liked the dissertation?"

"I wrote it thirty-five years ago, when to attack anti-Semitism in Spain was less easy than it is today. I argued," he made a little self-deprecating gesture with his hands that I would see often in the course of the evening, "that Jews in Eastern Europe were probably the descendants of the Khazars. How else explain that so many were there? They were not, strictly speaking, Semites, save in the religious sense of the word. That made their slaughter by the Nazis even more absurd, not that any killing of any people because of their religion was not a horrific crime. I'm afraid in the coda of the book, I went far beyond my subject matter and inveighed against Catholic anti-Semitism and demanded penance for our sins. I am told that some of the Corpus people, not knowing that the pope would agree with me, slipped him a copy of the book. So I became an archbishop and later a cardinal. Later, I think, he was unhappy with me, though he never said anything about it. All he ever talked about was whether I was able to continue my work. I told him that I got out an article every year or two, and that seemed to please him."

"He was no one's man but his own?" Ricki asked.

"When he wanted to be. He was predictable most of the time, but then unpredictable in unpredictable ways. I am told that he was very upset with me when I commented on his letter concerning the ordination of women. He had said, as I'm sure you all remember, that the Church cannot ordain women because it never has; my response was that as a historian I thought the evidence leaned in the opposite direction, as I said in answering questions after my lectures this week. It was the only time that I publicly disagreed with him. Everyone knew, however, that I had grave reservations about the centralization of power in his papacy and the harm it was doing to the Church.''

I was distracted from the conversation by lascivious thoughts about my ex-wife. Or wife, if I were to believe the wedding ring. Was the ring an invitation? Did she want me? During the final years of our marriage she seemed never to want me, so I didn't try very often to tell her I wanted her.

''Will you be elected pope next week?'' Patty asked in what was almost a whisper. ''Do you think you're going to win?''

He laughed ruefully. ''If I win, I will lose, and if I lose I will win . . . who can say? You must ask Cardinal Cronin—who does not look very well, by the way—or Cardinal Count Von Obermann or Cardinal DeJulio. They know better than I do. I pray every day that I will be serene no matter what happens.''

He looked around the table with his vulnerable brown eyes.

''It is like being elected dean. At first I didn't want to be dean. Then when I saw who was opposing me and why, I wanted to beat them. I became, internally, you must understand, as combative as my most ardent supporters. That has not happened yet in this election, but I feel each day that I am being drawn towards the desire to win, no matter what the personal cost might be in later years, because they desire so strongly to defeat me, even if it means destroying me in the process. Soon I fear I may become as determined to win as your Cardinal Cronin.''

He laughed again, as if to dismiss the folly in his own conflicting emotions. But there was a hard glow in his eyes. Until then I had wondered whether this charming, diffident, gentle scholar had enough internal fortitude to take on the Vatican power structure, even if he was elected. I no longer doubted it.

''But what do you think, Doña Patricia?'' He turned toward Patty Anne.

''I think you'll win, Don Luis,'' she said. ''I'm sure

you'll win, though it might still be a tough fight.''

"That is what my colleagues tell me; and you, Dinny,
what do you think?''

My imagination was planning the lewd details of a preliminary assault on Peppermint Patty in the car returning to
the Spanish Steps, an assault that I knew would never happen.

"I agree with my wife, Don Luis. As always. The cardinals are beginning to feel the pressure of world public
opinion. They don't understand it and they may not like it.
But they know what the Catholic laity want, and by the time
they go into conclave they will be more afraid of them than
of the Curia or Corpus.''

He nodded. "As a historian, I find the new importance
of the lay opinion to be fascinating. It could change everything. Put us back in the ninth century, when the rural land-
owners, like the Orianis, swarmed into Rome to restore
some semblance of order.''

"Just so,'' Ricki agreed. "Just so.''

"I suppose,'' he said thoughtfully, "that seemingly harmless little Bishop Ryan thought of it first.''

"Cardinal DeJulio will be your secretary of state?'' Tonia
asked with the most charming of smiles.

"I do not permit myself to think of such things,'' Don
Luis said. "But, yes, of course he will.''

"Is it not strange,'' I asked, surprised to note that my
pasta had disappeared, "that since so many of the cardinals
are the late pope's appointees, there is such a strong sentiment for change? Even Cardinal Monastero has to make the
required obeisance to change.''

"It has happened before, Dinny,'' he sighed, "though I
reject the comparison. In 1877 a man named Ruggerio Bonghi wrote a book about Pius IX, who had been pope for
thirty-one years and who had named every cardinal in the
Sacred College. He predicted that the next pope would be
Cardinal Pecci of Perugia, on the basis that he was the cardinal most unlike Pio Nono. He was right, and indeed his

prediction was confirmed the very next year. Many of the cardinals personally admired Pio Nono, but they were also tired of him; men tend to get tired of popes towards the end of their time, which is a good reason for limiting the length of the term, since death no longer limits it to just a few years. So the Church swung from being unbearably conservative to being quite liberal for that time. It would have continued down that path if the Austrians had not vetoed Cardinal Rampolla in 1903.''

"Sometimes, Don Luis," Ricki said thoughtfully, "too much history becomes a burden."

"It does, Ricki." The cardinal sighed. "But fortunately for me I do not compare myself to Giovanni Pecci, who became Leo XIII, the man who, as I'm sure you all know, wrote the first great social justice encyclical. I compare only the situations. I think it is 1878 again, and most of the cardinals, even some of the Curia, who rarely act in concert, by the way, want to see a change of ethos, even if they are not sure what such a change would mean or how far it would go."

I had calculated that Patty was wearing only panty hose and underpants underneath her dress. Not serious obstacles to a man who wanted to claim his wife again. The slit would provide me with easy access to critical areas. I knew that I wouldn't do it, but it was fun to imagine.

"You are more liberal than Leo XIII was," Ricki continued. "He would never have sat down at a dinner table like this when he was pope."

"He could not leave the Vatican," Paoli snorted, "because of those Piedmontese pigs."

"Paola Elizabetta," her mother said reprovingly. But also with a touch of pride.

"Sorry, Mama," she apologized, but with little sincerity.

"Well, if I am elected, I will continue to come here for dinner . . . if you will have me. However, everyone is more liberal now. Even Cardinal Count Von Obermann appears in a big purple sport shirt."

"Do you know anything," I said, changing the subject abruptly, "about the 'extraordinary' section of the APAS gambling in the derivatives market?"

The cardinal was startled. So was everyone else, except perhaps my guardian angel. I don't know what made me ask the question. Perhaps I was trying to take my mind off seducing my wife.

"You have evidence of this, Dinny?"

"Not enough to do a story yet. Nor do I have any solid reason to think that there have been major losses over there, though there are some hints."

"They will never tell us." The cardinal sighed. "They will hide and dissemble and if necessary lie."

"Until a pope makes them tell the truth."

"The late pope, Dinny, was not much interested in such matters."

"What impact do you think such a story would have on the conclave?"

He paused to think about it, his forehead twisted in a worried frown.

"I hope it is not true. The Church cannot afford yet another financial scandal. Yet they are not smart enough to engage in that dangerous market. If they have, then there will be a scandal. Your friend Cardinal Cronin, who is less sensitive to such matters than I am, would doubtless see it as an asset to his cause."

"If it turns out to be true, should I write about it?"

"Certainly you should write about it. The truth must be told. For too many centuries we have hidden the truth in the name of protecting the Church. That has corrupted us. To quote the late pope, the Church must be a glass house."

"Deep secret, guys." I looked around the room.

They all nodded.

Patty said, "I've never stolen a story from you, Dinny. Besides, I have a hard time adding and subtracting."

Then the *dolci* were served, principally a rich and creamy chocolate ice cream with chocolate sauce. Peppermint Patty ate a couple of bites and moved the dish aside. As did everyone else but Paoli, who ate with a young woman's immunity to worry about calories, and me.

I devoured the ice cream with an eight-year-old's fervor and would have asked for more if I would not have shamed myself. If you can't nibble on a woman's body, I told myself, the next best thing is Italian ice cream.

And the latter is a lot less dangerous.

"Let us offer thanks at the end of this wonderful meal." The cardinal extended his hands, Tonia on one side, my Patty on the other. We formed a circle of hands and bowed our heads.

"I offer thanks together with all of you for this marvelous dinner, for this night of peace in the midst of so much turbulence and uncertainty. I offer thanks for old friends rediscovered and for an old friend suddenly grown up and quite beautiful, like her mother . . . and for new friends, who I hope will become old friends. May they continue to be dedicated to their important vocation. I also pray for myself and all my colleagues who will go into conclave next week to choose our new pope. May the Spirit inspire us to work well and with openness and courage . . . and grant that our Church, our poor, battered Church, may shine once again as a light of radiant love to all the nations."

His voice seemed to crack at the end. I realized for the first time how much the ugliness of the Vatican must hurt those priests who want the Church to shine as a radiant light of love.

"Amen," we all said together.

After a few more minutes of quiet conversation, we said good-bye to Don Luis and our hosts, thanked the latter for a glorious night, and promised the former our prayers as he promised both of us interviews after the conclave, "though I imagine you will want them only if I win."

"You will get the Bonghi book for me, Paoli?"

"Naturally," she said as she hugged me and kissed me

good night—the first time she had kissed me. She must have felt that I had been a very good boy.

On our ride back to the Piazza Trinità dei Monti, Patty and I remained silent, hiding behind our own thoughts and fears and worries. My sexual desires quickly and inexplicably died. I took no advantage of the slit in the thigh area of her dress, though it was only a few inches away from my fingers.

"He will make a good pope, won't he, Dinny?"

"Yes, he sure will. He'll probably suffer a lot, but he'll never wring his hands and complain."

"Everyone suffers."

I didn't want to touch that one.

We were silent again.

"Do you think Cardinal Cronin does not look well, Dinny?"

"Tired. Worn out. Needs a rest."

"Don't we all."

I didn't want to touch that one either.

"Don Luis seemed to enjoy us—the women, I mean."

"Who wouldn't?"

"A lot of priests would have been embarrassed by the way we were dressed."

"Irish priests, not Spanish priests."

"Maybe. . . . Anyway, it would be nice to have a pope that clearly enjoys us."

"Yes, it would."

We shook hands at the end of the ride in front of her hotel.

"Thank you very much for insisting that I come, Dinny. I would have hated myself for the rest of my life if I had missed it."

"It was your decision, not mine," I said primly.

"You helped me."

"You were wonderful," I said lamely. "I was proud of you."

"Thank you," she said wearily. "Now I need a good night's sleep."

"So do I."

I walked into the lobby of the Hassler feeling that somehow I had not made a disastrous mistake.

Maybe, however, I had missed a great opportunity.

Dinny

I desperately wanted to sleep. I was still not over the jet lag and I had been on the run since I had left the plane at Fiumicino. But I was too keyed up to sleep. The images and the ideas of the dinner raced through my head. Don Luis had fascinated me. He was the perfect man for the job and he seemed likely to get it. Diffident and fragile as he was, he had a will of iron, deep piety, and a first-rate mind. Great pope.

Fantasies of the three lovely women gradually exorcised Don Luis from my imagination. I tossed and turned on my bed as these fantasies entertained and tormented me. Though it had cooled off outside, the hotel was still hot, like a summer night at the Jersey shore, thick with humidity. Or at the Lake Michigan shore, as far as that went.

I tried a shower. That had no effect at all. I glanced at the alarm clock next to my bed. Two-thirty already. No sleep for me tonight. I'd stumble around in a fog all day tomorrow.

Then I realized what I was going to do.

I did know her room number—144. One floor above the ground floor. With charm and my room key, which looked enough like hers, I could bluff my way past the concierge and the security guard, both of whom would doubtless be sleepy at this time of the early morning.

Why not? What did I have to lose? She might turn me away. Or she might not. Nothing ventured, nothing gained. A one-night brief encounter. Or at worst, a love affair until after the conclave was over. We were both lonely and probably both hungry for love. I sure was. After the conclave we would go our separate ways.

There were all kinds of weaknesses in that line of reasoning. But just then I wasn't looking for weaknesses. So I splashed myself with cologne, donned my brown slacks and beige knit shirt, picked up the room key, rode down in the elevator and out into that good night.

Both the security guard and the concierge at the Hassler were asleep. They didn't matter. If my luck held next door, I'd get to Room 144 without any trouble.

The concierge at the Hotel de la Ville was half awake, but at my confident and charming *"Buona sera,"* he nodded and slumped down even further behind his desk.

The security guard was utterly dead to the world. I tiptoed by him and up the stairs to what was in the much more logical American way of things, the second floor. One forty-four was halfway down the corridor on the left.

My heart was pounding. I was the ravisher, coming to take possession of the fair matron. In fact, I knew that if the fair matron turned me away I would run as fast as I could.

I knocked lightly on the door.

"Yes?"

"Dinny."

She opened the door slightly and peered out at me around the corner.

"It *is* you."

"I think so."

She had let her hair down and washed her face. No trace of makeup. She had also changed her scent. This one was pure invitation. And she was so beautiful and so attractive that my heart did a slow, lazy turn.

"Come in," she said, opening the door all the way. "Don't stand out there all night long."

No rejection. Just the opposite. Almost too easy. Dangerous, but it was far too late to run.

She was wearing a short white gown, gauzelike in texture and transparency. And the wedding ring.

"I couldn't sleep," I said lamely.

"I couldn't either. It's too hot."

Her eyes were liquid emeralds, brimming with desire and enticement.

"Maybe you'd be a little cooler," I said as I flicked the gown off her shoulders, "if you're not wearing this."

The gown fell to her ankles. Wonder, surprise, admiration, astonishment rushed through my body, trailing behind them imperious hormones.

She closed her eyes and gulped. But she made no attempt to fight me off or to cover herself. Her erect nipples glistened like rubies.

Far too easy.

She put her arms around me, hesitantly, tentatively, almost fearfully.

They were strong, muscular arms, difficult to escape from despite their present caution.

"I thought you'd never come," she said, opening her eyes. "If you had waited a half-hour longer, I would have gone over to your room."

"That would have been interesting."

My naked ex-wife was more beautiful than ever.

She leaned her head against my shoulder. "It's the loneliness, Dinny, the awful, terrible, empty loneliness."

"I know what you mean."

"I suppose this is Father Blackie's rubber band snapping back."

Now she was clinging to me.

"Could be."

My eager fingers began their explorations: first the long, silky red hair; then the smooth, curving back; next the solid buttocks, subtly designed to be cupped by a man's hands.

She sighed and squirmed slightly with pleasure as I rediscovered my wonderful prize.

"Don't hurt me, Dinny."

"Have I ever hurt you, Patricia?"

"No. . . . You know all my secrets."

"You don't forget secrets like that."

She giggled and then we both laughed.

I caressed her thighs, her smooth, firm belly, and at last her rich, full breasts, which I had wanted to grasp since the night in Trastevere. She pressed my hands hard, forcing them deeper into her breasts, and pressing them against her rib cage.

"Don't stop, Dinny, not now."

"Irresistible rubber band!"

"Damn his metaphors anyway." She sighed, snuggling closer to me. "This is only one night, Dinny. It means nothing more than that."

"Only one night," I echoed.

"Definitely."

I gently eased her away.

"I want to admire you," I said.

There was a lot to admire. Patty was neither Venus nor Juno but Diana, a tall, lithe goddess of the hunt. No, she was Maeve the Marvelous, an Irish goddess with a long, supple body that genes and exercise had blessed. I was as addicted to that body as all the kings of Ireland were addicted to Ireland. She was even more lovely than the last time we had made love. Experience and pain had left their marks but had enhanced her beauty, which was both earthy and ethereal. She bowed her head and closed her eyes.

"Look at me when I'm admiring you."

"If I see the love in your eyes, I'll die," she said.

"I don't think so."

She looked up at me and opened her eager green eyes. She blushed and smiled joyously.

"There's lots of pictures and statues of naked women all

around this city," she said. "Why don't you ogle them instead of me?"

"You know the answer to that," I said, undressing as quickly as I could.

We both giggled again.

"Enjoy me all you want, Dinny. Make up for lost time."

I had entered the room as a ravisher, a most improbable guise for the likes of me. But how could one ravish such a sad, unprotected, lovely woman? So I changed to a healer, a man sent to cure her of her pain and renew her confidence. My pleasure was less important than healing her. I would direct all my actions to make her happy.

As I fondled her, she seemed to realize what was happening and to resist this invasion of her suffering. But quickly she melted and abandoned herself completely to my ministrations.

I repeated my pilgrimage of caresses and I described her wondrous body as I went:

> Honeydew, your high and graceful breasts,
> One taste enough to break my heart.
> In the curve of your wondrous thighs:
> A deep valley flowing with perfumed wine
> Around which wheat and blooming lilies twine
> Whose sweetness invites my enchanted eyes.
> I will seize the fruit, press them to my teeth.
> Then, famished, impassioned, and lightly deft,
> Explore the valley's tantalizing cleft
> And your delicacy savor, drink, and eat!

"How beautiful! Did you write it, Dinny?"

"I wish I had. It's a modern paraphrase of a love song in the Bible."[1]

"Which you happened to memorize just in case you should ever need it?"

"With only one woman in mind."

[1] Sg. 7/1-6

"Your usual blarney, Dinny, but I love it."

Ever the neat homemaker, she scooped up her gown and my clothes and laid them out in neat piles. Then she fell back on the bed, heavy and lethargic now with awakened need and completely open to me.

I stretched out next to her and began to kiss her.

When my tender healing came to an end and we were happy and exhausted lovers, she sighed with satisfaction, then threw her arms around me and wept bitterly.

Rarely did the old Peppermint Patty weep. And never after lovemaking. Usually she was ready to bound out of bed and do something else, turn on the TV, grab for a book, rush to a table and write down notes that were surely not about our interlude of passion.

Now she wept.

I soothed her with my caresses.

Then she cuddled closer to me, sighed happily, and went to sleep.

Like young lovers, we slept naked in each other's arms.

Dinny

I was consuming the miserable continental breakfast that even the best of the hotels provide. OK, it was the Hassler, so you could eat more than a hard roll and a cup of coffee— red juice made from Sicilian oranges and hard corn flakes covered with skim milk.

After my night's exercise I needed more. I had to be content with a croissant and jam from a plastic container.

I was in great good humor from my triumph earlier in the morning as a lover. Patty Anne and I had never before been so sensitive in our lovemaking. I was also, however, worried about my wife . . . ex-wife . . . whatever. The weeping woman in my arms was not the old Peppermint Patty at all.

"You broke her heart when you left her," my shrink had insisted. "You like to think of yourself as the victim in the divorce. You lost a woman that you slept with occasionally. She lost a man she loved."

"That's definitely not true. She's free to marry anyone she wants now, someone who can keep up with her as I surely couldn't."

"As you didn't want to. . . . You have your self-pity to sustain you. You left her with nothing."

While I was prepared to admit most of the shrink's charges—no doubt that I was a wimp, for example—this one made no sense at all. Patty had filed for divorce, she had thrown me out of the house, she was the one who wanted her freedom, wasn't she?

"Without you, she will deteriorate," the shrink had predicted. "Mark my words. In a few years you will have your complete triumph. You will celebrate her decline as proof that you were right all along."

"I'd never celebrate anything she suffers."

Well, I didn't think I would, but I was still convinced then that she had wronged me.

Now I wasn't so sure. The suffering woman to whom I had brought peace, however temporary, last night was not the Patty I knew. Or maybe she was the Patty I never knew.

On one count the shrink had been wrong: I didn't rejoice at Patty's anguish. I wanted to do something about it. But what could I do? An occasional night like the last one could hardly sustain either of us in our loneliness.

I was lonely too, wasn't I?

Not lonely the way she was lonely?

"They don't do breakfast any better here than they do at the CNN hotel," Patty announced as she sat down at my table. "May I have that second croissant, please? And a tad of your coffee? I've worked up an appetite for some reason."

Dressed in jeans and a red T-shirt with "Turner Broadcasting Systems" emblazoned on it in gold, her hair secured in a ponytail and without makeup, my sometime wife was bright, clear-eyed, and cheerful, ready once more to take on the world.

So I had accomplished something.

I offered her the croissant and the plastic holder filled with strawberry jelly (which tasted like it had been made from plastic strawberries) and poured her a full cup of coffee.

"Sleeping late this morning, Patty Anne?"

"Just couldn't get out of bed." She giggled as she wolfed down the croissant in one gulp.

"I'll get some more."

"One of those cute little raisin rolls down at the end of the table."

I had missed them on my two previous trips. I brought back a half-dozen.

We munched on them in total contentment.

"Thank you very much for last night," she said shyly, touching my hand. "You were wonderful."

"I'm the one who should be saying thanks."

"You know what I mean, Dinny. You've changed since . . . well, since the last time."

I couldn't remember the last time, but I didn't think that would be a good thing to say.

"For better or worse?"

"For better, óf course. I almost don't know you anymore. Maybe getting rid of me was good for you."

"This morning I think I'll pass on that comment."

She swallowed a whole raisin roll in one gulp.

"Sorry, I shouldn't have said that. I came over here to thank you for being so kind and wonderful and to say that, as we agreed, it was only one night."

I hadn't agreed, not quite.

"It was a grand night," I said.

"It was all of that, but we both know better than to think

that we could ever get back together again. We'd destroy each other.''

''Maybe.''

''You know we would.''

I thought very carefully about what to say next. Nonetheless, afterward I felt that my reply hadn't been too swift.

''Maybe not.''

''No maybes about it.''

She rose from the table, drained her coffee cup, and apologized. ''Sorry, I've got to run.''

''I think we should talk sometime, Patty. At great length.''

She put the coffee cup back on its saucer and stared at me thoughtfully.

''Maybe, Dinny. Maybe.''

She hurried out of the dining room.

Did I want her back, this new Patricia who had changed even more than I had?

I thought about it as I finished my cornflakes.

Yeah, I wanted her back, all right. Hang the costs.

I smiled to myself, as though I were about to launch a vast campaign to recapture my Patricia, while in my heart I knew that I wouldn't make the next move.

CNN

ANCHOR: More trouble with the Vatican press office, Patty?

PM: (In front of the sala stampa, wearing windbreaker, blouse, and slacks, hair in ponytail.) Tessa, they're worse than the Kremlin was in the old days. We know from what Cardinal Cronin told us after he came out from the General Congregation this morning that there was a fierce argument about Vatican finances.

(Cut to SC, in front of the ugly audience hall, looking like he was ready to explode, gray against the dark gray sky.)

SC: We tried to persuade Cardinal Fletcher to tell us how the money from the patrimony, the Vatican's endowment, is being invested. Either he doesn't know or he won't tell us. We asked that a committee of cardinals might check last year's investments. Cardinal Moreau, the camerlingo, was somehow unable to put that to a vote.

PM: Do you think there is something wrong with the investments, Cardinal?

SC: One hears rumors that they might be playing around with derivatives. That's all right if you know what you're doing and are only hedging. But as someone who knows a little bit about the Chicago Board of Trade, I'd say that those who can be trusted to be competent in that kind of marketplace are few and far between. So, if everything is fine, why not tell us about it? We are, after all, the interregnum government and we have the right to know. We also have to take finances into account when we vote next week.

PM: Do you expect to get the details, Cardinal?

SC: No way, Patty, no way.

(Cut back to PM.)

PM: So we went back to the sala stampa to find out from the press briefing more about the discussion on money. My old friend Father Lenny Richardson did the briefing. He simply denied that he had any knowledge on that discussion and suggested that if we wanted further details we could ask Cardinal Cronin the next morning at his press briefing.

ANCHOR: Pretty nasty, huh, Patty?

PM: Nasty and arrogant. Confident that he's back in power again. But there's worse. He also announced that women will not be permitted on the tour of the conclave area tomorrow.

(Cut to Father Richardson, implacable at the podium,

as angry voices, mostly female, shout at him.)

LR: That decision is final. There will be no appeal from it. Only male journalists will be permitted inside the conclave area on the tour. The cardinals are all men and their privacy must be respected.

VOICE: None of them will be there tomorrow, will they?

VOICE: Sexism!

VOICE: Why does the Catholic Church hate women?

VOICE (PM): If we swear we're not having our periods, will you let us in then?

LR: (distaste written all over his face) That decision is final. Appeals to Cardinal Cronin will not accomplish anything.

PM: That's where we stand now, Tessa. Most of the men correspondents have agreed that they will boycott the tour. So the public will hear no descriptions of the conclave area.

ANCHOR: Any explanation of the reason, Patty?

PM: None. It makes no sense at all. The Church continues its steady backward march into the Middle Ages. Patricia McLaughlin, CNN, Rome.

Blackie

*N*o," I said firmly, "you will not go over to the sala stampa and throttle that young fool."

"What?" Milord Cronin whirled on me.

"I will not permit you to waste your time and energy on a bootless enterprise, however satisfying it may be."

"Bootless?"

"You will simply excite some sympathy for him among

those who are predisposed to be sympathetic."

"Yeah?"

The cardinal did not take kindly to being told what to do.

I sighed loudly. "What you will do is go to the General Congregation tomorrow and announce that, since the sala stampa will not permit women to tour the conclave area, you will lead a tour yourself in your role as the one responsible for physical arrangements. You will not ask Cardinal Moreau for permission, you will simply tell one and all what you propose to do. You will also invite such cardinals as wish to accompany you to feel free to do so. Your allies will cheer enthusiastically and there will be another and substantial victory for our side, without anyone being throttled."

"Indeed?" he said, slipping into my vocabulary again as he sat down on the couch. "Now you not only spill my coffee, you tell me what to do."

"When necessary," I said, this time quite firmly.

"Occasionally in error and never in doubt?" he said ruefully.

"Arguably."

"All right, you win. But I won't forget about that guy."

"I'm under no illusion that you will."

"Why did they do it, Blackwood?" he asked, abandoning all immediate plans for throttling. "What did they hope to gain?"

"Their principles say that women are inferior and that they would profane the sacred rooms in which the sacred college of sacred cardinals are to meet. Moreover, by enforcing the principles at this time they demonstrate that they are still in charge and send a message to the cardinals that their attempts to revolt will be frustrated and it will be business as usual. They also deny to themselves that their power is slipping."

"Do they know what they are doing to the image of the Church?"

"They don't care. The media are not an important audience. Only their own membership and their supporters matter.''

''Rich supporters.''

''Oh, yes.''

''What if they try to stop me tomorrow?''

''That is why you demand that your colleagues join in this solemn high procession through the conclave area—von Obermann, Sanchez, Llewelyn, DeJulio, Ulululu, Whelan, Kennedy, Michner, LeClerque. They will not dare to try to stop all of you.''

Milord Cronin grinned; of a lesser man I would almost say that he grinned fiendishly.

''That should be fun,'' he said.

CHICAGO STAR

Vatican Reasserts Control over Conclave

Rome.

Vatican authorities today moved to reassert their control over the process of electing the next pope, who will become the spiritual leader of one billion Roman Catholics throughout the world. Cardinal Moreau, the camerlingo, or acting pope, refused to permit a discussion on the floor of the General Congregation—the daily meeting of cardinals—of delicate matters of Vatican finance. The sala stampa, or Vatican press office, imposed stern restrictions on the behavior of journalists accredited to the conclave and criticized Chicago's Cardinal Cronin for holding his own press briefings each morning after the General Congregations adjourn.

''These two moves,'' said an experienced Vatican official, ''should serve as a bucket of cold water in the faces of those unruly cardinals who do not realize that solemnity and decorum are essential to such an important task as electing a pope."

Vatican authorities were especially critical of Cardinal Cronin's pandering, as they saw it, to the media. "He acts like he's running for office. Yet it does not matter how often he gets his picture on television, he will not elect the next Pope. He is deceiving himself if he thinks that will be the 'Gran' Elettore.' "

These officials are unanimous in their conviction that Cardinal Menendez will not be elected. "We simply will not permit it," one of them said.

TIME

Long Conclave Predicted

Hopes are fading in the Vatican that the conclave to elect a new pope will be a brief one. The group of radical cardinals aligned with the candidacy of Luis Emilio Cardinal Menendez y Garcia of Valencia has lost all hope of winning on an early ballot. Too many serious questions have been raised about Cardinal Menendez's record for him to be able to garner the necessary two thirds plus one votes required for election. But his supporters, led by Chicago's ultraradical Sean Cardinal Cronin and Düsseldorf's left-leaning Klaus Maria Count Cardinal Von Obermann, are determined to fight to the bitter end, no matter how long they prolong the voting. They probably can command enough votes to drag out the process for many days and thus block such moderate compromise candidates as Tampico's Jaimie Cardinal Suarez or old Vatican hands Vincente Cardinal Monastero and Brazilian Hans Schlossmann.

"They will eventually wear themselves out," said

a highly placed Vatican official, "and settle for a moderate like Cardinal Monastero. But it will take many days."

Vatican officials have taken steps to rein in the excesses of the world media, which, they believe, have turned the preconclave deliberations into a circus. The media, they believe, in their enthusiasm for Cardinal Menendez have become tendentious and even mendacious.

Dinny

At the bureau office, cool now that the heat had broken and the sky was gray and sullen, Paoli studied me carefully. She was trying to determine whether I had engaged in sexual intercourse after her family's dinner party. Apparently she could not make up her mind.

I wasn't going to help her solve the puzzle.

"Great party last night," I said.

"Naturally it was most pleasant."

"Good food, good conversation, good friends, beautiful women—"

"Your wife especially."

"Patty Anne is well-preserved. She works at it."

"She wore her wedding ring last night."

"So as not to shock the cardinal."

"She was very well-behaved."

"Patty knows when to put on her company manners."

Paola Elizabetta, as her mama had called her last night, gave me up as a bad cause. "Ms. Van der Stappen from Amsterdam wants to talk to you."

I called Amsterdam. Harriet's information was tantalizing

but not definitive. It was clear from the records that the International Agricultural Bank of Holland had contacts with the Vatican and made investments for them in the past several years. Neither the size nor the success of the investments, however, were clear from the available evidence.

Did I want her to probe further?

"Let me think about it and get back to you in a couple of days," I said.

I didn't have enough to go with a powerful story. The paper would not—and rightly so—tolerate a speculative story about corruption or incompetence in the Catholic Church's financial dealings without a smoking gun. I had no smoking gun and no idea where I might find one. Well, I'd had to give up great stories before because I couldn't find hard evidence. Maybe I would have to give up this one.

"Any idea where I could find the smoking gun, Pretty Princess?"

"Smoking gun?" She wrinkled her forehead. "Oh, you mean for the APAS? I'm sure there are people who know but it would be most difficult to find them. However, there is no true secret in the Vatican, despite all its secrecy."

I thought about it for a moment.

"You have no idea where we might start looking?"

"Some of the bankers might know, but if you try to talk to them, they will tell others and you lose your own secrecy."

"Yeah. . . . Well, I'll have to think about it."

Yet I must be close to something or the people in Den Haag would not have had the shade on my tail.

"Here's the book by Bonghi. It is in Italian. Naturally I have marked the appropriate passages."

NYT

Conclave Compared to 1878
Late Pope Another Pio Nono?
Cardinals Seen Wanting a Change

By Dennis Michael Mulloy
Rome.

The late pope had appointed almost all the cardinal electors, many of whom liked him and supported his policies. Yet inside the conclave they voted overwhelmingly for a man who was the exact opposite. They wanted a change, as did the whole Church.

The year was 1878. The pope was Pius IX. The man elected to replace him was Giovanni Pecci, the archbishop of Perugia, who became Pope Leo XIII. It was so clear to everyone that Pecci would be elected to replace the man who had been pope for 32 years, that, the year before, a papal biographer, Ruggerio Bonghi, had cheerfully predicted the election of Cardinal Pecci and almost no one had disagreed with him.

Historians are, by their nature, fond of discovering parallels from the past. Certainly there are parallels between 1878 and the present—a long reign, massive dissatisfaction in the grass roots of the Church, a sense that it is time for a change, an appealing candidate who, while still perfectly orthodox, is in many ways the opposite of the last pope.

However, as historians also realize, history does not repeat itself. On the one hand, in the last quarter of the nineteenth century there was great unhappiness with the definition of papal infallibility which Pio Nono had imposed on the First Vatican Council (and which has been used only once since then). On the other hand, at that time there were no powerful secret organizations like the Corpus Christi movement or the Opus Dei who would bitterly resist such a change.

It is obvious that a solid majority of cardinals, perhaps as many as 60 or even 65—close to the required 73—want a change. But, being cardinals, they would prefer to have the transition be slow and peaceful. Those forces resisting change here are determined that there will be a high cost in any transferal of power from the more conservative forces in the Church to the more moderate.

They continue their relentless attacks on Valencia's Luis Emilio Cardinal Menendez y Garcia as too radical, though there is nothing in his record that would confirm such charges (save that he wears a suit and tie when making an academic presentation, as he did earlier in the week at the North American and Germano-Hungarian colleges).

Recently the Vatican power structure (which in this fight does not include all the Roman Curia by any means) has grown more defiant. It has blocked a frank and public discussion of Vatican investments, which have been the source of scandal often in the past. It has also banned women journalists from a tour of the conclave area in the Vatican Palace. It is widely debated whether this defiance is the result of increased confidence that it will turn back the tide of change or of increased recklessness because it has been forced to think the unthinkable: The next pope may well be Luis Menendez or someone very much like him.

History books do not say how the Vatican establishment reacted to the election of Leo XIII. Perhaps many of them also thought it was time for a change.

Dinny

After I had filed my story about 1878, WHICH WAS JUST esoteric enough to make it into the paper, I decided to walk back to Piazza Trinità dei Monti.

"I need to do some thinking," I told my principessa.

"Naturally," she had agreed. "But it is raining."

"I will wear my rain sleeker."

"Slicker," she corrected me.

"Naturally."

The rain was little more than a mist, what the Irish would call a "soft" day. I walked and walked and walked, paying little attention to where I was or what I was seeing. Gradually my tense muscles unwound.

I had not even known I was tense.

Why was I tense?

Because I was juggling too many bowling pins, typical enough behavior.

Despite my entertaining experience the previous night, this assignment was beginning to wear on me. The unremitting dishonesty of the Corpus people and their journalistic allies was making me sick to my stomach. I had also eaten too much pasta and too much dolci. I still was not over the jet lag and probably never would be, doubtless because I had not listened closely enough to the admonitions of my guardian angel.

Most of all, however, I was worried about my ex-wife. Or wife. Or lover or mistress. Or whatever. I was worried about the demons that seemed to be ripping her apart. I was worried about what I should do to fend off those demons—as if I could! And finally, I was worried about my new and problematic resolution to get her back. Did I really mean it? And if I really meant it, did I realize the trouble it might cause?

She had been so wonderful in bed last night. Every man's dream of an utterly compliant lover.

The little bishop from Chicago had warned me that if we went the way of reconciliation—there, I'd said that word— it must be with the implacable resolution that it would work. Was I ready for that determination yet?

Not quite. However, if matters continued to drift I'd soon find myself in a situation where I would have no choice. The reconciliation had picked up a momentum of its own. One or the other or both of us would have to erect a large stop sign or it would rush on.

I stopped at a sidewalk cafe in the Piazza del Popolo for a croissant and a cup of coffee and a dolci under a Cinzano umbrella. Well, two dolci, to be precise. Also a second croissant.

Despite the coffee, I was lethargic after my snack. The rain became less "soft." I'd get wet, but I didn't care. Life had been good enough since Patty and I had split, not as bad as it was during the last years of our marriage, but not as good as during the earlier years.

We both had changed. For the better or worse? She thought better in my case. I thought better in her case. Maybe we had both learned something from our shrinks.

Was it worth the risk?

I decided that, no, it was not worth the risk.

The rain was worse. The drops were pelting against my face. My old suit was soaking wet despite the rain sleeker. *Slicker.* Fortunately I had several suits now, didn't I?

What I needed was a siesta.

Lover or no lover.

I hailed a cab and returned to the Hassler.

There was an envelope in my box. I opened it in the elevator. A key to Room 144 of the Hotel de la Ville next door.

I went into my room, sat on the couch in my suite, and thought about it. It was certainly not worth the risk. But to hell with the risk.

I thought about it for a few more minutes. Then I hunted for my spare key, put it in an envelope, and addressed it to Patty Anne.

I rode back down to the ground floor, ducked next door to avoid the rain, and deposited the key in her box.

The message should be clear enough: The ball is in your court, Patricia Anne Marie Elizabeth. You must make the next move.

I picked up my cellular phone and punched Niko's number.

"The guy is still on me, Niko."

"You led him and my men on a merry chase today through the streets of Rome."

"A lot on my mind."

"A woman perhaps? I know what it is like."

"I doubt it."

"Perhaps not. You had a fine evening last night, I am told."

"Naturally. But I missed you."

"I am," he chuckled, "how should I say it, not quite at that level of acceptance. But I progress."

"Good luck."

"I will need it, I think. We will continue to watch him closely. And the house in the hills. Do you have any idea why he is following you?"

"Is that an official or an unofficial question?"

"Unofficial, if you wish."

"I'm pretty sure that they think I am likely to stumble on to something about Vatican finances. I'll let you know if I do."

"I understand."

Perhaps he did.

I then punched his lady love's number.

"Paola Elizabetta Maria Angelica Katarina Brigitta, even

though I have no lover at hand, I think I need a siesta. Old folks do, you know. On occasion. Especially after such a stimulating dinner party like last night. So keep the world away from me for a couple of hours. OK?''

"Naturally. I am sorry that you don't have a lover. They, ah, facilitate siestas, I am told.''

"Sometimes.''

I called the desk to tell them to hold my calls, tumbled into bed, and, half hoping that a lover might show up, fell into a deep and peaceful sleep.

Blackie

*M*y virtuous sibling called to ask whether it would be possible for her team to venture down to Amalfi or Positano. I advised against it.

"About his psyche I know very little, Mkate@LCMH. But one could make the case that he is close to the breaking point.''

"Not a good time to be there, is it, Punk?''

"Alas, no.''

"OK. We can wait till after the conclave. I want desperately to swim in the Mediterranean.''

"Lake Michigan is much more salubrious.''

Then it fell my lot to accompany Milord Cronin to the General Congregation.

"It would be appropriate for your comments to be measured and controlled,'' I asserted. "You don't want to appear to be what certain media have called unruly.''

"Quod Deus avertat!" he replied.

Which freely translated meant "God forbid!"

Actually he was totally under control.

"Eminences," he began, with all the smooth charm of which he is capable, "it has been called to my attention that there is some problem at the sala stampa with regard to tours by the journalists of the conclave area. That seems to me to be unfortunate. With all due respect to the sala stampa . . ."

Slight snicker.

"I am, after all, the one responsible for the area and especially for the security. I am willing to conduct such a tour myself this afternoon, especially if some of my colleagues here will assist me since, as is well known, I am not a polyglot."

Instantly, as planned, a number of cardinals rose to say they would be happy to accompany Cardinal Cronin on the tour. Some of them were surprises, men on whose vote we had not counted.

"You will permit female as well as male journalists in the rooms?" Cardinal Moreau, characteristically, was nervous.

"I would not be inclined to discriminate. Am I correct that my eminent colleagues would agree with this proposal?"

Murmurs of assent.

"I think I can assure you, Cardinal, that no one, woman or man, will be permitted to linger in the conclave area. I will bring a squad of Swiss Guards to make sure of that."

Laughter from the cardinals.

"Well, I see no problem with that," Cardinal Moreau agreed.

"Was I restrained enough, Blackwood?" Sean Cronin whispered in my ear.

"A model of probity and prudence."

Either way we won. Our side would have supported the public's right to know (whatever that may be) and the rights of female journalists and would once more emerge as the ally of moderation and intelligence. If perhaps the people from the sala stampa tried to stop a dozen cardinals, the world media, and the Swiss Guard from entering the conclave area, then there would be bloody hell to pay.

I hoped it would go smoothly. The Curial hardliners and the Corpus gang had already given the Church enough of a black eye. We needed no more scandals.

Dinny

*H*i, Patty," I said to my once and future wife. "Do you think Cardinal Cronin will let me come on your tour?"

"It's not my tour, Dinny." She blushed furiously. "Everyone is welcome."

"See, I told you, Paola Elizabetta, they won't discriminate against men."

"Naturally."

Patty was wearing a tailored suit, black skirt, white jacket. Her hair was piled on her head again. Imperial professional woman.

However, if one pulled out a few hairpins and removed a few garments so that her wondrous hair collapsed on a naked back, she would be . . . what? An irresistible imperial professional woman? My ex-wife. Or whatever.

She had not come to my room last night, although I had expected her. The next move was still up to her.

There were some guys from the press office standing around looking dyspeptic. It wasn't their tour anymore but they figured they ought to be there.

Bishop Ryan, back in his Chicago Bulls jacket, was standing at the entry door, accompanied by two Swiss Guards in their fatigue blues. A tableau perhaps of the once and future Church. Some sort of small, infernal device rested on the table in front of the little bishop.

"What is that infernal device, Bishop Blackie?"

"A secret weapon for detecting bugs and other such things. It now tells me, Ms. McLaughlin, that your camera-person is carrying a video camera, which is permitted at the present time."

"What good does it do if you're letting all of us in?"

"When you leave we will sweep the area for bugs."

"You expect one to be left?" I asked.

"Oh, yes, many, as a matter of fact."

"I didn't know you were that interested in secrecy."

"I am interested only in a level playing field."

"Ah!" I said.

"If our guys are going to be bound by secrecy, so is everyone else."

CNN

PM: The cardinals who come into conclave in a few days to elect the next pope will do hard time. This is the typical cell for one of the electors. Indeed, it is the cell that Sean Cardinal Cronin, archbishop of Chicago and the man responsible for the physical arrangements, will occupy.

It is obvious that this is not a luxurious room, a simple single bed, a table, a chair, a dim light, a couple of sheets of paper, and a pad of Kleenex. The word *cell* is appropriate. Why the spartan circumstances, Cardinal?

SC: I think Pope Paul VI, who drew up the present regulations for the conclave, wanted the gathering to be something like a retreat. Also the ancient custom was that the people of Rome wanted a quick result, so they wouldn't permit the electors to be too comfortable.

PM: That bed doesn't look long enough for you, Cardinal.

SC: (laughing) I guess I'll have to scrunch.

PM: I thought that the new hotel on the other side of St. Peter's was built for events like this.

SC: A lot of people thought that. We could have designed a sealed passage through the Basilica to the Sistine Chapel. But the late pope never changed the regulations, perhaps because he thought that "hard time," as you call it, Patty, would facilitate a quick result.

PM: I suppose women have never been in the conclave?

SC: Never is a long time, Patty. We do know that when Pius XI died, Cardinal Pacelli brought his housekeeper, Sister Pasquelina, in with him. You could bring in a couple of assistants in those days.

PM: And he was elected pope, wasn't he?

SC: Yes, he was. Afterwards she became known as the Papessa.

PM: Were they lovers?

SC: They didn't sleep together, if that's what you mean.

PM: I think we'll go into the Sistine Chapel now.

(Cut to Sistine Chapel.)

PM: Under these astonishing frescoes of Michelangelo, the cardinals will gather twice a day until the pope is elected. They will sit in plain wooden chairs behind these plain wooden tables, which will be draped in crimson and white. Each time they gather there will be two votes. The cardinals will have a preprinted form which says, *Eligo in Summum Pontificem.* They will add the name of their choice, fold the paper, one by one walk up to this altar, and say the following prayer in Latin. (Reads from a slip of paper.) "I call to witness Christ the Lord, who will be my judge that my vote is given to the one whom before God I consider should be elected."

Then each cardinal places the folded paper on this gold dish called the paten and tips it into this chalice.

When all have voted, the ballots are counted by three cardinals and the results announced. The ballots are burned in this stove. If a pope is elected no straw is put in the stove and white smoke appears. If a pope is not elected, straw is added and black smoke appears.
ANCHOR: Very solemn stuff, isn't it, Patty?
PM: And very scary too, Tessa. A lot scarier than just punching a hole in a card, the way we vote.

Patricia McLaughlin, CNN, in the Sistine Chapel.

Blackie

*W*ill you stop playing with that infernal machine, Blackwood?" The *gran' elettore* complained. "You're driving me crazy."

The "infernal machine" was no larger though substantially heavier than a small portable radio of the sort that joggers have been known to carry.

"I am merely testing to make sure your room is not bugged."

"I'm sure it is not."

A loud buzz sounded from underneath his desk.

"Ah!" I said, reaching there. "But you indeed have been bugged!"

He jumped up from the couch on which he was slumped.

"Damnation! How dare they! I'm going to raise hell with Gene Schreiber! Let me see the thing!"

"Not very elaborate, I'm afraid. No more than fifty yards at the most. The receiver must be somewhere in the building."

"Sweep every room!"

We did indeed and found another bug in Mick Kennedy's room, one in the dining room, and one in the faculty lounge, where we met after supper. The other cardinals were horrified, and some of them just a little unhappy that they were not important enough to be bugged.

"Can you find where the receiver is?" Milord Cronin demanded.

"Let me see what it says in the instruction book. Ah, yes, one pushes this button . . ."

A new humming noise began. I walked into the corridor, trailed by a gaggle of cardinals, their eyes popping, and a few curious seminarians. I walked to the left and the hum faded. Then I walked to the right and the hum became louder. It led us into the bowels of the Nordamericano, indeed to a sub-basement where, in a tiny closet, a reel-to-reel tape was spinning very slowly. Into it was plugged a small transceiver, patently on the same wavelength as the tiny bugs in the pocket of my Chicago Bulls jacket.

"Get the rector," Milord Cronin said softly to one of the seminarians. That worthy rushed off, delighted, no doubt, that the hated rector was now up the proverbial creek without the proverbial paddle.

A few minutes later, an ashen Gene Schreiber, his jowls quivering, appeared on the scene.

He stared in fascination at the recorder.

"As God is my witness, I have never seen this before," he said in a terrified voice.

It was one thing to swear that you had never seen it and another to swear that you knew nothing about it.

"It's your house, Gene," Milord Cronin said ominously, "as you are so fond of telling us. You find out who did it or we'll hold you responsible."

He turned and strode toward the narrow staircase and up it at top speed, slowing appreciably at the top. One of these days, he's not going to make it, I thought.

I took the precaution of shutting off the reel-to-reel recorder, confiscating the receiver, and removing the tape.

"It's a good thing, Blackie, that you caught it," Cardinal

Kennedy observed. "Now we don't have to worry about them anymore."

I did not admit that only my ·recent assignment as sweeper, now in yet another sense than that of Harvey Keitel, and my obsession with ingenious gizmos and gadgets accounted for this amazing piece of intelligence work. Let them all continue to think that the inoffensive and innocuous little bishop knew everything.

"It is not unlikely that by tomorrow morning a whole new set of bugs will be found in this building," I said. "Our friends are nothing if not determined."

"How many did you find after the press tour today?" Cardinal Cronin asked as we returned to his suite. He poured a splash of Jameson Twelve-Year Special Reserve (now almost twice that age) for himself and Cardinal Kennedy.

I contented myself with a small sip of Bailey's Irish Cream.

"Fourteen," I replied calmly to the cardinal's question. "Of many different makes and varieties. Some like those we have found here. Others much less sophisticated. Our professional sweepers found only four of them. Doubtless, they were well paid not to find the others."

"The media bugged the conclave while they were in there?" Cardinal Kennedy said with a surprised gulp.

"The temptation of an exclusive was too great to pass up. I presume that others will appear before we are locked up—in response to more sinister motives."

"I can't believe it!"

"You saw the bugs in this building, Mick. We are fighting with desperate men and women. They will stop at nothing to keep their power, which they will tell you is God's power to protect His Church."

"Her Church," I corrected him.

"Should we go to the media with this one?"

"I don't think so. It might look like overkill."

I slipped away with my glass of Bailey's in my hand to file another pessimistic report to my virtuous sister.

Dinny

I returned to my hotel suite to work on a dull story about the tour of the conclave area. Most readers of the paper would have already seen the dismal place on television, so there was not much I could add.

I did have a good lead, however:

> Journalists from all over the world swarmed through the conclave area in the Vatican Palace today. When they left, Vatican security services, under the supervision of the Most Reverend John Blackwood Ryan, auxiliary bishop of Chicago, discovered fourteen separate listening devices in and around the Sistine Chapel.

> "A lot of journalists are obviously looking for exclusives," Bishop Ryan observed. "It remains to be seen how exclusive an exclusive is when fourteen different people have it."

> The bishop added that some of the listening devices may have been placed there before the journalists came.

Someone came into my room.

"I'm busy," I informed the housekeeper, as I thought it was.

"I can wait," my old wife and new lover replied. "I'm

in no hurry. . . . Don't keep me waiting too long. I may lose interest.''

I glanced up. Patty was wearing jeans and a blouse, one button too many of which was open, and, as best as I could tell, no bra.

I felt like I had been hit by a bolt of lightning. My strategy had worked. Whether I wanted her back or not, I had her now. I could worry about tomorrow or the next day or next week or next year when they came.

''Be with you in a minute,'' I said as, with trembling fingers, I ran the spell check.

''No rush. I'll straighten up this mess.''

Patricia could not stand mess. By my standards the suite was in reasonably good condition. By hers it was a mess. So while I saved the file and printed out the copy, she bustled around my rooms, smoothing out the bed, hanging up my jacket, stacking my papers and books in neat piles, rearranging the towels in the bathroom.

''Nice place,'' she said. ''The *Times* must like you.''

''They claim to.''

I turned off my notebook.

''Your piece for the day?'' she asked, picking up the output from my cigarette-carton-size portable printer. ''May I read it?''

She actually hesitated, waiting for my permission.

''Sure.''

She read it very quickly. Sex, which I presumed was what she wanted, would always take second place to a story.

''Nice,'' she said, returning the pages to my desk. ''You made a relatively dull day sound fascinating. But then, that's what they pay you for, isn't it?''

Her movements were languid, inviting. I was about to lose my mind.

''So they tell me.''

She sat on my lap, a large and therefore heavy woman. I did not mind in the least. Her breasts, indeed braless, were only a few inches from my mouth.

"The face is all right," she said, tilting my head and examining my face closely with magical fingers. "A little thinner than it used to be, but much more distinguished. I think we'll leave it the way it is."

"Thank you," I gulped.

"I like the hair too. Iron gray mixed with silver. Perfect, but I don't think we'll let it turn grayer. Much less white. It will have to stay the way it is."

"If you say so."

"I do."

This was not my Patty Anne. This was some strange Roman woman who had disguised herself as my former wife.

"And the body is in excellent shape, as I remember it from night before last."

She unbuttoned my shirt and began to explore.

"I want to make one thing clear before we continue, Dennis Michael."

"And that is?"

"This counts for last night, not tonight. When I'm finished here after our siesta, it is back in your court."

"Oh . . . Paola Elizabetta says the only reason for taking a siesta is that you have a lover in bed with you."

"The little brat is right, though she is not talking from experience." She peeled off my shirt.

I reached for both my phones and turned them off.

The stranger who had disguised herself as my wife had comedic intentions. That's why I knew she really wasn't Patricia Anne Marie Elizabeth. For Peppermint Patty, sex was always intense and serious, no joking around. But this woman wanted to make our siesta high comedy.

She shed her blouse and drew my lips to her breasts. "You'd better be good again today, Dinny Mulloy, because I expect only the best from my lovers."

I had no choice but to comply. Very gently I sank my teeth into first one then the other breast. She moaned deeply, on fire with sexual joy.

We had a very pleasant siesta.

After our first romp we lay quietly next to one another, hand in hand, my free hand on her belly—friends, companions, colleagues, who also happened, as chance would have it, to be lovers.

"I have a statement to make," she announced. "Only a statement. I will not answer questions about it."

"Fair enough."

Silence.

I began to stroke her stomach.

"Stop that! I have to make my statement.

"Make it, then!"

"No questions or discussion?"

"Absolutely not."

"Well . . . I love you, Dennis Michael Mulloy. I have always loved you since the first time I saw you in that run-down sports bar in New York. I will always love you. Dummy that I am, I let you get away once. I'll never make that mistake again.

"Oh."

"No questions." She rolled over on top of me, five feet ten and a half inches of solid woman, enough to take one's breath away even if we weren't both naked. She assaulted my lips with fierce kisses, to make sure that I didn't ask questions.

I was in no position to argue.

In the back of my head, however, I noted that she had not given me any choice in the matter.

When I woke up, it was after seven. She was gone. But she'd left a note:

"Must have supper with another one of my lovers. See you later, I hope."

Dinny

I lay comfortably in my bed. My siesta had lasted several hours longer than it should have. I knew I should get up and order myself some supper. I needed to restore my energy. The reckless harlot who had invaded my room under the pretext that she was my former wife had exhausted me. And she'd left a note saying that she expected more of me later in the night. How had I got mixed up with such a woman?

I also wondered what she could possibly see in me. I had wondered that the first time we fell in love. Now the puzzle was even greater: Why risk a second time with me?

Rolling over in my bed, I tried to dial room service and realized that my phone was off. I turned it back on, dialed room service again, and ordered pasta, *bistecca fiorentina*, several slices of salami, and a dolci. No, I didn't want any vegetables. Make it two plates of salami and two dolci.

I turned on the lights. Despite the rumpus that had occurred earlier, the suite was spotlessly neat. Someone had cleaned up everything but the rumpled, sweat-drenched bed sheets. That was part of the woman's disguise, the sort of thing my real ex-wife instead of this voracious impostor might have done.

Why hadn't housekeeping awakened me to pull down my bed for the night?

Perhaps someone had posted a DO NOT DISTURB sign, one of those warning cards that appeared in six European languages, Japanese, and two Arabic scripts. I better get out of bed and take it off the door before my dinner came.

I struggled out of bed, threw on a robe that someone had thoughtfully left on a chair next to my bed, opened the door to my parlor, and removed the card. She had probably put it on my door, not when she left, but when she'd come in.

I was still groggy and bemused. I should take a shower, but only after dinner.

Though I tried to explain to myself that the demon woman who had played with me wasn't really my wife, I had to admit that she was. Totally transformed, liberated, hungry, but still undeniably Patty Anne. The woman who yesterday at breakfast had insisted that ours was only a one-night stand had assaulted me in the privacy of my room and driven me out of my mind. What was going on?

It was an interesting academic question, but I didn't care much about finding an answer. I wanted more of her wanton abandon. Afterwards, whenever that might be, I would try to figure it all out.

Right.

I was sitting there, working on a story, and she had come in and overwhelmed me.

Story? I had not filed it. There was still time, but not much of it. I'd better send it off. I dashed over to my printer: The story was gone.

Had she stolen from me? What would have been the point of that? It was not all that important a story.

On the top of my tiny printer I saw an envelope with the Hassler letterhead. I tore it open. Inside was a note written on a sheet of Hassler notepaper in large womanly letters, Peppermint Patty's handwriting.

Dinny,

I don't know whether you're going to wake up before tomorrow morning. So I'm faxing your piece off to the paper. I found their address in your address book.

Love,

Patty Anne.

She was back in my life, all right. In full sail!

Well, so what?

Had I not won my wife back as I had threatened to do? Or had she grabbed me as I drifted by?

Or did it matter?

Would it last?

I refused to think about that question. Better that I eat my dinner, which room service had just set up in the parlor.

I devoured it like a man who had not eaten a good meal in weeks.

After I had polished off the second dish of ice cream, the phone rang. The hotel phone, not my magic cellular phone.

"Mulloy."

"Deeny?"

"Yes?"

It sounded like Paoli but not quite.

"Tonia."

"Yes, Tonia."

"I have some material for you. You will find it interesting."

"Ah."

I clearly was not supposed to ask what the material was.

"Paola Elizabetta does not know about it. Ricki knows I'm calling you, but he does not know precisely what the material is."

"I see."

"You wish this material?"

"Certainly."

"I will meet you at twenty three hundred on the Ponte Sant'Angelo."

"All right."

"You know where that is?"

"At the foot of the Castel Sant'Angelo."

"Excellent. I will be close to the opposite side of the bridge, near the Via di Banco Santo Spirito. I will find you."

"All right."

"Come alone. Make sure no one follows you."

Perhaps Tonia had read *All the President's Men*.

"Yes."

I put down the phone, thought about my shade and how to lose him, and dashed into the shower. I was wide awake now, all thoughts of sex temporarily suspended. That could wait till later. Now all I could do was smell the smoking gun.

Wearing dark slacks and a dark blue windbreaker, I popped out of the hotel. The clouds had rolled in from the Mediterranean. The night was dark and cool. Sure enough, my tireless shade was waiting for me. Casually I walked down the Spanish Steps and into the Metro. He kept close to me.

Didn't the man ever sleep?

I boarded the A line train and took it west toward Flaminio and the Piazza del Popolo. My shade stumbled into the same car. Just as the doors were closing at Flaminio, I jumped out and ducked behind a pillar. I saw his handsome, wasted face glued to the window as the train rushed past. I hurried over to the other side of the station and boarded the eastbound train. Let him think I wanted to go east.

I got off at Barberini, the stop beyond Spagna, and quickly walked to the Via Veneto. The beautiful people had long since left the street. But the tourists didn't know it yet. I mixed in the crowd, walked toward the other end of the street, spotted a cruising taxi, and asked the driver to take me to San Pietro.

There was no moon glowing over the Basilica but the floodlights still outlined it against the sky. Nice place, but the product of an earlier financial scandal.

I still had fifteen minutes to spare. I walked quickly down the Conciliazione toward the Tiber. The Castel Sant'Angelo was illuminated, but not the bridge beneath it. At the other end, where it fed into the Via di Banco Santo Spirito and then to Corso Vittorio Emanuele, Rome's fashionable shopping street, it seemed quite dark.

I glanced back repeatedly. I had lost my shade.

There were barriers at both ends of the bridge to block vehicular traffic, but pedestrians, even at that late hour of the night, poured across it—mostly tourists approaching the Castel and San Pietro, both shining against the night sky. Or young lovers who found the bridge a useful place to hold hands and to kiss, in the relative safety of the courtyard of twelve angels Bernini had sculpted on either side of the bridge.

Who was I on this day of all days to be critical of young lovers?

I walked to the other end, found a place on the rail facing upriver to lean in relative privacy, save for the massive angel who loomed above me, and waited.

I figured that no great harm would be done by praying to the angel. So I did.

Precisely at the time the bells rang eleven o'clock, I heard a voice next to me.

"Deeny?"

"Tonia?"

"Sì."

She was wearing slacks, a trench coat, and a slouch hat, her gender indistinguishable in the dark.

"These are the papers." She slipped a packet into my hand.

"Thank you."

"They are what you are looking for."

"Wonderful."

"I cannot tell you how I found them, but I have violated no moral laws."

"Naturally."

"As I told you, Paola Elizabetta knows nothing of this. My Ricki knows only that I am bringing you some documents. Wisely, he does not speculate."

"Good."

"You are a good man. I know you will tell no one."

"No one."

"Good night, Deeny."

In a few seconds she was gone, as though she had disappeared into the night.

I slipped the packet into my belt and held it through the pockets of my windbreaker. I shivered in the cold but the packet made me feel warm. The smoking gun!

I turned to walk the few yards to the east bank of the Tiber. Suddenly, a rushing figure hurtled across the bridge, bumped into me, knocked me to one side, and rushed on toward the Corso.

What the hell!

I had caught a glimpse of his face and recognized him from somewhere. Who was he?

I followed after him into the Corso and then remembered who he was—the kid with the burning eyes who had bumped into Paoli on the bridge to the Good Humor train at Fiumicino. Was he chasing her mother?

As I watched him he turned off on a side street, then reappeared, hurried back to the Tiber, looked around in confusion, and then recrossed the bridge. He seemed lost in the night, not so much trying to find someone as trying to find where he was. On the other side of the bridge, he turned around as if to orient himself and then walked south toward Trastevere.

I figured Tonia was safe by now. But I didn't like the kid. I would keep my eye open for him again and turn Niko and company loose on him.

I walked along the east bank of the Tiber, picked up the Via Clementina, which led to the Via Borghese, and then the Via Condotti to the Piazza de Spagna and up the Spanish Steps. Even at midnight on a cold night, crowds of people, many of them shivering, were sitting on the steps or leaning against every available leaning post. My shade was waiting for me in front of the Hassler, having done the only sensible thing by returning to his lair. I walked by him and into the hotel.

I could barely wait till I got to my room to open the

packet. Hastily I went through a sheaf of maybe twenty papers. Even a quick glance showed that they were copies of documents from the extraordinary section of the APAS and that they listed Vatican investments made through the International Agricultural Bank of Holland in Den Haag. The losses of the Vatican investors in derivative trades seemed to total almost half a billion dollars, a fifth of their endowment!

Bingo! The smoking gun.

Where should I hide them? Not in the safe of the hotel. A fat enough bribe might make them available to anyone. The safe in my suite would do for storing jewelry, but a rogue CIA agent would have no trouble blasting it open if he thought it necessary. I could hardly walk around with the documents on my person. Any place I might hide them in my suite would be an easy target for even an inept shade.

Then I had a brilliant idea.

I sat down and memorized the key facts with the help of an obscure code that I jotted down on a piece of notepaper. That would be enough to write the story. Then I called New York on my magic phone and got the boss.

"I've hit pay dirt."

"Figured you would."

"I'm sending you the documents to back it up."

"How?"

"FedEx. There's a box right around the corner. Hang on to them till I file the story. If anything happens to me, if I disappear or something, break it wide open."

"Dinny, I don't want you taking chances, you hear?"

"I hear, and by sending you this stuff I am eliminating the chances."

That's what I thought then, anyway.

"I still say no risks."

"Fine, I don't plan to take any risks. They're for your eyes only till you hear from me—one way or another."

I wrote a couple of sentences on a sheet of notepaper to

explain what the sheets were about and that a rogue CIA guy named Peter Rush was tailing me. I put the whole batch in a FedEx envelope, addressed it to the boss at the paper, put the paper's account number on it, and sealed the envelope.

Now the only problem was my shade. I had a hunch, however, that he did sleep at night. I looked out the window. No sign of him. Perhaps he had gone to ground for a couple of hours.

Hiding the FedEx package in my jacket again, I casually drifted out. No sign of him in either direction. I ambled toward the FedEx box. Next pickup at 6:00 A.M. For the morning flight to New York. I walked by the box, glanced around in both directions. No one in sight, no one watching me. I shoved the package into the box and drifted away. No one watching.

Even if they were watching, the FedEx box was built like a fort. They would have to blast it open.

I strolled back toward the Hassler and reached for the key in my pocket. Two of them, actually. One to my room. The other?

To the room of that abandoned woman that claimed to be my wife.

I had forgotten her in my excitement over the smoking gun. Shame on me. What time was it? Almost one o'clock? Too late?

Never too late. I walked into the Hotel de la Ville, waved my key at the concierge and the security guard, and strode up the stairs to the first floor.

I was on a roll. Why stop now?

Patricia Anne

What are you doing here at this hour of the night? You have no right to come into my bathroom when I'm taking a shower. A key only gives you access to the bedroom, and only when I want you. No way does it give you the right to try to force your way into my shower without asking.

No, it's too late at night. I've had a hard day. No, it's too late to ask. Please go away. I don't care whether you're already naked. I said *go away!*

You've already had enough of me for one day.

I disagree. You can too have enough of me. Who do you think you are?

My lover? Don't be silly!

Please don't touch me that way . . . well, you're already here. So I suppose it's all right. Next time give me some advance warning. You do have a phone, don't you?

Oh, Dinny, I'm talking like a fool again. Yes! Yes! I love it! Don't stop! You can come into my shower with me anytime you want! I love you so much! Don't stop! Don't ever stop!

Dinny

Our first love in our new relationship had been healing. Our second had been comic. The third time turned out to be sweet and tender and nostalgic. Bishop Blackie's rubber band had snapped us firmly back in place. For the time being, anyway.

This new wife of mine was insatiable. That was all right, so was I.

I knew why I was, but I couldn't figure out why she was.

I was awakened in the morning, the woman in my arms, by a ringing phone. I reached for it.

"My house." She laughed, beating me to it.

"Yes, Dee Dee. Sorry, I overslept. Hard day yesterday . . . what! . . . My God! Yes! I'll be right down! It finishes him, I suppose."

She hung up and turned to me, her eyes wide with horror.

"It's on the AP line and in the conservative papers. Don Luis was married when he was twenty years old. In a civil marriage in Valencia. This will destroy him, won't it?"

I shook my head, trying to clear the cobwebs from my brain. "I guess so."

Patty was dressing hurriedly. "Forgive me for running, but—"

"I understand."

Another telephone ring.

"McLaughlin. . . . Yes, Bishop Blackie, I've heard. It's terrible, isn't it? He's having a press conference at the Spanish College at ten? Before the General Congregation? Surely we will be there. In our earlier broadcast, we'll say that he has yet to tell his side of the story. All right? . . . Dinny? No, Bishop, I don't know where he is.''

She grinned at me mischievously.

''Sometimes he's eating breakfast in his hotel about this time. I'll look and see if he's there. I'll give him the message.

''What? I should remember that Saint Peter was married? The first pope? How do we know that? Jesus cured his mother-in-law? Well, that's pretty good evidence, isn't it? Thanks for calling. Yes, I'll look around for my husband, er, ex-husband, whatever he is. Bye.''

She hung up. ''Did you get the drift of it, Dinny?''

''Their third shoe. They must be terrified to have dropped it so soon. Let me use the phone.''

I dialed the bureau. Sure enough Paoli was there.

''Deeny, I have been calling you!''

''I was in the shower. I've heard the news. Don Luis is having a press conference at ten at the Spanish College. I hear there's more to the story. You know where that is? OK. Pick me up in forty minutes. Don't cry, kid. It's not over till it's over.''

Patricia kissed my lips, patted my cheek, and rushed out the door.

A P

Menendez Marriage Revealed

Rome.

Italian newspapers this morning published a document purporting to be the record of a civil marriage between Luis Menendez and Maria Elena Bustamente in Valencia forty-four years ago, both were students. He was twenty years old and she nineteen. Apparently he is the same Luis Menendez who is now the cardinal archbishop of Valencia and has been prominently mentioned as a leading candidate in the papal election next week. The stories say nothing about the present whereabouts of Ms. Bustamente. Cardinal Menendez was unavailable for comment this morning. The papers reporting this news assume that it will end his candidacy, which has been widely supported by European and North American cardinals. It is also expected that he will also be forced to resign from the College of Cardinals.

CNN

PM: . . . the cardinal has not yet replied to the charges, but he has scheduled a statement at ten this morning at the Spanish College. CNN will cover it live.

In fairness to the cardinal, the papers that carried this story are the same ones which reported a financial scandal in Valencia during his administration, when in fact he inherited the scandal from his predecessor and cleaned it up immediately. We should withhold judgment until the cardinal himself responds.

ANCHOR: Will this end his chance of being pope, Patty?

PM: It's hard to tell yet until we have the full story. It certainly won't help.

Patricia Anne McLaughlin, CNN, Rome.

Dinny

$\mathcal{I}$ watched CNN from the lobby of the hotel while I waited for Paoli and the car.

Her eyes were red when I bounced into it.

"I have been unable to reach my parents. They would know," she sniffed, "but they are in court today."

"I just saw my ex-wife on television. She pointed out that it was the same papers who phonied up earlier charges against him. We have to wait to see what he says out at the Spanish College."

She nodded. "I will not believe he did anything wrong."

"A lot of us do foolish things when we're turning twenty, Paoli."

"Bah! I never did. Sometimes I wish I had."

Dinny

$\mathcal{I}$ found my wife near the CNN van in front of the Spanish College. We were there along with half a thousand other journalists waiting for the promised statement by Cardinal Menendez. She and my girl guide embraced like long-lost friends. Paoli quickly looked from one to the other of us and smiled triumphantly.

Little brat.

"They're saying that he will have to announce his resignation and go into a monastery for the rest of his life. Do your parents know anything, Paola Elizabetta?''

''I cannot find them. They are both in court.''

''This is a time,'' Patty Anne said with a melancholy shake of her head, ''when I hate being a reporter. We're in a feeding frenzy. Look at the eagerness on all these faces. We can nail a cardinal to the wall this morning; great story, right?''

''Nail him to a cross,'' Paoli said bitterly.

''I kind of doubt it,'' I argued. ''Note over on the fringe of the crowd an almost invisible little man wearing a Chicago Bulls jacket. I don't think he'd be here for a wake.''

Promptly at ten, Cardinal Menendez emerged from the door of the college and stood at the top of the steps while a microphone was set up. He was wearing a simple black cassock and looked grim and solemn, perhaps a priest ready to say a funeral Mass for members of his family. He carried a manila folder in his hand. A group of seminarians followed him with large piles of paper.

He tapped the microphone to make sure it was working.

''I will speak in English,'' he said, ''because that is the international language. I'm sure others can translate what I have said. I will make a statement but I am not yet ready to answer any questions. Perhaps later.''

CNN

(Cardinal Menendez is standing solemnly on the steps in front of the Spanish College, delicate blue sky in the background, flowers everywhere. He carries no manuscript or notes.)

LEM: This is a very painful moment for me. Agonies from my past which are with me every day now almost overwhelm me. I am shocked and dismayed by the use that has been made of my personal tragedies.

Nevertheless, I must say something to you. I will talk of several documents I have here in this folder. When I am finished my young colleagues will distribute copies to you.

You have doubtless seen in some of the Italian papers this morning a photocopy of the civil marriage certificate issued to me and Maria Elena so many years ago. As the Spanish journalists here could doubtless tell you, in Spain many of us are married civilly for financial and inheritance reasons even if we also intend a religious ceremony.

(Murmur in the crowd.)

The custom in our country is to have a quiet civil ceremony on the afternoon before the church wedding. It is not unlike—in the United States—obtaining a marriage license.

I have here a copy of the marriage certificate of Maria Elena and myself to show you that we did receive the sacrament of matrimony the next day.

(He holds up the certificate. Camera zooms in on it. It looks official but the words cannot be read.)

My second document is the baptismal certificate of our daughter, Maria Rosaria, who was born thirteen months after our marriage. I emphasize thirteen months.

(His voice is low now and deeply melancholy, as though he is reciting a funeral dirge.)

I add that whoever is responsible for printing the first document this morning certainly had access to the rest of these documents and must have deliberately chosen to omit them.

The third document in my file is one that still brings great sadness to my being. It is a news story recounting the death of my wife and daughter in a plane crash at the Madrid airport during a thunderstorm. They were on their way to the Costa Brava for a brief summer vacation. I was to join them the next day. Like many wives of our generation, Maria Elena did not believe both parents should fly on the same plane.

(He looks down for a moment and fights to control his voice.)

In case there is any doubt about this story, I also have in this file copies of their death certificates. Three years later I went to the seminary. The reasons for this decision need not be detailed this morning. I was not, however, motivated by despair. I do not, incidentally, travel with these documents. They were faxed to me from Spain within this hour.

(He pauses again and takes a deep breath.)

The papers this morning claim that the fact of my marriage is a "startling revelation," if I translate the Italian properly into English. One can have a revelation, however, only when something is secret. The fact of my marriage was never a secret. To confirm that, I have a newspaper story from the day of my appointment to Valencia which mentions my wife and daughter. My marriage was something I never discussed at length until today. But neither did I try to keep it a secret. Here is the final document, an excerpt from my "official" biography in which my marriage, my child, and the death of my wife and child are explicitly mentioned. I doubt that there is a Spanish churchman who is unaware of it. Little was made of it because I chose for reasons of personal taste not to make much of it. I cannot imagine that the pope was unaware of it when he sent me back to Valencia from Salamanca.

I therefore feel that there is nothing for which I must apologize. One does not apologize for receiving a sacrament, even if it is a sacrament which most priests do not receive.

In conclusion, I do not wish to answer any questions at this moment, not because of grief, though I will grieve all my life for the losses on that terrible day. Rather, I remain silent until I can be confident that I am in better control of my anger than I am at the present moment.

Thank you.

(Cheers and applause.)

(Cardinal turns and, ignoring the scores of questions which are being hurled at him, walks slowly back into the Spanish College. Seminarians distribute copies of his file.)

PM: Well, you've just heard Cardinal Menendez's version of the story from his own lips.

It remains to be seen what impact both the so-called revelations this morning in right-wing papers will have on his chances of being elected pope in the conclave, which begins next week. . . .

One can hardly blame the cardinal for being angry. There is apparently no trickery too vile, too dishonest, too evil for his opponents to stoop to. If I may speak again as a believing, practicing Roman Catholic, these men are a disgrace to our Church. For them to continue their hold on power would be intolerable.

Patricia Anne McLaughlin, CNN, in front of the Spanish College, Rome.

Dinny

The woman is, I think, furious. Most appropriately, if I may say so."

I was startled by the voice. Without my noticing it, Bishop Blackie had materialized at my side.

Reporters were running in all directions trying to get to telephones to call in their story. I had plenty of time to meet a deadline. I wouldn't sit down at my notebook until more of the events of the day played out.

"At least not at me," I said.

"I presume that phase has finished."

Now what the hell did he mean by that? Had he read something in my eyes as I watched her wrap up? Like adoration?

None of his business either, him and his damn rubber band. Anyway.

Patty joined us and, of all people, hugged the little bishop.

"I hope I didn't go too far, Bishop Ryan?"

"Hardly."

"Dinny?"

"My eyes were wide with admiration and adoration!"

She blushed, as she was wont to do.

"It has been called to my attention," the bishop continued, his kindly blue eyes blinking rapidly, "by usually unimpeachable sources, that when Cardinal Menendez y Garcia walks into the General Congregation this morning, he will receive a standing ovation from most of the cardinals present. It has also been called to my attention by the same highly reliable sources that he might answer a few questions when he comes out of the General Congregation."

"I'll be there." Patty grinned.

"So, I believe, will I be there," the bishop went on. "Moreover, it is altogether possible that I will entertain at lunch in the Borgo one or two journalists who might want some background briefing about the sexual behavior of popes, should anyone be interested. You know the place I mean, Principessa?"

"Naturally, Monsignore. I should make a reservation for four in a private dining room?"

The bishop seemed to count heads to make sure that the three of us plus him made four.

"Excellent idea, Principessa. Now I must return to the Nordamericano to assure Milord Cronin that what he saw on television really happened."

"You think, Bishop, that this will help or hurt Cardinal Menendez's candidacy?"

"Just now I wouldn't want to be the bright publicist who thought of the idea of this morning's revelations, even if he happened to be, as I think not improbable, the director of the sala stampa."

That idea had not occurred to me before. However, it figured.

"I will see you shortly at the Vatican. Oh yes, and if I may venture a rare personal opinion on these matters, the Principessa's word to describe those responsible for this cruelty is most appropriate. They are indeed pigs."

CNN

PM: This is Patricia Anne McLaughlin again with a special report from Rome. We are standing outside the hall where the cardinals meet every morning. We are hoping to get some hint of how the other cardinals reacted when Luis Emilio Cardinal Menendez y Garcia entered the hall this morning.

(Cardinals appear on screen walking out of the meeting.)

PM: I see Sean Cardinal Cronin of Chicago, who is usually willing to comment on these meetings. . . . Cardinal Cronin, good morning!

SC: (charming as always but looking dead tired) Good morning to you, Patty Anne.

PM: Can you tell us how the other cardinals reacted when Cardinal Menendez entered the meeting hall this morning?

SC: Delighted to. They rose and gave him a tremendous ovation. You must have heard it out here.

PM: We did, but we weren't sure. . . . Could you estimate how many cardinals rose?

SC: A lot more than two thirds plus one. Incidentally, your friends at the sala stampa won't tell you this.

They're still too angry that their clever little plot back-fired.

PM: Are you hinting, Cardinal, that the sala stampa is behind these ''revelations''?

SC: No, I'm not hinting it. I'm asserting it as a fact of which I am very confident. We know who these reporters are and we know their relationship to the sala stampa. And you can tell them I said so.

(Strides off camera.)

PM: Chicago's Cardinal Sean Cronin just accused the Vatican press office of orchestrating the attacks on Cardinal Menendez. Now I see Cardinal Menendez himself . . . Don Luis, may CNN have a word with you?

LEM: (smiles wanly) Surely, Doña Patricia.

PM: (flustered) How do you feel after the standing ovation from your fellow cardinals?

LEM: I feel much better. Exhausted but reassured. The cardinals were very good.

PM: (getting a focus) Do you still miss your wife and daughter, Cardinal?

LEM: (shrugs) But of course. I miss them every day. How could I not miss them? Love like that never dies.

PM: Do you think that God permitted their death so that some day you would be pope?

LEM: (sighs) I gave up long ago trying to understand the crooked lines of God. I know that he loves me and Maria Elena and Maria Rosaria. That is enough.

PM: You think of them every day?

LEM: Certainly. They are my wife and daughter. (Opens his breviary.) I carry their picture in here so that I will pray to them every day.

(Shows faded black-and-white photo to PM.)

PM: A very beautiful woman and a lovely little girl.

LEM: Yes, aren't they? I prayed to them with special fervor this morning so I would not lose my temper. They helped me, I am sure.

(Puts picture back in his prayer book.)

PM: (fighting her own tears) The first pope was married, wasn't he, Cardinal?

LEM: (familiar charming smile returns) San Pietro himself, you mean? Yes, he was.

PM: One more question, Cardinal. The archbishop of Chicago just suggested to CNN that the sala stampa was behind these series of "revelations" about you. Would you comment on that?

LEM: (His lips tighten, perhaps dangerously.) I hope that is not true, but if Cardinal Cronin says so, he must have good evidence. It is very sad.

(He slips away.)

PM: Thank you very much, Cardinal Menendez. . . . Now I see John Cardinal Meegan of Miami Beach. Cardinal Meegan, may CNN have a word with you?

JLM: I'm always happy to talk to an employee of my good friend Ted Turner. I am usually called John Lawrence Cardinal Meegan, by the way.

PM: (hardly intimidated) Sorry, Cardinal. Might I ask you what effect you think these so-called revelations about Cardinal Menendez will have on the conclave next week?

JLM: (flutters hands) Well, Patty, I certainly cheered this morning with all the others for the cardinal. He's a fine man and I think the revelations this morning gave the wrong impression. I certainly didn't know about the marriage. It might have helped if he had been more forthcoming about it earlier. We can hardly elect a man who was married, however validly, as pope. It would shock the good Catholic people and suggest that perhaps the celibacy requirement would soon be abolished.

PM: Do you think many cardinals agree with you on this point?

JLM: Oh, I think most of them would. The Church is not ready for a married pope at the present time.

PM: Even if his wife died more than four decades ago?

JLM: That is not the point.

PM: What is the point, Cardinal?

JLM: (impatiently) The point is that he has not been a lifetime celibate. The Catholic people expect their pope to be a man who has had no carnal knowledge of women.

PM: (almost chokes on that) But we know from the Bible that Saint Peter, the first pope, was married, because Jesus cured his mother-in-law.

JLM: (impatiently, hands fluttering wildly) Well, Patty, Catholics have always believed that after Saint Peter was named head of the Church, he took a vow of celibacy and abstained from carnal knowledge of his wife. Or she may have already died. Besides, those were very different times. What was perhaps acceptable then would certainly not be acceptable now.

(Cardinal, visibly upset, leaves camera. Blackie Ryan drifts into view, looking befuddled. However, those who know him would suggest that he only crosses the vision of a camera when he wants to say something. He has exchanged his Bulls jacket for a black suit with clerical collar.)

PM: Here's Bishop John B. Ryan of Chicago, an auxiliary to Cardinal Cronin. Bishop Ryan, may we ask you a few questions?

JBR: Possibly.

PM: Cardinal Meegan has just suggested to us that Saint Peter was not married at the time he became the first pope because his wife was already dead and because he took a vow to abstain from carnal knowledge of women after he was named pope by Jesus.

JBR: (blinking as if confused) Oh, that is what we were told as a matter of piety in grammar school. But I don't think that those positions will stand up to the test of what we know about history. Surely his mother-in-law wouldn't be living in Peter's house unless his wife was still alive. And a vow of celibacy would have made no cultural sense at that time. An occasional holy man like Jesus might have practiced it. But most Jewish young men in that era felt they had an obligation to marry and thus to perpetuate the people of Israel. Many of the early popes may have been married. Celibacy as a condition for ordination to the priesthood only arose later in the Church's history. That is not to say that it is inappropriate, only that it came to be the norm somewhat later.

PM: Cardinal Meegan suggested that times were different then, and while a pope who was married could be acceptable in those days, the Catholic people would no longer tolerate it today.

JBR: I can think of one important difference.

PM: And that is?

JBR: Jesus picked Peter. He doesn't get a vote next week, but Cardinal Meegan does. I'm not sure that's an improvement.

PM: (taken aback by Blackie's blunt reply) Are you suggesting, Bishop Ryan, that the first pope had "carnal knowledge" of a woman while he was pope?

JBR: Doubtless that is Cardinal Meegan's felicitous phrase. Sexual love exists to bind men and women together and to draw them to reconciliation when they quarrel. If Mrs. Peter truly were alive—and the evidence suggests that she was—then I would devoutly hope and pray that she and Peter made love often.

PM: Thank you, Bishop Ryan.

And now we must return to Atlanta. Patricia Anne McLaughlin, CNN, Vatican City.

Dinny

"Your wife was very good this morning, was she not, Deeny?"

"You mean in her interviews?"

We were walking across the vast Piazza San Pietro, angling toward the left side of the Bernini colonnade so as to turn into the Borgo. After the bomb Sean Cronin had dropped on the sala stampa, neither of us had any desire to drop by that place.

I knew that I had to write my story about the smoking gun, but in the excitement of the day, the story had slipped a bit on my priority list. I still had plenty of time.

Paoli was wearing a white suit with navy trim today, still carrying her clipboard, still every inch a professional.

She pretended to be offended by my question.

"What else would I mean?"

"I dunno . . . but, yeah, she was very good. These days Peppermint Patty is good at just about everything."

Paoli decided to play along. "Well, at least you find siestas useful now."

"After Bishop Ryan insisted on world television, what choice do I have?"

"He wasn't talking to you and Patricia."

"The hell he wasn't. That guy never says an unconsidered word."

She pondered.

"Well, perhaps he was. But no one else would know, would they?"

"Only those who know Patty and me."

We entered the narrow Borgo. A young man with a tense

face and wild eyes strode past us. Same guy as last night. What the hell was he up to? I'd have to remember to tell Niko about him. I glanced back. He rushed past my inevitable shadow. If they knew each other, they gave no sign. I doubted they played on the same team. The punk was not cool enough for a rogue CIA agent, even a clumsy one. Still, maybe they did. The honorable company was capable of astonishingly stupid mistakes.

"You both seem very happy." Paoli glanced at me sideways.

"Reasonably happy."

"You must not quarrel again."

"Oh, we'll quarrel every day. But I lost her once and, count on it, Pretty Princess, I don't intend to lose her again. Not ever."

"May God bless you. Both of you," she said fervently.

"And may She protect us both, too. Especially from one another."

CHICAGO STAR

Prominent Nun Opposes Menendez

Rome.

Protest against the papal candidacy of Luis Emilio Cardinal Menendez y Garcia increased today in the light of revelations that he had married as a young man. Even if, as he claims, his marriage was valid in the eyes of the Catholic Church and his wife died forty years ago, many Catholics in Rome are horrified at the possibility of a pope who was once married.

Sister Megan O'Neill, an Irish nun who has given many retreats to bishops and priests in the Vatican, and whose work was frequently praised by the late pope, expressed vigorous criticism of Cardinal Menendez.

"It would be terrible," she said in a rich Irish brogue, "if Catholics would have to live with the fact that a man we call 'His Holiness' had once laid lustful hands on a woman. We expect our popes to be pure and decent men. There's nothing wrong with marriage, of course. It's a sacrament, but not for a pope. A woman waiting in line to be presented to him would naturally fear that he might have lustful thoughts about her."

Sister O'Neill, a trim and attractive woman in her early forties, dressed in a modern religious habit, said that she thought it would be hard to respect a married pope.

"I'd be uneasy with him," she said. "And many other religious women would be, too. We would wonder if he was evaluating us as sexual objects. As I tell my priests when I give them retreats, once a priest becomes involved with a woman, he loses something of his priesthood. He may do penance and continue to be a priest, but he is a priest under a cloud and the laity sense it even if they don't know exactly what the cloud is. It would be horrible to have a pope under a cloud."

There is much discussion in Rome today about the Menendez marriage. But the growing consensus is that the cumulative revelations about him have eliminated any chance of his election. It is expected that his strongest supporters, Sean Cardinal Cronin of Chicago and Klaus Maria von Obermann, will seek another, more moderate and less controversial candidate.

Timothy "Ty" Williams, the powerful American layman who is the head of Save Our Church, even went so far as to suggest that Cardinal Menendez might have been responsible for the death of his wife and daughter. "Damn convenient for him, wasn't it, that he wasn't on the plane that crashed!"

Dinny

The pretty princess was raising hell about our dining room not being the right one. Maeve the Mad and I were left alone for a moment.

"I talked to the kids this morning."

"Good."

"Deirdre, the little brat, asked if you and I were sleeping together."

I was not sure that I liked that. It was none of her business.

"And you told her?"

"I told her that she was a little brat and that it was none of her business. I try not to lie to them, Dinny."

"That's a good practice."

Was I ready for three smart, perceptive, and obnoxious teens? Well, if I wanted their mother, I didn't have much choice, did I?

Besides, they were alleged to adore me.

Fat lot of good that would do.

"You know what she said?"

"Do I want to?"

"She said that was wonderful because she knew you and I wouldn't be content with just a brief affair!"

What's getting into kids these days that they say something like that about their parents? Even if it is true?

"And you said?"

"I just laughed."

"As good a response as any."

"Dinny, we have to talk about this."

"You told me that you didn't want to talk."

"Don't give me that shit. You didn't want to either. Now because your daughter is on to us, I figure we'd better." She drew a deep breath as if the galleon was about to open fire with all guns. "I have to talk, Dinny, regardless of Deirdre."

"I'll be happy to listen," I said with a smile. "Maybe I'll have some things to say, too. But we're not going to waste the siesta this afternoon on talk, are we?"

She grinned wickedly at me and said, "Of course not."

Just then Bishop Blackie materialized, looking bemused as always. So we changed the subject.

Blackie

Milord Cronin lay on his couch looking like he had just been run over by a Roman tram.

He opened his eyes when I entered his suite—after a discreet knock.

"Just taking a little siesta, Blackwood. How are we doing?"

I resolved at that moment to summon our medical team to the Janiculum and find a place in the guest house where they might hide. My sibling, Mkate@LCMH insisted that under no circumstances should he be taken to an Italian hospital if he should collapse.

"The way I hear it," she had commented with more than her usual vigor, "they almost killed the pope. We are not going to let them kill Sean, are we?"

I had agreed, perforce, that no way were we going to tolerate that outcome.

"This unfortunate series of events," I replied to the cardinal's question about how we were doing, "might be made to redound to our advantage. But it has not done so as of yet. It would appear that the other side assumed that Don Luis would respond to the charges, though, as is consistent with their low level of intelligence, they did not anticipate how effective he would be."

"Figures." He closed his eyes.

"You saw your prince brother from Miami Beach lecture Patty?"

"Oh, yes," he said, his eyes remaining closed. "What an asshole!"

"Doubtless."

"Then there was a guy I did not recognize because he wasn't wearing his usual jacket who kind of ate poor John Lawrence alive . . . good line, though. Jesus Christ doesn't vote and John Lawrence does." He opened one eye and grinned.

"Nonetheless, his opinion, I would judge, may have some resonance with a few of the more nervous cardinals and with some conservative Catholics around the world. The idea of a pope who has in fact had carnal knowledge of a woman, to use your colleague's elegant phrase, may appear threatening. Especially since our mutual friend gives every indication of having enjoyed it. I have just briefed *The New York Times* on this matter and I suspect they will take their usual high line. Possibly even another pompous editorial."

"Good for us. A lot of Catholics around the world would think it is not a bad idea, for a change, to have a pope who has slept with a woman, especially in married love."

"I believe our side can make that point. But it would be most useful to back it up with a survey. I would wager that the responses will be overwhelmingly in favor of our mutual friend."

In the rhetoric of Chicago politics, the candidate is often referred to as "our mutual friend." He is even more often referred to in that fashion if he is elected.

"You have already suggested that to your lovely friend at CNN?"

"Oh, yes."

"She's sleeping with her husband again? She seems radiant these days."

"I find that highly likely."

"Yeah, me too . . . but all right." He struggled off the couch with some difficulty. "I'll call Klaus and get the survey ball rolling. It should be very interesting to see the results."

"Doubtless."

The question in my mind now was not whether Sean Cronin would collapse but when. And of what?

Mark

All day, every day, Mark felt that the top of his head would blow off. He was consumed by passionate and, as he thought, justified anger at what was happening. These foolish men and cuntish women were playing their stupid games while tens of thousands of babies died every day. He wanted to kill all of them. Often, especially at night, he would rush through the streets, a knife in his jacket pocket, looking for people to kill. He had not killed any of them yet. He would not permit his passion to sweep from the face of the earth all the lesser evil ones interfere with his primary mission to do God's work. That foolish spick must die first, then he would kill as many others as he could.

He would die a martyr's death, but he had known that all along. He was on a suicide mission. That was all right. After the rejection by stupid and immoral men of his God-given call to be a priest, there was nothing left in life for him. Death would bring peace. He would be welcomed into heaven as a conquering hero, one of the great white-robed army who had died for the faith. His courage would be celebrated for an eternity. He would watch his enemies twist forever in the torments of hell!

So he would kill no one until he killed the new pope and then the cunt from CNN.

Yet, rushing through the streets of Rome with the sharp dagger under his jacket gave him a feeling of vast exaltation. They might ignore him, they might shout rudely after him as he pushed them aside. They did not realize that he held in his hand the power to bring them to their knees and make them beg for their foolish, sinful lives. When he did that, and he might do it soon, he would ask the women if they ever had an abortion. If they lied he might kill them anyway. The world would suffer no loss if one more cunt was eliminated.

Then he would tell himself that such a reign of God's justice must wait. He would grit his teeth and repeat over and over again: *the new pope first.*

So each day he would climb the steps to the roof of his operational point and smile at those he met on the stairs. Everyone would smile back except the girl with the long black hair, who would gaze at him with such loathing as though she could read his soul and detested what she saw.

Perhaps she would have to die before the pope did.

N Y T

Some Popes Did Have Love Lives
Not All Were Lifelong Celibates
One Fathered Child While Pope

By Dennis Michael Mulloy
Rome.

Catholic historians today dismissed the idea that popes in past ages were always "lifelong" celibates, as the opponents of Luis Emilio Cardinal Menendez y Garcia are claiming in the wake of his admission that he married as a young man and fathered a daughter.

Rodrigo Borgia, Pope Alexander VI, almost certainly fathered one of his children, a daughter (by a sixteen-year-old mother), while he was pope. Yet, in terms of his intelligence and skill in administering the papacy, he is ranked as a "good" pope by many Catholic historians. He was also kind to his many mistresses and loved his numerous progeny with a doting father's concern. Living at a time when the nobility firmly believed that they had innate rights to sexual pleasure, perhaps he did not even think of his sexual adventures as serious sins.

He has a bad reputation, one expert said, but he was by no means the worst of the popes.

Other men were widowers at the time of their election and had sons and daughters for whom they had to provide. The first five or six successors of St. Peter were simply important men in the Christian community of Rome. It is unthinkable that, in those times, they were not married or at least had been married, just as Peter was.

The popes of the early Middle Ages, the so called Dark Ages, were little more than tribal chieftains, presiding over a small and barbaric town of only a few thousand people. They lived riotously and died quickly. Some of them were celibates, but many of them were certainly not. Later, when the papacy ruled large sections of central Italy, the pope was thought of and thought of himself as more a temporal leader than a spiritual one. The popes of that era lived in great luxury and spent much of their time partying and hunting as did other late medieval and early Renaissance monarchs. Their attitude was typified by Leo X, the Medici pope, who excommunicated Martin Luther and is supposed to have said after his election, "The papacy is at last ours. Let us at least enjoy it."

It is difficult, according to these historians, to return to the mentality of those years. Most of these papal monarchs were also concerned about the good of the Church they were governing and did their best to rule it well. The distinction between their own temporal powers and the welfare of the Church was one that never seemed to enter their heads. Nor did they seem to understand that their public role as head of the Church imposed restraints on their private lives that did not limit the pleasure of other important archbishops. Many people disapproved of their behavior, but few thought it important—or safe—to object.

In the last two centuries of papal political power, a custom prevailed among many men who worked for the pope's civil service: They would take minor orders early in their careers and postpone till later years ordination to the priesthood. During their time in the lower levels of the civil service they would acquire mistresses who often became, for all practical purposes, common-law wives. Then at a certain point in their live, when it appeared that they might have important careers in the papal bureaucracy, they would accept ordination and pension off their women. Some of these men became popes and, according to rumors of the time, appointed their sons cardinals. One great papal secretary of state of the nineteenth century, Cardinal Antonelli, never accepted ordination to the priesthood and seems to have lead a dissolute life till the very end. Only in this century, after the elimination of the papal states, could one be confident that the popes were lifelong celibates.

Most popes, one historian noted, were celibates when they were popes and many were indeed lifelong celibates; but many were not. No useful service is done to the papacy or to the truth by pretending otherwise.

Cardinal Menendez differs from many of them only in that his marriage was a sacramental marriage and that his wife was not pensioned off but died before he became a priest.

Catholics were not taught these historical facts in the English-speaking countries in this century because pope worship had become so strong that the pretense had to be made that all popes were saintly men. A brief visit to the papal apartments on the top of Castel Sant'Angelo and an inspection of the frescoes would reveal that the Popes responsible for these apartments had sex on their minds constantly.

Nor must we overlook the fact that St. Hormisdas, who died in the year 523, was a widower when he became pope and that his son, St. Silverius, also became pope. Perhaps if Cardinal Menendez's daughter had not been called home as a child, the historical source added with a twinkle in his eye, she would have been elected pope some day.

The Church, he said, is made up of human beings. Popes through the ages have been just as human as everyone else. Some have been great saints and poor popes. Some have been great sinners and effective popes. Most have been good men who struggled to be good popes under always trying and often impossible circumstances.

Dinny

We've got to talk, Dinny." My new lover, who sometimes posed as my old wife, snuggled close to me.

"Talk," I said, moving my fingers back to her nipples.

"I can't talk under these circumstances," she said, squirming happily. "You won't let me think."

"I'm the one that can't think."

We were in my suite with the drapes drawn. We were making the most of the siesta, as I had been advised. Now we were in my bed, though we had not started there. My piece on papal marriages, an ironic counterpoint to our festivities, lay on my desk in the parlor, next to a fax machine that Paoli had produced which would enable me to file my stories to the boss's New York office without risking interception at the hotel fax or the complexities and risks of trying to send it to the paper's computer online.

She had called from the lobby with the machine just as Peppermint Patty and I had begun our amusements. Should I bring it up? she had asked.

No, I had responded with a sigh, I'll come down and get it.

My pretty princess had not even looked at me as she handed over the machine to me and explained how it worked.

"I will not trouble you any more at siesta time," she had murmured as she turned around and left the lobby.

"No problem," I had said.

She had merely sniffed in reply.

I returned to the room and put the machine on my desk. It could wait till later.

While I had been out of the suite, Patricia Anne had stripped down to her panties.

"Little brat is a pest." She had laughed.

"Anticipation increases the pleasure," I had proclaimed as I fell upon her and dragged her, unprotesting, to the floor.

Later she proclaimed the need to talk.

"I did not think a man could be as sweet and gentle as you are, Dinny."

Involved as I was in the processes, I still did not lose my gift for blarney.

"You're such an appealing woman I can't be anything else."

That was surely true. With my wife, my real wife as opposed to this delightful impostor, sex had been a mixture of wild passion and unpredictable shame, with intermittent bouts of compulsive modesty. It was normally a rewarding conquest but rarely an easy one. This new woman, however, gave herself easily and generously. There was no choice but to be sweet and gentle in response. I still could not imagine why she loved me.

"Am I really that appealing?" she said dubiously.

"You really are. You have the kind of appeal that demands a man cherish and treasure you."

It was not flattery or blarney, but simple truth, though it does take a touch of blarney to express a simple truth effectively. Doesn't it?

"I'll have to think about that . . . but still, I am worried about the future. I don't want us to return to the old ways."

Now, at any rate, she was willing to admit that there might be a future.

"We won't," I said firmly, rolling over on top of her. "I lost you once. I don't intend ever to lose you again. Understand?"

She sighed peacefully at the suggestion—absurd, out of the present context—that I had subdued her completely.

"Are we committing a sin, Patty Anne?" I asked. "You had more Catholic school than I did. Is this sinful?"

"Why would it be sinful, Dinny?" she said, stroking my face.

"Because we're not married anymore."

"Well, it would only be fornication. But we are still married in God's eyes. So maybe the State of Illinois would consider us fornicators. But they don't arrest people for that anymore. And God thinks we're still married and Bishop Blackie's rubber band is working the way it should, however belatedly."

"That makes sense," I agreed. "I'm glad, I think."

"It's not you I'm worried about," she said, changing the subject. "That's why I have to talk while there's still time."

"But not here."

"I'll have a hard enough time even if I can think, which I can't now."

"All right, where?"

"Paola Elizabetta says there's a place called Nettuno which is only an hour from here by train and has some very nice hotels right on the beach. She also says nothing ever happens on Saturday and Sunday. We could go down tomorrow morning. We'd only be away for twenty-four hours. And our portable phones would be with us. . . ."

Paoli had suggested that, had she?

The bratty guardian angel never missed a trick.

Instead of accusing the child of reckless interference, I gave in. "Sounds fine with me."

Twenty-four hours on the beach or close to a beach would not do any harm. I could write the story about the Vatican investments on Monday morning and file it so it would appear the day before the conclave.

N Y T

(EDITORIAL)

We continue to be astonished at the high jinks—no other description seems appropriate—marking the papal election campaign in Rome. All elections, even the most sacred, have similar dynamics. Dirty tricks of one sort or another regrettably mark most elections. But the mix of fanaticism, depravity, and disregard for world public opinion that have characterized the attacks on Cardinal Menendez of Valencia the last week have finally become almost comic. His opponents do not seem to be aware of how foolish they seem not only to those who are not Catholic but also to the one billion Roman Catholics who are watching their television sets in disbelief.

The cardinals who assemble in conclave on Tuesday evening must vote their consciences. But they cannot afford to ignore the damage done to the Catholic Church by the deplorable behavior of some of the Vatican insiders this past week. Those who aren't Catholics are astonished. Those who are Catholics must be deeply embarrassed by this display of immorality and stupidity.

Blackie

The weekend, it was alleged, would not be busy, mostly because the Italian journalists all took the weekend off. Absolutely and completely. There would be no more "revelations," no more planted stories, no more rumors of new "compromise candidates," no more alarms and excursions. An appropriate time for Milord Cronin to relax.

But how could he relax with the smoke of battle teasing his nostrils?

Moreover, I was not altogether sure that the dedicated and zealous enthusiasts of Corpus Christi would take the weekend off.

I personally would rather fight the corrupt journalists than the selfless enthusiasts.

The surveys from around the world were showing what one would have expected: Most of the Catholics in the countries where quick surveys were possible thought that an occasional pope who once had a wife was a very good idea indeed.

For understandable reasons, it seemed to me.

Moreover, they now knew enough about the personalities involved in the conclave to strongly support Cardinal Menendez—by a four-to-one margin. More than half of the American Catholics (in the wording of the questionnaire for them I had played a minor role) said they would be "very disappointed" if he were not elected.

None of this was particularly surprising, though it generated considerable skepticism among conservative journalists and among some of our American cardinals, most vocally, as one would have expected, John Lawrence Meegan, who insisted that they should have surveyed only good Catholics.

He did not swerve from this judgment even when it was explained to him that support for Cardinal Menendez *increased* among those who went to Mass every week.

Moreover, we had received positive editorials from *Le Monde, The Times* of London, *Frankfurter Zeitung, The Irish Times, The European, Corriere della Sera,* and naturally, the good and gray (and unbearably pompous) *New York Times.*

Presumably *Time* would continue its slanted coverage in the edition that would appear here on Monday. I could not figure out why *Time* was so opposed to change in the Catholic Church, but it did not matter, given the weight of support on our side.

Editorial writers, in any event, did not vote.

I did conclude, tentatively, that the "revelation" of Don Luis's marriage had finally redounded to our side.

Naturally I had been aware of it. I had read his official biography and discounted the matter because I failed to see how anyone could have turned it into an issue. Such a mistake was unpardonably stupid on my part.

However, at least I had all the facts available when Sean Cronin, in pajamas and a robe, had exploded into my room early yesterday morning. It was then relatively easy to devise a strategy of response. I had counted on the mix of grief and anger that would characterize Don Luis's mood that critical morning. I also no longer feared that he would withdraw from the election at the last moment. The honor of his wife and daughter were now at stake. The men who had violated that honor were not likely to enjoy long and prosperous careers in the service of the Church.

I had, early on Saturday morning, scanned the premises of the Nordamericano and discovered four more bugs of the same make as the day before, somewhat more cleverly concealed but not immune to the sensitivity of Mike the Cop's bug detector. However, the utility that was supposed to find the receiver refused to reveal it. Perhaps it was outside in a car that came by only at what was thought to be key moments to pick up transmissions. Or perhaps the informal weekend truce applied even to that activity.

I had no doubt that Archbishop "Mean Gene" Schreiber was still in the game, knowing now that the only hope for his career was a victory for the other side.

I had assembled a paper bag with those bugs and the ones from the day before, as well as the ones of the same make I had confiscated from the Sistine Chapel, commandeered a car, and borne the package to the sala stampa, empty on Saturday morning, and presented the contents of the bag to the inestimable Father Leonard F. X. Richardson.

"Bishop Ryan . . ." he had said nervously when he discovered my presence next to his desk in the press room.

"I am returning some of your playthings," I had said, peacefully enough. "You perhaps should warn your principals that as quickly as they put them in the Nordamericano we will discover them."

I thereupon had opened the paper bag and poured the twelve insects on his desk, perhaps with more flourish than was absolutely required.

"Have a nice weekend, Father Richardson," I had said, taking my leave.

It will be said by my critics that I was gratuitously nasty and vindictive in that interlude. It will be said that the Ryans of County Tip have always been rogues (though they do not exhaust the rogue population of that justly famous county)[1] and everyone knows it.

Such comments are arguably true. Nonetheless, I thought it useful to contribute to the panic that was doubtless seizing our opponents.

I had recounted this minor incident to Milord Cronin, who laughed longer and louder than necessary.

By that time, I was estimating the probability of a victory for Don Luis at approximately .9 if Milord Cronin was able to walk into the conclave. But, unfortunately, my estimate of the probability of that latter event happening had fallen to between .45 and .5.

Therefore I called Washington and suggested to the good Senator Cronin that she might fly to Rome that evening and bring along her husband, unless he was irrevocably committed to covering the successes of the Chicago Bulls that night. Nora said that she and Ed would catch Delta Flight 148 from JFK in the evening.

I then phoned my sibling Mkate@LCMH in our guest house and suggested that she and her associates join me for lunch at our little restaurant in the Borgo.

---

[1] In the County Tipperary, it is said, all the Ryans are rogues but not all the rogues are Ryans.

Before I left, the cardinal strode into my room to announce that we were having lunch at the same restaurant the next day with the count cardinal of Düsseldorf.

"On Sunday?" I asked mildly.

"That's what he said, too. But there's some details I want to be sure we nail down. A week from today it will be too late."

Then he departed as abruptly as he had come, crimson cape trailing behind him like the tail of a scarlet comet.

I sighed in loud protest.

I reported this incident as typical to my guests a half hour later.

"He is at his limit," I told them candidly. "You will remember that his brother sailed a boat into a storm on Lake Michigan and was never seen again."

"Sean isn't that self-destructive, is he?" my sibling demanded as she consumed the excellent Frascati I had ordered.

"Not quite. But he was tired when he came here. He has this odd resistance to taking vacations. Moreover, he has driven himself without restraint ever since we came. He has indeed put together a winning coalition but in his absence it may pull itself apart, like all disparate coalitions do when their leader disappears."

"Do you think he'll have a stroke or a heart attack?" Ron Stewart asked me.

I shrugged. "My only instinct is that he will collapse in some fashion."

Joe Murphy, a.k.a. Jmurphy@NUH.ed, observed, "That may give us a chance to intervene—if he survives."

"How long will the conclave take, Punk?"

"It is highly improbable that if he is inside it will last more than twenty-four hours."

"So if we can put him back together, medicate and sedate him, we can expect he'll be out shortly."

"Arguably."

"That may be what we will have to do. I would worry about his long-term prognosis if he should blow this conclave."

My virtuous sibling had caught conclave fever.
Why should she be different from anyone else?

TIME

Third World to Block Don Luis

Rome.

A last-minute coalition of Third World cardinals is
meeting in Rome over the weekend to block the election
of Luis Emilio Cardinal Menendez y Garcia as the next
pope. While the Menendez steam roller received a jolt-
ing blow earlier in the week with the revelation that he
had married as a young man and fathered a child
(mother and daughter, fortunately for the cardinal's papacy bid, dying in a plane crash), it still is believed to
command enough votes to come close to the required
seventy-three in early balloting. The Third World coalition intends to run a candidate of its own, most likely
the old (74) but vigorous and respected archbishop of
Goa, Manuel Cardinal deSilva. They hardly expect Cardinal deSilva to win, but they believe that he will garner
sufficient votes to derail the Menendez bandwagon and
open the way for a more moderate, compromise candidate, like Cardinal Monastero, who served for five
years as papal nuncio to Peru and hence knows the
Third World from the inside.

The coalition's members feel that Menendez's em-
phasis on the rights of women will not be understood
in their countries. Moreover, given the importance of
celibacy to distinguish Catholics from others in Third
World countries, they find the fact of his youthful marriage very hard to accept.

"He should have at least told us about it at the very
beginning," one of them said. "Now he casts doubt on

the whole issue of priestly celibacy. We can't accept that for our countries.''

NATIONAL CATHOLIC REPORTER

Progressives Have Doubts About Menendez

Rome.

Many of the Catholic progressives in Rome to present their wishes to the cardinal electors have expressed grave reservations about Luis Emilio Cardinal Menendez y Garcia, the front-runner in next week's conclave.

''He's the late pope with a warm smile,'' said Tad Martin, Jr., chairman of the Gay and Lesbian Catholic Alliance. ''He hasn't taken a forthright stand in support of gay and lesbian Catholics. He has equivocated on the issue of clerical celibacy. For all his visits to the Third World and especially Latin America, he does not seem to understand the absolute necessity of liberation politics. His response to the question of the ordination of women does not reveal any forthright commitment to equality of women or understanding of the holiness of the feminist movement. His marriage, as he describes it, sounds like a typical macho relationship. He opposes anti-Semitism but he does not speak out on the rights of Palestinians. He does not respond to the letters of Catholics for a Free Choice on abortion. We don't need another pope like the last one. If Menendez is elected he will be the last pope with a slick Spanish smile.''

Progressive protesters in the Piazza of St. Peter's are now carrying signs which attack Cardinal Menendez. Some of them proclaim ''Menendez, Go Home!''; ''Menendez, Get Another Wife to Abuse!''; ''Menendez, How Many Gays Have You Bashed Today?''

A coalition of progressive Catholics are preparing a

petition to distribute to the cardinals just as they enter the conclave.

"We want our words to be the last thing they hear before they go in to vote," said Cruz Carmelita Caraffa of Catholics for a Free Choice. "We want them to know that we speak for tens of millions of Catholics whom they have excluded from the discussion."

Dinny

The train ride from the Termini to Nettuno required only an hour. Carrying two small bags each and dressed for a warm day at the beach—shorts and T-shirts—my lover and I departed at 10:25 in the morning.

"A brief second honeymoon?" I suggested.

"No way," she replied. 'If we do have a second honeymoon it won't be brief like the last one. This is a day off for me to talk."

"Fair enough. Do I get to talk, too?"

"Only when I'm finished," she said firmly.

I thought about resisting her claim on a monopoly and then decided against it. Sometimes her demands might be reasonable. Talking was important to her, so she had the right to talk.

But what was it she wanted to talk about? Perhaps she wanted to warn me against drinking again.

We arrived at the little seaside town just before noon. The railroad station was two blocks away from the beach, which also was the main street. Remnants of the walls of the old city stretched in one direction; the marina, filled with boats, and the beach in the other direction. North of the town was the *castello* that had provided the setting for the summer fun and games of Rodrigo Borgia (Alexander VI) and his delightful family. Behind the town was the cemetery for some seven thousand Americans who had died in the folly of the Anzio landing in 1944.

It was a perfect summer day, light breeze, clear sky, a touch of sea mist on the beach, warm air, sailboats drifting slowly on the water, power boats skidding by. No one was swimming, but a bunch of teens were frolicking in the water in a halfhearted game of volleyball, in which most of the young women were topless.

Peppermint Patty was shocked. "Those young women are not wearing bras!"

"Gee, I hadn't noticed."

"They're no older than Deirdre!"

"I don't think she's among them."

"Stop staring!"

"Who's staring?"

"You are! Most of the younger women are topless!"

"It's Rodrigo Borgia's country, after all!"

Also General Mark Clark's, the commander of the United States Fifth Army, who had bungled the Anzio invasion and most other operations in Italy but never was replaced. What would the GI's who had huddled on the beach as the German .88s pounded away at them think if they could see the beach now?

They would probably be as dazzled and delighted as I was.

"Well," she sniffed, "don't expect me to do *that!*"

"I had no such expectations," I insisted. "Besides, I know what your breasts look like."

"*That* will have to be enough."

We registered for our room and, after some argument, persuaded those responsible that we had reserved a seaside room, which they claimed was not on their annotation. When we threatened to storm out, they managed to find a room for us on the second floor.

That's the way it is done in Italy.

The room was clean and neat, if not too big. Sea breezes, slipping through the open sliding door, stirred the transparent curtains. Patty Anne, if indeed it were she, and of that I was not sure yet, stripped off her clothes, stretched luxuriantly, and exulted in the warmth of the air and the smell of the sea.

"I feel revived already," she informed me contentedly.

I had been watching her with my mouth hanging open.

"I feel something else," I admitted.

She whirled and swept me into her arms.

"You're cute, Dinny Mulloy."

"And thoroughly aroused."

"Fine." She disengaged from me, opened one of her bags, and pulled out an orange swimsuit. "But we talk first, OK?"

"OK," I agreed.

"Thank you, Dinny." Still naked, she kissed me. "You're a darling."

"You keep on kissing me that way and I always will be."

"That's what I want to talk about."

Quickly she donned her suit, a two-piece affair that was hardly a bikini but which left no doubt about this woman's many charms (certainly not my wife, she would never dress like that—nor kiss me before she put on her swimsuit).

Naturally, as my girl guide would have said, she hung up our clothes and tidied the room before we left for the beach.

I assumed the suit was intended to call attention to her, as if her flaming red hair, knotted on top of her head, would fail to attract notice. As it was, every eye on the beach turned in her direction as we hobbled on the gravel sand toward the water. And she had left her top on.

"Ouch," she protested. "This sand is no better than gravel. It's not like Long Beach in Michigan."

"Or Oceanside."

We dropped our junk—towels, a rug, the pack of sandwiches and Diet Cokes, and the Cinzano beach umbrella— and anointed ourselves and each other with suntan lotion.

She watched me skeptically as I smeared oil on her belly.

"I'm not sure those rhythms are appropriate for suntan lotion," she said.

"Why not?" I tried to look surprised.

"OK. That's fine and it's also very nice and it's enough for now. More maybe later."

"You're the boss," I agreed.

She tiptoed cautiously toward the water, tested with her foot, and exclaimed happily, "It's not cold, Dinny, come on!"

She dove into the water, came up sputtering, laughed loudly, and began to swim with long, powerful strokes.

"It's great. Like Lake Michigan in June."

That's what I was afraid of.

But not to be outdone by this strange woman who surely was not my wife, I dove in after her, screamed in protest, and then began to swim.

"Scaredy cat." She laughed at me when I had caught up with her.

"I can't touch bottom," I complained.

"Don't worry! I passed my lifeguard test!"

"How long ago?"

"Twenty-two years, but I can still do it. Want to see my dead man's hold?"

"I don't think so. Let's swim back."

Lake Michigan, I thought, was a lot cleaner than the Mediterranean.

We finally pulled ourselves up on the beach, myself winded, herself exultant.

"Wasn't that wonderful!"

"Yes, ma'am."

Everyone on the beach was watching us, no longer merely because of my lover's striking beauty but also because we had been so foolish as to swim before it was the appropriate time. How could anyone swim before May 15? The date mattered, not the water temperature!

"Now we gotta talk," she announced, gathering up our

paraphernalia, after we had dried ourselves. "No, what I mean is I gotta talk."

As we collected all our stuff, I glanced up at the hotel veranda. Our shade had appeared there. I thought we'd lost him at the Termini but he must have found out where we were staying. I started to dislike him intensely.

We wandered over to a far end of the beach with the sea wall behind us and a fence separating us from the hotel next door on the other side. She put up the beach umbrella, arranged the towels and the blanket, put our sandwiches in the deepest shade, and then, still standing, tossed aside the top of her swim suit!

"Patricia Anne!" I exclaimed in surprise.

"I will not be the only overdressed woman on the beach! Even if you don't like it!"

She unknotted her hair and let it fall; it was not long enough to provide any more than a hint of a cover for her breasts.

"I never said I didn't like it."

"You're old enough to know that women like to display their charms as well as hide them, depending on the circumstances and their mood. And you're *not* supposed to stare!"

She sat down next to me and stretched out her legs in contented self-satisfaction.

"What you mean is that I am definitely supposed to stare but to pretend that I'm not staring."

"Whatever," she sniffed.

I picked up the Coppertone 35 sunscreen and began to smear it on her torso. She did not protest. I was very gentle.

"What are you thinking?" she demanded.

I paused to analyze my thoughts.

"I'm thinking how utterly beautiful you are and how vulnerable and fragile. I'm thinking that I can't figure why you still love me. I'm thinking how much protection you need."

I went back to my careful anointing.

"It's strange, Patty my love, I never thought of you as needing protection before. You never seemed to need it at all. But just now I want to protect you for the rest of my life. Does that offend you?''

"I need protection, all right, Dinny. Lots of it. I always have.''

I put the top back on the Coppertone and put it back in the bag.

"You are going to talk now?''

"Yes," she said. "But you're going to have to be patient with me. I'll probably mess it up a couple of times.''

"It's easy to be patient with you, Patty," I said, astonished at the words. It wasn't usually easy to be patient with her.

"No, don't put your arm around me, please. That will make it more difficult.''

"All right.''

She began to make marks on the gravely sand next to her.

"Why didn't you stand up to me?" she exploded. "Why the hell didn't you ever fight back? Why didn't you stop me? Why did you let that bitch therapist and me tear you apart!''

"Well, I guess I didn't know how to fight with a woman and I didn't want to learn—''

"No! I mean, yes, of course! But that's not what I want to talk about. I want to talk about what I did wrong, rub all that out.'' Impatiently she rubbed out the marks on the sand. "I didn't say any of it!''

"All right.''

"What I mean is," she began with renewed determination, clenching her fists and stiffening her shoulders, "what I mean is, why were you such a wimp all the time?''

"I don't think I am anymore, not as bad.''

"Oh, damn.'' She pounded the sand. "That's not the point. . . . No, you certainly are not a wimp anymore. You're wonderful.'' She touched my chest with a quick caress. "I know you're not a wimp now. You've changed. But that's not the point, is it?''

"I don't know what the point is, Patty.''

"How *could* you know what it is when I haven't told it to you?" She punched the ground. "I must try again."

"I'm in no rush."

"The point is that I am a bitch. I've always been a bitch and I always will be a bitch."

Oh.

"That's not a fair description, Patty."

"Yes, it is, damn it." She punched my leg this time. "Oh, I'm sorry, Dinny. I didn't mean to hit you that hard."

"Didn't hurt!"

"I'm trying to say ... I'm trying to say that ... that if ever a woman drove a man to drink, I drove you to drink."

She stopped, exhausted by her outburst.

"Patty, that's not fair, there was a lot more to it than that."

"Damn it, I know *that*." She grabbed my arm and hung on as if for dear life. "But I don't want to talk just now about what *you* did. I want to assume my own responsibility."

"I understand."

"You see," she plunged on, gaining momentum like a beach ball in the wind, "being a bitch was the way a woman survived in our family. Everyone shouted at one another. If they started shouting at you, you shouted back. It seemed to work out, but you had to hide a lot. I ... I really didn't know how else to live. I guess I hoped you would shout back like everyone else did. Only, you didn't."

"I didn't know how."

"*Of course* you didn't know how. But I wanted you to do it just the same. Maybe deep down I figured you'd shut me up and then discover the woman that maybe lurked under the bitch, only, I wasn't sure she was really there. . . . I'm not making any sense, am I?"

"Yes, you are. You're making perfect sense."

"Am I? I mean I thought I was protecting myself from you, but deep inside I wanted you to sweep away the protection and find out who I was. You never did. I hated you for that so I became even more of a bitch.''

''And I ran away.''

''Sure, you did.'' She squeezed my arm. ''But that's not the point. I drove you away, too. I demanded more of you than any woman can reasonably demand of any man. Didn't I?''

''I guess so, Patty.''

''You *know* so. All right, you gave me less than a woman might reasonably demand. Until we both came to Rome and I realized that you'd changed. But that's not the point. I mean, it *is* the point in our lives just now, but it's not the point in what I am trying to say. Does that make sense?''

I extended my arm around her. She leaned against me.

''I fouled up, Dinny. Terribly. We both did, but if I wasn't such a bitch, none of it would have happened.''

''You're not a bitch anymore.''

''That's because you won't let me be a bitch. But I'm afraid—''

''Of what?''

''That I'm incurable.''

''You're not.''

She twisted away from me, turned onto her stomach, buried her face in the towel, and murmured, ''I am terribly sorry and beg you to forgive me.''

I stroked her back with one hand and then rested my hand on the small of her back.

Blarney failed me.

Finally I was able to say, ''Of course I forgive you, Patricia Anne Marie Elizabeth. I forgive you because I love you and always will love you. I expect you to forgive me, too, when I go through my litany of offenses.''

''Oh, I will,'' she said, turning toward me with a wicked grin. ''Definitely. But that will have to wait till tomorrow. I've had enough strong emotion for one day.''

She rolled over on her back and smiled complacently.

"As I said in the bed yesterday, I have no intention of ever losing you again."

"I won't let you sneak away either."

"Fair enough," I said, caressing her belly. "More stomach muscles here than four years ago."

"There ought to be after all the exercises I've done."

"I do resent one thing, however."

"What's that?" she asked, her face clouding.

"For the rest of our lives, you're going to have the moral advantage over me because you apologized first."

She squealed with joy. "I'll never let you forget it. . . . Come on! I need another swim."

She did not bother with the top of her swimsuit. Needless to say, our swim this time stirred up even more astonishment.

"God! This is wonderful!" she exclaimed as we swam out to sea. "I feel like a new woman! Maybe I am!"

"You are," I agreed. "New and much better."

She was not my wife, I was sure of that now. She was someone else, but I was willing to pretend for the rest of my life that she was my wife. So it didn't much matter.

We returned to our umbrella and rested for a few moments to regain our breath after the exertion of our swim. I found that I felt like a new man, too.

"Maybe we ought to go back to our room," I suggested.

"For lovemaking?"

"I thought we might go to church, catch a late afternoon Mass. Thank God for Bishop Blackie's rubber band."

"I thought you didn't believe in God," she said with a mischievous grin.

"Once a Catholic, always a Catholic!"

"I checked the schedule by the concierge's desk before we came out here. There's a Mass at six-thirty. We could do both . . . if you want."

"I think I could live with that."

She pulled on a T-shirt and tossed her swimsuit top into her bag.

"This seems to be the way we do things here on Italian beaches."

"Are you going to tell your daughters that you went topless in Nettuno?"

"*Our* daughters. Certainly not! It is none of their business. They might get the idea that it's all right for them to do the same thing."

She laughed as she said it, which led me to believe that she would in fact do just the opposite.

"The conclave is a great story, but isn't it wonderful to get away from it?" she continued blissfully. "After all that crooked garbage, a gorgeous day on a beautiful beach with a man you have a terrible crush on. That's the way to live, isn't it?"

I hadn't thought about the conclave for hours. I didn't want to think about it till noon tomorrow.

"Crush?"

"Humungous crush. I expect I may never get over it."

She laughed exuberantly. This new partner of mine was exuberantly in love with life. Not bad at all.

We gathered up our stuff and, hand in hand, strolled back to the hotel. We were followed by every eye on the beach. If my new woman noticed the attention she was garnering, she gave no indication of it. But then, if you are an internationally recognized journalist, you are used to public attention, whether or not you're half naked and whether or not you have a hulking, silver-haired companion holding your hand.

I noted that my shade had vanished. I thought nothing about that then. Looking back on it, I should have been alerted to potential dangers.

Dinny

So we made love and went to Mass (in Italian). I thanked God for bringing me this wonderful new wife. I figured blarney ought to work with God even though He could see through it, because it meant I cared:

Thank You very much, just when I was getting old, for bringing me this new wife who will keep me young for a long time to come. You may argue that it is the same old Peppermint Patty, with her moods and her tantrums and her erratic energies. And You can believe that if You want. You can also say that You poured out a lot of Your grace to get us the right therapists and to make us finally admit our contributions to the breakup. I'll go along with the game, if it will make You happy, because I know You like to be happy just like we do. But it's a new model wife You've sent me and I'm very grateful for her.

As You know, because You eavesdrop on our love-making, she's more afraid of the future than I am. Maybe she's right. Despite all the therapy and despite our willingness to admit that she can be a terrible bitch and I can be a total coward, I am confident about the future. Male ego? Maybe. But I have a secret which I won't tell her yet. I figure You wouldn't have gone to all the trouble You did to make the old rubber band snap us back into place unless You really wanted it to happen. So You'll give us the grace we need. I should be the special target of grace because it is really up to me. When I wimp out, the problem starts again. As long as I don't wimp out it will be all right. Won't it? Things got very good again this trip, around when I found the guts to stand up to her and say Stop it, Patty. It won't ever be easy, but it's worth it and I've done all right so far, haven't I? Pretty good, in fact, huh?

Moreover, I've learned how much she needs my love—which, let's face it, is a big help to my male ego. Especially when the woman is someone like Patty.

So I take it for granted that You are going to continue to help me.

If You don't, I'll tell Bishop Blackie on you.

"What were you grinning about all through Mass?" this new woman demanded of me.

"I was bargaining with God."

"Oh?"

"I told him that if he didn't help me to be a better husband than I had been before, I'd tell Bishop Blackie on him." My new wife thought that was hilariously funny. So she hugged and kissed me right in front of the old church, much to the wonderment of the other people coming out.

We ate fresh seafood on the veranda (Patty Anne in an ankle-length blue tank dress under which there was nothing at all), walked the beach in the dark, went back to our room, and sealed our love again. Afterward, I was exhausted. Too much for one day, I told my wife.

She laughed at me.

We ate a late breakfast, swam again (she wore the T-shirt out of the hotel and peeled it off as soon as we reached the beach), sunned a bit, took a ferry out to one of the Pontine Islands, returned for an early siesta, and then caught the three o'clock train back to Rome for the last couple of days before the conclave began.

Blackie

The cardinal looked gray when we walked down from the Janiculum to the piazza and over through the Bernini columns towards the Borgo. It was a hot and humid day and I suggested we take a car.

"Can't do that!" he insisted. "You'll report that to your sister and she'll have more points against me. By the way, I hear she and Joe and the two heart people are on the grounds. Is that true?"

"Arguably."

"You really expect that I'm going to have some kind of attack?"

"Yes," I said flatly. "Odds are ninety percent."

"Nonsense. I never felt better."

But he didn't sound very confident.

"Well," he continued, "at least they're not Corpus people."

I took the precaution nonetheless of ordering the driver to bring the car and follow us both ways.

The session with Graf Von Obermann was yet another review of the votes. The good Teutonic knight rolled his eyes but patiently went through the list yet again.

Including "certain"'s and "probable"'s we were now counting on a minimum of sixty-four votes on the first ballot and a pickup of ten more on the second ballot, which would put us over the top.

"It's going to be a near thing," Milord lamented. "One or two guys could do us in."

"Damn fine thing," I observed, quoting the Duke of Wellington's comment after Waterloo. Neither of them heard me. By "fine" the duke meant "close," as well he should have. I began to think of James Joyce's outrageous word play on Waterloo at the beginning of *Finnegan's Wake*. Anything to kill the monotony of going through the list again. However, it was useful because it kept Milord from going around to the various dwelling places of the cardinals and strangling a few of them.

"Ja, but there are many whom you have listed as doubtful who will come along at the last minute when they see that we are not exaggerating in our estimates."

"We could also lose some of the probables," Sean Cronin said, pounding the table. "I could name a dozen I don't really trust."

The cardinal had estimated at the beginning that we had to win the first morning. If we were short even by one vote at the end of the second scrutiny that morning, our support would ebb.

I agreed that we must peak early but I did not think that a man who came within a couple, or even ten, votes could be denied the papacy. Reading the history of previous papal elections, it was hard to deny the papacy to someone who had a large majority of the votes. Cardinals always wanted to be able to say that they had voted for a winner (and to say it with a clear conscience), and once the movement toward a candidate had picked up steam, a few more would join on each ballot. Moreover, this was different because for the first time world public opinion would put a lot of pressure on them not to offend the watching and waiting spectators. Finally, it was patent to almost everyone that anyone besides Menendez who won would find the papacy an insurmountable burden from day one. His election would very probably be booed in the piazza and around the world. By my calculations, which I kept to myself, most of the Curia would finally jump on the bandwagon because, they would say to themselves, they too were fed up with the Corpus people and did not want to try to govern the Church in a papacy that would be discredited the day it started.

Thus I had estimated that at the most only twenty-five would finally vote against Don Luis. I judged that, more than likely, we'd be out by supper.

I kept silent because my technique of counting only the certain or probable opponents did not suit Milord Cronin's passion for winning. It was not, he seemed to think, the votes we would never get that mattered, but only the votes we would have to get.

He also drank four cups of coffee during lunch.

"Ja Ja," Klaus Maria assured him as we rose from the lunch table, "I will be in touch with all our precinct captains, as you call them. But nothing will be done today. Everyone will have a long siesta."

"I won't," Sean Cronin grunted.

We left the restaurant and headed up the Borgo toward the piazza. Our car followed us at a discreet distance. We turned the corner and walked through the colonnade toward the back route up to the Janiculum on the other side.

We were only ten steps into the steaming piazza when Sean Cardinal Cronin grabbed his heart and with a loud scream fell to the cobblestones.

AP

Cardinal Cronin Collapses

Rome.

Sean Cardinal Cronin, archbishop of Chicago, collapsed of an apparent heart attack in the hot sun of the piazza of St. Peter's this afternoon. A powerful influence in the preparations for the conclave, Cardinal Cronin was a leader in the campaign to elect Cardinal Menendez of Valencia.

He was taken immediately to the North American College on the Janiculum Hill, just above the Vatican. He is being treated by private physicians from Chicago.

There was no immediate report on the cardinal's condition.

REUTERS

Cardinal Reported "Critical"

Rome.

Rumors circulating at the North American College here late this afternoon reported that the condition of Sean Cardinal Cronin is critical and that he is hanging between life and death. He has already received the last rites of the Catholic Church. The cardinal apparently had a heart attack while returning here from a luncheon conference with Cardinal Klaus von Obermann of Düsseldorf. Asked why he was not taken immediately to the Gemelli Clinic where Pope John Paul was treated, seminarians at the college reported that a team of American doctors, concerned about the Cardinal's health, had been in attendance at the college for several days.

C N N

ANCHOR: According to reports we are receiving from our team in Rome, Italian radio is reporting that Sean Cardinal Cronin, archbishop of Chicago, is hovering near death in the North American College in Rome after a massive heart attack in the Vatican on this hot, quiet Sunday afternoon. If Cardinal Cronin should die, the outcome of the conclave, which only yesterday seemed all but certain, would be very much in doubt.

Blackie

I discussed the matter for some time with Herself in the ornate chapel of the North American College. I noted that all our lives are in Her hands and that indeed She was at liberty to take away what She had given us whenever She wanted.

Nonetheless, and despite his terrible record at taking care of his health, it appeared from my purely human perspective that it would be useful if She could arrange to spare him for a somewhat longer period of time, the exact length of which I would leave to Her discretion.

I did not request, I observed to Her, that he recover soon enough to go into conclave, though if that would be arranged too we would also have been grateful. It seemed to me, I said, that She definitely wanted Don Luis to be the next pope and that She could arrange for that outcome any-way she wanted. Personally, I suspected that Sean Cronin absent would have almost as much impact as Sean Cronin present, because cardinals would tend to be superstitious enough to believe that he might come and haunt them if they didn't deliver the expected votes.

On the other hand, it might be altogether possible, I thought, that some of them would say that the cardinal's "seizure," as my virtuous sibling called it, was Her judg-ment on him for his presumptions in attempting to elect a decent pope. It seemed to me that She might want to obviate such a regrettable conclusion.

But, I concluded, as in all such matters, not our will but Hers be done.

I went through variations on this theme for some time, then returned to my room. Almost at once the phone rang. It was my good friend and ally, the Pretty Principessa in tears.

"Deeny and his wife are down in Nettuno. . . ."

"Excellent."

"And they are saying on the radio that he is dying."

"I believe that is somewhat of an exaggeration."

"Someone should make a statement."

"A point well taken. Where are you?"

"Outside in a car."

"In fifteen minutes we will have a statement."

I went to the sickroom where our four doctors and a hast-ily assembled team of Italian technicians and nurses were hovering over the cardinal. I motioned my sibling out of the room.

"How's he doing?"

"Reasonably well, Punk. We've got him sedated, which we should have been doing for days. We haven't got a di-agnosis yet, but I think he'll make it."

"The Italian radio is saying that he's dying."

"That's not true!"

"We need someone to make a statement."

"Like who?"

"Like whom."

"I gather you want me to say something to the media."

"Who better than someone who deals with sick minds?"

She grinned. "I always wanted to do something like that. Let me talk to the gang inside and put something together."

No one ever accused my exemplary sibling of being a shrinking violet.

Precisely fifteen minutes later, said sibling appeared in front of the reporters, silver hair properly arranged, makeup discreetly applied.

As those who know her will testify, Mkate@LCMH is a very attractive woman and, when she elects to be so, extremely charming. She dealt very effectively with the media. The question about her field of expertise came from the principessa. Naturally. My sibling hesitated not a second before she gave her answer. She had now established affability and trust among the reporters. They would believe her.

I introduced her after she was finished to said principessa, who immediately launched a litany of praise of me.

I slipped away, paused at the chapel to thank Herself for Her cooperation thus far, and retired to my room to try to think things out. I called all the precinct captains I could reach and told them of the doctor's statement and warned them that they should not believe any more pessimistic reports. They asked about visitors and I assured them I would let them know.

While I waited for further developments I read the oaths that one must take upon entering the conclave. If one had not known it already from other sources, one would have immediately realized that Paul VI was an obsessive-compulsive deeply troubled by scrupulosity. The cardinals got off easily. They merely had to swear that they would follow all of the pope's rules, to defend the rights of the Holy See, to refuse all secular vetoes, and to keep the whole conclave secret.

The words of the secrecy pledge made interesting reading:

> Above all, we promise and swear to observe with the greatest fidelity and with all persons . . . the secret concerning what takes place in the conclave or place of election, directly or indirectly, concerning the scrutinies, not to break this secret in any way, either during the conclave or after the election of the new pontiff, unless we are given explicit authorization from the same pontiff.

One wonders why the obsession with secrecy. Conclaves in the past had never been that secret. What did the pope fear? Or was it merely that the atmosphere of secrecy that pervades the Vatican as infectious diseases once pervaded the Tiber swamps has become an end in itself?

For folks like me the oath was even more demanding:

> I, John Blackwood Ryan, promise and swear that I will observe inviolate secrecy about each and every matter concerning the election of the new pontiff which has been discussed or decided in the congregations of the cardinals, also about whatever happens in the conclave or place of election, directly or indirectly, and finally about the voting and every other matter that may in any way come to my knowledge.

> I will not violate this secret in any way, directly or indirectly, by signs, words, or in writing or in any other

manner. Moreover, I promise and swear not to use in the conclave any kind of transmitting or receiving instrument, nor to use devices of taking pictures; and this under pain of automatic excommunication reserved in especial manner to the Apostolic See.

I will maintain this secret scrupulously and conscientiously even after the election of the pontiff, unless special permission or explicit authorization be granted to me by the same pontiff.

In like manner I promise and swear that I will never give any help or support any interference, opposition or hostility or other form of intervention by which the civil powers of any order or degree or any group of individuals, might wish to interfere in this election.

So help me God and these Holy Gospels which I touch with my hand.

All of this in the service of the one who said that what was whispered in the chambers would be proclaimed from the housetops, a comment that was as good as a prediction as it was a norm. You can't keep anything secret, so there is no point in trying. Everyone knows how the voting went in the 1978 conclaves, despite Paul VI's rules. They would know this time the day the cardinals came out. Perhaps the new pope would dispense everyone from the oaths anyway.

As it was, however, the conscientious would keep the oaths, and the unscrupulous would ignore them—as they were already planning to do with their bugs. My job would be to try to keep the playing field level, especially against those who thought their careers or their cause was too sacred to be bound by oaths or indeed by any strictures of the moral law.

NYT

Cardinal Cronin's Condition "Serious"
"Resting Comfortably," Doctors Say
Collapse Occurred Near Vatican

By P. E. Oriani

A spokesman for the doctors treating Sean Cardinal Cronin here at the North American College told reporters late this afternoon that Sean Cardinal Cronin was "resting comfortably" after a seizure in the Piazza San Pietro earlier today.

Dr. Mary Kathleen Ryan Murphy declined to characterize the seizure as a "heart attack" and said that the cardinal's condition was "serious but stable."

"We are still in the process of running tests to determine what happened," she said. "We will have another statement tomorrow."

She denied that he had received the last rites of the Catholic Church. The Sacrament of the Sick had been administered, she said, but added that was for people who are sick and not for the dying.

Asked if the cardinal was in good spirits, she replied that he was very happy to still be alive.

In reply to the question of whether he would be able to participate in the conclave which begins 48 hours from now, Dr. Murphy replied, "We shall do everything in our power to see that he does, but now we can make no guarantees."

Dr. Murphy said that she was not a heart specialist

but a psychiatrist and that's why she had been asked to talk to the press.

Dinny

I collapsed on the bed in my suite, exhausted and discouraged, a man who had been disappointed by a difficult trip to a far country, like India. The ride back from the beach had been hot and bumpy, with long and inexplicable delays. I was edgy and tense, ready to blow up at the slightest provocation. The strange woman who claimed to be my wife was in a similar mood, a let down, she claimed, after an orgy of exercise and passion. We agreed not to bother each other on the ride in and to take another siesta in our respective rooms as soon as we got to them. There will be times, she said, when no matter how much we love each other, that either or both of us would need to be alone.

I had agreed and tried not to sound irritable in that agreement. "Human limitations are awful, aren't they?" I had said.

"We'll survive," she said, it now being her turn to be confident and my turn to be doubtful.

We left open an outspoken option for supper and a night together. I felt that I would just not be up to it. The woman was insatiable.

I was only half asleep when the phone rang.

"Dinny?"

"Yes?" I snapped.

"They're saying on Italian radio that Cardinal Cronin died this afternoon."

"Good God, no!"

"We'd better go over there, don't you think?"

"Certainly. I'll meet you downstairs in a few minutes."

I put on jeans and a sport shirt. When I met her I saw that this new woman had chosen the same wardrobe. It was unbearably hot. We had a hard time finding a taxi but at last hailed one at the foot of the Spanish Steps after we had decided to settle for the Metro.

At the Nordamericano the crowd of journalists seemed thin. But the CNN van was parked in the lot, and even from a distance I recognized my principessa leaning against the van. We hurried over. She hugged both of us.

"He is alive," she said. "Do not believe the radio stations. It is Corpus again. They will do anything."

Dee Dee, Patty's producer, appeared. "Thank God, you're here. We have a clip from the press conference. Atlanta wants you to watch it and to go on live at once."

The clip showed a smooth and attractive and utterly credible woman assuring us that Cardinal Cronin was still alive.

"Who is she?" Patty asked as she pulled a light blue jacket out of the van and put it on.

"Father Blackie's sister," Paoli replied. "She is neat, isn't she?"

Patty grinned. "That clan may own the whole Church before this is over."

"Perhaps," the princess said quietly, "they are the Church."

That seemed just then a very profound observation.

"Why don't we try to get her out here for an interview?"

No one thought it was a bad idea.

"Maybe we should request Paola Elizabetta to go in and ask her, if she doesn't mind doing a favor for CNN?" I proposed.

The princess didn't wait for an answer.

Ten minutes later she emerged with Dr. Murphy in tow, a striking woman with a handsome and intelligent face. This, I said to myself, will be an interesting exchange.

"You had a good holiday?" the princess whispered to me as CNN set up the camera.

"Honeymoon, Principessa," I said. "And it was great." She hugged me again. "I am so happy for both of you."

"So am I. As you know, however, the woman is not my wife."

"What!"

"No, she is a clever impostor who looks like my ex-wife, but she's quite different. Much nicer and much *sexier!*"

"You are terrible, Deeny," she said, "Just terrible."

C N N

PM: I am speaking with Dr. Mary Kathleen Murphy, spokesperson for the team of doctors caring for Sean Cardinal Cronin of Chicago, who collapsed in front of St. Peter's earlier today. Dr. Murphy, Italian radio is reporting that the cardinal is already dead. Is that true?

MKM: As my mother, God be good to her, would have said, the wish is the father of the thought. No, he is certainly not dead, far from it. At the present time we do not see him in any danger of dying.

PM: Will he be well enough to enter the conclave tomorrow night?

MKM: That remains to be seen. We certainly hope so.

PM: Wasn't it fortunate that a team of American doctors who know his medical history happened to be in Rome?

MKM: Yes, it was.

PM: You have all the equipment you need to treat him?

MKM: What we didn't have we managed to borrow.

PM: There is no thought of bringing him to a hospital?

MKM: At the present time we see no need of that.

PM: You expect a full recovery?

MKM: With the help of God.

PM: You're a psychiatrist, aren't you, Dr. Murphy?

MKM: (large smile) That's what they tell me.

PM: Does that not suggest that some of the cardinal's problems may be partly psychological?

MKM: (even bigger grin—she's been waiting for this one) No more than everyone else's problems are partly psychological.

PM: We've just been speaking with Dr. Mary Kathleen Murphy, one of the medical team treating Chicago's Sean Cardinal Cronin. She has told us that rumors of the cardinal's death are false, that the team expects a complete recovery, and that it is possible that the cardinal may be able to enter the conclave on Tuesday evening. Thank you very much, Dr. Murphy.

Patricia McLaughlin, CNN, at the North American College, Rome.

Dinny

We went back to the Hassler. I invited this purported wife of mine to dinner on the rooftop.

"I'm not dressed for it."

"On Sunday evening they are tolerant."

"I must pay for my own dinner."

"I'll let you be a colleague until dinner is over. Then you become a wife again."

She laughed, somewhat uncertainly, I thought.

I stopped at my suite to pick up a jacket.

The roof of the Hassler, six floors above the street, is a perfect place to eat—if you or your employer have the money to afford it. You look down the Spanish Steps and then over toward the Tiber and the Vatican and St. Peter's, whose dome shines like a crimson and gold Fabergé Easter egg in the glow of the setting sun.

"How lovely!" Patty exclaimed.

The maître d' and the waiters bowed us across the room to a window view.

"I'm glad I let you talk me into this," she said with a happy light in her eye. "It hasn't been a good afternoon in a lot of ways."

"I know."

"Isn't that Murphy woman a knockout?"

"I won't fight that. She claims the little bishop is a changeling. She calls him 'Punk.' "

"And obviously adores him, like everyone else."

"His damn rubber band."

"Right." She smiled. "His damn rubber band. . . . Do you think the Corpus people are finished, Dinny?"

"I think they've just about run out of weapons. Tomorrow and the next day are probably going to be anticlimaxes."

As it would turn out, I couldn't have been more wrong.

After we finished off our dolci at the end of the meal, we watched the sun set behind the dome. My hand explored her thigh, solid and firm inside her jeans. She merely smiled.

Finally, after I had signed the bill, I took her hand and led her out of the dining room.

"You're my wife again," I said.

"I'm not sure, Dinny . . ." she said hesitantly.

"Yes, you are," I insisted.

She sighed and gave in. "Yes, of course I am sure. How could I not be? All right, husband, drag me off to your lair. You did pay for the dinner and you are entitled to a little pleasure."

Her verdant eyes glowed in anticipation.

Like I said, insatiable.

In the parlor of my suite, I unbuttoned her blouse and teased her breasts beneath a plain white bra.

She held my hand, not so much to stop it as to keep it in place.

"Can we talk a little more, Dinny? There was something I didn't say yesterday that I have to say now."

"Sure," I said as I guided her to a couch, my hand still on her breast. "May I continue to play while we talk?"

"Why not?"

She paused. "This will be hard to say, but I have to say it."

"My feelings won't be hurt."

"It's not that which worries me."

She took a deep breath.

"You're a wonderful lover, Dinny. Sweet and sensitive and tender. You know all my secrets and all my fantasies and all my needs. I fall apart when I see you. My legs turn to water. I want to melt into your arms. I can't wait till I get rid of my clothes and lie in bed with you."

"My feelings aren't hurt yet."

She slapped my arm, very carefully. "Don't be silly. . . . I knew that you were that kind of man when we were married. I was terrified of you. I was afraid that you would sweep away all my disguises and take away all my defenses. I was terrified that you would own me body and soul like you do now. So I fended you off. You let me. Don't let me do that again."

"I don't own you body and soul, Patty."

"Yes, you do. In the way I mean it. And you know the way I mean it. My shrink said my biggest fear was sexual surrender. I fought her every inch of the way on it but she was right, literally right. In my family you never thought of letting down the barriers. You caught me this time when I was unprepared for you. All the barriers were gone. I couldn't fight you off and I didn't want to anyway."

I drew her close. "I think I noticed that."

She giggled. "Don't let me get away with fending you off ever again."

"I don't intend to."

I wondered whether I could really keep my word on such an intricate and delicate subject. I'd have to try. No, I must succeed.

Then my mind turned to other matters.

As she was falling asleep, Patty murmured something I didn't quite catch.

"Hmm?"

"I *said* that the other night, when you were so tender and loving that I had to surrender, it was no big deal."

"Oh?"

"I don't mean that it wasn't wonderful." She rested her head on my belly. "I mean that I didn't stop existing or anything like that."

"Oh."

"I suppose," she said in a drowsy voice, now almost asleep, "that it's like that with God and death."

I didn't want to try to figure out that metaphor. Still don't.

WALL STREET JOURNAL

(EDITORIAL)

We note with some interest that the Catholic Church seems to be thinking seriously of returning to the "touchy-feely" style of religion that flourished during the 1960s. Just at the time when virtually every government in the civilized world has abandoned completely the leftism of that era, the Catholic Church seems ready to try it again.

Luis Emilio Cardinal Menendez y Garcia may be a virtuous man, but the fact remains that he has been identified with the Marxist "liberation theology" that many left-leaning priests (including American missionaries) in South America have embraced.

It is hard to understand why the cardinal would be

sympathetic to Marxism, since his early years were spent under the regime of the Spanish Republic, which murdered tens of thousands of priests and nuns.

Having emerged safely from the turbulence of that era, the Catholic Church astonishingly seems ready to plunge back into it. Religion that ties itself to fashion runs the risk of losing all claim to express the eternal verities for which it is supposed to stand.

We hope that the cardinals keep this in mind when they go into conclave tomorrow night.

Dinny

The woman and I had breakfast in the Hassler dining room. She kissed me good-bye and promised she'd see me later in the day. It was a casual parting, too casual for what was ahead of us. As the day went on I wished to heaven I had been more affectionate.

I returned to my room, removed my coded notes from my wallet, opened the notebook computer, and began to work.

I had hardly started to pound away, when the phone rang. The boss in New York.

"This is incredible stuff, Dinny. It's another prize for you, I'm sure."

"We'll see."

"Look, we'll have our Wall Street people go over it and prepare an in-depth analysis of what these sheets seem to mean. You won't have to worry about that. OK?"

"Fine."

I had assumed that's the way we would play it.

"You write just a general piece about what happened

and the issues involved and maybe the impact on the conclave. . . . What do you think the impact will be, by the way?"

N Y T

Vatican Loss Put at Half-Billion
Investor Traded in Derivatives
Secret Catholic Group Involved

By Dennis Michael Mulloy
Rome.

During the last six months a secret Vatican investment group has lost approximately a half billion dollars in trades in the so-called "derivatives" contracts. The losses of the Catholic Church in these trades, which amount to between a fifth and a fourth of its total endowment, appear to be second in size only to the losses sustained by Baring's Bank of London.

According to documents obtained by *The New York Times*, these trades were made through the International Agricultural Bank of Holland in The Hague by Arturo Buonfortuno, the chief investor of the Administration of the Patrimony of the Apostolic See (APAS). The International Agricultural Bank is currently under investigation by Dutch banking authorities and is reported to be in grave danger of seizure and liquidation.

The chief source of the funds of the patrimony was a grant of 90 million lire made by Fascist dictator Benito Mussolini in 1929 at the time of the Lateran Treaty in settlement of Vatican claims against the Kingdom of Italy for losses suffered when the kingdom confiscated all Church lands. The level of the patrimony until six months ago was, according to those familiar with it, consistent with the increase in the Dow Jones stock average since 1929. Virtually all of the income from the patrimony is used to meet regular operating expenses, and most of the salaries of the Vatican's employees. The Vatican, by its own admission, is chronically short of funds, as it strives to raise the salaries of its employees so that they are comparable with those of their counterparts in Italian firms.

Last year a modest raise in salaries became possible because of an increase in endowment income. Cardinal John Fletcher, the American who presides over the Prefecture for Economic Affairs, attributed this increase to wise investments but categorically denied to *The New York Times* that any investments had been made in "derivatives" contracts. The prefecture is the oversight agency which theoretically supervises all Vatican financial operations but which in practice has little authority over the secret APAS.

An inspection of the records made available shows that indeed the "derivatives" trades—mostly a highly complex combination of various hedging maneuvers—produced a net gain of more than a quarter of a billion dollars in the summer months of last year and accounted almost entirely for the money that was used to increase Vatican salaries.

However, since then, changes in the marketplace created heavy losses for the Vatican. Apparently Buonfortuno poured more money into similar investments to try to stop the losses. Just as in the Baring's Bank affair, these later investments increased the losses. It is not clear that the Vatican's exposure to further losses has ended.

This is not the first major Vatican financial loss. During the pontificate of Pope Paul VI, the Vatican appeared to have lost more than a hundred million dollars because of poor investments made by one of Buonfortuno's predecessors, Michele Sindona, in the real estate firm SGI (Società Generale Immobilare). Sindona was later indicted in the Franklin Bank Scandal on Long Island.

Allowing for inflation, that loss would appear to be approximately half the present loss—if the Vatican has no further exposure in problems of the International Agricultural Bank.

In theory the investments of the APAS must be approved by a supervisory board of cardinals. However, either the cardinals did not understand the risks that were being taken in derivatives trading or have done their best to cover up the losses.

It is generally believed in Rome that Buonfortuno is a member of the Corpus Christi Institute, the highly secretive association of priests and laypeople which is said to have enormous power in the Vatican at this time. It is also believed in the Netherlands that the International Agricultural Bank, closely held by a conservative Dutch family, has strong links to the Corpus Christi Institute.

From the records available to *The New York Times*, it is not clear that either Buonfortuno or the APAS violated any civil laws, either Italian or Dutch. The Catholic Church simply made unwise investments, not the first organization or the last to do so.

However, the problem in the Vatican is not unlike that at Baring's Bank—a single inexperienced investor, operating without proper oversight, ran up a huge debt in a matter of weeks which will work havoc on the organization.

It is not clear that the problem will ever be solved for the Vatican unless it is willing to give up its habits of secrecy, which make effective oversight practically impossible.

What impact will this have on the conclave which begins on Tuesday evening? After the revelation of financial disaster, the cardinals may have a hard time giving the papacy away. How many men would want it when the nature of the financial catastrophe becomes clear?

Dinny

I carefully went over the piece, word by word, looking for any exaggeration or misstatement, changing commas, inserting periods, modifying paragraphs.

I thought for a moment about what I was doing. Was I creating a terrible problem for the Church, with which I had just formally reaffiliated? Would this scandal create a worldwide crisis of confidence in the Church, which even a man like Don Luis could not solve? Would it not be better just to let sleeping dogs lie? No laws had been broken, except perhaps the Vatican's own laws. Did the public have a right to know about what the usual mix of secrecy and incompetence had done to the Church? It was a private institution, after all.

But it had a public trust, a sacred trust. The only way the Vatican would ever change would be if its monumental ignorance and stupidity were revealed. If there were ever a time to do this, it was now.

No one would leave the Church. Catholics, even theoretically fallen-away Catholics like I claimed to have been, did not leave because they discovered that their leaders were bungling fools. Most of us knew that all along. Nor did we stay because we thought that our leaders were financial geniuses or brilliant administrators. We knew all along that they were not.

"Right," I said aloud and pushed the "CTL P" instruction. My slow-moving printer began to print out the piece.

The phone rang again.

"Dinny? Dee Dee. Have you seen Patty lately?"

"No," I said, my stomach turning uneasily. "What's happened?"

"We can't find her. She left a couple of hours ago to buy a can of hair spray over on the Borgo Santo Spirito. She's very particular about that, as you know."

I didn't know.

"And?"

"She just never came back. We're looking all over for her."

"Keep looking. Let me know."

I was shivering. I had always assumed that they would kidnap me. But Patty!

There was a knock at the door. I rushed to it and flung it open. No one there. But there was an envelope on the floor. I picked it up. There was a note inside and a video cassette.

The note, in distorted block letters, read, "NO STORY UNTIL AFTER THE CONCLAVE!"

I was shaking so badly I could hardly hold the tape. I tried a number of times to put it in the video player that was part of my suite's TV.

I finally succeeded. I turned on the set and pushed a number of buttons. Nothing happened. Finally I hit the right button. The tape began to play.

A picture of Patty, her face bruised, her blouse torn, her lips tight, a gun pointed at her chin.

"Do what they tell you Dinny or they'll kill me," she said in a stricken voice. "They'll release me after the conclave is over."

The tape went blank.

I knew they would not release her. When the conclave was over they would probably rape her and certainly kill her.

CHICAGO STAR

Cronin Illness Seen as "God's Will"

Rome.

The sudden and almost fatal illness of Sean Cardinal Cronin is being viewed by many Catholics in this city as a sign of God's displeasure. "He tried to treat the conclave like an American election campaign," said a devout old churchman, "and God struck him down for his presumption."

"That's what happens to those who support sodomites and socialists and sell-outs," said Timothy I. Williams, a prominent Catholic layman.

While not going that far, other Vatican experts feel that Cardinal Cronin's heart attack will destroy the plans of a large group of left-leaning cardinals to elect as the next spiritual leader of the world's one billion Catholics the Spanish radical Luis Emilio Cardinal Menendez y Garcia. Menendez is seen largely as Cardinal Cronin's creation. In Cronin's absence from the conclave it is expected that the Menendez candidacy will collapse and the cardinals will turn to another and more moderate candidate, even if such a change of heart will lead to a conclave that could last a week or longer.

"Cronin works like a bulldozer," said a highly placed American official here. "He sold the others a bill of goods and keeps them in line like Mayor Daley keeps the city council in line. But that's not the way conclaves are supposed to work. The cardinals will sigh in relief when it becomes clear that he won't be inside hounding and harassing them."

No one here believes the optimistic reports coming from the cardinal's personal physicians that the cardinal is recovering speedily from what they call a "seizure."

It is generally thought that he almost died yesterday. There is also serious question as to why he is being treated by American doctors when the highly esteemed Gemelli Clinic, which treated the late pope, is readily available in Rome.

Blackie

Sean Cronin favored us with his most charming smile, a smile normally reserved for the presence of lovely women.

There were three of such in the room—his sister-in-law (and once adopted sister) Nora, Janet Stewart, and Mkate@LCMH. Their spouses lurked in the background along with the innocuous little bishop.

All the medical equipment had been pulled away. The cardinal had been permitted to shower and shave and to don navy-blue pajamas. He looked rested and tranquil and only slightly haggard.

"So what's the verdict?" He smiled at my virtuous sibling, who apparently was the spokesperson in the sickroom, too.

"Through no fault of your own," she said crisply, "you're going to live a while longer."

"I know that."

"Your heart is undamaged and is functioning normally. Your brain, to use the word loosely, is in good shape. Your blood pressure is well within limits. You suffered, we believe, from an attack of tachycardia—a sudden quickening of the heartbeat which can be very dangerous, but in your case, this time, apparently was not. It could occur again or it may not. We will provide medication which you should carry with you at all times in case it should recur."

"Should I ask why it happened?" he said, his smile becoming all the more charming—and with a touch of diffidence that I'm sure he did not feel.

"You know damn well why it happened, Sean Cardinal Cronin. You're exhausted, you don't sleep at night, and you drink too much coffee. We absolutely forbid all those things. You need a long rest, more than one good night of sleep, and two cups of tea a day. We can give you some medication that will help with the caffeine addiction in the short run. In the long run, cold turkey."

"Yes, ma'am. . . . Now, about the conclave."

"We don't want you to go in—"

"Wait a minute." He sat up, ready to protest.

"I am *not* finished," she said, tapping her pen on her clipboard, a sign that Mother Superior was close to anger. "We would *like* to be able to keep you here for observation for a week. We take a risk if we let you go out of our care, even for a few hours—"

"It'll be only a half day," he said pleadingly.

She ignored his interruption.

"On the other hand, we have to calculate the strain on your organism of keeping you here while the conclave continues, incredibly, without your presence and wisdom. It would certainly be much harder on us and arguably, as someone in this room says often, harder on you."

"Hooray!" The cardinal yelped.

"Please, Your Eminence," she said with a faint but deadly hint of a smile, "act your age!"

"Touché." He laughed.

"We will continue to monitor you up to the time when it becomes absolutely necessary for you to leave for the conclave tomorrow afternoon. Then we will drive you over there in something of a solemn high procession. My elusive brother will materialize intermittently—when he is not playing with Mike the Cop's ingenious little toys—to make sure you take your medication on time. Today we tell the media that we are continuing to monitor your condition and we will make a decision tomorrow."

"Tomorrow morning?"

"Tomorrow afternoon."

"It would be quite effective for our cause," I interjected, "if you join the line of the cardinals at the very last minute. A sign from heaven, if you will, for the more superstitious of your colleagues. Along with the exemplary Cardinal DeJulio, I shall make sure that all preparations are executed with my usual diplomatic tact."

General laughter.

"We will, however, permit your charming Norseman friend," Mkate@LCMH continued implacably, "Count von Obermann to pay his respects later in the day. He will tell everyone how well you are doing."

"Teutonic knight," I murmured.

"And thus put to rest the rejoicing of the Corpus people that your alleged brush with death was a sign of God's displeasure with you."

"They never stop, do they?"

"Now, tell me how many cups of coffee you had at lunch before your attack?"

"Two or three—"

"Five," I insisted.

"Sean Cronin," my sibling pointed a warning finger at him, "did you enjoy the pain in your chest when you collapsed on the pavement in front of that gosh-awful church?"

"No," he said solemnly, "not a bit."

"If you want that to recur, you will continue to drink five cups of coffee at a meal."

"I'm only drinking two cups of tea a day."

"You are duly warned."

"Yes, ma'am."

I personally figured that if Sean Cronin had been able long ago to give up the lovely Nora, he certainly would be able to give up coffee.

Dinny

After a half hour of pure panic, I finally became clear-headed enough to call Niko.

"They've taken her, Niko. My wife."

"Are you calling from your room?"

What the hell? "*Yes*! I repeat, they've taken Patty."

"Call me back on your cellular phone."

"Oh." I did as he said.

"We know they've got her, Deeny. We are in touch with our people up there. She is all right so far."

"They'll kill her after the conclave."

"We know that, too," he said, his voice tense and distracted, like that of a man under terrible pressures. "We plan to free her tonight. I promise you that we will do so. I absolutely promise that."

"I will come along."

"I understand . . . but you must give us time."

"Very well."

"Stay in your room. Do not go out for any reason. Make no phone calls on the hotel phone."

"Fax to New York?"

He hesitated.

"That will do no harm. Is your, ah, shade still outside?"

"Let me look . . . yes, he is. Your two guys are there also."

"You are able to recognize my men, Gianni and Rico?"

"Yes."

"You may trust them absolutely. Trust no one else. I will

call you soon on your cellular phone. I know how difficult it is. But please trust me. For now you must wait.''

"All right," I said.

What else was I to do?

Mark

*M*ark smiled at everyone as he climbed up the stairs, a trip he now took every day. They recognized him now and took him for granted. They nodded and smiled back. No one asked him who he was or where he was going or for whom he worked. He still experienced terrible temptations to give up his sacred mission. Now the devil was trying to tell him that Mom didn't want him to kill anyone.

He always waited till the stairwell was clear before he pushed open the door and walked out on the roof. The tar on the roof was hot, as hot as the hell to which he would send many people the day the new pope was elected— whether it was the baby murderer or not.

He placed his attaché case on the ledge at the edge of the roof, at the most three inches of stone. He was now carrying the case every day so that no one would be surprised when he appeared with it on the Big Day.

He opened the case and removed the small telescope, the only thing he carried with him. It would have been foolish to bring the gun until the day itself.

He drew out the parts of the telescope and peered into the piazza. It would be a long shot, very long. He would have the opportunity for only one try, two at the absolute most. He must make the shots count.

He smiled to himself. He did not look like he had ever

been a marine, but he had won a medal for his skill as a marksman, sometimes shooting at targets even farther away than this one.

They had thrown him out of the marines, too. He would get even with them. They would be blamed for his training as a marksman.

He laughed softly.

CNN

ANCHOR: Ted Turner, president of Turner Broadcasting Systems, delivered this morning a strongly worded message to the president and prime minister of Italy concerning the disappearance of CNN reporter Patricia Anne McLaughlin

TURNER: (grim and somber; reads from paper) My letter reads as follows: I strongly protest the seeming indifference of the Italian government to the apparent kidnapping of CNN correspondent Patricia Anne McLaughlin. Although Ms. McLaughlin has been missing now for many hours, the minister of the interior seems utterly indifferent to her fate and the Roman police refuse to respond to CNN's telephone calls. I warn the appropriate leaders of the Italian government, and especially you, Mr. President and Mr. Prime Minister, that we hold you personally responsible for Ms. McLaughlin's fate. Your behavior is as criminal as that of the persons who have kidnapped Ms. McLaughlin. Should anything happen to her, Turner Broadcasting Systems and all affiliates will do everything possible to drive you from public office and hound you out of the company of decent, civilized human beings.''

(He folds the paper and returns it to his jacket pocket.)

I have sent copies of this letter to the President of

the United States and the secretary of state. I want to repeat in my own personal words what I have just said. If anything happens to Patty, the president, the prime minister, and the minister of the interior of Italy will regret it to their dying day.

ANCHOR: And now we take you back to Rome, where a spokesman for the medical team treating Sean Cardinal Cronin is about to issue a bulletin.

MKM: (in a light blue double-breasted suit with white buttons and collar) Sean Cardinal Cronin continues to rest well in his rooms here at the North American College. All the cardinal's vital signs are normal. He is ambulatory and in excellent spirits. There is no sign of damage to his heart functions and his brain is fine. . . . Well, in so far as the brain of any male of the species can be said to be fine!

(Laughter.)

MKM: (regaining a straight face) We have diagnosed his seizure as an attack of nonchronic tachycardia induced by fatigue, overexertion, jet lag, heat, and excessive consumption of coffee. Such seizures can be fatal but in this case it was not. We think that recurrences are unlikely as long as the cardinal obeys the instructions of his doctors, takes his medication, and forswears coffee. Permanently.

We will continue to monitor his condition to confirm our diagnosis.

I know you all want to ask whether the cardinal will be able to participate in the conclave, which opens tomorrow night. We have yet to make a determination on that matter and will not do so until tomorrow afternoon. We will do all in our power, short of seriously endangering Cardinal Cronin's health, to assure his participation.

Herr Cardinal Klaus Maria Johann, Count Von Obermann, visited the cardinal this afternoon. They had a long and affable conversation. I do not know whether they discussed the conclave. I would not be surprised, however, if they did.

Q: Are you aware that many media outlets say that the Cardinal is a much sicker man than you have reported him to be?

A: They lie.

Q: Are you suggesting that the cardinal is suffering from a caffeine addiction?

A: You bet. There are worse addictions. (smiles) I could name a few. . . .

Q: Can you explain why the cardinal was not brought immediately to the Gemelli Clinic?

A: Certainly I can. We were not about to trust the cardinal's life to a medical team which was so tardy in diagnosing the late pope's colon tumor. We don't want doctors who are too delicate to look up the pope's rectum to make decisions on Cardinal Cronin.

Q: Are you suggesting, madam, that the medical care being provided here is better than that of one of Italy's best clinics?

A: You got it.

CNN

ANCHOR: CNN has just learned from Roman sources that the bottleneck blocking the search for our missing Patty McLaughlin is the general director of the Ministry of the Interior, that is, the chief civil servant of the ministry. We have also learned on reliable authority that this gentlemen, Benedetto Longhi, is thought to be a member of the Corpus Christi Institute, of which Patty has been very critical in her preconclave coverage. We at CNN take the liberty of extending Ted Turner's warning to Mr. Longhi and to the Corpus

Christi Institute: If anything happens to Patty, you will wish you had never been born.

Λ P

Vatican Denies Involvement in Kidnapping

Rome.

A Vatican spokesman this afternoon dismissed as "absurd," charges by the Cable News Network that a secret Catholic organization was involved in the disappearance today of Patricia Anne McLaughlin, a reporter for the network.

Alphonse de Tassigny, director of the sala stampa, the Vatican press office, dismissed Ms. McLaughlin's disappearance as "another example of her well-known hunger for publicity."

Asked about allegations from CNN that Benedetto Longhi, the general director of the Ministry of the Interior, has blocked investigations of Ms. McLaughlin's disappearance, de Tassigny replied that he is not privy to the decisions of the Italian Ministry of the Interior. He also stated that whether Longhi was a member of the Corpus Christi Institute was purely a personal matter for him and no one else's concern.

De Tassigny is also widely believed to be a member of the Corpus Christi Institute.

Blackie

ℱather Ryan.''

"This is Tenente Niko Colona, Monsignore, Paola Elizabetta's young man. I work for the intelligence section of the carabinieri, the military police.''

"So I understand, Principe.''

"Paola Elizabetta thought I should inform you that we plan to free Signora McLaughlin tonight.''

"Ah?''

"Only my unit knows that we will do this. Our struggle with the general director of the ministry is over the release of a squad of their commandos to my team. Neither he nor anyone else there knows what we intend to do. Thus we believe that the dangers to Ms. McLaughlin are not substantially enhanced by this controversy.''

"Indeed.''

What the young man was telling me is that he knew where Patty Anne was being held but no one else knew that he knew.

"We wonder if you could provide us with any information about the reasons for the kidnappers' actions?''

"It seems patent to me that they are agents of the International Agricultural Bank of Holland, which, I have reason to believe, is faced with liquidation. I presume they want to keep secret until after the conclave the involvement of the Vatican in highly risky investments made through that bank, in the hope that if their side wins, the Vatican will deny their losses and the bank will survive.''

"So,'' the young voice tightened in rage.

"Just so, Tenente.''

"And the Corpus Institute is involved with both the investor and the bank."

"I should note that I doubt that the leaders of the institute would be involved in the kidnapping. Even they are not so foolish. But I further doubt that they are unaware of it."

"This has been a great help, Monsignore; I will inform you instantly when Ms. McLaughlin is free."

"Thank you, Tenente. Be careful."

Indeed. The young man, who must be both very brave and very intelligent if he were involved with that young woman, did not say "if she is free" but "when she is free."

Presumably he knew what he was doing. But it was a very risky business.

Damn the fools!

I solemnly made my own the vows of Ted Turner.

Dinny

Dinny Mulloy."

I was still trembling, like someone about to undergo dangerous surgery.

"Niko, Deeny."

"What's happening?"

"We plan to free Ms. McLaughlin at eleven tonight. We will pick you up at eight. Is that appropriate?"

"Absolutely."

"I am most grateful for your patience. You have been watching television, I presume."

"Yes."

"We have hoped and still hope that a squad of the ministry's anti-terrorist commandos will be released to my command. The general director of the ministry has blocked this release. Paola Elizabetta's mama and papa have made the strongest possible representations to the prime minister and the president. They continue to do so. I fear that the minister of the interior will have to relieve his general director from office and perhaps arrest him. With or without the anti-terrorist team, we will go ahead. In their absence, it will be somewhat more dangerous, but we will still be successful."

"Does this infighting put Patricia any more at risk?"

My stomach warned me that it wanted to vomit again.

"I do not believe so. No one knows except the members of my team that we know where she is. My team is completely loyal to me. No one will be expecting a raid tonight. That is why we must do it now."

"I understand."

"I will call you at seven-thirty to give you further instructions. . . . The man is still outside?"

"Yes. Your men Rico and Gianni are still on him. I presume they do not want to risk calling you from the street."

"Very good. *Ciao*, Deeny."

"*Ciao*, Niko."

As I hung up I realized that I didn't even know Niko's last name, only that he had a face like a Giotto angel. Or a Fellini waif.

I revised my piece one more time and printed it out. I tore up the earlier versions and flushed them down the toilet. I then sat on the easy chair in my parlor and tried to think the alternatives through.

When we left for the Alban Hills, the die would be cast. We would either free Patty Anne, or in the attempt one or both of us might die. There would be no turning back from these alternatives.

I might just as well send off the story to New York and ask the editor to hold it either until he heard from me or heard of my death. In either event it would be in the next day's morning edition and perhaps in the *Herald-Tribune*, too.

It was not a story worth dying for. But if one or both of

us was going to die, at least we would have our revenge on those who killed us.

At seven-fifteen I called the boss on his private line, using my cellular phone.

"Dinny here."

"Yeah, Dinny, what's up?"

"I'm going to fax you the story in a couple of minutes. Your private fax and your eyes only."

"Got it."

"They've taken Patty."

"We know she's disappeared, but who has her?"

"The bad guys. They say they'll kill her if I tell anything about what's going on. I presume they work for the bank up in The Hague."

"Good God, Dinny, don't take any chances."

"For reasons we may have in a story later on, we have to get her out tonight. This is for your ears only."

"Got it."

"I don't know how risky it will be. Any time you got a lot of guys with guns running around at night shooting at one another, it gets dangerous. We have to move now, just the same."

"Got it."

"So hold the story until you hear from me, maybe a little after midnight our time. Or until you hear one way or another that we're dead."

"Sure, we'll hold it, but, Dinny, I don't like the sound of this."

"Neither do I. But if we do get killed, I want to know that you're going to get the guys that did it."

"We sure will. There's a lot of stuff on Turner today about this crazy, what do they call it, Crapus crowd being involved. Sounds like they are."

"Corpus. And they're involved up to their fucking necks. They've blocked police action all day. Take care of them for us, too."

"We sure will. But the whole thing sounds deadly dangerous. Are you sure, Dinny. . . ."

I thought about that.

"Not at all. But from where I'm sitting it's what we gotta do. If anything happens to us, you guys take care of the kids."

"Yeah, sure. Give my love to Patty Anne, Dinny."

"I will."

"And, Dinny . . . God bless you!"

First time I ever heard that word on his lips save as an expression of surprise. So, all right, you go out like Dinny Mulloy, hell, like any Irish journalist, should—with a wisecrack.

"I'm sure She will."

I sent the fax, thought about tearing it up, and then folded it and put it in my jacket. Show it to Peppermint Patty on the way home. Please God.

The minute clock moved from 7:21 to 7:30 with tedious indifference, like a line at a government office. I dressed in dark blue slacks and a black sweater. I put the text of my piece in my hip pocket.

I was in good condition and my martial arts techniques were passable. But I was not a young anti-terrorist commando and I had no weapons.

Precisely at seven-thirty, the cellular phone rang.

"Niko. Is the man still out there?"

"Yes."

"Be careful, Deeny, he is a killer. They may want to take you out. My men will be right behind you. But he is very quick."

"So am I, Niko. And very angry."

"Naturally. You will leave the hotel now and take the Metro to the Stazione Termini. We do not want to be seen picking you up at the hotel. My men will pick you up at the Metro station there and lead you to my car. Be careful, Deeny."

"You too, Niko."

I left my room, rode down the elevator, casually dropped my key at the concierge's desk, and walked out into the failing sunlight. Trying not to look like I was in a rush, I ambled down the Spanish Steps, ducking around the crowds of young people who were utterly unaware of me.

I could feel Peter Rush's eyes boring into my back. If it were now his job to kill me, how would he do it?

Probably he would be an opportunist—stick a knife into me in a dark corner, an ice pick into my ear on a crowded train, a stealthy injection on a street.

Or push me into an oncoming train just as it was pulling into a station, but still moving fast enough to grind me apart under its wheels.

Sure, that made sense. Why try to dispose of me in the crowds along the Spanish Steps, like he tried to do the last time, when he could quickly push me off the train platform and then make a speedy getaway before the onlookers realized what had happened?

So I was safe until I got to the platform. Then I'd better be ready for him.

Trying to give the illusion of unconcern, a man out for a stroll and a bit of a train ride on a hot spring evening, I walked down the stairs into the cool semi-darkness of the Metro station. I now sensed him right behind me. I bought a ticket, walked through the barrier, and rode down the escalator to the platform. I caught a glimpse of him in a reflection from a glass-covered advertisement. He *was* right behind me.

Where were Niko's guys? Had I been set up?

I tried to remember my revered master's instructions for relaxation and self-possession before an encounter. I endeavored to center my life, to feel the flow of the cosmos running within me, to put aside anger and a desire for revenge, and stay in contact with my own positive energies.

I was never very good at that kind of contemplative thing, but this time it helped. A little anyway.

When I heard a train coming, I would know he was about

to attack. I hoped I would sense when he had launched himself at me. It would not be a gentle tap, but rather a quick and massive shove. You don't roll a six-foot-two, hundred-and-ninety-five-pound former power forward under a train with just a gentle push.

At the precise moment he would be upon me, I would simply collapse on the floor, fall apart, like my bones and muscles had been disjointed, and permit him to throw himself over me. He would land on his face, astonished and temporarily immobile. I would then pounce upon him and beat the shit out of him.

Always remaining in contact with the flow of cosmic energies through my soul!

Yeah.

Were Niko's guys still there? Were they on my side?

I thought so, but finally I didn't care. This was between me and Peter Rush.

The rumble and roar of a train thundered on my left. I tensed and then, astonishingly, relaxed. The revered master's techniques did work. I would have to try them the next time I made love to Peppermint Patty.

Five more seconds before he struck.

Four.

Three.

The train ground into the station, crunching and lurching as though it were not sure it should stop.

Two.

I felt him right behind me. I smelled the alcohol on his breath.

One.

The train was only twenty yards away.

I collapsed.

Then everything went into slow motion. Or maybe it had been in slow motion for the last ten seconds.

Two feet kicked into my ribs. Shocks of pain raced through my body. Then Peter Rush sailed over me, like a linebacker on whom a wide receiver had made a switchback block. He took off like Michael Jordan going to the hoop, flailed in the air for what seemed like an eternity, and then fell in a heap at the very edge of the platform.

The momentum of his charge carried him farther still. He tumbled over the edge and right into the path of the braking train.

I heard a terrible sound of something splattering.

Peter Rush flew into his death without uttering a sound.

"Poor man," I said as I rolled to my feet.

I'd better get out of there before anyone realized what had happened.

I turned and there were Niko's two men, with snub-nosed revolvers in their hands. They quickly put them away.

"*È morto,*" one of them said in astonishment.

"Pretty much, I think," I said, trying to control my stomach muscles.

"He killed himself trying to kill you, Signore."

"Looks that way."

"Niko sent us."

"I know that."

"Come with us. We will arrange matters."

We sped up the escalator into the terminal and then climbed back into the Piazza di Spagna, once the hangout, I found myself thinking, for crazy teenage English poets.

Only then did the need to vomit rise from my stomach to my lips. Alas, after my spasms of retching in the hotel room, I had nothing left to give to the enterprise.

My new friends, Rico and Gianni, hustled me quite gently into their Lancia and we sped off, ignoring in the effort swerving cars and fleeing civilians.

Cops are cops all over the world, even when they all have faces like Giotto angels.

Gianni called someone on his portable phone and spoke in very rapid Italian. The voice on the other end of the call sounded astonished.

Gianni handed me the phone.

"Deeny?"

"Niko."

I found that I still had reserves of cosmic forces flowing into me. That was nice.

"They say you killed him!"

"Not really, Niko; as our mutual friend Rico here says, he killed himself trying to kill me."

"Astonishing!"

"Well, I don't do it every day, thank God."

"But—"

"The trick, Niko, is to let the cosmic forces flow through you."

"Naturally. Ciao, Deeny."

"Ciao, Niko."

At that moment, the cosmic energy—or whatever it was—was still bubbling inside me. Could I activate it when I was making love with Patty after all this nonsense was over? Why not? It would really blow her mind! At that moment of exaltation I had not the slightest doubt that Patty and I both would survive. On the ride up to the Alban Hills, that confidence would fade, but never completely.

We pulled alongside a line of similar black Lancias across from the Termini. Rico helped me out of the car, Gianni opened the door to another car, and I hopped in. Three men replaced me in the car in which I had come, all dressed in black shirts and slacks and carrying an array of odd-looking weapons. A driver and another man were in the front of the new car. Niko sat at the other end of the backseat. Between us, also dressed in black, but tastefully fashionable black, was my girl guide.

"You are well, Deeny?" She took my face in both her hands and searched in the fading light, as if looking for signs of an infectious disease.

"Breathing in and out, Pretty Princess," I managed to say, though the enormity of what had happened and what remained to be done was catching up with me.

"Paola Elizabetta insisted on coming," Niko said with an expressive sigh. "She said she was covering the release of

Ms. McLaughlin for *The New York Times.* It is useless to argue with her. She will not, however, leave the car when we climb the hills. That is understood.''

"Yes, Tenente Niko," she said impatiently. "You are the lord and master, Tenente Niko."

She abandoned her examination of my face and held my hand instead.

"We will save her, Deeny. We will. I know we will."

"Naturally," I said.

"We have at least some news that is good," Niko said, his voice strained in the dark. "Our people up in the hills report that our friends and their friends know nothing. They merely laugh at the television reports. They do no additional harm to Signora McLaughlin, other than to threaten her. Moreover, the general director of the ministry has been removed and indeed arrested. The anti-terrorist squad of the polizia, the state police, has been released to me, though I have yet to hear from their leader."

"The general director is a pig," Paoli said firmly. "And a fool to think he could stand up to my mama and papa."

"You have not sent your story to New York?" Niko asked. "The one they're trying to stop?"

How did he know that? Or had he figured it out? Or had Paoli figured it out and told him? It didn't matter, not now anyway. We had to get Patty out of the mess she was in first and then worry about everything else.

"I sent it."

Paoli gasped. So did Niko, though not so loudly.

"My editor will hold it until he hears from me or hears that either of us is dead. I figured that we would not go quietly into that good night."

Silence.

"I understand," Niko said finally.

"Naturally," Paoli had agreed.

His transceiver buzzed.

"Tenente Colonna qui. Sì, Commandante, sì. Mille grazie."

The *commandante*—presumably of the commando squad—spoke too rapidly for me to grasp all that was being said. Apparently he was asking questions of place and time and directions. The target house, I gathered, was on a direct line across Lago Albano from the papal villa at Castel Gandolfo, ''an excellent sighting point, because of the lights on the Specola Vaticana.''

''Vatican observatory,'' Paoli whispered to me.

The helicopters would take off from Ciampino, the military airport, fly over the *specola*, across Lago Albano, over a place called Roca di Papa, and join us on the other side of the old volcano that had created the Alban Hills.

There were lots of ''sì, sì''s being exchanged.

''Guy sounds like he's totally cool,'' I said to Niko when he had ended the conversation.

''They are all that way. That's how they deal with danger. They are, however, very good. I hope only that they are punctual. We will not wait long. If their helicopters are more than fifteen minutes late we must go in without them. We cannot run the risk of being discovered.''

''Won't the bad guys hear the noise of their copters.''

''They will come in very low and very fast. The bad guys will hear them only for a few seconds. We will immediately throw our concussion and smoke grenades. We will use these weapons.''

He held up an odd, tubular gun for my inspection.

''They make no noise. They eject a tiny stream of liquid that immediately immobilizes the target, even more rapidly than a bullet wound would. There are no stray bullets and no ricochets. I say they would be very useful for keeping a wife quiet.''

Paoli snorted derisively.

We sped out of the southeast side of Rome and on to the Autostrada Uno (A-1). I gathered that we would pull off the autostrada beyond Frascati on the other side of the hill on which the villa was located. We would scale the hill, which was covered with forest, and come in the back way. There were three guards outside and four men inside. We would pick off the outside guards, one by one, with our silent toys, wait for the commandos, throw our grenades, and rush the house. Our spies inside would depart at ten-fifty, leaving the door and the gate open. After we threw our grenades Niko and three others would rush up the stairs, subduing any guards they encountered, and break into the room where Patty was bound and now also gagged. The others would pour in through the other doorways and windows as the commandos landed on the roof and rappelled down the sides of the villa like mountain climbers.

He also showed me the computer-produced design of the house using a penlight to illumine it.

"In this room on the first floor, Signora McLaughlin is being held—"

"Deeny's second floor," Paoli corrected him.

"Naturally."

"I will lead men in this door, which our people will leave open before they depart the house for the night. We will cross the kitchen, which will be dark, exit through this door on the other side, climb these stairs on the right, then run down this corridor to the room and smash the door open. It should take no more than fifteen seconds. Our opponents will be dazed for at least a half minute."

It sounded like an absolutely crazy scheme to me. I didn't have a better one.

"I see," I said dubiously.

"It sounds quite mad, Deeny," Niko said. "But it really is not. There are twelve of us and another twelve commandos. By that time there will be only four of them. And they will be startled and disoriented by our grenades."

"You and four others will climb the stairs, not three. And I'll have one of your guns."

He hesitated and then agreed. "Very well. But you will stay behind us. We could not keep you out anyway. Paola Elizabetta, naturally, will stay with the cars."

"Naturally."

If you believe that, Tenente Colonna, you'll believe that chickens have lips.

Colonna—wasn't that a black noble family too? It hardly looked like an arranged relationship. Maybe they had known each other all their lives and happened to fall in love.

For they surely did love each other. My poor princess's facial expression alternated between pride in him and fear for him.

We pulled off the autostrada at a rural interchange, passed some small villas, and then began climbing a winding path up a hill. Finally we stopped at a dead end.

"Good," said Niko, "We are virtually on time. It is nine-ten. We will be at the top of the hill by ten-fifteen. We will have plenty of time to pick off the guards and await the coming of the anti-terrorist squad."

We parked our four cars under the trees. We put on ski caps and blackface just like they do in the movies. He gave me the water pistol, as I thought of it, and instructed me how to use it.

"It will hurt no one, but use it only if you have to. Too much of this in the house will incapacitate our own men."

I nodded in silent agreement.

Niko addressed his men. His last words were *"Silenzio, silenzio, silenzio!"*

"Silenzio" was easier said than done. There was a touch of moonlight when the moon wasn't slipping into cloud cover. But we were to use no lights climbing the hill. Rather, we were to ease our way slowly up the hill, feeling our way through the trees, dense with the brutish smells of early spring—which it was up in the hills.

It was not an easy task. We stumbled and slipped and pulled and fell as we labored up the hill. Not as young as any of the others, I gasped and gulped for air. The higher we got, the more I felt that I would never make it.

It was cold. We were up in the mountains now where the spring temperatures, according to my guidebook, often fell to the middle forties.

Colder than that, I thought as I bumped my knee against a tree. My ribs were hurting now from where the late Peter Rush had kicked me on his way into the hereafter.

As we struggled and fought and cursed our way up the hill like a bunch of amateur mountain climbers on Mount Everest, Niko whispered two commands approximately every thirty seconds:

"Presto! Presto!" and *"Silenzio! Silenzio!"*

I would have told him that they were incompatible if I were not too breathless to speak.

Finally, after what I knew were hours of agony, we stumbled to the top, Niko heaving me up the last two yards with a sweep of his arm.

We were all suddenly quiet except for our heavy breathing. Gradually that faded into total silence. Ahead of us was a gray stone wall with floodlights on the top. Two of them, however, seemed to be burned out. Our enemies were hardly professionals in this kind of game, unlike the kids who were terrorists in Italy twenty years ago.

"Ten-forty," Niko whispered. "Rudi, Gianni, Fredi, now! *Presto.*"

Three men slipped off soundlessly into the night on their black sneakers. We waited and waited and waited. It seemed like it must already be the day after the Last Judgment.

I had a momentary image of the Sistine Chapel. I had forgotten about that since noontime. My Patty was all that mattered.

I heard slight hissing sounds on the other side of the wall, like a snake biting, one right after another, followed by three soft sighs. Next to me in the faint light of the reappearing moon I saw a sardonic smile of satisfaction on Niko's face.

His principessa was nowhere to be seen, but I had not the slightest doubt that she was lurking in the darkness. He probably knew it, too.

Gianni, Rudi, and Fredi drifted back to us, each giving the thumbs-up sign.

"Only four left," Niko whispered to me.

I hoped they had counted right.

Almost immediately a gate in the wall opened and a tiny Fiat burped out. The servants leaving. They left the gate open. Niko motioned us toward the gate. We divided into two groups, one of which quickly rushed to the other side of the gate. We waited expectantly.

The minutes slipped by: eleven-oh-five, eleven-ten. Maybe someone had stopped the commandos again. At eleven-fifteen we were supposed to go in without them. Let's get it over with, I thought.

Then a voice crackled briefly on Niko's transceiver.

"Sì, sì," Niko said. *"Pronto."*

I turned on all the cosmic forces I could find. They began to flow again through my body. The revered master was right. You could link up with the universe. I had to learn more about this sometime soon.

He flicked off the transceiver and led us through the gate. He held up two fingers and motioned his men to positions around the house. He grabbed my arm and pointed at a lighted window on the second floor (American style). Then he pointed at a door just beneath it. I nodded.

He lifted one finger. From the bags they had slung over their shoulders, his men removed odd-shaped and danger-ous-looking devices and held them ready to throw.

Niko signaled a half-minute. His men watched expec-tantly. He reached into his bag and pulled out a large bomb-like contraption. He signaled twenty seconds by extending the fingers of both hands twice. Then he held the ten fingers up and lowered them one by one.

I heard the dim whirl of the copters as they came up the mountain.

At one second, Niko hurled his grenade through the win-dow on the ground floor. The world went mad. Glass crashed, bombs exploded, smoke whirled out of the house, floodlights from the copters illumined it and the courtyard all around us.

Our men rushed the house. Niko led some of us toward

the back door. Confused, dazed, uncertain, I did not know where I was or what I was supposed to be doing. Then I saw the lighted window partially obscured by smoke and remembered whom we had come to save. I rushed after Niko and his crew.

As I entered the house, I heard more smashing glass. Men in black were rappelling down the side of the house, smashing windows and climbing into the upper floors.

We bumped our way across the kitchen floor. I banged my other knee. I'm too old for this, I thought irrelevantly.

But the cosmic forces cut in and suddenly everything went into slow motion. Niko kicked open the swinging door at the other side of the kitchen. A burly blond giant of a man loomed up, a pistol hanging limply in his hand. He struggled to raise the gun, very slowly, like he was a sleepwalker. Niko hit him in the face with a jet from his water pistol. The man crumpled to the floor.

The inside of the house was now illuminated by a spectral light—the glare of the copters' floodlights on the courtyard reflected into the house.

We dashed up the steps. I had somehow managed to get right behind Niko. That was all right, I was floating on air, caught up completely in the energies rushing through me. We turned at the head of the stairs and rushed toward the door at the opposite end. Light streamed out the slit beneath the door.

Suddenly a door swung open between me and Niko. Another large blond man emerged from it with an Uzi in his hand, ready to fire.

Without giving it a second thought, I blasted him with my water pistol. He keeled over with an expression of great surprise on his face. Behind me Gianni gasped. *It's all right kid, I'm the last knight of Europe, the last and lingering troubadour to whom the muse had sung when all the world was young.*

Niko glanced quickly at the falling man and, still running ahead, flicked a quick salute in my direction.

The concussion grenades continued to explode. More smoke swirled through the house. Sirens blasted. Horns blared. Heavy feet trampled on the floors above.

In very slow motion, Niko hurtled toward the door. It occurred to me, as I floated along after him, that Niko was a very brave young man.

He smashed against the door; it sprung open. The room was small, a servant's bedroom, perhaps. A single bare bulb cast a dim light. A bound and gagged figure slumped on a hard chair in the middle of it. A dark-skinned man stood in front of the chair, rubbing his face with his hands, an Uzi in one of them. He looked up at us, confused by our sudden arrival, and tried to swing the weapon in our direction.

Gianni, who had pushed around me, popped him with a squirt from his water pistol. With a sigh of infinite relief, the man swayed and, as leisurely as someone settling in for a long night's sleep, dropped to the floor.

Still in slow motion, Niko drifted across the room to Patricia, a knife in his hand.

"It is Niko, Signora, Paola Elizabetta's young man. Deeny is with me. You are safe."

He pulled the gag out of her mouth and cut the ropes at her wrists and ankles.

I swept her into my arms and said, "Seventh Cavalry, ma'am, reporting for duty. Colonel John Wayne at your service."

She swayed and slumped against me, still confused and disoriented by the noise and smoke. But she did giggle.

"Is it you, Dinny? In blackface?"

"Just a little disguise I whipped up, ma'am, to fool the savages."

She clung to me. "I knew you'd save me, Dinny. I knew you would."

The other wife I once had would have chewed the ass off of me for taking so long.

Her face was badly bruised and swollen, most of her blouse had been ripped off, but she was alive.

"I love you more than ever, Dinny."

Two big men in black wearing gas masks and with a variety of fancy rappelling equipment hanging on their bodies swung easily into the room through the broken window.

"Tenente Colonna?" The larger man pulled off his gas mask and glanced around the room.

"Commandante Brunello." Niko saluted.

"Benissimo, Tenente." The Commandante saluted in return and, with a big grin, extended his hand.

They babbled in Italian at each other, the commandante apologized for being late, Niko insisting that he was enormously happy to have them join us. Someone tossed me a jacket for my woman. I slipped it over her shoulder; she courteously shook hands with her saviors and thanked them for coming. She continued to cling to me with her other arm.

An astonishingly resilient woman, this new redhead of mine.

Two more commandos came into the room dragging a couple of sleeping Italians they had knocked out on the upper floor. An alarm went off in my head. *Let's see, we had disposed of three of them outside. Gianni, Niko, and I had each of us knocked one over. That was six, two more by the commandos. That made eight. There was one too many.*

"Niko!" I shouted. "There's eight of them. There were only supposed to be seven!"

He looked up, momentarily confused.

"Yes, there are eight," he said, frowning.

"Maybe there's nine!"

The issue didn't remain in doubt long. Another blond, this one small and nasty looking, stumbled into the small room, bleary-eyed but in firm possession of an AK-47. In very slow motion I saw him lift it and prepare to sweep the room. I heard Patty scream. This time something like my whole life passed before my eyes. I'd made such a hash out of so many things. Now I was going to die.

Sorry, I said to whoever was in charge. Or maybe Whoever.

Suddenly an explosive black bundle smashed into the gunman's back, sending him pitching forward. The weapon jumped out of his hands and fired a short burst at the ceiling. Rudi and a commando fired their squirt guns at the same time. The man barely moved. He had already been knocked out by his fall.

With a sharp cry of pain, Niko scooped up the black bundle. *"Carissima mia!"* he screamed.

The bundle, instantly recognizable despite her black face, opened one eye and then the other. She spoke in English, doubtless for the impact on her English-speaking audience.

"Naturally, it is quite pleasant to be in your arms, *caro* Niko," she said. "But you may put me down whenever you wish. I am perfectly all right."

He eased her to her feet, she swayed a little, and then steadied herself with a hand on his chest.

He told her that she had saved the lives of all of us.

"Naturally," she replied, quite happy with herself. "But it is good, *caro*, that I disobeyed your orders, is it not?"

She and Patty Anne embraced each other and wept in each other's arms.

Naturally.

It was agreed that one of the helicopters would fly Patty and Paoli and me back to Ciampino. Niko and Commandante Brunello would remain at the villa to clean up the mess. Niko and the commandante led the two women down the stairs to the kitchen.

I remained behind, looking for a telephone. I climbed the steps to the next floor and found at the head of the steps a large, late-nineteenth-century parlor, the floor of which was covered with broken glass. On a table at the far end of the room, beneath a shattered bay window, was a flat red telephone. Modern Italian.

I picked up the phone and heard the dial tone. I figured that I would use my credit card number. Then I thought,

No, let whoever's going to have to clean up this mess pay for it. They owe the *Times*.

So I punched in the boss's private line. In a few moments he was on the line with his usual greeting.

"Yeah?"

"Dinny. We're both all right. Go with the story."

"You sure?"

"Sure I'm sure. Go with it."

"Patty?"

"Indestructible."

"You'll file a story about this?"

"I think I'll ask our friend P. E. Oriani to file it. I'm too involved personally on this one."

"Fine, she's good. By the way, Dinny, how old is she?"

"Old enough. Hey, you might add this, because she won't tell you, that a guy that we weren't expecting showed up with an AK-47 and could have wiped out the whole bunch of us. She knocked him over. And out."

"Wow! Yeah, we'll put it in a box. Or maybe run another story tomorrow. You'll be able to file by then?"

"I think there'll be a lot of follow-ups on the story I filed a couple of hours ago. Now go with it before it's too late!"

He laughed.

"Are you sure you're all right, Dinny? Patty too?"

"Bumps and bruises, but we're breathing in and out and that's what counts. Go with the story."

I hung up and walked down the stairs to the courtyard, where the helicopter was waiting. The cosmic forces were drifting away again. I was shifting back into ordinary consciousness. I was tired, I hurt in every inch of my body, and I wanted to sleep—with or without a woman, which shows in what bad shape I was.

The elation of the victors was so great that they didn't notice my tardiness. They were all sipping from a brandy bottle and singing "Santa Lucia"—the good saint, perhaps, knowing why. I didn't. Someone offered me a swig of brandy. I shook my head and said, "No, thanks, I'm the designated driver."

Finally, we were helped into the copter and it lifted slowly off the ground.

I've always felt that if a copter really had its way, it wouldn't take off but would rather sit on the ground and spin around and around like a top.

Peppermint Patty huddled in my arms. Paoli, perhaps still shaken by her sudden encounter with the Dutch thug, promptly went to sleep.

"What was it all about, Dinny?" my possible wife asked. "I'd like to know."

So I told her the whole story, except about Peter Rush. It would be a long time before I told anyone that part of it. I was certain that I'd see his last desperate efforts to save himself in my dreams for a long time. I also omitted the source of my papers, referring only to a certain "Deep Crimson."

I partly read from moonlight and partly recited from memory my piece for the paper.

"When will that appear?" she asked.

"Tuesday morning. It should be on the street in a couple of hours."

"You sent it before you came up here?"

"With instructions to the boss not to use it till he heard from me. I figured that if either or both of us were killed up here, the people who did it would pay a price."

She shivered in my arms.

"Thank God, we're both still alive!"

"I'll buy that."

"You've called him?"

"Found a phone in the house."

She stiffened. "Goddamn it! It's my story!"

"No, it's not! I did the work on it!"

"And I did the suffering! You took my story away from me!"

"Patty Anne," I said, "you're under a lot of strain, so

I'll let you get away with saying that. But you're a bitch and an asshole if you actually believe it."

I wished I could have bit my tongue off. That was really overkill.

However, the fight went out of her.

"Am I? I don't know. Maybe I am. It hasn't been one of my best days."

"Besides, what happened tonight is your story. CNN will be at the airport waiting for you. Your friend Mr. Fonda—oops, his name is Mr. Turner, isn't it—has the Italian government so scared that he knows already what time we're setting down. Dee Dee and company will be there. And you'll probably be on *Larry King Live*. And we won't get our story about tonight in till Wednesday's paper. It'll be back page because the big news will be the conclave. You'll be the big heroine and I'll be the big bum who is half married to you."

"Bum in blackface," she said, snuggling closer to me.

We were already over the lights of the sprawling city of Rome, flying right toward St. Peter's, it seemed.

"How's the cardinal?"

"Seems to be getting along pretty well."

"Will he go into the conclave? What impact will your story have on the election?"

"I don't think they'll be able to give the triple crown away."

CNN

ANCHOR: We just have had very good news from Rome. Our Patricia Anne McLaughlin has been freed from the kidnappers who seized her this morning. She is at a military airport south of Rome. Patty Anne, it's good to have you back!

PM: (wearing white slacks, a black commando jacket,

and no makeup and looking battered but resilient) Believe me, Tessa, it's good to be back. I want to thank Mr. Turner and everyone at TBS for helping to get me out. I also want to tell my kids that I'm fine and need a good night's sleep. But I will call them immediately.

(Begins report.)

I was freed at approximately eleven-fifteen local time by two Italian commando teams, one from the carabinieri, the military police, under the command of Lieutenant Niccolo Colonna and the other from the polizia, the state police, under the command of Major Francisco Bruncllo. They used the typical methods of anti-terrorist teams—concussion and smoke grenades and men from helicopters rappelling down the side of the villa where I was held. I was released unharmed. Nine prisoners were taken, four Italian and five Dutch nationals. I was deeply impressed by the professionalism of the raid. The two teams carried it off perfectly, thank God.

I should add in the interest of accuracy that my once and future husband, Dennis Michael Mulloy, apparently figured out what had happened to me and accompanied the interior ministry team.

I'm still confused about why they kidnapped me. Apparently they feared that a Dutch bank would be liquidated if the bank's auditors found out about a scandal in which the Vatican is involved. The full story will be in Tuesday's *New York Times*, which will be on the streets in the U.S. in a couple of hours.

ANCHOR: We're already planning a special Larry King interview with you tomorrow, if it's all right with you.

PM: It's fine, Tessa. I'll be back at work in a couple of hours. We have a conclave to cover.

The cardinals will go into the sealed area in the Vatican in about fifteen hours. I cannot estimate what impact the story of the Dutch bank and its Vatican connections will have on the conclave, but it will be a major new problem for the cardinal electors to ponder.

Patty Anne McLaughlin, CNN, at the military airport, Rome.

Blackie

I flipped off the television. A certain princess had called me with the good news and warned me of the impending CNN special report.

There would be no need to wake the cardinal or those monitoring his condition. The good news could keep until the morning.

So the story would break in the *Times* and presumably the *Herald-Tribune* in the morning. Poor Church, it would have one more large batch of rotten eggs on its face. Maybe we would be able to change the rules of the game down there in the Sistine Chapel. It was long past time.

And what a classy way of telling the world—and him too—that you were reconciling with himself: once and future husband.

Nice going, Patty Anne. Soon we'd have the two of you back in Chicago. Where you belong!

Dinny

The doctors at the airport ministered to Patty's hurts and gave her some strong anti-irritant pills. They assured me that my ribs were not broken and that my knees were not seriously damaged. They gave me some of the pills, too.

She then phoned the kids in Chicago. The noises coming out of the phone suggested they were whooping and hollering for Mom. As well they might.

She handed the phone to me and made the head gesture Irish women make when they mean you better talk to whoever's on the phone.

"Daddy!" they yelled enthusiastically, each of them on their own phone.

"Is Mom really all right?"

"Did you really save her life?"

"Are you really coming home?"

"Yes, Mom is really all right. No, I really didn't save her life. And, yes, I am really coming home."

"Forever?"

"Forever!"

They whooped and hollered again. Deirdre wanted me to watch her team's softball finals. Kevin said he had a baseball game. Nothing from Brigie, just thirteen, and a delicately sensitive thirteen at that.

"Don't you have anything lined up for me, Brigie?"

"I'll be so happy to see you, Daddy, that I won't need anything else."

"You'll get tired of my hanging around."

"No way, Daddy," she said, tears in her voice. "Not ever."

My eyes stung with a few tears, too.

"You sound like you made a lot of commitments," this once and future wife said to me, cocking an eye and arching an eyebrow.

"You did, not I," I replied, "and on worldwide television."

"I know *that*. But you can't really live in Chicago, can you?"

"Why not?"

"You can't leave the paper!" she said in a tone as if she were forbidding me to leave the paper.

"Who's talking about leaving the paper?"

She rubbed her forehead dubiously.

"Maybe it's my aches and pains or the medicine they gave us, but how are you going to stay on the paper and live with us in Chicago?"

"We do have a Chicago bureau."

"Is it open?"

"Yep."

"But they haven't offered it to you, have they?"

"Yep."

"Really?" Her face lit up in a glow of delight.

"Really."

"When?"

"A couple of weeks ago."

"And you didn't turn it down?"

"I told them I'd think about it."

She leaned her head on my shoulder.

"You wanted me back?"

"Hell, Patty, I've always wanted you back, even when I didn't want you back."

She rested her head for a moment, then laughed, then said, "Let's go home, Dinny."

"To Chicago?"

"No, silly! To the Hassler. We have work to do tomorrow."

We found Paola Elizabetta harassing some commandos

about their being ten minutes late. She never gives up.

"You both are all right?" she demanded.

"Fine," Patty replied.

"You are *not* fine!"

"Do you talk to your mama that way?"

"Naturally. You may be all right, Patricia, but you are not fine."

"I will be fine tomorrow or the next day. I do appreciate your love . . ." Her eyes teared. "You are so much like my daughter." She hugged Paoli.

"And you are so much like my mama."

"I'm sleepy," I announced.

They both glared at me. Paoli pointed at a Lancia. We got into it. She boarded one behind us.

Let the old married folk have some privacy.

"And how are you *really*, Peppermint Patty?"

She hesitated.

"All right, but not fine, like your young colleague said. They humiliated and beat me and messed around a little, not much." She spoke in a casual tone, as though these things happened every day. "They threatened to rape me to death after the conclave was over and I think they meant it. And they told me you were dead. So I hurt, mentally and physically. But I'll be damned if I'll let those bastards ruin the rest of my life."

"Good," I said.

"Especially," she said, sounding grimly determined, "my life with you, my funny, blackfaced, once and future husband."

"Maybe talk it over with your shrink when you get home."

"Probably a good idea. I'd kind of like to take tonight off, if you don't mind."

"All I'm going to do is fall asleep . . . and take as many nights off as you want!"

"One will be plenty . . . same bed, though."

"Naturally."

We both laughed.

She did cuddle naked in my arms, however.

"I guess I won't have to buy any nightgowns anymore."

"Yes, you will. They're fun to take off."

She laughed softly, only half awake, and then slept. Since I had kind of renewed diplomatic relations with the deity, I said a few prayers of gratitude. Before I too ventured into the land of Winkum, Blinkum, and Nod, I think I said the grace before meals. Maybe I should learn some more prayers.

I rolled over in what seemed like a half-hour. The sun was peeking through the drapes, not exactly a rising sun either. Patty had departed from the bed, but the shower was running. Then it stopped. She emerged from the bathroom, modestly wrapped in a towel. Well, Peppermint Patty in a towel could never be all that modest.

"I wish I had a cushy job with the delayed media," she announced. "Stay in bed as long as you want, ride around with pretty and adoring young women, file one story a day. Such a deal!"

She tossed the towel away.

"Delayed media?"

"Sure. I work for the instant media. We bring you the news the instant it happens. So we have to work hard all day long and often into the night. . . . Stop staring at me. You're a lewd old man. Can't a woman dress in privacy in this place?"

"There's always the parlor."

She laughed, walked over to me, and planted a kiss on my cheek.

"I'll see you later. If you think of it, you might call the kids about one o'clock. They'll be up and getting ready for school by then. They'd love to hear from you. Here's the number."

She scribbled on a piece of paper, pulled on the jacket the interior ministry had donated to her, and said, "I gotta go over to my place to get some more decent clothes."

"Look your best for *Larry. King Live.*"

"Definitely!"

Since I do work for the delayed media I went back to sleep.

A P

Cardinal Denies Financial Scandal

Rome.

John Cardinal Fletcher, the American who heads the Vatican's Prefecture for Economic Affairs (PEA) has denied categorically reports published this morning about a huge loss in Vatican investments.

"It's all a fake," he said. "The story, the documents, the kidnapping, they're all totally phony. It's an anti-Catholic attempt by the media to discredit the Church just as it is engaged in the sensitive task of electing a new pope. I think it's diabolic."

Asked about reports from The Hague that Dutch bank examiners had already seized the International Agricultural Bank of Holland, the bank allegedly involved in the Vatican's massive losses, and had confirmed the basic outlines of the story, Cardinal Fletcher denied that he had heard about those reports and added that if there were such reports, "They are all part of this anti-Catholic plot."

The cardinal refused to release a list of the investments of the Administration of the Patrimony of the Apostolic See (APAS), which technically is part of his office.

"That material is confidential and we are absolutely not going to reveal it just to contribute to the notoriety of a couple of hack journalists."

Dennis M. Mulloy, the reporter for *The New York*

Times who first reported the loss, said in response to Cardinal Fletcher's comments that he stood by his story. "Either the cardinal is not telling the truth," he said, "or he doesn't know the truth."

CNN

PM: (wearing a white dress and crimson jacket with gold trim) We're talking with Dr. Mary Kathleen Murphy, who is the spokesperson for the doctors treating Sean Cardinal Cronin of Chicago. Dr. Murphy, what is the latest report on the condition of the cardinal?

MKM: The cardinal is doing very well. All vital signs continue to be normal. He is eating healthy food and drinking only tea—and two cups a day at that. We now confidently expect a complete recovery.

PM: And the conclave?

MKM: We are naturally reluctant to release a man from treatment who so recently suffered a severe assault on his system. On the other hand, we understand the importance of the election. We know there will be doctors inside, but we are not certain that they will understand the cardinal's condition. We'll make a decision late this afternoon.

PM: Could you give us a hint?

MKM: No. How are you doing, Patty?

PM: (blushing) Much better, Doctor.

MKM: Did that cardinal really say that it was all a fake to gain publicity?

PM: Yes, he did.

MKM: What a jerk he must be, even for a cardinal!

PM: (not altogether displeased) Thank you Dr. Murphy. We'll be watching the procession of the cardinals this afternoon to see if Cardinal Cronin is in it. Patricia Anne McLaughlin, CNN, Rome.

ITN

REPORTER: We are talking to Commandante Francisco Brunello, head of the polizia's anti-terrorist squad. Commandante, you were in charge of the mission last night which freed an American television correspondent from captivity in the Alban Hills, were you not?

FB: (He looks wonderful in a black uniform with medals, gold trim, and red tabs. His black beret is trimmed in red and black.) I had the honor of cooperating with Tenente Niko Colonna of the military police, who commanded the entire mission.

Q: You are aware that Cardinal Fletcher of the PEA charged this morning that the raid was a fake perpetrated by anti-Catholic forces to embarrass the Church just as the cardinals are going into conclave.

FB: Yes, I have heard of it.

Q: Would you care to comment on it?

FB: I am personally insulted. I have a brother who is a priest, an aunt who is a nun, and an uncle who is a bishop. I go to Mass almost every Sunday. I am a good Catholic. I would never want to embarrass the Church. Never!

Q: And you think the reporter was truly kidnapped?

FB: (angry) Signora was kidnapped and tortured! If Cardinal Fletcher had seen the damage to her face when we arrived, he would not have said such a foolish thing.

Q: What about the alleged scandal in the Vatican?

FB: I know nothing of that, but I do know that two of the men we arrested were security personnel from the Dutch bank. They confessed that they were sent here to make sure that Signora would be killed after the conclave ended. They also confessed that some-

one was supposed to murder her husband, Signor
Mooloy.

Q: Thank you, Commandante.

Mark

Mark hated the stupid Italian police. On the day before
what he knew would be his Big Day, they were everywhere.
When he came to "his" building he saw a uniformed cop
asking everyone who entered it for their identification card
and checked their names off on a list.

Since his only ID was an American passport and since he
could not explain why he needed to get into the building
and since his name was certainly not on the cop's list, he
walked rapidly by the building.

He would have to find a way to get by them tomorrow
morning. Perhaps if he came early enough, they would not
be checking anyone.

This was a terrible setback. They had told him in the
marines that when plans went awry you had to improvise.
But no matter where he went on this street, the cops were
checking. How do you improvise against that?

It was unfair of God to permit this to happen.

Dinny

I wandered down the Conciliazione trying to absorb enough background to get a story out for tomorrow morning. If the cardinals did elect someone on the first scrutiny, then I'd have to rewrite the story at desperate speed in the hope that I could make the deadline. All right, I could do a piece about the Menendez election beforehand and put in a few additions. No real problem.

A background piece about the cardinals going into the conclave and about whether Sean Cronin would appear (and I'd bet my last ten-thousand-lire note he would) would be fine if there were no victor tomorrow morning. But it would be kind of dull, especially compared with P. E. Oriani's piece about the rescue at Cutoff Pass. The editor would want more from me.

Well, he wasn't going to get any more, unless something happened today. I'd prepare a draft for the Menendez election.

Fine.

Except the instant media would show Sean Cronin in line and that would kill anything someone like me in the delayed media might have to say.

What impact would my story have? Fletcher was already denying it, though the denial would not hold up much beyond early afternoon.

Would it cause the cardinals to circle the wagons and defend the Church, a not entirely improbable reaction? Or would they realize that Peppermint Patty's bruised face on the screen would cut the ground out from under Jack (-in-the-Box, as I heard he was called) Fletcher and they would have to elect a pope who would come clean on the finances?

I figured it was a toss-up. However, I told myself, my job was to write the news that was fit to print and not worry about the outcome of the election.

Except, I did worry. It was my Church as well as Jack Fletcher's.

I almost collided with Blackie Ryan on the piazza. Damn, he *was* usually almost invisible!

"Ah, the once and future husband."

"The woman will upstage me for the rest of the day and probably tomorrow. What she calls the instant media have all the advantages over us delayed media."

"Arguably. But how does said woman fare?"

"She'll be OK. She has enormous resiliency. Now she feels rotten. Understandably."

"Indeed."

"Will your man march today?"

"What do you think?"

"I think you're delaying the announcement to the last minute to squeeze one last bit of political advantage out of it, that's what I think."

He smiled. "I will tolerate nothing that would be a serious threat to his fragile health."

"If indeed it were fragile."

"Of course," he said, turning toward what would be the entrance of the conclave.

"What are you up to?"

"As I said when we had supper in Trastevere, I am a sweeper for Milord Cronin. It is therefore appropriate that I be given the charge of sweeping the conclave area for electronic devices."

"Have you found any since the last time we talked?"

"Five or six every day."

"That violates the rules!"

"Arguably."

"My friends at Corpus?"

"And lots of others, too."

"Why?"

"So they can leak information to the media types while the conclave is in process, and so certain radio stations can broadcast this information back into the conclave to those who have brought in portable radios and thus possibly destabilize the process."

"What do you do with the bugs you confiscate?"

"I turn them over to our mutual friend Leonard F. X. Richardson so that they may be used again."

Dangerous man. But I always knew that.

"Doesn't the Vatican have sweepers?"

"Oh, yes, but their instruments seem not to discover all those that my state-of-the-art playthings will pick up. As a special advantage, one of my playthings will also detect portable radios that are being smuggled in against the rules that the cardinals legislated for themselves."

"Indeed?" I said.

"Oh, yes."

"I didn't know you were so big on secrecy."

"I'm not, but I am big on level playing fields. Incidentally, I also possess another high-tech device that will cast a magic net around La Cappella Sistina. It will prevent any bugging from within or without. Naturally, if you will excuse the expression, only Milord Cronin and I know about this latter device."

"Now I do, too, Bishop Blackie."

"That is true."

"Is this discussion off the record?"

"As I once said to you, I can't imagine that I would have anything of sufficient importance to say off the record."

"Especially since by the time my story might appear, the cardinals would already be locked up?"

"That is true also."

"So you're telling me this so that one will not believe the stories that one might hear on some of the Italian radio stations?"

"Arguably." He sighed loudly.

"Very interesting."

We had arrived at the door to the conclave. The Swiss Guards saluted as if Blackie himself were a candidate.

"Incidentally, Bishop Blackie, your metaphor about the rubber band was not all that inaccurate."

"Patently."

Dinny

$\mathcal{I}$ walked into the sala stampa, just to see what might be happening there. My old friend Father Len Richardson was waiting at the door.

"You may not enter," he snarled. "Your credentials have been revoked."

"Ah," I said happily. "I was hoping that might be the case. Can you tell me why?"

"I don't have to answer that question."

"I guess you don't, Len baby. By the way, where do you plan to work the day after tomorrow?"

While he sputtered, I walked away.

Did they really think they had a chance of winning? Maybe they did. If God is on your side, by definition how could you lose?

Well, I had my story.

As I walked back up the Conciliazione, I saw the kid with the burning eyes again, striding toward the Tiber. He was wearing a black suit and a black turtleneck. He looked exactly like a priest.

CNN

Larry King Live—Special Interview

LK: In this special interview, which we will replay several times today, we talk with Patricia Anne McLaughlin, CNN correspondent, who was rescued early this morning by Italian commandos from the state police and intelligence officers from the military police. How are you feeling, Patty?

PM: All right, Larry. I'll be fine in a day or two.

(Throughout the conversation, PM's tone is flat and unemotional.)

LK: How were you kidnapped, Patty?

PM: I had gone into a *farmacia* on the Borgo Santo Spirito to buy some hair spray. I came out and these four men pounced on me and dragged me to a car. There were people who watched it, but they did not try to help me.

LK: Is it true that you were tortured by your captors?

PM: I haven't used the word. They pushed me around and beat me up and molested me in some minor ways. They threatened to gang rape me and kill me. I think they meant it.

LK: Isn't this gratuitous violence unusual for terrorists?

PM: They weren't terrorists, Larry. Not even really very professional kidnappers. They were common thugs from the International Agricultural Bank of Holland.

LK: The bank that was seized today by the Dutch government?

PM: That's right.

LK: You know that Cardinal Fletcher denied all of the

charges today and said it was an anti-Catholic attack on the Vatican.

PM: The cardinal doesn't know what he's talking about. That's probably why they gave him the job.

LK: You were kidnapped to prevent your former husband from reporting the story of the financial loss the Vatican seems to have suffered?

PM: I called him my once and future husband last night.

LK: What does that make him now?

PM: (does not change her expression) My lover, I guess.

LK: Instead, he led the commandos to the villa where you were being held and saved your life.

PM: He turns out to be a useful guy to have around.

LK: You think this was all a part of a conspiracy by the Corpus Christi Institute, Patty?

PM: I kind of doubt it. I can't imagine the higher-ups getting involved in a brutal kidnapping. Mind you, the former general director of the Ministry of the Interior, who is known to be a member of the institute, tried to stop the participation of the polizia commandos in the operation. I suspect that there may have been a rogue element of the institute at work. But not the prelate or his staff. I hope not, anyway.

LK: What impact do you think Mr. Turner's threats had on the Italian government?

PM: (smiles for the first time) I saw the clip only this morning. I'd say he scared the daylights out of them.

LK: Who is going to be elected pope, Patty, and when?

PM: Cardinal Menendez, probably the first morning.

Blackie

We watched Patty Anne's totally cool performance on television after lunch, since all of us would be in conclave when it was played again.

The cardinals, just returning from the final General Congregation, were wearing their fancy robes, though with their Roman collars pulled off. Save for Sean Cronin, who since he had not attended the congregation, was wearing tan slacks and a light white sweater. He was his old vigorous self again, though still pale from his experience. He was drinking Perrier water because the vigilant doctors had also vetoed Diet Coke.

"Are you going in Sean?" they had asked, almost in unison, when he had strolled into the lounge.

"Don't know yet. My medical team won't tell me till the end of the day, just before the procession."

That was the technical truth. But Sean Cardinal Cronin knew quite well that he would be at the conclave—if only because, should his doctors say that he could not, he would defy them. The other American cardinals suspected much the same thing.

"It will make a great deal of difference if you're with us," Mick Kennedy had said tentatively.

"No, it won't," Milord Cronin had laughed. "After that article in the *Times* this morning, Don Luis will win in a walk."

As is doubtless patent, that is not what he would have said if left to himself. However, someone had suggested this might be a prudent response.

Then we had watched Doña Patricia hold Larry King at bay.

"Very impressive," Mick Kennedy had observed. "That woman has lots of courage."

"She admitted that she's fornicating with the man," Cardinal John Lawrence Meegan said, his head shaking, his hands fluttering.

"No, she didn't," Sean Cronin said, dismissing the flutter with the wave of his hand. "She's still validly married to him. Canonically they are separated, but there has been no effort on either side to seek an annulment. She lives in Chicago, so I would know. She merely proclaimed their reconciliation in a lovely way."

Silence for a moment.

Then John Lawrence took up the cudgels again.

"Well, I think we ought to stand behind Jack Fletcher. He's one of ours, after all."

More silence.

"He did flatly deny the story again at the General Congregation, didn't he, Mick?"

"I'm not sure many cardinals believed him, John Lawrence. The ones around me snickered."

"We all know how dumb he is," Milord Cronin added.

"Still, I would hate to see us rush to judgment and cast our votes on the basis of a scandal that has yet to be verified."

Yet more silence.

"We should cast our votes for the man we think will be the best pope," Cardinal Cronin said, looking around the room. "I have a hunch that Jack-in-the-Box won't get many votes."

Milord was certain that Cardinal Meegan would not vote for Cardinal Menendez. My position was more guarded. He wouldn't cast the decisive vote, but once the outcome became certain, he would join the bandwagon on the final vote.

Like a lot of others.

Because, even if they were not from Chicago, they didn't want to back a loser.

CNN

(Picture shows PM standing right next to a barricade with the processing cardinals only a few feet away from her. She stills wears the stunning crimson jacket. A Swiss Guard stands close to her, apparently to make certain she doesn't jump over the barricade. The guard remains impassive through the broadcast as the Swiss Guards always do.)

PM: This is Patricia Anne McLaughlin with a special report from Vatican City. We are watching the cardinal electors in their full robes processing into the conclave area of the Vatican, where they will begin tomorrow morning to vote for the next spiritual leader of a billion Roman Catholics. The elaborate robes must certainly be very warm on this hot spring day in Rome.

This is the question of the moment—will Chicago's Sean Cardinal Cronin join his colleagues in the conclave? We have not seen him yet and it now seems probable that he will not enter the conclave.

(Huge cheer from the crowd as Cardinal Menendez appears in the procession.)

They're cheering now for Luis Emilio Cardinal Menendez y Garcia, who is the favorite of Romans, as he seems to be for most of the lay Catholics throughout the world. However, the laity do not get to vote, not even the Roman ones, though a long time ago they did vote.

(Cardinal Menendez spots Patty, comes over, and

blesses her with a warm smile. Another wild cheer.)

(Patty is nonplussed for a moment, then continues.)

The last cardinals have walked out of St. Peter's. There is no sign of Chicago's Cardinal Cronin. His presence is thought by many to be essential to a victory for Cardinal Menendez. . . .

(Another big cheer. A Mercedes, led by two cara-binieri on motorcycles, pulls up to the barricade at the foot of the steps of St. Peter's. Sean Cronin in full robes emerges from the car and joins the procession at the very end. He waves to the crowd of well-wishers.)

Wait a minute, here is Cardinal Cronin, arriving at the very last minute! He must have talked his doctors into releasing him. . . .

(PM loses her cool. After all, it is her own bishop.)

Cardinal Cronin, it's wonderful to see you alive! I'm so happy to see you're back with us.

(The cardinal looks up, sees Patty, strides over to her, hugs her very briefly.)

SC: Not as happy as I am, Patty Anne, to see that *you're* back with us!

PM: (flustered) Well, there it is. The College of Cardinals has now gone into locked quarters near the Sistine Chapel, from which they will come out only when they have elected a pope.

This is a slightly flustered Patricia Anne Mc-Laughlin, CNN, at the entrance of the conclave.

Mark

Mark caressed the barrel of his rifle with proud affection. All his human friends had let him down. But he could still count on the weapon to stand by him, if he treated it right. He cleaned and oiled it every day. He would take no risks of it jamming at just the moment of glory. When he marked the head of the baby killer with the weapon's crosshairs and squeezed the trigger, the weapon would operate perfectly. The baby killer's head would explode and his blood and brains would come pouring out, smearing forever his fancy white robes.

Mark smiled to himself. It would be so easy. The police were fools. They had checked people going into the building in the morning, but they had left it unguarded the rest of the day. Before the procession into the conclave, he had simply walked up the stairs, smiled and bowed to everyone, and walked out on the roof. Only the cunt with long black hair stared at him with a mixture of fear and contempt. He picked up the dagger he had had hidden in the luggage he had checked. In the marines they had praised him for his skill with a bayonet. He had loved to stick the blade into a dummy and twist it. He would stick it into the cunt tomorrow and twist it slowly. She would die with a look of surprise on her face and a scream of pain. It would serve her right.

They had thrown him out of the marines because of a bayonet. Another gyrene, a man he had admired and respected as a close friend, had said a dirty thing about him. Mark had lost his temper, as any man would who was accused of being a pansy, and drawn the blade out of its sheath, just to scare the man. They had all jumped on him and dragged him off to the brig. The next day he was given a dishonorable discharge and hustled off of the base.

He was not a pansy no matter what anyone said. He did not desire men any more than he desired women. He did not trust men any more either. Those men whom he had thought of as friends had all turned against him.

There could be some problems in the morning. Light rain was predicted. He would have to keep his weapon under his raincoat till the last minute. Only light winds were expected. That was fine. Heavy winds might cause the bullet, with its hollow head, to drift off course. He could allow for that, but it made the operation more problematic. He said a little prayer to God asking that there be no heavy winds.

Perhaps he should have shot the baby killer this afternoon. He could have easily done so.

When he had emerged on the roof of his sniper's post, Mark had timed himself in his task of opening the case, assembling the gun, falling on the roof, loading the magazine with his dum-dum bullets, focusing the sight, aiming the gun, and pressing lightly on its trigger. When he had practiced the routine in his room, he was able to do it all in thirty seconds. On the roof it had taken only thirty-five seconds. Not bad. He would have to make the whole routine automatic. If he paused to think while he was doing it, he would foul it up.

He had pointed the gun at the procession of cardinals to make sure he could focus the sight quickly. He had made only a slight turn, and the heads of the cardinals had come into sight. By chance he had focused right on the head of the murderer.

Pull the trigger now! a voice screamed in his head. Get it over with!

His finger had tightened on the trigger, then he rebuked the voice. What good would it do to eliminate the man when he was not yet pope? The glory would belong to the man

who had actually killed a pope. The world would never forget that.

He could wait another day or two.

He had relaxed his finger and quickly disassembled the
gun, put the parts carefully in the case, and softly descended
the steps. On the Big Day, the Day of Glory, he would not
bother with the gun or the bag. Rather, he would walk
calmly down the stairs and disappear in the crowds. Perhaps
they would catch him, perhaps not. That didn't matter, but
he would not make it easy for them.

When would he kill the girl? Perhaps if he saw her while
climbing the stairs. Perhaps afterward. He would have to
seize the opportunity when it came. But he probably should
wait till after he had shot the baby killer. If he killed the
girl first and a pope was not elected, they would come after
him.

The cunt on CNN would be his second target after the
baby-killer pope. He would have plenty of time to scout her
out before the pope appeared on the balcony.

Still stroking the weapon, Mark imagined her head ex-
ploding and her brains and blood spilling down on her dress.
One second she would be alive and babbling into the tube.
The next second she would be burning in hell where she
belonged.

Then his thoughts turned to the infinite pleasure of driving
his bayonet into the gut of the girl with the long black hair
and twisting slowly as he dragged it across her belly and
drained away her life.

He felt a smile of contentment on his face.

Dinny

Maeve the Marvelous was sitting at the vanity in her skimpy underwear, brushing her gorgeous red hair. I remembered a ritual of the past. I took the brush away from her and burnished her hair with slow, loving movements. She slumped on the vanity bench, giving herself to my care in total relaxation.

I discovered that I really didn't need the revered master's cosmic forces.

"You remember, Dinny?" she murmured.

"How could a man ever forget?"

"I've missed you so much."

"Me too."

"I suppose we have to consider these last four years as an investment in the rest of our life."

"Precisely. . . . Oh, I forgot to tell you, I called the kids today, just as you suggested. It will be useful in your career as a member of the instant media to have a husband in the delayed media to make your calls."

She snickered. "More useful to have a husband who likes to brush my hair. What did the little brats have to say?"

"They wanted me to reassure them that you were really all right. I said something silly like their mommy was a champ. Then they began to give me advice on how to cope with you."

"They did not!" she said with a laugh. "Loud mouths!"

I eased the bra strap off her shoulder. She sighed appreciatively.

"Yep." I continued brushing. "The consensus is that Mom was neat and totally cool, but sometimes you had to stand up to her and shout her down. It always worked because Mom would melt and hug you when you shouted back."

"Oh," she said meekly. "I guess they have Mom figured out pretty well."

"Better than I did for a long time. So I had to promise that I would shout back. They even said that after a while it was kind of fun."

"Poor kids."

She unhooked her slinky, lacy bra. A WonderBra, though heaven knows my Maeve the Passionate didn't need one.

"I don't think so. . . . How are you doing, Peppermint Patty."

"Fine, Dinny. And this time I mean fine."

She reached up, extended her hands around my neck, pulled my head down to her lips, and kissed me, sweetly, gently, affectionately.

"More brushing?"

"Not of my hair," she drew it together in a braid and led me to our bed.

She was still hurting, I knew. So I had to be very careful and very delicate. I guess I was successful because when we were finished, she whimpered, "Memorable."

I said something inarticulate.

"Dinny, you can shout at me all day long if you do things like that to me at night."

"I'll keep that in mind."

A little later, while we relaxed companionably in each other's arms, she asked, "You think it's certain that Don Luis will win?"

"Nothing is ever certain in politics, Patricia Anne Marie Elizabeth. Anything can go wrong."

Blackie

"Nothing is ever certain in politics," I said to Sean Cardinal Cronin. "Anything can go wrong."

He nodded. "Don't make no waves, don't back no losers."

"Yet we are in a relatively good position," I added. "I assume you agree with my point that on balance, the exposé this morning helped our cause."

"Yeah, it sure did. There was a tendency to rally around poor Jack-in-the-Box, but most of the men know he's a fool. They also know that they have to do something to impress upon the folks out there that they're aware of the problem and are responding to it."

"Indeed."

Sean Cronin was lounging on his bed, if one might call it that, and seemed relaxed. He was still pale but on the whole he looked much better than he had since we came to Rome. I had come to his "cell," as the conclave room is not inaccurately called, to make sure that he had consumed his late-evening medication.

As soon as I had entered, he removed a stack of pills from the shaky table that was to be his desk, held them out in his hand so I could see them, and then gulped them down with a half glass of water.

"So, you can report back to that terror of a sister of yours that I am acting like a responsible convalescent."

"Arguably."

"I met with our guys after we took those terrible oaths and before supper. They say there is no other real candidate.

Even the Curial people seem kind of resigned. Alabastro hugged me when I came into the dining room. Monastero shook hands with me and said that he agreed with me that we need a very different kind of pope. I don't know whether we should completely trust them, but they look beaten and, to tell the truth, not all that unhappy about it."

"*Timeo curiales et dona ferentes*,"[1] I replied, showing off my experience long ago as a teacher of Virgil to high school students who were innocent of poetic sensibility. "Still," I added, "they probably had grown weary of the late regime. And the fervor of the Corpus Christi Institute must unsettle them."

"How many portable radios did you confiscate?"

"Fourteen. There was some considerable protest but my assistants had a copy of the resolution that had been unanimously accepted. Your brother-in-the-Lord, John Lawrence Meegan, had a particularly ingenious and quite expensive little device; he almost jumped out of his robes when my infernal machine turned it on. He protested quite loudly when we confiscated it. However, one does not argue with the Swiss Guards. He can collect it from them when the conclave is over, though I imagine, like many of the others, he will be too ashamed to seek it out."

"How many bugs did you collect while we were eating supper?"

"Only four. I will return them to your good friend Leonard F. X. Richardson at the sala stampa on completion of this exercise."

"I doubt that you will find him there or any place else in this city. And your other infernal machine will cloak the whole Sistina?"

"Oh, yes. It will be a level playing field. Moreover, this

---

[1] "I fear curialists, especially when they're bringing gifts." In the original, Pius Aeneas, as he called himself, used the word "Danaos," which meant Greeks.

concern keeps my mind occupied during our stay in this terrible place."

"I'm glad of that."

I wandered out into the corridor and through the quiet building. It was a hell of a way to elect "the spiritual head of one billion Roman Catholics," as the mass media called it. The conclave was quaint, archaic, and kind of charming. Good theater. However, it entrusted the fate of a large, cumbersome, and confused voluntary organization to electors, many of whom, one suspected, would have a hard time reading and writing and some of whom were so dumb that even the other cardinals noticed it. Better that the pope-designate be brought out on the balcony and subject to cheers or jeers, as in the time when the ancestors of Princess Paola Elizabetta Maria Angelica Katarina Brigitta Oriani—"call me Paoli"—were running things.

Well, we had to work with what we had. Maybe the injection of a little Chicago-style politics would give us a chance of electing the best man among the candidates. However, good man that he is, I mused, he will inherit a gosh-awful mess.

These elderly gentlemen would argue that their ignorance and incompetence (though they were hardly likely to accept my words) simply made room for the Holy Spirit to work, a spirit who would whisper a name into their ears at the right time—oddly enough, the name of the man who looked like a sure winner.

In the theology I was taught, this failure to do one's homework in the name of trusting in God was called *tentatio Dei*, "tempting God," and was viewed as a grave sin.

However there have been occasions in human history, like the surprise election of Pope John XXIII, when the Holy Spirit, just to show that She could do it, turned human weakness and ignorance and presumption into a situation where She could take over. Normally, however, we humans, especially we churchmen, endeavor to give Her large obstacles to overcome, something to shoot at, as it were.

At the end of a long corridor I looked out on the nearly empty piazza. There was a light rain falling. A few carabinieri walked slowly back and forth, two by two as they always did.

They had surely done a good job in saving the fair Patricia Anne.

I walked back to my own "cell," muttering my childhood prayer, "Come Holy Spirit." When all the expected votes had been counted, one must still pray. In Chicago we take seriously the adage, "Never count on nothing till all the votes are in."

CNN

PM: I am standing in the Piazza San Pietro in clear view of the chimney of the Sistine Chapel, which you can see on your screens. Father Jamie Keenan of Holy Name Cathedral in Chicago is with me.

(PM is wearing a white dress, more of a shift this time, and a rain slicker.)

(Cut to Father Keenan, handsome, laid-back young man with a pleasant smile.)

PM: Good morning, Father Keenan.

JK: Good morning, Ms. McLaughlin.

PM: We expect that in a few minutes smoke will pour from that chimney, don't we, Father?

JK: Yes, we do.

PM: If the smoke is black it means that in their first two ballots this morning, the cardinals did not give two thirds plus one of their votes to anyone. White smoke will mean that there is a new pope. What will happen if there is a new pope, Father?

JK: In a relatively brief time, Cardinal Gregorio Alabastro will emerge up there and announce that we have a pope and give his name and then the name he will use as pope. There will be, in all probability, wild cheers from the crowd. Some time later the pope himself will emerge on the balcony and make a few remarks.

PM: How long will that take, Father?

JK: Perhaps an hour. The new pope must be fitted in his papal robes, though Vatican tailors will certainly have a number of different sizes ready based on their estimates. The procession will be organized, the pope will choose the men he wants with him on the balcony. Then everyone will process out.

PM: Many observers expect that we will see white smoke this morning. They assume that Luis Emilio Cardinal Menendez y Garcia will be elected on the first or second ballot. What do you think, Father?

JK: That's certainly possible. He was the heavy favorite going in.

PM: Others say that if he is not elected this morning, his support will erode. Do you agree?

JK: That remains to be seen. As we say back home in Chicago, you can't beat somebody with nobody.

PM: (Suddenly very excited, she grabs the priest's arm.) Father! There's smoke! It looks like it's white!

CROWD: *È bianco! È bianco!*

JK: (mildly excited) It sure does look white.

(Then the smoke turns black, first black mixed with white and then pure black.)

CROWD: (confused) *È bianco! È nero! È nero!*

PUBLIC ADDRESS SYSTEM: *È nero.*

PM: That settles that, doesn't it, Father Keenan? The new spiritual leader of the world's one billion Roman Catholics was not chosen this morning.

JK: No, he wasn't, Ms. McLaughlin.
PM: Do you think we will see white smoke this afternoon, Father?
JK: Maybe.

Mark

Mark was disappointed. He was sure the baby killer would be trapped in his crosshairs this morning. But he had escaped for another couple of hours at least. Damn. Should he stay here on the roof? No, that would be foolish. He might be spotted by a cop. He would walk back to his apartment and clean and polish his weapon again.

The young woman with the black hair came into the building as he was leaving. She was with another bimbo like herself.

"Per dolore," she said to her friend. *"È nero!"*

"Sì, Laura, è nero."

So her name was Laura, was it?

He would shout it at her while she was dying.

"Die, Laura, die and go straight to hell!"

He felt the power of the final judgment stir within himself. He would be God to the people he killed.

Dinny

$\mathcal{I}$ led the Pretty Princess over to the Borgo for lunch. I carried my notebook and my portable printer in a computer bag. I would do the story this afternoon, either story, on the notebook, print it out and try to send it from the sala stampa, credentials or no. Otherwise I would call New York on my cellular phone and read it to the desk.

"That was disappointing," I said to her.

She shrugged. "Rarely is anyone elected in the first scrutiny. Many make complimentary votes for their friends, especially when it is clear who is going to win. However, they will not want to spend another night in that terrible place, sleeping in someone's office."

"I hope so. Cardinal Cronin thought he had to win this morning."

"Bah! Chicagoans are an impulsive people!"

"Tell me about it!"

She laughed. "I didn't mean that but I suppose it may be true too. Mama and Papa have said that I should invite you and your, ah, once and future wife—"

"Lover."

"*D'accordo*. Mama and Papa wish that you should come to supper tonight at our *casa*. To celebrate, naturally."

"They think we will have something to celebrate?"

"Naturally."

"Sure. I can't speak for the woman who is involved in instant news, but—"

"She has already consented."

"Naturally."

And naturally she was asked first. Oh well, I didn't mind

being the second-rater on this team. Not so long as I could sleep with her every night.

We passed the old Carmelite church, Santa Maria in Transpontina, one of the contributions of the Borgia pope. The kid with the wild eyes emerged from the modern office building next door. What the hell was he up to?

"I have taken the liberty," the girl guide informed me, "of acquiring the use of a fax machine on the first floor of this building. It would be better to send your piece to New York from there instead of from the sala stampa."

"You don't think they'll let me in?"

"Our friends will have taken their leave. They will know that their time is over."

"I wish I was as sure as you are."

"We have, after all, been here for twelve hundred years."

"Naturally. . . . Incidentally, that was a nice piece you sent on the raid. I noticed that a certain Niccolo Colonna received a substantial amount of attention."

She turned on me, ready to be furious, then smiled.

"He deserved it. He will be at dinner, too."

"Does that mean your relationship has changed?"

"Perhaps a little bit, *un poco*."

The rain was drifting away, the sky clearing from the west, the air was cool and fresh. Would we really see white smoke this afternoon? I found myself feeling very pessimistic. I wondered what Sean Cronin was thinking up there in the Vatican Palace.

And Bishop Blackie.

Blackie

"We lost by one vote, one stinking vote! Sixty-four on the first ballot, nine more on the second. We were almost there. Now it's all in jeopardy."

Sean Cronin had stormed into my room. I was sitting at my table pondering three more bugs, most likely brought in before the cardinals arrived (though not necessarily without the knowledge of some of them). My trusty Vatican sweepers had managed to find only one of them. I had also checked my cloaking device in the chapel. Working perfectly. I had decided to leave it on.

"So I am told."

"That lousy rotten bum John Lawrence Meegan voted against us. I'll break the bastard's neck. We have to meet with the precinct captains and spend the rest of the day trying to keep our votes in line and pick up a few more."

He paced up and down anxiously, rather in violation of the norms imposed by Mkate@LCMH. This would never do.

"I would advise against it."

"What!"

He turned to me in fury.

"You have it locked up. We will win on the first ballot at the next scrutiny. I take that as a given. If you and your precinct captains flit around trying to collar votes, it will create the impression that you think you are going to lose. Rather, you should scatter among the crowd, two of you together in all cases, and celebrate. It is all over. You should make a lot of noise, laugh loudly, consume more wine than is absolutely necessary, and then retire for a pleasant si-esta.''

"You realize what is at stake?'' He stared at me, Donner and Blitzen in his eyes.

"Arguably. That is why I offer a strategy which will guarantee victory.''

"The Daleys never take victory for granted.''

"This a different electorate. They want to go home and say truthfully that they voted for the winner. I suspect that your friend from Miami Beach will change his vote without any urging. So will most of them. I predict as many as eighty-five votes. I have here a list of the small number that will vote against us. It is all over, unless you create doubts about that by your behavior.''

He sunk to my bed, ran his fingers through his thick hair, and thought.

"You're usually right, Blackwood.''

"Arguably.''

"It is a pretty clever strategy at that. On occasion I tend to be a little too headlong.''

"Some have actually said that.''

He stood up.

"All right, we'll do it your way. I'll whisper to the other guys how we'll play it. I'm sure they'll agree.''

"No one has ever accused Graf Von Obermann of being headlong.''

He laughed his wild West of Ireland battle laugh and launched himself forth from my room.

We had better get him out of here before supper, I thought.

Perhaps I would have a word with Luis Emilio Cardinal Menendez y Garcia and whisper that suggestion in his ear.

I then settled down to the pasta they served at lunch. I thought it quite tasty. However, I am notorious for thinking that there is no such thing as bad pasta. It is merely that some kinds are better than other kinds. In any event I had two helpings.

What if I were wrong this afternoon?

I have been wrong on occasion, sometimes intolerably so.

Then I would have to figure out Plan B.

Blackie

Looking well rested from their heavy Italian lunch and their siesta, the cardinals, still yawning, ambled into the Sistine Chapel. I made sure that my ingenious machine was still working properly. I hoped that I could return it to Mike the Cop in another day or two.

Our precinct captains were laughing happily. The atmosphere I had suggested to Milord Cronin had certainly permeated the college. From the look on Jack-in-the-Box Fletcher's face, he had made up his mind to vote for the winner. So had the cardinal of Miami Beach.

That's what it looked like.

I hoped.

If I were wrong this would be the biggest blunder thus far in a life that has been marked by more than the occasional blunder.

Don Luis looked calm but pensive. He would look that way, however, no matter what he expected to happen.

Cardinal Ulululu slapped me on the shoulder as he came by and gave me a thumbs-up sign.

"Go Buckeyes!" I whispered.

"Go Blue," he replied with a grin.

If Don Luis won, we had done the man no great favor. On the other hand, he was what the Church needed.

I closed the door to the chapel from the outside, leaving the local friendly neighborhood Swiss Guard in charge.

He saluted me with considerable fervor. I was becoming all too visible in this place.

We would know very soon whether my estimate of the situation had been correct.

I said the prayer to the Holy Spirit again.

CNN

(It is six in the evening; on this spring day, the sun is right behind St. Peter's.)

PM: (Now minus the rain slicker. The summer knit white dress clings closely to her form. Her hair is piled up on her head.) We are back here in the piazza of St. Peter's again, waiting for the afternoon smoke. Father Jamie Keenan is here with me. It seems almost certain, doesn't it, Father Jamie, that if Cardinal Menendez doesn't win this afternoon, we will have a long conclave?

JK: Arguably, Patty Anne.

PM: Some Italian radio stations that are said to be affiliated with the Corpus Christi Institute have been reporting all afternoon that Cardinal Menendez votes fell from the first ballot this morning to the second. Do you think that's likely, Father Jamie?

JK: (thoughtfully) I'm not sure, Patty Anne. The only way they could know anything about what's going on up there would involve automatic excommunication. I don't think anyone has broken through the seal. So they may well be whistling in the dark as they pass the cemetery. Besides, I hear that someone has installed a cloaking device inside the Sistine Chapel.

PM: (visibly jumpy) There's a certain tension in the air. The crowd seems edgy, don't they?

JK: They sure do. Cardinal Menendez is the favorite of the Roman people and of most other Catholic laity around the world. I would be afraid that if someone else wins, he is likely to be greeted with loud boos. That would not be a happy beginning for a new pope.

PM: We should know any minute now, shouldn't we?

JK: I'm sure most of them took advantage of the siesta time, so they may not have begun punctually. If they did begin on time they would be on the second ballot now.

PM: (tense and distraught) There is the smoke, Father! It looks like it's black again!

(The camera focuses on the smoke.)

CROWD: (sullenly) *È nero! È nero!*

JK: It certainly looks black, Patty.

(As the camera watches, the smoke gradually loses its dark black color, shifts to gray, and then to wisps of white.)

PM: It's changing color, Father Jamie! It's changing color!

CROWD: (uncertain) *È bianco? Non, è nero. Non, non, è bianco!*

JK: It certainly looks white now. The PA should confirm in a couple of seconds . . .

PA: *È bianco!*

PM: (hoarse with excitement) That confirms it! The one billion Roman Catholics of the world have a new spiritual leader! He was elected on the first day of the conclave on the second scrutiny, perhaps on the first ballot of the second scrutiny, so that would mean on the third vote of the day! The crowd here in St. Peter's is ecstatic! Somewhere an Italian military band is playing. People are dancing and celebrating. They obviously think that the new pope will be their favorite, Luis Emilio Cardinal Menendez y Garcia of Valencia. What do you think, Father Jamie?

JK: We'll know in a few minutes, Patty Anne. Cardinal Gregorio Alabastro, the senior cardinal deacon, will appear on the balcony up there, yes, the one on the monitor now, and announce the identity of the new pope.

(Suddenly the high door of the balcony swings open, a cross bearer and two acolytes emerge, and then, the tiny figure of Gregorio Cardinal Alabastro.)

GA: (in a frail old voice) *Annuntiabo Vobis gaudium, gaudio magno* . . .

JK: (Even he is excited.) I announce to you a very great joy . . .

(Wild cheer from ecstatic crowd.)

GA: *Habemus Papam* . . .

JK: We have a pope . . .

(More cheers.)

GA: *Ludovicus* . . .

(Crowd becomes ecstatic.)

JK: That's it. There's only one Louis in the college, Menendez.

GA: *Aemilianus, Cardinalis Sanctae Romanae Ecclesiae* . . .

JK: Poor old guy got the second name wrong—it's Emilio, not Emiliano . . .

GA: MENENDEZ Y GARCIA . . .

(Crowd goes bonkers.)

JK: He screamed it loud enough. He sounds happy.

GA: *Qui imposuit sibi nomen* . . .

JK: Who takes for himself the name . . .

GA: JOHANES!

(Crowd is deafening.)

JK: John. That's all she wrote, Patty Anne, Pope John XXIV!

PM: (frazzled) It's all over now. The Catholic Church has a new leader, Luis Emilio Cardinal Menendez y Garcia, John XXIV, the 267th successor to Peter the Fisherman (voice cracks with emotion), who was also a married man.

Patty Anne McLaughlin, CNN, Vatican City.

Dinny

*P*aoli hugged me and kissed me. Everyone in the piazza was doing it. Great joy indeed. They had pulled it off, with ease, apparently.

We hurried over to the office building next to the Carmelite church and fed my hastily completed article into the fax. I'd do a follow-up after the new pope's first speech.

As we left the building, I saw the kid with the wild eyes coming in. What the hell was he up to?

The Conciliazione and the side streets leading into it and into the piazza were swarming with laughing, shouting people. Good lead for the next piece.

We hurried back to the sala stampa to watch Pope John's acceptance speech up close on large-screen television. There was apparently no one in charge of the place.

We settled down and watched the big screen as Vatican functionaries draped the balcony of the Basilica with scarlet and white hangings. They moved quickly as if infected by the exuberance of the crowd. It looked like the new pope would be right out.

Something gnawed at my mind. Something was wrong. What was it? What the hell was wrong?

Then I realized what the hell was wrong.

I grabbed my cellular phone and pushed Niko's button. No connection.

I rushed outside, the princess trailing after me.

I pushed the button again. This time there was a connection and the phone rang.

And rang and rang and rang. No answer.

I was desperate. What should I do now?

"Niko."

"Niko, this is Dinny . . ."

"Yes, Deeny?"

"There is a kid with a crazy gleam in his eye and an attaché case in his hand that has been hanging around the new office building next to Santa Maria in Transpontina. I'm afraid that when the pope comes out—"

"Got it, Deeny. We're on our way."

"Buon Dio!" Paoli cried out.

"You get the pope's speech and that's an order. I'm going down there."

Mark

Mark was sky high. Everything had worked perfectly. He had fit in with the crowds pouring into the streets around St. Peter's. Only the suspicious woman called Laura had seen him ascend to the top of the building. She was no problem. She would die soon anyway.

In the failing light, no one would see him. It was a piece of cake. All his uncertainties vanished. He would make history this night.

The damn fools in the crowd were singing and dancing and celebrating. They were baby killers, too. He would bring their celebration to an end in just a few minutes.

Lying on the roof, he carefully focused the scope. The lights around the church were just as good as sunlight. Not a bit of wind blowing.

He thanked God for that help.

Today would be his Big Day, his Day of Glory.

He focused on the priest setting up the podium and the microphone. He could send him off to hell in a second.

Kill him!

The voice was shouting in his head again.

But he was not the target. The baby-killing pope was the target.

He swiveled the gun around in search of the CNN cunt. She was clearly visible right next to the CNN van, asking for death with her cuntish white dress and big tits. A perfect target.

He swiveled back and forth from the podium to the woman.

A piece of cake.

The doors swung open. The murdering pope came out.

Mark tried to catch him in his crosshairs. Other people got in the way. Impatiently he waited for them to get out of the way of his target.

Kill them all! the voice shouted.

No, not yet. If he fired a shot at someone else, the pope would duck or someone would pull him down. The first shot would belong to His Fucking Holiness.

Then he heard Mom's voice: "No, Mark, no! What will people say!"

He hesitated.

Maybe killing wasn't the way to stop a killer.

Then the crowd on the balcony straightened itself out. The pope stepped to the podium. God damn his handsome, smiling spick face.

A perfect target!

NOW!

Dinny

I had almost caught up with Niko. I was only twenty yards behind him and two other men—Rudi and Gianni, it looked like. They were fighting their way through the crowd that was coming from the opposite direction. It was getting darker. I couldn't see the roof of the office building.

The crowd hardly noticed the three men with drawn Berettas who were fighting against them. What does a cop with a gun mean on the night a new pope has been elected?

Behind me there was a buzzing sound in the public address system, as someone adjusted it

Dear God, I prayed, don't let us be too late.

Mark

Very carefully, Mark increased the pressure of his finger on the trigger. The pope was still in his crosshairs. He must not jiggle the weapon by pressing too hard.

NOW!

As he was squeezing the trigger, Mark felt a sharp blow on his head. The weapon lurched in his hand, the bullet flew off on the wrong course. Then someone hit his head again and he lost his grip on his weapon. He rolled over and looked up.

The cunt—Laura—was attacking him with a broom! She dared to assail the most important martyr of the twentieth century with a fucking broom!

He rolled to his feet, grabbed his bayonet from the sheath on his belt, and charged her.

"Die, Laura, die! You fucking cunt!"

She hit again and again with her stupid broom.

One of her blows hit his right hand; the bayonet jumped out of his hand, just as he was about to stab her.

Astonished, he looked at his empty hand. How dare she hit him this way!

He'd kill her with his rifle, a couple of shots in the belly. Then he would turn and kill the pope. In all the noise no one had heard his shot. He still had a chance.

She was beating his face with her broom. Damn the cunt! His fingers grasped the weapon. He tried to shield his face from the flailing broom. He moved the weapon into position.

"You'll die now!" he screamed.

She jammed his stomach with the broom, punched it solidly into him. He gasped for breath.

Then she jabbed at his testicles.

He howled in pain. But determined to eliminate this annoying insect, he pointed the weapon at her.

She grabbed the barrel of the weapon and shoved him. He tilted backward.

"Stop!" he yelled a command at her.

She kept pushing. He stumbled, lost his balance, strove to regain it, and straightened up. She shoved again, harder. He tried to push back but he was off balance. He drew a deep breath and pressed with all his strength against her. She let go of the weapon and dropped back to the floor of the roof.

"Now you die, cunt!" he bellowed.

Somehow she managed to reclaim her broom. She shoved herself to a sitting position and hit him in the nose with it.

He howled again, dropped the gun, and fell backward.

Suddenly there was no roof beneath. He was falling. He flailed desperately to stop his fall.

"Mom!" he yelled.

Then the lights went out.

Dinny

I heard the firecracker sound of the rifle shot. It pinged into the sidewalk behind some revelers on the other side of the street. I caught up with Niko and his men. They stood, paralyzed, as they watched a bizarre combat on the roof of the office building between a man with a rifle in his hands and a young woman with a broom.

"Don't shoot!" Niko cried. "We don't want to kill her!"

She hit the man in the face with her broom handle. He dropped the gun and stumbled backward over the ledge of the building He screamed once before he hit the concrete of the Conciliazione headfirst. He lay still on the ground, a crumpled puppet.

The young woman, a mere child with long black hair, stood there looking down at him. She held her broom like it was a pike or a battle sword.

Gravely, Niko saluted her.

Just as gravely she raised the broom in a return salute.

CNN

(The camera focuses on the pope at the balcony. He has no notes.)

PM: The pope is about to give his first message to the

world. There are a number of cardinals up there with him. I see Sean Cardinal Cronin of Chicago, who made it into the conclave just twenty-four hours ago, at the very last minute.

Father Jamie, who else is there?

JK: Cardinal DeJulio and Cardinal Graf von Obermann, who I presume will be called the Great Electors of the conclave, along with my boss, of course.

(Did his voice catch? It might have.)

JOHN XXIV: I will speak first in English which is something of a world language, then in Italian, then in my native Spanish.

(The sound of a firecracker is heard faintly. No one notices.)

First, to the people of my new diocese here in Rome: I want to thank you for your enthusiastic welcome. You are now my people and I am your bishop. I promise that I will never forget that and I will seek to serve you well as your own bishop.

I want to thank my fellow bishops in the College of Cardinals for their great support and confidence in me. You know as well as anyone does my limitations and my faults. Having forced this task upon me, you will certainly not neglect me in my times of need.

I want to thank God for all his blessings.

I have chosen the name of John, not by accident . . .

(Laughter from the massive crowd.)

I hope that the name indicates my great reverence and loyalty to that astonishing man and my determination to carry on, towards its fulfillment, the great work he began.

I ask for the prayers of all Catholics and indeed all women and men of goodwill around the world that God will assist me in this difficult and complicated task.

I have four special messages tonight.

The first is that there is no room anymore for secrecy in the Church. As my predecessor of glorious memory said, the Church must be a glass house. Secrecy always leads to the abuse of power and to corruption. I have released all the cardinal electors and everyone else who was in the conclave from their vows of secrecy. I have also released them from the conclave itself so they may go back to their residences. I do not want to make Cardinal Cronin's doctors any more angry at me than they already are!

(Laughter.)

The second is about the environment. The earth has been given to us for our use and our protection. To abuse it is to insult the God who has given it to us. I will try to address my first encyclical to this subject.

Thirdly, I want to address the women of the world. I firmly believe that the struggle of women around the world for full human equality is one of the most powerful of what the Conciliar document, *Gaudium et Spes*, called the signs of the times. Granting that in all social movements there are some abuses and some irrelevancies, I nonetheless think it is folly not to recognize the fact that God's Holy Spirit works in this movement. I dedicate myself to furthering the progress of this movement. I ask the three important women in my life, all of whom are now with God—my mother, my wife, and my daughter—to ask God's help in preventing me from ever forgetting this pledge.

Finally, I beg everyone to remember that the Church exists to spread the message of the Lord Jesus about God's great love for us. We have a Church and we have a pope to talk to the world about the importance of love. Many times through the years we have made the Church and the pope ends instead of means and have forgotten about our message of love. We must try our best never to do that again.

God bless you all.

Now I turn to Italian.

PM: We have just learned that there has already been

an attempt on the new pope's life. We are told that the carabinieri found a man with a high-power, long-range sniper rifle on one of the buildings near here. He was stopped just before he shot at the pope. It would appear that the man is now dead.

Dear God, Father Jamie, what is happening!

JK: (gulps) Next time they should have bulletproof glass up there.

Dinny

The young woman's name was Laura Silvestri. She was just eighteen and from the Campagna, the rural area around Rome. Her father was a farmer; she was a computer operator. She had never liked the man with the hate in his eyes. Only when she had seen him with the bag did she realize what he was trying to do. She had attacked him with the only weapon available. She was sorry he was dead. But she was glad the pope was still alive.

No, she did not want to go on television. She wanted only to go home to the little apartment she shared with three friends. She did not want to worry her mama and papa.

She clung to Paoli, who had embraced her.

Very well, they would take her home and post a guard around her house so that no one would bother her.

Was there anything in all the world that she wanted?

She had wanted to go to the university. But there was not enough money for that.

There will be, Niko promised her. You will go to the university. A grateful Italy will see to that.

She seemed puzzled by the promise, but she nodded shyly. *"Mille grazie, Signore, mille grazie."*

Naturally, my girl guide had accompanied me despite my instructions. She took rapid notes as the young woman spoke to us.

"You write that up," I said. "You can describe her better than I can."

"Yes, now we must listen to what Pope John says in Italian. I will translate for you."

She reached in her vast purse and produced a Walkman television. We watched his Italian address; I took notes as she translated for me. We went into the office where she had leased the fax (naturally she had a key for it). I worked on my notebook, she on one of the local computers. We fired our stories off to New York. Both should make the deadlines. What fun the boys in layout would have with all the stuff we had sent in the last twenty-four hours!

"If the cardinals are coming out of the conclave, we should go over to the North American and see what they have to say."

"Sì," I agreed. "That is one hell of a brave woman, Paoli."

"Yes, and she doesn't realize it. I will insist to Mama and Papa that we take care of her. I've always wanted a little sister."

The press conference at the North American was a bit of a flop. At the beginning Cardinal Cronin described the voting.

"Pope John had sixty-three votes at the end of the first ballot, seventy-three at the end of the second, and eighty-nine at the end of the third. Since he was only one vote short at the end of the first scrutiny, we knew that it would be all over by suppertime. I'm happy about that. Only someone with a cast-iron stomach like Bishop Ryan could enjoy the pasta they served in there."

Much laughter. Blackie better watch out. He was becoming quite visible.

Then Cardinal Meegan took over and dominated the conference with his fluttering hands and high-pitched voice. He

praised the new pope to the heavens, said he was just the
right man for the time, and that God had been good to the
Church to send to us a "man named John."

I guess that was some kind of scriptural reference.

He then implied strongly that he and the new pope were
the closest of personal friends.

Cardinal Cronin did not bother to hide his contempt at
this outburst. Neither did any of the others.

Every time another cardinal tried to answer a question,
Cardinal Meegan either jumped in and interrupted him or
waited impatiently so he could answer the same question.

He ruined the conference, the jerk.

Anyway, we had our stories.

"Cardinal Cronin, do you know anything about the attempt to assassinate Pope John just as he was beginning to
talk?" My Patty Anne, still under full sail, asked.

"I've heard about it," he said. "But just that it happened.
Our friends from *The New York Times* over there look like
the cats who cleaned up on the canaries. Maybe they can
fill us in."

I had to say something.

"This is the first time I've been on CNN," I said, "so
you must excuse me if I seem embarrassed."

My Patty Anne turned purple, but she was laughing, too.

"You can read all of this tomorrow morning in copy-
righted stories in *The New York Times* newspaper, as Jimmy
Breslin calls it.

"A young man, an American apparently, was on the top
of an office building with a sniper's rifle. Someone suspected him and phoned the carabinieri. When they arrived
they saw him struggling with a young woman equipped with
a broom. In the struggle he fell over the side of the building
and was killed."

"The young woman saved Pope John's life?" Patty asked
me.

"She sure did."

"And you were the one who summoned the police?"

I squirmed at that one.

"Uhm, I don't think I'd better comment on that question."

More laughter. Loud applause. A handshake from the cardinal. A big hug and kiss from the Pretty Princess. This was getting to be a pleasant habit.

Dinny

I rubbed the soap suds into my once and future wife's lovely body, giving special and loving attention to its most tender parts.

"You look like Pauline Borghese," I said, referring to the statue of that mostly naked young woman (Napoleon's sister) sculpted by Canova in the Borghese museum.

"I don't really," she insisted. "She was at least twenty years younger than I am. . . ."

"Fifteen. She was twenty-five."

"And she was a larger girl than I am, taking my height into account."

"I like you better."

"You should."

The celebration at the Orianis' had been great fun, quietly exuberant relaxation. My arguably future wife had worn a scandalous strapless white summer dress with a fitted bodice (accompanied by the usual symbolic scarf) that was about as close to a corset as one could wear and still appear in public. She justified her choice on the grounds that "the two of them won't be wearing much either," an accurate enough prediction.

Niko had arrived late, singing the praises of Laura Silvestri. She was a child of natural grace and poise. She must be protected from those who would turn her into a celebrity and destroy her. Paola Elizabetta did not seem jealous of his praise.

"We will protect her. Naturally. But no one will ever violate her dignity."

Maeve the Marvelous and I were exhausted. But we persuaded ourselves that a warm shower would relax us. I don't know whether it did or not.

Before the shower, however, she had to straighten out the mess in what she was pleased to call "our apartment."

"The paper," I had said, "will have to charge you for using my suite."

"The paper," she had responded with a derisive sniff as she put in order a pile of papers on my desk, "owes CNN for giving you a new lease on life."

"Arguably."

"I need a vacation, Dinny," she pleaded after I compared her with Pauline Borghese.

"So do I. But what about the kids?"

"They'll give us three days off, especially if you tell them you had to fight me to get it."

"Cardinal Cronin and his medical team are going to Amalfi."

"I want Nettuno." She sighed.

"Nettuno it will be."

And it was.

Blackie

The day after the election and several days before the in-augural (as it now must be called) of Pope John, the pope appeared in a jammed sala stampa. Invisible once again now in my Blackhawks jacket, I loitered at the side.

The pope wore a Roman collar and a black suit. He announced that he would reserve the white robes for "liturgical events." He said that he was sure that the articles in the world press about the bad investments were "substantially accurate." He added that Cardinal DeJulio, who had agreed to be his secretary of state, would immediately determine what further exposure the Church might face.

He hoped that Catholic people all over the world would realize that this would never happen again and understand that those who would suffer would be the families of Vatican employees, who were already underpaid, and come to their help.

He had already ordered that the APAS be folded into the PEA, which Cardinal Cronin would administer from Chicago. All the telecommunication technology that now existed made it possible for the PEA to be directed from anywhere in the world. For a time it would be better that it not be administered in Rome.

This appointment, he warned with a smile, was conditional on the cardinal's resolution to drink no more coffee.

Laughter from Milord Cronin.

He would speak to the prelates of the various institutes and "suggest" that the Church would be better served by the elimination of secrecy, which was counterproductive in the modern world. He was sure they would agree.

' He had asked Cardinal LeClerque to act as the new president of the Commission for Social Communications. He would oversee the "renewal" of the sala stampa.

He had already invited the archbishop of Canterbury and the patriarchs of Constantinople and Moscow to visit him as soon as it was convenient. He promised return trips to their cities.

He was also establishing other commissions to investigate the various problems the Church was facing. He intended to present for discussion very shortly a new set of rules for papal elections, but he was not ready to be specific about what he had in mind.

Furthermore, since all bishops of the world are required to retire at seventy-five, so should the bishop of Rome. If God gave him that much life, he would step down on the day of his seventy-fifth birthday.

Finally he was awarding the medal Pro Papa and Ecclesia to Signorina Laura Silvestri, "the wonderfully brave young woman who saved my life last night." He would use his own personal money to match that of the Italian government to see that this extremely intelligent young woman could obtain the university education she desired.

Also he was awarding the same medal to another young woman whose bravery had saved so many lives at the time of the commando raid in the Alban Hills, the Principessa Paola Elizabetta Oriani.

That latter worthy turned to her colleague from the paper and wept. With pleasure, I thought.

As a very last word, he said, he hoped that everyone would be patient. There were so many things that needed to be done. Some would require time because they were so complex. He hoped that we Catholics and all women and men of good faith around the world—a phrase he used frequently—would be patient with him.

Pope John XXIV had charmed them all.

That night I ate supper in Trastevere with Patty Anne and Dinny. They thanked me for the help and especially for my rubber band metaphor. I warned them that since they would both be living in Chicago I would keep a close eye on them. They laughed and said that their kids would be doing that, too.

Doubtless.

She had lost him once because she had not understood how to keep him. She would not make that mistake again. Nor did it seem likely that he would tolerate such a mistake.

They dropped me off, at my request, near San Pietro. I looked up at Pope John's new quarters on the fifth floor of the Vatican Palace. All the lights were blazing. Still working hard.

We had done him no favor, but he had done us a big favor. In the parlance of Chicago politics, we owed him one. He was entitled to pick up his marker.

We had not lost. It remained to be seen whether in the final analysis we had won.

But to paraphrase the sainted sage Vincent Lombardi: While it is true that winning isn't everything, losing isn't anything.

Author's Note

This novel is a fictional simulation of the next papal election based on an analysis of the forces and ideas and factions and pressures and incredible intrigues that are at war with one another in the contemporary Catholic Church. I have no idea when the next conclave will occur, nor do I have any desire to hurry the day.

Within the framework of a love story and an adventure story, I try to give life to the issues and the emotions that shape Catholicism today and that will shape the next conclave and perhaps its outcome.

The arguments in this book are not about the substance of Catholicism but about the style of institutional leadership. I think there is a good chance that the outcome the next time the white smoke billows above the Sistine Chapel will be similar to the one I project.

To the issues of plausibility:

The vicious backbiting and defamation in the Vatican is known to anyone who has dealings with the Curia. Thus Giovanni Montini (later Paul VI) was banished from the Vatican by Pope Pius XII without the red hat because of slander. So was Giovanni Benelli banished by Paul VI, but with the red hat. At this moment, the Vatican inner circle is defaming a cardinal who is thought to be a possible successor to the present pope.

A financial mess was created by another "genius," Michele Sindona (later convicted of fraud in the United States) in the SGI affair.

A complete reversal of former policies occurred both in 1878 and in 1914.

While the Corpus Christi Institute is a fiction, there are, nonetheless, secret organizations in the Church that have very great power and are very dangerous to those who disagree with them.

The often biased and inaccurate press reports from Rome appear frequently. Consider, for example, the obsequious *Time* Man of the Year story that praised the pope for bringing unity back to the Catholic Church while the sidebars of the article, based on *Time*'s own surveys, indicated that just the opposite had happened. Often the reason is the ideological biases of the authors or the editors. Perhaps more often it is the inadequate sources the authors use, especially disreputable Italian journalists.

The ban on female journalists inspecting the conclave area was actually issued before the first 1978 conclave and rescinded because of pressure from male journalists and from many cardinals.

The power of corrupt Italian journalists to create a mood to shape the conclave is illustrated by the second conclave of 1978. The journalists claimed that the cardinals had come together in a somber mood of fear for the future of the Church and thus created that mood, which came close to turning the papacy over to the arch-reactionary from Genoa, Giuseppe Siri. The kidnapping and murder of innocents has been part of Italian life for many years, though perhaps less in most recent years. It must be noted, however, that despite the violence of the Mafia, the murder rate in Italian cities is much lower than in American cities: It is safe to walk the streets of Rome at night.

There is no Federal Express box around the corner (on the Via Gregoriana) from the Hasslet. But there should be.

A civil marriage in Spain before a religious marriage was required during the brief and bloody years of the Spanish Republic, but not at the time that Don Luis was married. However, for various reasons, I am told, some couples followed the custom.

Finally, attempted assassination has already happened once in this half-century.

Thus, while the events in this story are fictional (as are all the characters), many events not dissimilar from them have already happened.

I rest my case for plausibility.

The issues raised in this story are not doctrinal. They are rather about the style of ecclesiastical administration. I write out of my conviction that the Church would be much better served and would serve much better if it were more pluralistic and decentralized and less authoritarian and obsessed with secrecy.

This issue is not theological. It is sociological. My studies of Catholicism around the world for the last three and a half decades persuade me that such an administrative style would be far more effective than the present style in furthering the Church's central mission of preaching God's love. I tell this story not as a theologian but as a sociologist.

I also believe that Catholics worship God and neither the institutional Church nor the pope. I believe that the cult of personality in which Catholics sometimes engage is immodest.

It is ridiculous to contend that a story about the weakness of Church administration will shock the Catholic laity. Anyone who has studied lay attitudes and behavior for the last thirty-five years, as I have, knows that the laity are beyond shock and that their faith does not depend on the intelligence or the virtue or the skill of their leaders.

I question no Catholic doctrines in this story (and refute as false any charges that I do). Rather I question organizational style from the perspective of one who can claim to be an expert on that subject. I deny that criticism is either disloyal or disrespectful. On the contrary, to remain silent after my long years of studying the sociology of the Church as an organization would be disloyal.

In effect I am arguing on grounds of sociological and organizational analysis, the Church should return to the style of the late Pope John XXIII.

Such an argument in story form will hardly drive faithful Catholics out of the Church. If we have learned anything in the last thirty years, it is that nothing will drive the faithful out of the Church. They haven't left despite all the turbulence and are not about to leave. The plea that one should remain silent lest the faithful be scandalized is self-serving and self-protecting dishonesty.

As should be clear, the organizational style of the Church has been different from what it is at present at many times in history. It is time, I think, for another change in style.

AG
Friday in Easter Week, 1995

Appendix

(A reprint from *The New York Times*—the real one, not my imaginary one.)

Why Do Catholics Stay in the Church? Because of the Stories

By Andrew M. Greeley
Chicago, July 10, 1994.

"If you don't like the Catholic Church," the woman in the *Donahue* audience, by her own admission not Catholic, screamed at me, "why don't you stop being a priest and leave the Church?"

I had been criticizing what I took to be the insensitivity of some Catholic leaders to the importance of sex for healing the frictions and the wounds of the married life and perhaps renewing married love. I was taken aback by the intensity of her anger. Why did it matter so much to her that I had offered some relatively mild criticism? Why did such criticism seem to her to demand that I decamp from Catholicism and the priesthood?

"Why should I leave?" was the only reply I could manage. "I like being Catholic and I like being a priest." Later I remembered the response to a similar question by my friend Hans Küng: "Why leave? Luther tried that and it didn't work!"

Yet the question persists. In its most naked form it

demands to know, "How can someone who is intelligent and well-educated continue to be a Roman Catholic in these times?" The question is not a new one. It has been asked by anti-Catholic nativists for 150 years. Often the latent subtext is "How can anyone who is intelligent and well-educated believe in any religion, especially Catholicism?"

The question is worth a response, if only to clarify what religion is and what there is about the Catholic religion that explains its enormous appeal even to men and women who think that the pope is out of touch and that the bishops and the priests are fools.

Catholics remain Catholic because of the Catholic religious sensibility, a congeries of metaphors that explain what human life means, with deep and powerful appeal to the total person. The argument is not whether Catholics should leave their tradition or whether they stay for the right reasons. The argument is that they do in fact stay because of the attractiveness of Catholic metaphors.

You can make a persuasive case against Catholicism if you want. The Church is resolutely authoritarian and often seems to be proud of the fact that it "is not a democracy." It discriminates against women and homosexuals. It tries to regulate the bedroom behavior of married men and women. It tries to impose the Catholic position regarding abortion on everyone. It represents dissent and even disagreement. The Vatican seems obsessed with sex. The pope preaches against birth control in countries with rapidly expanding populations. Catholics often cringe when the local bishop or cardinal pontificates on social policy issues. Bishops and priests are authoritarian and insensitive. Lay people have no control of how their contributions are spent. Priests are unhappy, and many of them leave the priesthood as soon as they can to marry. The Church has covered up sexual abuse by priests for decades. Now it is paying millions of dollars to do penance for the sexual amusements of supposedly celibate priests while it seeks to minimize, if not eliminate altogether, the sexual pleasures of married lay people.

One might contend with such arguments. Research indicates that priests are among the happiest men in America. The Church was organized in a democratic structure for the first thousand years and could be so organized again. But let the charges stand for the sake of the argument. They represent the way many of those who are not Catholic see the Catholic Church, and with some nuances and qualifications the way many of those inside the Church see the Catholic institution. Nonetheless this case against Catholicism simply does not compute for most Catholics when they decide whether to leave or stay.

Do they in fact remain? Are not Catholics leaving the Church in droves? Professor Michael Hout of the Survey Research Center at the University of California at Berkeley has demonstrated that the Catholic defection rate has remained constant over 30 years. It was 15 percent in 1960 and it is 15 percent today. Half of those who leave the Church do so when they marry a non-Catholic with stronger religious commitment. The other half leave for reasons of anger, authority and sex—the reasons cited above.

How can this be, the outsider wonders. For one thing, as the general population has increased, the number of Catholics has increased proportionately. Still, how can 85 percent of those who are born Catholic remain, one way or another, in the Church? Has Catholicism so brainwashed them that they are unable to leave?

The answer is that Catholics like being Catholic. For the last 30 years the hierarchy and the clergy have done just about everything they could to drive the laity out of the Church and have not succeeded. It seems unlikely that they will ever drive the stubborn lay folk out of the Church, because the lay folk like being Catholic.

But why do they like being Catholic?

First, it must be noted that Americans show remarkable loyalty to their religious heritages. As difficult as it is for members of the academic and media elites to comprehend the fact, religion is important to most Americans. There is no sign that this importance has declined in the last half century (as measured by survey data from the 1940s.) Skepticism, agnosticism, atheism are not increasing in America, as disturbing as this truth might be to the denizens of midtown Manhattan.

Moreover, while institutional authority, doctrinal propositions and ethical norms are components of a religious heritage—and important components—they do not exhaust the heritage. Religion is experience, image and story before it is anything else and after it is everything else. Catholics like their heritage because it has great stories.

If one considers that for much of Christian history the population was illiterate and the clergy semiliterate and that authority was far away, one begins to understand that the heritage for most people most of the time was almost entirely story, ritual, ceremony and eventually art. So it has been for most of human history. So it is, I suggest (and my data back me up), even today.

Roger C. Schank, a professor of psychology at Northwestern University who specializes in the study of artificial intelligence, argues in his book *Tell Me a Story* that stories are the way humans explain reality to themselves. The more and better our stories, Schank says, the better our intelligence.

Catholicism has great stories because at the center of its heritage is "sacramentalism," the conviction that

God discloses Himself in the objects and events and persons of ordinary life. Hence Catholicism is willing to risk stories about angels and saints and souls in purgatory and Mary the Mother of Jesus and stained-glass windows and statues and stations of the cross and rosaries and medals and the whole panoply of images and devotions that were so offensive to the austere leaders of the Reformation. Moreover, the Catholic heritage also has the elaborate ceremonial rituals that mark the passing of the year—Midnight Mass, the Easter Vigil, First Communion, May Crowning, Lent, Advent, grammar school graduation and the festivals of the saints.

Catholicism has also embraced the whole of the human life cycle in Sacraments (with a capital *S*), which provide rich ceremonial settings, even when indifferently administered for the critical landmarks of life. The Sacrament of Reconciliation (confession that was) and the Sacrament of the Anointing of the Sick (extreme unction that was) embed in ritual and mystery the deeply held Catholic story of second chances.

The "sacramentalism" of the Catholic heritage has also led it to absorb as much as it thinks it can from what it finds to be good, true and beautiful in pagan religions: Brigid is converted from the pagan goddess to the Christian patron of spring, poetry and new life in Ireland; Guadalupe is first a pagan and then a Christian shrine in Spain and then our Lady of Guadalupe becomes the patron of poor Mexicans. This "baptism" of pagan metaphors (sometimes done more wisely than at other times) adds yet another overlay of stories to the Catholic heritage.

The sometimes inaccurate dictum "once a Catholic, always a Catholic" is based on the fact that the religious images of Catholicism are acquired early in life and are tenacious. You may break with the institution, you may reject the propositions, but you cannot escape the images.

The Eucharist (as purists insist we must now call the Mass) is a particularly powerful and appealing Catholic ritual, even when it is done badly (as it often is) and especially when it is done well (which it sometimes is). In the Mass we join a community meal of celebration with our neighbors, our family, our friends, those we love. Such an awareness may not be explicitly on the minds of Catholics when they go to Church on Saturday afternoon or Sunday morning, but is the nature of metaphor that those who are influenced by it need not be consciously aware of the influence. In a *New York Times*–CBS News Poll last April, 69 percent of Catholics responding said they attend Mass for reasons of meaning rather than obligation.

Another important Catholic story is that of the neighborhood parish. Because of the tradition of village parishes with which Catholics came to America, the dense concentration of Catholics in many cities and the small geographical size of the parish, parishes can and often do become intense communities for many Catholics. They actuate what a University of Chicago sociologist, James S. Coleman, calls "social capital," the extra resources of energy, commitment and intelligence that overlapping structures produce. This social capital, this story of a sacred place in the heart of urban America, becomes even stronger when the parish contains that brilliant American Catholic innovation—the parochial school.

Perhaps the Catholic religious sensibility all begins with the Christmas crib. A mother shows her child (perhaps age 3) the crib scene. The child loves it (of course) because it has everything she likes—a mommy, a daddy, a baby, animals, shepherds, shepherd children, angels and men in funny clothes—and with token integration! Who is the baby? the little girl asks. That's Jesus. Who's Jesus? The mother hesitates, not sure of exactly how you explain the communication of idioms to a three-year-old. Jesus is God. That doesn't bother the little girl at all. Everyone was a baby once. Why not God? Who's the lady holding Jesus? That's Mary. Oh! Who's Mary? The mother throws theological caution to the winds. She's God's mommy. Again the kid has no problem. Everyone has a mommy, why not God?

It's a hard story to beat. Later in life the little girl may come to understand that God loves us so much that He takes on human form to be able to walk with us even into the valley of death and that God also loves us the way a mother loves a newborn babe—which is the function of the Mary metaphor in the Catholic tradition.

It may seem that I am reducing religion to childishness—to stories and images and rituals and communities. In fact, it is in the poetic, the metaphorical, the experiential dimension of the personality that religion finds both its origins and raw power. Because we are reflective creatures we must also reflect on our religious experiences and stories; it is in the (lifelong) interlude of reflection that propositional religion and religious authority become important, indeed indispensable. But then the religiously mature person returns to the imagery, having criticized it, analyzed it, questioned it, to commit the self once more in sophisticated and reflective maturity to the story.

The Catholic imagination sees God and Her grace lurking everywhere and hence enjoys a more gracious and benign repertory of religious symbols than do most other religions. On measures of religious imagery I have developed for national surveys (and call the GRACE scale), Catholics consistently have more "gracious" images of God: they are more likely than others to picture God as a Mother, a Lover, a Spouse and a Friend (as opposed to a Father, a Judge, a Master and a King). The story of the life, death and resurrection of Jesus is the most "graceful" story of all—the story of a God who in some fashion took on human form so that he could show us how to live and how to die, a God who went down into the valley of death with us and promised that death would not be the end.

How do they reconcile such gracious imagery with the often apparently stern and punitive postures of their religious leadership? It must be understood that religious heritages contain many different strains and components, not all of them always in complete harmony with one another. However, in any apparent conflict between images of a gracious God and severe propositional teaching of the leaders of a heritage, the latter will surely lose.

Consider the matter of sexuality, a subject on which Catholicism is thought to be particularly repressive. Under the grim and dominant influence of St. Augustine, the Catholic high tradition has always been suspicious of "too much" marital sex. It was all right for married people to make love for the purposes of having children, so long as they didn't enjoy it too much.

Whether this cold and harsh teaching was ever accepted by married lay people, whether in fact it was ever possible for anyone but a celibate theologian to believe it, remains open to question. But the problem did not bother most Catholics because they didn't know about St. Augustine and they learned about marital sex from their parish priests (some of whom had wives of their own), their mothers, their friends and neighbors and especially from the marriage liturgies which praised the union between man and woman as reflecting the union between Jesus and his people. The Sarum ritual from Catholic England provided a blessing for the marriage bed and for the bride that she might be vigorous and pleasing in bed—a blessing that today we would doubtless want to extend to men. While the Anglican ritual of the Book of Common Prayer follows Sarum closely, it discreetly omits such references.

In any contest between St. Augustine and Sarum for the hearts and the bodies of the common people, Sarum was bound to win. But surely the Sarum tradition and what it stands for cannot have survived to the present, can it? Does not everyone know that Catholics are sexually repressed and that Catholic husbands and wives do not enjoy marital sex? Like a lot of other things "everyone" knows about Catholics, this happens not to be true. Or to put the matter more cautiously, while Catholics may be sexually repressed, they are on the average less likely to be sexually repressed than other Americans.

According to two different national surveys, Catholics have sex more often than other Americans, are more playful in their erotic amusements than others and apparently enjoy sex with their spouse more than do others.

Moreover, if I use my GRACE scale I can account for all of the differences between Catholics and others in their sexual pleasures. Catholics seem to enjoy sex more precisely because they have more benign religious images. I do not claim that they are aware of the link between their enjoyment of sex and religious images; metaphors work usually on the preconscious level. Yet one can hardly find a better proof that religion is imagery before it's anything else and after it's everything else.

A new school in the psychology of religion, which bases itself on the so-called attachment theory of psychological maturation, supports my perspective. A happy and playful attachment between mother and baby prepares the child for similar attachments later in life, especially to God, who is in some sense a surrogate mother—an all-powerful source of love and reassurance. Professor Lee A. Kirkpatrick of the College of William and Mary has suggested recently that Catholicism is an especially powerful religious heritage on the imaginative level precisely because it offers so many objects of potential attachment. It has been suggested that the most powerful of all the objects of attachment is the metaphor of Mary the Mother of Jesus representing the mother love of God.

I believe that is absolutely right, although some progressive Catholics have tried to play down the role of Mary in the Catholic tradition lest it offend our ecumenical dialogue partners. Research on Catholic young people reveals that the Mary image continues to be their most powerful religious image. Who would not find appealing a religion which suggests that God loves us like a mother loves a little child? Who would not be enchanted by a story which suggests that we are, as the Chicago theologian John Shea has argued, not just creatures, not just sinners but, more than anything, beloved children?

When I was in grammar school in the mid-1930s, the nuns told a story that sums up why people stay Catholic. One day Jesus went on a tour of the heavenly city and noted that there were certain new residents who ought not to be there, not until they had put in a long time in purgatory and some of them only on a last-minute appeal. He stormed out to the gate where Peter was checking the day's intake on his Compaq 486DX Deskpro computer (I have edited the nuns' story)—next to which, on his work station, was a fishing pole and a papal crown.

"You've failed again, Simon Peter," said the Lord.

"What have I done now?"

"You let a lot of people in that don't belong."

"I didn't do it."

"Well, who did?"

"You won't like it."

"Tell me anyway."

"I turn them away from the front gate and then they go around to the back door and your mother lets them in!"

It is the religious sensibility behind that fanciful story that explains why Catholics remain Catholic. It might not be your religious sensibility. But if you want to understand Catholics—and if Catholics want to understand themselves—the starting point is to comprehend the enormous appeal of that sensibility. It's the stories.

Patrick

*H*e'll meet her out on the road at the foot of the hill by the tree where the accident happened. The first time he's seen her since my Ordination almost a quarter century ago. He says he's just going out for a breath of fresh air, but that fools no one. He came back to Chicago to renew a love affair that's been dead for thirty years. A second chance. They'll probably mess up the second chance like they did their first chance.

My best friend and the woman I've loved since she was in eighth grade.

Obscene fantasies fill my mind, actions in which I'd never engage with her in the real world. Does she know how much I desire her? Does she know that my imagination now automatically undresses her? Women usually know, don't they? She *must* know. Yet she glows whenever she is with me. So she does not object.

Is it not my turn? Have I not taken care of her through the years? Did I not urge her to leave her sociopathic husband? Do I not have some rights in the matter? Have I not been a priest long enough? Is it not time to break away from the insane Church and its stupid cowardly leaders?

The smell of blossoms is overpowering tonight, like the empty flower car returning from a cemetery.

I had my turn too and I lost my own first chance. It's only fair to give him his second chance before I take mine.

If I'm really serious about leaving the priesthood and I'm not in some dumb mid-life crisis.

It's all fantasy isn't it? Jane and I could never be lovers, could we? Surely not.

Am I sure of that? I don't know. I'd like to find out.

Anyway I must give the two of them my best possible advice. They are entitled to their second chance without my trying to spike it. The Lake seems sinister and brooding tonight, dark and restless out there. Water. Baptism. The symbol of life and death and new life. It meant life for Leo and Jane once. Then death. New life? Maybe.

What does it mean for me?

Three times I might have possessed Jane—that evening here at the house, the day she told me she was pregnant, and that dazzling night in Rome. What I thought was respect overcame my desire. Now I wonder if I am a coward just like Leo, a wimp who is also an occasional hero.

I can tell that I am still special for her by the way she smiles at me and the lilt in her voice when she talks to me. I'm not out of the running yet.

Does anyone know how I feel? Even my preternaturally perceptive sister-in-law?

I don't know. Only once did she speak to me about my feelings towards Jane and that was long ago.

Leo

In those rare moments when I am honest with myself, I have to admit that I accepted the offer from the University and returned to Chicago because I had heard that Phil had walked out on Jane. Finally. Yet I've made no attempt to see her until this improbable stroll on a May evening with the odor of spring so dense on the night air that it reminds me of the pungency of that luxuriant Brazilian rain forest I was in a couple of years ago, the smell of rapacious fecundity.

Will I find her? Will she find me?

Will the old magic still be there? Or, as seems more likely, will we find that at the age of fifty—almost fifty for her—we are not the same persons we were at the age of twenty? Will an encounter, even on a lovely and romantic night, dash cold water on the foolish dreams we had when we were young?

That's the likely scenario. Academic that I am, I analyze and reanalyze and come up with the same conclusion: You can't go home again.

But why else am I here but that I am trying to go home again?

The place has changed, the road is paved now. The sub-divisions are crowding in from the other side of the lake. The streetlights are newer and brighter—old gaslights long since gone—but the road seems darker, perhaps because the trees are so much taller and the foliage so much thicker. The Old Houses have been remodeled and repainted and look faintly modern and commonplace instead of elegant and ro-mantic as they once seemed to me. The glitter and the ro-mance have vanished. Or were they ever here? Do not we humans spread a nostalgic sheen over the site of our ado-lescence and our first love and make it more dazzling in our memories than it ever was in reality? And don't we thus run a risk of profound disillusion when we discover how ordi-nary it is when we try to come home again?

She is likely to have changed too. Plain Jane instead of Magic Jane. Maggie, who is her ally, insists not, but she is a prejudiced witness.

What if she hasn't changed? What if it's gasoline that gets poured on the embers instead of water?

Will the fury and the guilt of the past come back to haunt us again? Or the ghosts that lurk on this road, the ghosts of dead friends? Can I have her, if I want her, without putting those ghosts to rest?

Will I have to find out what happened that night?

The last time I saw her was at Packy Keenan's ordination. She already had two children and was probably expecting a third. She looked terrible. I was still trapped in my fury and was barely civil.

When we meet tonight, if we meet, will I be anything more than barely civil? I feel the rage stirring within me again.

Jane

I know what I'm doing. Unless Leo has changed completely, he'll wander towards the tree where our friends died and I'll meet him there. He will be expecting me. He always was an incurable romantic even when the romance was with death.

Only a few days before the accident, he had asked me to marry him, more or less. I didn't say no, but like a fool I didn't say yes either. I talked about a lot of foolish objections and problems with our families of which I didn't even realize I was aware. Then on the day of my twentieth birthday I betrayed him. He never forgave me. Instead he ran out on me just at the time when I needed him the most.

He's the only one who thought he made a fool out of himself. The others all thought he was a hero. When I heard what he said at the jail, I was terribly proud of him.

I would have married him before he went to war on a day's notice if he'd asked me. He didn't ask.

What will he think of me? An old woman—almost fifty, worn out by an unhappy marriage, unable to satisfy her husband sexually, and unable to save two of her kids, and probably a third? I was pretty good-looking at twenty but that was long ago.

Not counting doctors, three men have seen me naked— my husband who quickly lost interest, another man whom

I unintentionally terrified before I was marred, and Leo. He didn't see much in that fragmented moonlight, but I think he liked what he saw. If he should get another look at me, will he still like me? Or will he be disappointed?

Will he guess that I think a lot about ending my life? He always knew what was going on inside my head.

He was so sweet at Packy's Ordination, same gentle smile and so nice to young Phil and poor Brigie, my two lost kids. And as friendly to me as though we'd seen each other the day before. He didn't look like a man whose soul had been torn apart by war.

Maggie Ward Keenan, who thinks she knows everything, says that Leo and I should have a Catholic summer, one in which we allow the summer heat to rekindle the warmth of the love that once existed between us. She quotes a liturgy from some place about the bride being buxom and bonny in bed. Well I suppose I'm buxom enough but not very bonny in bed. Not much practice in a long time.

I tell myself that my husband is wrong when he says that he fools around because I'm not very good in bed. But I wonder often whether maybe he's right. Would I have been any better a lover with Leo?

Or with Packy? If he had not been committed to being a priest I might have married him after Leo died. That night in Rome ten years ago we were so close . . . I must not think about that.

Would I be any better with him if we made love tonight?

Was that an adulterous thought? I would have confessed it a few years ago. Now I'm not sure that Phil and I were ever really married.

Maggie quotes some poet called Friar Thomas of Hales about cuckoos singing in early summer. I don't quite know what that means.

Maybe she's right about being Catholic. We do know in our hearts that our lover is kind of like God to us. I wish I could really believe that. I certainly was not God to my husband nor he to me.

If I invite Lee back to our empty house, would he come? Should I try? Would You want me to?

I bet You wouldn't object all that much. I think You always wanted us to be together.

The scent of the lilacs and the jasmine and the flowering crab apple trees reminds me of the scent of a wedding mass.

Now I wish he'd never come back to Chicago. I wish I was not walking down the hill on this road with its terrible memories, hunting for him like a horny teenager searching for her latest crush.

Leo was my first crush, even before my crush on Packy. I was his first crush too.

I hope he likes me.